Memory
Clouds

Books by Tony Moyle

'The Circuit' Series
MEMORY CLOUDS
MEMORY HUNTERS
(Pre-Order now – Release Date Nov 2020)

'Ally Oldfield' Series
THE END OF THE WORLD IS NIGH
LAST OF THE MOUNTAIN MEN

'How to Survive the Afterlife' Series
THE LIMPET SYNDROME
SOUL CATCHERS
DEAD ENDS

Sign up to the newsletter
www.tonymoyle.com/contact

Memory Clouds

TONY MOYLE

PUBLISHING

First published: July 2020

ISBN

Limbo Publishing, a brand of In-Sell Ltd

www.tonymoyle.com

Cover design by Damonza

In memory of…

Brian 'Sleepy' Nelson

"I heard the storm from far away
The days grew dark I heard them say
The lightning flashed, screamed for blood,
Came the thunder, came the flood."

From the song 'I Saw the Storm' – Brian Nelson

- Chapter 1 -

Ascension Eve

Almost everyone in the world received the letter. The only one you'd ever see, and it always arrived on Ascension Eve, the occasion of your eighteenth birthday. Over the last three decades those in the West who'd already passed the milestone knew its contents only too well. If you were younger, then you'd spent years anticipating its delivery and were in no doubt of its significance on the next chapter of your life.

The rest of your life.

The letter wouldn't be dropped on your doorstep. It wasn't left carefully under your porch, sheltered from the somewhat erratic weather patterns only too common in the middle of the twenty-first century. Neither was it posted through your letter box, a device long since removed from the collective memories of door designers. Without fail, and always promptly at nine o'clock in the morning, it would arrive in the hanging basket of an automated delivery drone, which would hover impatiently outside your door until you accepted it. Rumours persisted that if you left it waiting too long the drones were fully equipped and instructed to blow your home's front door off.

No one risked it, not in the age of the Circuit.

In the West, where he lived, every letter looked the same. It was identical irrespective of which country, city or street you lived in. Was it the same for the people of the East? Few on this side of the divide really knew for sure. No regular citizen had travelled that way in decades. The 'Proclamation of Distrust' made sure no one wanted to. Here in his half of the world there was no such doubt over the momentous occasion of your own Ascension Eve.

Even those who hadn't received their letter yet certainly knew what it looked like. It had a distinctive envelope, crisp white paper with black and gold parallelograms along the edge. There was no address listed on the front, just the recipient's name, on this occasion one Jake Montana. In the top right corner, where the older generation would recall a thing called a stamp once lived, a familiar embossed emblem shouted for attention.

The Circuit.

Although its branding was predominantly gold it possessed a reflective quality that tricked the eye into believing there was more to it. The logo had an elaborate modern font which was both iconic and unavoidable. It was emblazoned everywhere these days. Plastered on the sides of public transport vehicles, liberally splashed within the frequent broadcasts from political parties of all ideologies, laser-etched on the side of fruit and vegetables in a way that meant they were still safe to eat, projected on the side of every tall building in the city and, most importantly, inside your own mind.

No one needed the branding to know who the letter came from. Apart from their own, the Circuit abolished this type of correspondence years ago. It wasn't the only method of communication that had disappeared. Email, the internet, mobile phone networks and video conferencing had all been consigned, like the humble homing pigeon before them, to the historical dustbin, only to be worshipped in museums. Not that there were any of those left anymore either. Initially no one bemoaned the loss of emails or text messages. When you had access to the Memory Cloud they were as redundant as writing letters. The Memory Cloud facilitated the collection, delivery and receipt of every thought, message, emotion or memory to anyone, anywhere in the West of Earth and you didn't need to lift a finger. That's how the vast majority of people communicated with each other in the year twenty fifty-four and it was only possible because of the Circuit.

Over the last thirty years every aspect of modern life had been affected by their presence. Simple acts, like how people entered into a contract, had changed immeasurably. You could pay for goods and services, enter agreements and sign your life away with a single simple thought, and once you'd done so there was no going back. Thinking was legally binding, and nobody got away with arguing they'd been a little bit drunk at the time, so it didn't really count. Not these days. Arguing was pointless and incredibly dangerous. In the early years of the Memory Cloud swathes of people mistakenly purchased expensive sports cars they couldn't afford, offered proposals of marriage to perfect strangers, and falsely volunteered for excruciating plasma grafts all because they were unable to control their own enhanced minds. Their ineptitude prompted the original system developers to reconfigure the rules.

Rules that were designed to protect and govern the actions of the collective and the individual.

Rules that were presented to you on Ascension Eve.

The Circuit's letter contained your future life rules. The process wasn't random. It was based on a complete assessment of the candidate's past memories and emotions, collected and stored permanently in their Memory Cloud throughout their developmental years. The rules strictly enforced your future path, selected for you from your own innermost desires. Every letter contained the same basic information each time, yet the details were unique to the person it was addressed to.

Today Jake would learn his fate.

Ascension Eve was quite simply the biggest moment of your life and no amount of reassurance prepared you for it. It was a rite of passage that more than ninety-nine percent of humans had to navigate and, in the eyes of the authorities, it marked your transition from childhood to adulthood. If you were a Circuit subscriber there was no alternative and no appeal, if you didn't like the outcome you only had yourself to blame. After all, the decisions were generated from your own cloud.

People trusted the Circuit to interpret their desires correctly, but that didn't quell the anxiety of the moment. There were so many unknowns that you couldn't predict until you saw it in black and gold. The rules assigned you a life partner, a job within the system, the country where you'd spend the rest of your life and the role you'd play within society. It even determined how you'd spend your free time, the small amount that you were allowed at least. After all of these choices there was still one revelation that raised your pulse rate the most. The letter stated, rather than predicted, how important you were in the eyes of the Circuit.

Your 'importance factor'.

In the middle of the twenty-first century this rating mattered far more than your position in any class system or demographic. After your eighteenth birthday it didn't matter where you were born, who your parents were, what colour your skin was or how affluent you were. In future your standing in the system was tied to one of five ascending levels of importance. From the minority who occupied the top level of vital, through essential, and then necessary. The final two levels were the ones nobody wanted to see written on the page. Trivial and the fifth level, superfluous. Once you were appointed to a level you were stuck there indefinitely, and people associated themselves with their importance factor as much as they did their own name. They'd include it, often spontaneously, when introducing themselves for the first time. This was particularly true if you occupied the top levels.

"Hi, Peter Harris, essential, and you are?"

"Brian."

"Yes, but what's your importance factor?"

"Um…"

Allocation to one of the bottom levels was an instant passport to social isolation from those above. No one wanted to be seen fraternising with a superfluous. Where was the value in it for someone of a higher rank? What would be gained and, more importantly, how would it make you look to others if you did? The Circuit had already judged you, so why wouldn't everyone else?

According to Jake's Circology teacher, not even the importance factor was random. The permanent and immovable prognosis of your relevance to others was also down to the individual. You'd made the choices for yourself, even if you weren't completely aware of it. The selection was reached by studying your deepest fears, personality type, intelligence, creativity, ambition and achievements since birth. All easily accessed by the Circuit by mining your Memory Cloud. To ensure balance, your profile would be benchmarked against the vast wealth of data generated by others. The system had been designed on the basis of fairness and equality, but there had to be limits. Not everyone could be vital and not everyone should be superfluous. Everyone had to compete for their place. The final decision was based on a robust formula from the billions who'd gone before you.

The Memory Cloud made a decision that you would be too selfish to make. A choice that combined your potential and the necessity of the West.

Since building the Memory Cloud, the Circuit had been responsible for collecting, analysing and deciphering every memory since subscribers were born. They knew more about people's lives than they did. They knew what was good for each individual, and everyone else who'd subscribed to their world. The Memory Cloud was a masterpiece, a brilliant piece of innovation created by an influential global software conglomerate to solve one of modern life's biggest problems.

Capacity.

Since the turn of the millennium humans had exceeded their natural age limits and their brains had been exposed to an ever-increasing volume of data. Yet physical capacity for data evolved slower than their desire to consume it. The Memory Cloud solved the problem. Rather than wait for physiological development to catch up, technology enabled subscribers to upload their thoughts, knowledge, memories and emotions to a secure cloud-based application free of charge. In turn, humans liberated large portions of their brainpower, safe in the knowledge that if they needed to retrieve the past a backup file could be accessed at any time and in any place. Memories were never forgotten, and knowledge would never be lost because they would always be there. Long after your body failed you.

But the Memory Cloud was more than a storage facility.

The Circuit presided over a priceless database of human opinion that it quickly used to reshape the world. If you held the collective thoughts of seven billion people, then you understood exactly what they wanted. In turn, if you knew their innermost frailties and fears you could use it to help them achieve their goals by making their decisions for them. Thinking on behalf of subscribers was one of the additional benefits of membership. A function that began as an optional extra gradually, and almost unnoticeably, became mandatory.

Procrastination is a very human instinct. Rarely do people have a clear picture of what path to take, influenced as we are by the media, our peers and our own assessment of logical information and illogical feelings. Often emotions and facts clash, confusing us to make a biased decision that actually damages our physical, mental, financial or emotional well-being. That's where the Circuit steps in. It modelled the various options from the data available and made a decision that was in your best interest. The choice would be validated against millions of other people who'd been in a similar situation. After the event the outcome would be thoroughly analysed for its relative success and the data submitted to the control group to constantly improve the accuracy of the system.

Its impact swept through every aspect of society like wildfire spreads through dry grass. In the early days, even the political elites contracted the Circuit to help them. Here was a tool that could identify policy decisions that appealed to a majority of voters. It didn't take long before the Circuit was more instrumental in people's lives than the politicians themselves. By the twenty-forties governments were no more than proxy management teams for a new global power and voting became just another decision that was taken on people's behalf. If the masses desired change then there was no dispute. The Circuit's influence was unavoidable, and in time uploading to the Memory Cloud became law. The punishment for non-subscribers or rule-breakers was severe. But even then, the brave new world didn't appeal to everyone and when freedoms are suppressed there will always be outliers.

A minority refused to comply with authorities. There was no single reason for their defiance. Across a spectrum of motives that unified their position, some disagreed ethically, frightened that their data would be misused. Some refused, or were physically unable, to wear the technology that enabled access to the cloud. Some simply had no desire to utilise the benefits of membership. These non-conformers were colloquially referred to as speccies and most were forced into hiding to remain unmarked and untracked. But it didn't end there. Pursuing a policy of universal coverage, the Circuit recruited teams called 'Archivists' to patrol, locate and convert them, although not even their vast knowledge knew how many speccies existed in the world.

None of them would ever receive a letter.

For everyone else approaching their eighteenth birthday its arrival meant two things.

Firstly, you no longer had control over your future aspirations. Your only hope rested on the Circuit making a fair assessment of your own desires and accurately choosing a life you wanted. For the vast majority of people this turned out to be the case. An analysis of satisfaction on the subject, measured through the memories stored in the cloud and having a one hundred percent response rate, gave an average score of six-point-nine-nine 'light bulbs' out of seven. No one seemed overly concerned with the zero-point-zero-one who were less than satisfied. That's the problem with statistics. People focus on the majority and ignore the minority. Every year millions of letters were sent out and the statistically small fraction of people given lives they hated equated to tens of thousands. Not quite so insignificant.

It didn't bother the Circuit. The figures were used to prove the system worked and to subdue potential disquiet. Every day a stream of propaganda was drip-fed into memory feeds and delivered to people's subconscious whilst they slept. Sleep was prime time in the cloud. Advertisers paid aggressive sums to promote products at a time when the masses weren't able to switch them off. A five-second night slot to a defined target group sold for tens of millions of credits.

The second realisation that accompanied the arrival of your letter was the knowledge that departure for your new life, if you were male, happened one day later.

Ascension Day.

But you wouldn't be leaving alone.

Every eighteen-year-old was gifted two guides.

They weren't just responsible for escorting you to your new life, which might just be thousands of miles away, they became temporary caseworkers keeping a virtual eye on you while you integrated into your new lifestyle and surroundings. For most users they were helpful, a value-added feature of membership. For a minority they felt like a sinister extension to the constant surveillance over their lives. It was one final surprise on Ascension Eve.

Jake Montana was about to find out what it was like. His letter was due this morning. Its arrival would be disappointing even if it wasn't a surprise. He'd been receiving regular alerts through his cranial implant for a month. Each internal 'ping' sent a shiver through his body like the harbinger of doom.

Jake loved life how it was. He liked living with his parents, Kyle and Deborah Montana. He liked his younger sister, Tyra, at least when she wasn't goading him about his impending misery. He liked his sleepy little New Hampshire town nestled on the coast and near his beach. He liked his local hovercraft softball team, the 'Dream Centre' down the road where you could plug yourself into the very latest in virtual technology, and all the natural delights of the American East Coast.

Most of all, though, he loved Christie Tucci, his childhood sweetheart.

Whatever his destiny was, Christie wouldn't be part of it. She couldn't be. It was a few months before she reached her own Ascension Eve, which meant her destiny had yet to be determined. How could his letter include her, if Christie hadn't received the news herself yet? That wasn't how the Circuit worked. The process started during the 'Great Segregation' of the twenty-twenties, when protectionism forced people to exist in small circles of society. Back then it was impossible to know who your best match was across seven billion people because everyone lived in enclosed sects. Not so now.

Now there were no limits.

They were doing Jake a favour.

Based on their profiling of him, somewhere out there was a more suitable match than Christie. The same was true for her, and every other eighteen-year-old. But there was more to it than matching someone to your own preference. The survival of the human race relied on couples who'd produce genetically superior and resilient offspring, less susceptible to modern disease and capable of surviving on an increasingly inhospitable planet.

Everyone had to make sacrifices for the greater good.

Jake couldn't care less about the rest of the world. He cared about his world. He'd always been independent and strong-willed. He didn't care about politics, or how other people behaved. It didn't have anything to do with him. All he really wanted from life was to be left to get on with it.

When did he ever get what he wanted?

Jake watched the drone nervously from his first-floor bedroom window. It had landed twenty minutes ago and was acting a little jittery. Nothing for it. Either he faced destiny, or he'd be forced to explain to his parents why a small drone was impatiently firing rockets at their front door.

- Chapter 2 -

Third Generation

Access to the Memory Cloud was normally facilitated by technology implanted inside the body. There were two standard devices. One embedded in a region of the brain called the amygdala, and a second attached to the optic nerve. The duality of these microchips provided a connection to a virtual world of almost unlimited knowledge and a portal to a repository of everything you'd ever experienced.

The surgical procedure to achieve this higher state of consciousness was usually performed during infancy. It was recommended by medical experts that it should be completed no more than three months after the birth of the recipient. Human behavioural scientists insisted it marked the point at which our earliest memories and emotions formed. Anyone receiving the implants later than this date would lose vital data about their early development. All of these claims were backed up by the manufacturer, who just happened to be the Circuit.

Everyone else believed there was a second reason for it.

It didn't matter how many powerful new age anaesthetic drugs were used during surgery, people knew from experience that the recovery period was long and extremely painful. It took months for the host to adjust to the foreign objects burrowing into their flesh. Metal and wire fought with tissue and bone to see which would reach optimal performance first. Babies found verbalising their distress particularly challenging. Which meant they couldn't complain. They resorted to screaming their heads off, a behaviour that didn't deviate from what every mother had experienced for generations.

The physical pain was just the beginning. Eventually it relented but for some the trauma associated with the event lasted much longer. Jake knew this only too well. He'd suffered from the consequence of having two small, wirelessly connected microchips embedded in his organs for years.

He was one of the unlucky ones.

Most users experienced no side effects from the surgery. Jake, on the other hand, endured debilitating headaches that felt like storms had broken out inside his head. They were as common as the passing of the months. When he suffered natural headaches, the real world could be stopped. He'd just send himself to bed, turn off the lights, pop a few painkillers and sit it out. Not with these headaches. The Memory Cloud never stopped. The connection was permanent, and until the cause relented the pain in his head was constant. Occasionally it would intensify over a period of several weeks and months. When it reached a state of permanency only one remedy was successful.

It was always the same.

An upgrade.

He'd lost count of how many he'd had. When it became impossible to think straight, move or remember past memories without screaming in anguish, he knew he'd get the message. An alert would arrive in his cloud feed mandating him to visit his nearest Conversion Room for more invasive surgery, more recovery and normally an even greater level of pain sometime in the future. The more advanced the upgrades became, the more they hurt. The last implant, grafted to his nerves just after his seventeenth birthday, had more power, greater processing speed, more capacity and more functions. His fragile body couldn't keep pace with the rapid rate of mechanical advancement. Which meant it was only a matter of time before the donor electronics rejected the host and the whole process cycled around again.

But even then, Jake's headaches and countless upgrades were not the worst part of being connected to the cloud. Another phenomenon haunted him.

Flashbacks.

But they weren't his.

It had long been rumoured, usually quietly and in secret code, that the Memory Cloud was not as secure as the Circuit pronounced. Anyone who'd received the regulation implants, whatever version they wore, became connected, twenty-four hours a day. Every second was extracted, recorded and, if prompted by the owner, shared with others. What if this interconnectivity was more fluid and the mathematical sluice gates allowed more data through than the Circuit acknowledged? Or maybe the flashbacks had something to do with the East? After all, their network was a different system all together. Theirs was called the Realm, at least that's how people in the West translated it. The Realm and the Circuit had battled for subscriber supremacy for decades. They'd do whatever it took to disrupt the other. Perhaps the East had infiltrated the Memory Cloud and Jake was suffering as a consequence? Whatever the reasons, Jake was certain he wasn't just passing his memories into his own cloud, he was receiving them from somewhere else.

He didn't know why it was, but he knew what it was.

He felt things.

THIRD GENERATION

Things he'd not directly experienced for himself. Which meant the feelings weren't from his own memories. Which meant he was trespassing on virtual land that didn't belong to him. What if it worked both ways? What if others could access his personal experiences? Although he had no control over these flashbacks, he was certain the Circuit wouldn't believe it was innocent. Their control over their intellectual and ideological property was total. Step out of line and the Circuit stepped in. Often that resulted in a mandatory upgrade of new technology or, in the rarest of cases, confinement at the Source.

The Source wasn't one specific place.

It was a series of secretive central hubs that occupied large swathes of territory in all countries under the Circuit's control. The largest one he knew about was on the East Coast not far from where he lived. He'd learnt in Circology class that the Source was closed to citizens and only contained those deemed a threat to the rest of society, sometimes temporarily, sometimes permanently. Although this was how the authorities portrayed it, Jake didn't know anybody who'd been there and returned again. Few people were foolish enough to put themselves in a position where they might find out.

Jake did his best to hide his flashbacks from the army of Memory Hunters that monitored the cloud for abnormalities and bugs. Maybe they already knew? After all, when everything was recorded, almost nothing could be hidden. Maybe that was the real reason he'd been prescribed so many upgrades over the last seventeen years? Maybe they were trying to stop the flashbacks rather than the headaches? But for whose benefit? His or theirs? Today, mercifully, he was pain-free and channelled both the visual and virtual worlds to help him focus on what would happen next.

THIRD GENERATION

Outside the window the drone had reacted to an internal sense of annoyance at being left to wait, and its metal shell had turned a light shade of pink. Nothing for it, thought Jake, time to face the music.

He lumbered out of his bedroom to the first-floor landing, having hurriedly thrown on the first T-shirt he could lay his hands on and a pair of ripped shorts. The sound of the escalator, clicking perpetually as each step fell monotonously away from the top before being replaced by the next, was just part of a familiar soundtrack. Jake sucked in a breath of anticipation and looked nostalgically around at his surroundings. This was the only home he'd ever known. The only house he'd ever lived in. Today was the penultimate day he'd wake up here. Down both sides of the landing a series of videographs played out a comforting procession of Montana family outings or notable personal achievements. They changed daily to reflect the mood of the viewer, an instruction direct from their cloud. Today they were sombre and one in particular caught his eye.

A six-year-old Jake was experimenting in the backyard with his brand-new physics bike. They were all the rage back in the early twenty-thirties. It was designed to help teach children to cycle without the fear of falling. Four canisters, either side of each wheel, instinctively adjusted the stability of the bike by discharging jets of high pressurised air that eliminated the chance the child fell off. Looking back now, it seemed a pointless contraption given how bikes were no longer in use outside of history lessons. As he remembered it, and as the videograph confirmed moments later, Jake had disappointed the marketeers of the product by careering head first over the top of the handlebars. Face struck concrete at force, dislodging a front tooth in the process, before his mother dashed to his aid, shrieking with worry. Jake instinctively stuck his finger in his mouth and ran it over that day's enamel victim. Today it looked and felt much like its white siblings, perfectly replaced on his gums by the wonders of modern dental reconstruction. It wasn't the only time he'd had work done on his appearance, but it had been the first.

Many of Jake's physical features had been improved down the years. His wavy, blond hair was only partially original having been enhanced to avoid the genetic weakness of the Montana family's receding hairlines. His lips, nose and chin had all been sculpted to remove minor inconsistencies or injury. Only the sparkling blue of his irises was authentic but that was only because eye surgery was outlawed in case it disrupted the signal of the chip in the nerve behind it.

Everyone invested in enhancements, at least here in the West. Money was no barrier to improving how you appeared in the visual world. In any one of the dozen walk-in clinics within a mile of his house, most work could be completed within the hour. All you needed to operate such establishments was a Circuit licence and a state-of-the-art cellular mogrification pen. Body surgery was as easy as getting a tattoo. As with everything in life, standards varied. It was immediately obvious when you met someone with the really expensive work. Jake's wasn't, but Christie liked it and that was all that bothered him.

Jake stepped on the escalator and both of his worlds slid gently by as he descended. Subscribers to the Memory Cloud saw two distinct worlds at once. On one dimension the physical world passed by as real as it had been for as long as man had noticed it. The fake plastic flower arrangements that poked rigidly over the rubber of the moving bannister; the subtle green ceiling lights that dimmed and brightened in response to the external conditions; the windowless windows that projected a realistic representation of the outside world onto what was basically a section of wall: all of these existed in Jake's visual world.

On the other dimension you experienced the virtual world of the Memory Cloud. It projected a visual representation of what you saw, thought or felt. These neural interactions were then grafted inconspicuously within or next to what you saw in the physical world. Visual memories from the past could be accessed at leisure and replayed in front of you, no less real than the videographs on the Montana family's walls. Occasionally an unexpected figure might pass through the scene on the off chance you wanted to buy toothpaste or upgrade your life insurance. The world of the Memory Cloud was your television, computer, museum, library, school, cinema, shopping centre and photo album all in one. It was the internet inside your head, and it took most people a while to adjust to it.

Each generation had had their own unique experience of it. Jake's dad, Kyle, had been one of the early adopters of the internal implants back in the thirties. Unlike today's infants his microchips were fitted while he was a young boy, although he never talked about the experience openly. Even though Kyle had been tethered to the cloud for decades he still had occasional bouts of 'cloud over' where the real and virtual worlds got confused. On one memorable occasion Jake found him hiding up a tree after he believed he was being chased by a pack of vicious dogs. In fact, he'd unwittingly allowed a dog food advert into his memory feed. It was easily done. The Memory Cloud was so lifelike everyone experienced 'cloud over' once in a while.

Jake's grandfather, Paddy von Straff, had even more trouble adapting to his, but it wasn't just down to user error. Paddy was born in the last millennium when the Memory Cloud was nothing more than a futuristic wisp of an idea. He was the only one in the family who truly knew the remarkable difference between now and then. Paddy's access to the cloud was via equipment best described as base-level. It wasn't even an official implant; the vital components being housed inside a small metal box that was attached to a belt around his waist. It interfaced with his consciousness via two sticky sensors that had to be attached to the sides of his head. From there wires ran down his back to the receiver on his hip. It worked about as well as a faulty hearing aid. Any signal he did receive rapidly disappeared and was immediately followed by a bout of swearing and his demands for life to return to the old days.

Paddy objected to the whole concept of the Memory Cloud. In his view it was a waste of time and a suppression of his human rights. Should any of the Montana family ever express dissatisfaction with their membership, blame always sat squarely with him. He'd signed up for the Circuit in the early days and as a consequence so had every other member of the family. In the Montana household only Paddy had chosen his own future the old-fashioned way. Everyone thereafter had, or would be instructed, to follow the rules laid out in their letters. Kyle and Deborah had been coupled together on their own Ascension Eve in the same way Jake would be today.

At the bottom of the escalator his family had gathered to wish Jake a happy birthday and to dish out the moral support for what might come next. At least most of them had.

"On a scale of one to ten," goaded Tyra before Jake had taken the final step off the escalator and onto the photo-fluorescent carpet. "How nervous are you? I'd say eleven!"

"Very funny."

Tyra reinforced her verbal taunt by sending Jake a virtual one that involved a holographic version of herself laughing on a continual loop. He swiped it from his mind, something he'd got used to doing when it came to her.

"Happy Birthday, son," said his mother. "How are you feeling?"

"Tense."

"Remember everything will be fine in the end. We've all been there, and it worked out great for me and your dad, didn't it?"

"Crap it did!" bellowed Paddy. "You've got very short memories. Maybe you should go back and check them again on that fancy cloud of yours. The two of you have had more ups and downs than a roller coaster."

"Not now, Dad," scowled Deborah, growling under her breath.

"It'll be a disaster, Jake. Mark my words, nothing good will come of it. It was better in the old days when…" Paddy paused while he fumbled underneath his silicon shirt to adjust the small metal box on his hip. "Why am I hearing Radio Seattle? I didn't ask for that racket. See what I mean, it's a nightmare…now what have I got? Bloody interference. No, madam, I'm not your Uncle Stanley, you've connected to the wrong member. Don't tell me who I am! No, I'm not him. I don't care if I do sound like him! Stop calling me, crazy bitch. Get out of my memory feed…"

"Have they arrived yet?" asked Tyra more through curiosity than malice on this occasion.

"No," replied Jake.

"I wonder what they'll be like," added Tyra. "Probably losers like you. That's how it works. They're designed by the Circuit to replicate an individual's characteristics, I learnt that in Circology."

"Do they!? You're screwed, then, aren't you?" replied Jake who sent a couple of his own pernicious memories into her feed.

"Mum, he's doing it again!"

"Jake, what have I told you about virtual bullying? It's banned in this house, do you hear me? Until your guides arrive, I still have parental controls and I'm not afraid to use them."

"She started it!" grumbled Jake.

"And I'm finishing it."

"Debs, how do I block someone again," barked Paddy, still arguing with his own virtual world somewhere near the living room door.

"Just think it, Daddy, and it will happen automatically."

"Oh Christ," he replied.

"What is it?"

"I think I've just blocked Aunt Lou instead," he said, grinning. "The mind knows what it wants! No…I wasn't talking to you, madam, whoever you are, hang up your end!"

"Are you ready then, son?" said Kyle with a friendly smile, placing a comforting hand on Jake's shoulder. "You won't know what the future holds until you go out there."

"I know."

"And I'd rather not replace the front door," Kyle chuckled. "We all got nervous on Ascension Eve. It's normal."

"I think I'm ready," said Jake. "I've been preparing for it my whole life after all. I just wish Christie were here."

Anxiety welled in his chest and generated a flood of adverts for antidepressant medication and replayed some of his darkest memories as a result. Christie always put him at ease. There was nothing he couldn't face when she was at his side in full support. How he needed her warm, infectious smile right now.

"Is she coming around?" asked Deborah.

"Later," replied Jake. "I don't think she can face the reality either. It'll be better once we know what's in the letter."

"Just remember son," said his mother. "This doesn't change who you are. We love you whatever happens. Whatever the letter says you'll still be the strong-minded, independent, caring, quirky and spontaneous boy you've always been."

"I hope so. It's just…" He stopped and stared around at the people who'd been there to support him his whole life.

"What?" asked Deborah.

This moment might be one of the last when they were all together. There was so much he should say, yet he was consumed by self-interest and the words escaped him. His parents had done their best, and he'd not always repaid their encouragement the way they'd deserved. He'd been an unruly child, often blaming the behaviour on his regular flashbacks, although it was more often down to teenage hormones. He had a habit of arguing with people over the slightest difference in opinion and his rebellious nature caused his parents to see too many head teachers and hospital wards. The opening of the letter wasn't just for him, it was for them also. A reward for their hard work and patience. Which meant opening it increased the pressure on him further.

None of his childhood misdemeanours were particularly planned or purposeful, but they'd supported and protected him whatever the circumstances. They were the first to stick up for his interests, even when he probably didn't deserve it. It was true to say they held him to their high standards, which he felt were often impossible to reach, but they meant well even then. As they waited for him to finish his sentence, he tried to express his feelings, but the words and emotions ran for cover, unable to make the jump from the virtual world of his cloud to the visible one where they might appreciate it more.

Kyle gave him a little nudge towards the door before it was forced open from the outside.

Jake sucked in a gulp of air and confidently strode through it. On the other side, hovering perfectly still and making a quiet humming noise, the pink chrome-coloured drone stared back at him. An unseen function analysed his identity before the basket that held the letter dropped down and towards him slightly. As he inched closer the name on the letter reinforced the magnitude of the moment. The drone fixed its small camera on his face and made a noise that suggested it sympathised with how Jake felt but it was also impatient and had other stuff to do.

He stretched out a shaky hand and the tip of his finger touched the paper. It was real. He'd always wondered what paper felt like. Paddy had talked about it, but his description hadn't done it justice. It was an exhilarating feeling, like the first time he'd kissed Christie or plugged himself into the Dream Centre. He lifted the paper prophecy out of the basket and immediately felt a shadowy presence just behind his right ear. Moments later, a second entity expanded behind his left ear.

A gravelly voice broke his subconscious.

"Strap in, Jake, this is when it gets really interesting!"

- Chapter 3 -

Brother Job and Sister Dinah

The projection of an old man strolled purposely towards the drone and gave the machine a gentle pat with a virtual hand. It slipped through the metallic shell, but the motion was enough for the drone to register some unknown command. Its solar engine hummed gently, and a few seconds later it shot into the murky sky and out of sight. The old man swivelled around with a disapproving look on his face.

Jake knew about the guides, even if he'd not seen one before. Family members had described their own escorts in great detail. There were always two of them, normally a man and a woman. Each one had a unique responsibility in your future development. Although they felt very real to you, they were invisible and unavailable to others in either world. One of the rare times when the Memory Cloud carried a protected programme, locked and secure. The guides were strictly bound to the virtual dimension.

Kyle had described his own guides in glowing terms when Jake asked him about them once. One of them was a tall, twenty-something girl with blonde hair and Amazonian stature. The other cut the pose of a muscly surfer dude, laid-back and interesting. By all accounts they'd been helpful, wise and offered the right words of comfort at times of stress. Jake got the impression his father actually missed their company, and he mourned them like old friends he'd lost contact with. In Kyle's opinion they had left him too quickly, and before he was ready. Perhaps they thought he'd formed an unhealthy dependency on them?

The guides never indicated how long they would be in your company and their departure was always unexpected. Until the guides decided otherwise, they were a permanent feature of your memory feed and were never far away. Sometimes they'd be close at hand, like the one staring disapprovingly at him right now, or miles away somewhere in the background. But they were always there somewhere, watching and listening. Scott, a cousin of Jake's who'd been through Ascension Day some years ago, reported that he'd been quite successful at negotiating with them. His guides had agreed to periods of inactivity to allow him private moments when he wanted to navigate the more intimate moments with his new bride.

The scowling face of Jake's guide suggested he wouldn't be so easily persuaded.

Although their primary responsibility was always to the Circuit, their appearance, feel and personality were very much a reflection of their host. The 'sibling programme' was built into the implants and started running the first day they were fitted. Over the next eighteen years the software coding evolved patiently in the recess of your mind, mirroring and replicating your own unique characteristics and behaviours. No two guides were the same and each was conceived to reflect different sides of your character. One was a reflection of, and represented, your natural, childlike state: curious, feisty, creative, playful, joyous, vulnerable and free-spirited. The other's personality was influenced by your adapted behavioural state: self-controlled, compliant, rebellious, polite and manipulative. They were the futuristic equivalent of the 'shoulder angel' but appeared as high-definition holograms.

"What time do you call this?" demanded the old man.

"What?" said Jake, rather surprised by the apparently scolding.

"It's twenty past nine. You're late! We've been waiting in there," he said, pointing a translucent arm broadly in the direction of Jake's head, "literally for years. Where are your manners?"

"But it's my birthday."

"Oh, lah-di-dah! So, he thinks he's 'special', does he?"

If Jake had doubted which part of his psyche the old man represented it was no longer in question.

"Sorry," whimpered Jake.

"So you should be. Eighteen years we've been marinating inside your mind, waiting patiently to come out and help you. What with all the upgrades you've had it's not been much fun for us, you know."

"At least they weren't laser-cutting your prefrontal cortex every other year," he mumbled under his breath.

"Less of your cheek!"

"Huh?"

"You know I can hear everything you say, don't you? We're inside you, remember. Nothing you do, think or say will ever escape us."

"Brilliant," he replied sarcastically.

"It's the lowest form of wit," the old man replied knowingly.

"Is it?"

"Yes. I won't put up with any insubordination on my watch."

The only upside of Ascension Day, as Jake saw it, was the chance to gain freedom from your parents' rules. Finally, he was in a position to make his own choices without worrying about whether they'd approve or not. It was obvious that the guides were a substitute, permanent babysitters who had none of the blind spots he'd often use to manipulate his parents' decisions.

"If it's alright with you, Mr Guide, I'm going back inside to open this," he said, brandishing the letter as a first-class excuse to retreat.

"Job."

"Yes, I suppose it is."

"No, not Mr Guide. My name is Job. Brother Job to be precise."

"Brother Job…can I call you BJ for short?"

"No," snapped Job.

Somewhere behind Jake someone broke out into a fit of laughter, but as soon as he swivelled around to locate the source it disappeared. He jumped with surprise when he found Brother Job facing him once more.

"How did you do that?"

"Do what?"

"Get over on this side of me so quickly."

"I'm a projection of your memory feed. You do know how that works, don't you?" replied Job scathingly. "The cloud goes where you go, and I'm a regular feature until I decide otherwise."

Jake blushed with embarrassment. Of course, that was how it worked, he thought to himself. Whatever appeared in your cloud stayed there until you swiped it away with your mind, although he was pretty sure that tactic wouldn't work for the guides. They were as fixed in this world as the trees and mountains were in the real one.

Jake was struck by how much Brother Job physically resembled his grandfather, Paddy. Similar in height, build, hair colour and age, but not in a fashion sense. Job's was a perverse style all of his own. Everything about it was wrong. Job tapped his foot impatiently. The imagined flip-flops made no audible sound, partly as the floor didn't exist in his dimension.

"Why are you wearing Bermuda shorts, flip-flops, a Hawaiian shirt, and fancy sunglasses? It's the middle of Solar Winter."

"Don't ask me, this is your party. These clothes came out of your memory bank, not mine. Plus, I'm basically a projected hologram so the outdoor temperature doesn't really come into it."

"I don't like it," said Jake. "It doesn't suit your personality."

"You mean your personality."

"I'm not wearing it, am I!?"

"Yes, but I'm you, or part of you, so you sort of are."

"I'd never wear that, EVER!"

"Then where do you think I got it from?" replied Job. "Tell me that."

Jake wanted to say flashbacks but quickly suppressed the impulse in case it made Job even more judgemental.

"I still don't like it."

"Then you'll have to log a complaint."

"Ok. How do I do that?"

"You know how the…"

"Right, yes…" he sighed. "I know how the Memory Cloud works!"

Jake scrolled through a virtual menu bar that cascaded down from an area above his forehead. He focused on 'Help', then selected 'Contact Us' and finally, in the last set of menus, 'Complain'. It wasn't a function anyone used very much. The fear associated with disagreeing with the Circuit created a compulsion to threaten it a lot more often than executing it. He logged a short verbal request before logging out of the menu bar.

"What now?"

"Wait…" said Job. "Right, I've got it."

"Got what?"

"Your complaint," replied Job.

"They go to you?!"

"Yes."

"Then why did I have to go through all that menu nonsense?"

"Rules."

"Brilliant," he said, revisiting sarcasm.

Job tutted loudly in umbrage.

"I think there are enough rules already," huffed Jake, "and I haven't even opened the letter yet."

"I've considered your complaint and have decided to act upon it."

"Oh, right," he replied with surprise.

"What would you like me to wear instead of this?"

"Anything but that."

"Right you are."

"Not that!" screamed Jake, averting his gaze but finding it didn't block it out. Brother Job was standing in the street wearing what Jake could only describe as a skimpy swimsuit.

"There's no pleasing some people. What about a fireman's outfit?"

"No."

"You love firemen, I checked the backup files."

"I liked them when I was five! Can't you just go with jeans and a T-shirt? Please!"

Brother Job morphed into the requested outfit faster than a catwalk model perfecting a costume changeover.

"That's better."

"Brother Job is here to please," he scowled with a deadpan expression and an unconvincing bow.

"Why are you called Brother Job?"

"All guides are named after Bible characters, a sentimental touch by our original developers, I believe. My specific name is symbolic and chosen for you. In the Bible the character known as Job lost God's protection as a test of his faith. Over the coming months your faith will also be tested."

"Happy birthday me," moaned Jake.

"I'm looking forward to it," replied Job sadistically.

"Why brother, though?"

"Siblings look out for each other, and we are here to watch over you."

"You've obviously not met my sister."

"Oh, but I have. I've got access to all of your memories, don't forget. Personally, I think you've been a little cruel to Tyra down the years if I'm honest."

"Does your so-called help include judging my every word and action?"

"Yes. But don't forget my opinions are still your opinions, half of them at least."

It dawned on Jake that only one of his guides had made a personal appearance. He'd certainly felt the presence of another when he placed his hand on the letter, but he'd not seen or felt her in his feed since.

"Where's my other guide?" asked Jake.

"Hiding!" came a softly spoken female reply.

"Where?" asked Jake.

"If I told you that then I wouldn't be hiding, would I!?"

Jake scanned the vista for both real and virtual life. It was Wednesday morning and the street outside his house was completely deserted. Most residents had either left for work, via the electrified trams that passed his house every ten minutes during the prescribed working hours of eight until six, or were already plugged in from home offices. The town of New Hampton Falls was small compared to the sprawling cities that penned it in. It clung to the coastline about forty miles north of Boston, although the trams reached it in less than fifteen minutes these days. The estate he lived on ran in a straight line down the main road. Opposite the front of his house a strip of identical buildings reflected back at him.

All of these buildings had emerged in the last twenty years, driven by the necessity to build more sustainable homes. Regulations demanded that they were constructed from a composite material that was half reclaimed concrete and half high-density ferrocon. Ferrocon had been specifically developed to absorb carbon dioxide from the atmosphere and was a combination of steel dust, sand and laboratory-grown plankton. In front of each house a strip of solar panels led down to the main road. Jake remembered a time when they were concrete driveways where everyone parked their cars. Other than in his Memory Cloud, he hadn't seen one of those in more than a decade.

In the gaps between the houses a dense forest of carbon rods stood to attention. Beyond that, just out of sight, the river delta cut the land like a lightning strike on its journey to the ocean. Across all of this familiar scenery there was no sight of his second guide, but he certainly heard her. An insane and protracted giggling rebounded around his mind, occasionally changing in pitch and proximity.

"I give up!" shouted Jake.

"I win!"

"If you like."

"Suckers!"

"Is she always like this?" Jake asked Job with a sigh.

"Probably."

"Why?"

"Don't ask me. You've only got yourself to blame," said Job, peering over the top of a virtual tablet that had materialised in his hands. "Can we get on now, Dinah? Jobs to do."

"Saucy!" She burst out laughing at the innuendo.

"Just come out," demanded Jake. "I have enough on my plate today without chasing around after a fictitious hologram."

"I'm very real, thank you."

"Prove it," replied Jake, hoping it might tempt her out.

"Don't spoil my fun. Keep looking for me. I literally won't stop hiding until you...wow, look...a cat!"

The projection of a woman materialised on the solar driveway of the house next door. She bent down to pet the ginger cat, out for its morning hunt. It completely ignored the newcomer: the Circuit had yet to see the value of equipping felines with their own virtual world. Even if it did have one it still wouldn't have shown the slightest interest in the woman's attention.

Jake couldn't imagine which twisted part of his personality was responsible for generating this peculiar, rather plump, middle-aged woman. Her frizzy red hair stood to attention like she'd suffered from a localised bout of static electricity. Standing about five feet tall and covered in offensively bright, tie-dyed coloured clothes, her broad grin showed off crooked, blackened teeth circled by incredibly brave purple lipstick.

"Jake!" she hollered, attempting to give him a virtual bear-hug. "We're going to have so much fun."

"We're not here to have fun, Sister Dinah, we're here to make sure Jake follows the rules."

"Rules are for fools! Let's invade Tyra's memory feed and play a prank on her?"

"Are you listening to me?" asked Job.

"Not really."

"Which of you is in charge?" asked Jake assertively.

"The Circuit," they replied simultaneously.

"That figures."

The commotion of his new guides' arrival drew his attention from the initial reason he was out in the cold street in the first place. His letter.

"What do I do now?" asked Jake, timidly staring nervously at the envelope.

"Go back inside and open it," directed Job.

"Or…we could make a paper airplane out of it," added Dinah.

Brother Job scowled.

"What if I don't like what's inside?"

"Tough. You're kind of stuck with it."

"Can't I just send you another complaint?"

"You can."

"Would that work?"

"No."

"Why not?" asked Jake.

"You signed up to the Circuit like everyone else did," replied Job sternly. "So, you agreed to it."

"No, I didn't."

"Ok, so technically you didn't sign up, but your grandfather did."

"What's that got to do with me?"

"Everything," scoffed Job. "Did he read the terms and conditions?"

"Does anyone!?" laughed Dinah.

Brother Job raised a hand and projected a wall of text into the sky above them in large-sized font. It was titled 'Circuit Terms and Conditions'. He scrolled through the virtual pages before stopping on page ninety-four.

"Ah, here it is."

"Here's what?"

"The small print. 'By agreeing to these terms any participant accessing the Memory Cloud does so for the entirety of their life and that of all future descendants of their bloodline for a period of one thousand years. Details of the cancellation policy can be found on page seven hundred and eighty-one.' Seems pretty clear to me," added Job, reading the page aloud.

"Show me the cancellation policy," Jake asked eagerly.

After several minutes of tiresome scrolling Job reached the aforementioned page. It simply read – 'cancellation of your subscription is only possible in a ten-minute period immediately after the agreement is signed'.

"That's ridiculous. Who's going to change their mind that quickly and before they've even been booked in for the implants, which might be months later?"

"Maybe your grandfather should have read it, then," replied Job. "Sadly, he didn't, and you're stuck with it."

"Don't worry about it, Jake," added Dinah joyfully. "I'm convinced the contents of your letter will be awesome. I'm seeing an exciting career as a Memory Hunter."

Being a Memory Hunter was a prized role in the Circuit and almost guaranteed your vital importance factor within the system. Hunters were recruited to recover and rebuild memories that were lost amongst the billions of geopbytes of data if a glitch or bug occurred. They were also assigned to monitor the collective thoughts of billions to identify those most likely to engage in any form of criminality. It certainly wasn't Jake's ambition to become one. If the Circuit had done its job correctly, he'd soon be reading 'Boat Designer' in the pages of his letter.

"Sister Dinah, don't oversell it," said Job.

"Whatever it says, it doesn't look like I have any choice," said Jake.

"That's the spirit," said Job. "Why don't you go in and find out?"

Jake nodded. "Are you coming in?"

"We're not allowed," replied Dinah sadly.

"Really?"

"No," confirmed Job.

"What if I just stay inside and never come out?" asked Jake, hopeful that he'd found a loophole.

"You could," added Job, "there's not a lot we could do about it today."

The instinctive emotion of relief permeated Jake's cloud and immediately revealed its hand to Job.

"Tomorrow, though, would be different. Tomorrow is Ascension Day and that means, if we choose to, we have the authority to order a team of weaponised drones to level your house and everyone that's in it. Tomorrow, you're our responsibility."

"I literally can't wait," replied Jake sarcastically as he headed back into the house.

- Chapter 4 -

This Is Your Life

If guides were supposed to put protégés' minds at ease, his had failed miserably. A day that started with a heavy dose of apprehension had been firmly overdosed on panic. Not only was Jake holding his future in his hands, but he also had no way of escaping it or the insufferable Dinah and Job whose contribution would endure until it was no longer necessary. In Jake's view that moment had passed about thirty minutes after their arrival.

Back inside the temporary safety of the house, the living room had been transformed to recognise the happier side of today. Virtual decorations adorned every wall in bright, bold, glittery colours. Birthday banners, balloons, streamers and music had all been sent to his memory feed by different members of his family. Tyra joined in, although all of her virtual balloons said 'Happy Birthday Loser' on them and exploded loudly as soon as he read them. Paddy's celebratory offering was the only object that physically existed: a tatty birthday horn that produced a rather reluctant spitting sound as he blew through it while simultaneously making no attempt to move from his sprawled position on one of the large leather entertainment chairs.

"Thanks," said Jake rather reluctantly.

"Happy Birthday!" they replied.

He knew it was a charade, there was only one thing on everyone's mind.

"Show us!" shouted Deborah overexcitedly.

Jake held the letter aloft like it was an unflattering award for 'world's lamest walk' or 'first place in very disappointing mornings.'

"Oh, it looks exactly like mine did," she replied.

"Nice to keep some traditions," added Kyle.

Paddy snorted. The idea of the Circuit caring about tradition was laughable. There would be a highly practical reason for the continuity: they'd probably bulk ordered a few billion a decade ago when they were on a discount.

"So…what are they like?" asked Kyle. "I bet they're amazing like Elijah and Rachel."

"Who?" snapped Deborah.

"Those were my guides, love. Don't you remember?"

She shook her head, clearly less enamoured by their memory than her husband was. It wasn't a surprise she didn't instantly remember. She'd never met or spoken to them in the time they spent in the early part of the couple's relationship.

"They're mental," said Jake, piercing his parents' minor domestic disagreement.

Outside the house two virtual faces peered through the windowless windows, one scowling and the other attempting a poorly choreographed dance that was somewhere between the conga and twerking.

"Cats don't make dogs," offered Tyra.

"Not true," interjected Paddy, who had removed his hip box completely to avoid further interruptions from nuisance callers. "I hear the Circuit have already perfected interspecies cloning but they can't find a market for it. Meddling with nature never turns out well, mark my words!"

"You know what I meant," huffed Tyra. "I meant you get what you give. Jake's guides are mental and so is he."

"I wish I was going to be here to pour misery on your Ascension Eve, Tyra," said Jake.

"Shame you won't be," she taunted.

"Have you opened it yet?" asked Deborah, moving the subject back to what most interested her.

"Not yet."

"I'll never forget my Ascension Eve," said Kyle. "I thought I was going to be sick. I was desperate to be rewarded with one of the highest importance levels, nervously curious about my new life but also sad to be leaving my old one behind. God, there was so much pressure not to disappoint the entire family when I opened that little white envelope."

"Thanks, Dad," Jake replied despondently.

"Oh, sorry, son, I didn't mean to make it worse. It was a lot easier in my day, too. We were still in the era of the 'Great Segregation' and the Circuit's rules were still building. At least I knew my future life would be somewhere local. Who knows where in the world you'll end up?"

Deborah broke down in tears at the realisation that her only son might soon be settling into a new life thousands of miles away. Jake still didn't fully appreciate their feelings about today. The adjustment would be as difficult for them as it was for him. Even so, his focus remained squarely about self-interest. After all, it was his letter not theirs.

"You're all deluded. It will never be better than it was in my day," Paddy blurted insensitively, ignoring his daughter's emotional pain. "We've brought all of this on ourselves because of an unquenchable thirst for abundance and an addiction to perfection."

"How did it work in the old days, Grandad?" asked Tyra partly through genuine interest and mostly in the hope of dragging out her brother's discomfort.

"Um...I can't actually remember," he said, rubbing his head.

"Sorry, I don't understand," said Tyra, bewildered by the concept of forgetfulness.

Memory loss was an alien condition for the younger generation of the West. They never forgot anything. It was a physical impossibility. Everything they'd ever thought, felt or seen was instantly accessible through the power of the Memory Cloud. It worked to both their advantage and disadvantage. It was impossible to lose anything important because you could always backtrack in your memory feed to see where you'd left it. Song titles never evaded recognition and people's names and ranks were recalled instantly, even if you'd only met them once when you were four years old.

On the downside it became a lot harder to use your memory as an excuse for why you hadn't done something. Avoiding chores or schoolwork was identified for what it really was, laziness or a lack of ability, not as it had been in the distant past because you'd 'forgot'. The very word itself was about as common in today's vocabulary as hearing someone say aeroplane.

"Wait, I'll remember it," gasped Paddy, screwing up his face in a vain attempt to jump-start his cognition.

"Dad, plug it in!" said Deborah pointing at the little metal box.

"I don't need it! I'll remember eventually, give me a second." After a few minutes of deep and visible concentration Paddy's recollection returned. "Ah yes, twenty-sixteen, that was the year it happened for me. Most people hated that year, but as far as I was concerned it was one of the best, a pleasure cruise compared to twenty-twenty."

Everyone nodded in agreement, even those who weren't born until a decade or two later.

"I'd taken a job as a junior sales assistant in a little office just outside Boston."

"An office?" interrupted Tyra.

"Yes."

"Which is?"

"What do they teach you in school?" he huffed.

"Important stuff rather than ancient history," she replied with a classically teenage tone.

"It's where lots of people used to work back in the day."

"Ugh, that's grim. Think of all the physical contact, must have been horrendous."

"It was wonderful. People actually used to talk to each other. Not through this fake reality that we have to put up with now. Real conversations. Person to person. That's where I first learnt to flirt."

"I think I'm going to be sick!" screamed Tyra hysterically.

"That's just how you did it back then. You met someone at work, or in the gym, or at the bus stop and you struck up a friendly conversation. You might compliment them on how they looked or offer a cheeky smile before politely asking if they'd like to go out for a drink or maybe even dinner. No algorithms, no rules and no letters. Well, unless they were love letters. I miss those. Much simpler. We didn't need to infiltrate the memory feed of the person we fancied before bombarding them with a collection of unauthorised virtual emotions like an artificial sex pest!"

"I prefer it our way. Saves time," argued Tyra who at fourteen was already on her seventh serious boyfriend as a result. None of them lasted that long before someone more interesting came along. What was the point of getting attached? It would all change on Ascension Day anyway.

"Pah! I didn't need some powerful higher consciousness to tell me when I was in love. I knew it as soon as I laid eyes on your grandmother, God rest her soul. My Nina. It was a perfect match."

"I know that feeling, too, Grandad," added Jake. "The first time I saw Christie I thought my heart was going to leap out of my chest. Even now, every time I think about her or see her, I get butterflies in my stomach and a powerful energy surrounds my body."

Tyra pretended to retch in disgust.

"Exactly!" replied Paddy so excited by his grandson's empathy he almost lifted out of his chair. "Don't let it go, Jake. Never."

"I don't think I'm going to be as lucky as you were, Grandad," replied Jake solemnly. "It's just not as simple as it was."

"Let's not get all depressed. The Circuit knows what's good for us," replied Kyle. "There are billions of people out there, and not one of us can truly know which one is perfect for us. But the Circuit can. They do all the hard work for us. You never know, Paddy, if you'd had the benefit of the system there was probably someone out there who was an even better match for you than Nina."

"That's my mother you're talking about," said Deborah angrily. "Half of the people in this room wouldn't be here if it wasn't for her, remember."

"No offence, my love, I was just trying to comfort the boy."

"It's not working," replied Jake.

"Oh, just open it," sighed Tyra, who was already distracting herself from the conversation by chatting to her friends in her cloud feed. "Let's just see what awful trauma the Circuit has in store for him and then all laugh!"

Jake took a seat as far from the others as possible. He caressed the letter under his finger and thumb. How did he open it? He'd never held one before. He searched for a button or sensor that might make the envelope dematerialise to reveal the letter underneath. There was none to be seen. When he turned it over, there was a small flap at the top and a code was printed in tiny letters. These codes were extremely common. As soon as your eyes noticed one, the chip in the optic nerve sent a message to the amygdala to immediately launch an instructional video in your cloud feed. Everything you bought had a code these days. Clothes, medicine, groceries, kitchen appliances, pets and anything that the Circuit deemed to be ancient in origin.

Jake watched intently as the brief instructional video was projected on the living room floor. In it a small child was demonstrating the most efficient method of opening a letter without disrupting the contents. They always used a child in these videos. It was how the Circuit kept you grounded. If an infant could complete any given task, then you could, too. If it transpired that you couldn't, then no doubt they'd have a record of that emotion and it would work against you in the future. Maybe this was how they worked out someone's 'importance factor'? thought Jake He reflected on all the times the smug little 'know it all' in the projection had outwitted him in the last ten years. Too many to count.

Not this time, though.

In no time Jake had carefully removed the letter from its wrapper. Like the Circuit logo on the envelope, the letter was in gold and black print. The paper had been scented with something pleasant yet indescribable. Jake checked his cloud feed for the smell, but it came up blank. Whatever the scent was it was new and would be logged forever, along with the memory of this day. The memory might be replayed frequently if he got what he hoped for today. The fragrant aroma that danced off the page had the unusual effect of lowering his pulse rate and shrouding his senses with a beautiful sense of tranquillity. Whatever was coming next, he no longer had reason to fear it.

Jake read the contents of the letter a couple of times. Most of it would need further explanation but, on this occasion, there were no more codes to help him out of his confusion. Perhaps that was the purpose of the two guides currently pressing their faces up against the windowless windows. The information did somersaults around his mind desperate to fix the landing and avoid falling flat on its arse. He'd need more practice.

"Tell us, then," burst out Deborah, unable to suppress her nervous excitement.

"I don't really understand what it all means."

"I remember that feeling," said Kyle. "Take us through it one line at a time. Who have they paired you with?"

"It just says, Sam Ragnara Goldberg, importance factor – necessary."

Almost immediately, and unnoticed by those around them, everyone other than Paddy scanned their Memory Clouds to get a first glimpse of Jake's future bride. It wasn't difficult to find her with such a unique middle name. Anyone's details and biography could be found on the cloud even if you weren't connected directly to them. If you wanted a more intimate interaction, however, you'd have to formally request access to their feed.

"Oh well done, my son," boasted Kyle, clapping his hands together gleefully. "You've done well."

"She's alright, I suppose," added Tyra. "Shame for you that she's not more important than necessary, though. Life's going to be a struggle, that's for sure."

"Do any of you remember Christie?" said Jake sternly. "You know, the girl who's been coming to this house for the past six years. The one you all get on with. The one I'm actually in love with."

"Yes, of course," said Paddy. "She's cross-eyed?"

"No, that's Tyra's friend Evie and don't mock, there's no surgery allowed on eyes, remember."

"I'll actually miss Christie," said Tyra. "She made you more bearable."

"Well, I shouldn't worry because in twenty-four hours I won't be here to annoy you. I'll be in Sweden, wherever the hell that is!"

Again, everyone mined their virtual platforms to check for themselves. The 'Great Segregation' may have ended two decades ago, but most adults had very little experience of travelling outside of their own borders. If practical, most couples were still selected locally, and the cost of travel by any means other than tram was exclusive to those with vital or essential importance factors or very rare exceptions.

"Holy moly," said Tyra. "It's on the other side of the Atlantic in the United States of Europe."

"Is it?" gulped Jake. "I thought most of Europe was in the sunken lands."

"Jake, connect your feed to mine for a moment," said Kyle.

As they coupled their cloud feeds, Kyle pointed out the regions of the U.S.E. that were still inhabitable after the catastrophic sea surge of the late twenty-thirties. He pointed out the location of the Low Countries before they were submerged, and then traced his finger across the virtual map to point out what remained of the Scandinavian region.

"Everything to the south of here," he said authoritatively with his finger pointing at somewhere called Turkey, a place Jake had never heard of, "all of this is uninhabitable until you get as far down as Tanzania. Although you can live there, no one wants to."

Jake quickly forgot about the calming influence of the scent in the letter and decided instead to engage full throttle hyperventilate. He'd never even left the country, let alone travelled across the sea. The ocean had always been a great comfort in his life. It was less than ten minutes' walk away and he and Christie went most days. They'd sit on the beach, relax, chat and watch while the waves half-heartedly broke on the sand, knackered from their extensive journey from a place thousands of miles away that he was viewing now on a fake map. When you lived your whole life by the sea you learnt how to respect it, whether you were swimming, sailing or diving. It had never held any fear for him until today.

"Oh God! I don't want to move to Sweden. I thought if I had to marry someone I'd never met before it might at least be somewhere nearby, then at least I might still see Christie…as a friend obviously," he added just in case the Circuit was listening and took offence.

They always were.

"I think that's why they do it," said Deborah whose face had gone pale with shock. "Take away the temptation. They must know how you feel about her."

"If they know that I love Christie, why are they doing this? They're supposed to be making the decisions for me based on my innermost desires and emotions. At what point did I beg to live in Sweden and have a job as an Archivist?"

"Is that the job they've given you?" said Deborah.

He nodded reluctantly.

"I hear it's a good one," added Kyle. "Lots of travel, exciting missions, and they have an important role in upholding the integrity of the Circuit."

"Huh," gurgled Paddy. "Welcome to the Gestapo, boy."

"The what?"

"Look it up on your fancy cloud."

He did.

He didn't like the comparison.

"Oh, that's perfect," he replied falsely. "I wanted to design boats, a fun form of transport that the Circuit haven't abolished yet. Where the hell is that on here?" he said, shaking the letter. "Nowhere! Instead I have to spend the next forty years chasing after speccies and enforcing the Circuit's laws. It'll probably be dangerous, dirty and demoralising. No one likes Archivists, do they?"

"You never were very popular," sniped Tyra.

"People like them more than speccies. They're the true enemy," added Kyle sternly. "Most are criminals. We can't track where they go and what they're thinking. It's totally irresponsible of them. Why would people do that unless they had something to hide? I think they're plotting against the rest of society. I bet they're already planning to invade so they can kill our children and steal our homes."

"Rubbish!" said Paddy. "You're being poisoned by your own mind. The Circuit wants you to be scared. That's why they broadcast the 'Proclamation of Distrust' every other day and fill your feed with mistruths. The Spectrum just refuse to live under an oppressive regime. They just want to be free, that's all."

Midway through Paddy's rant his metal hip box vibrated, and a light flashed like it was signalling a late wake-up call or urgent notification. He knew what it was but ignored it as usual. Even when he wasn't wearing the device, the Circuit tracked him through his connection with the other clouds associated to him.

"There is nothing oppressive about the Circuit," argued Kyle. "They keep us safe by tracking all those people who desire to do us harm. The technological advancements under the cloud have been nothing less than transformative, and I'll remind you that without them our race might not have survived at all."

"That's what they want you to believe, isn't it?" said Paddy. "They feed you lies and fear, even when you're asleep. Not me, I sleep naturally, no cloud, no Circuit and no clothes."

Tyra stuck her fingers in her ears and rushed out of the room.

"When was the last time you heard a report of a crime being perpetrated, Paddy?"

Paddy folded his arms and stared over a shoulder.

"Or a war. There hasn't been one of those for a while, has there? It's all thanks to the Circuit. You're just living in the past and can't find anything worth moaning about anymore."

Jake listened intently but found it hard to completely agree with either of them. His dad was right about illegality, there was almost none these days, but some niggling doubt in Jake's brain had always felt it was too perfect to be genuine, and his flashbacks proved that it wasn't. Now the horrors in his letter added to his doubts.

"What else does it say, Jake?" asked Deborah who always camped somewhere between her husband and father in her world views.

"I've been enrolled in a variety of clubs and societies for activities I've never previously shown any interest in. BASE jumping, quilting classes and chess club, whatever that is. Oh, and I've been signed up for Alcoholics Anonymous."

"You're not old enough to drink," said Deborah sternly.

"It's dated twenty fifty-nine so the Circuit are obviously predicting I soon will be, and quite heavily. After today I'm considering starting early to be honest."

THIS IS YOUR LIFE

All in all, the letter was a worst-case scenario. There was nothing in it to offer hope. It was as if his letter had been mixed up with someone else's. Maybe there was another Jake Montana in the West equally confused right now. The Circuit didn't make mistakes of this magnitude, everyone believed that to be true, but this had to be one. None of his desires and wishes had been factored in, and to top it all off there was one final gargantuan kick in the teeth at the end of the letter. He knew before he'd opened it that he would lose Christie, but he never imagined he'd lose himself at the same time.

"And I'm superfluous," announced Jake, a tear rolling down his face.

The room fell silent.

No one checked their clouds for confirmation of what it meant, they all knew. The Montana family gazed nervously at each other, struggling to make eye contact with him. Not even the returning Tyra thought it was funny. What did you say to someone who was superfluous? It was like reacting to a patient with a terminal illness. Kyle finally broke the silence after his wife jabbed him in the ribs with her elbow.

"It's not the end of the world."

"Yes, it is. How many of your friends are superfluous?"

"Well, none."

"There you go, then," whined Jake.

"They're not to be trusted," said Paddy, expertly mimicking Kyle's voice.

"I never said that!"

"You always say that, Dad," replied Jake. "You've been saying it since I was a little kid. Well, now you do know one. Me!"

"I really don't understand this," said Deborah. "How can you be superfluous if your new bride is necessary? The Circuit usually put people with the same importance factor together. You just can't achieve a harmonious relationship if you're occupying different levels. It's a recipe for disaster."

"I think the Circuit's rules are the least of my worries right now, Mum. In the space of thirty minutes I've lost my girlfriend, my home, my life and my hope. All because of someone called Alison."

"Alison?" said Tyra.

"Yes. That's who signed my letter. Principal Conductor of the Circuit, Alison."

- Chapter 5 -

Calm Before the Storm

Jake ran up the escalator before reversing its direction, making his escape to solitude somewhat slower than anticipated. His bedroom door swung open unaided, as it always did, and closed gently before he had the opportunity to slam it and dissipate his anger. He slumped down on his bed and closed his eyes. The virtual world washed across the insides of his eyelids, released from its competition with the physical world.

A torrent of birthday messages flashed through his feed. Most were from people he liked; some were from people he barely remembered. He swiped them away like an invisible hand threatening an irritating fly. As soon as the virtual space was cleansed of family and friends, a barrage of Ascension Eve-related corporate leeches invaded his privacy. Everyone from major chess manufacturers to Swedish quilting groups to travel insurers knew the contents of his letter and wasted no time in trying to profiteer from his misery. It was easy enough to switch them off if you were proficient with the cloud, but they'd never disappear completely.

They always found new and innovative ways of infiltrating your thoughts. Sometimes they'd wait for you to access an old memory before surreptitiously placing a sneaky product placement amongst the scenery. It might be on an advertising hoarding in the background, or a passer-by might be holding or wearing the product. On some occasions they'd even hack a historic conversation you remembered and sneakily place a reference to their business within the dialogue. The answer to why they went to such lengths was simple. It generally worked. But not today.

What Jake needed right now was clarity.

Something had gone horribly wrong and he wanted answers.

He'd always feared losing Christie, even though he knew it was inevitable. His plan had been to fight for that love. To find a way to continue seeing her even after the revelations in the letter. Those thoughts had betrayed him, even though he did his best to keep them out of his mind. Writing them down wouldn't help either, even if paper was still widely available. When you wrote you thought, and when you thought they were aware of it. Their letter was punishment for attempting to cheat the system. The Circuit had him in a headlock but at least now he had an individual rather than a system to aim his anger at.

Alison.

Why had he never seen or heard that name before? He scanned back through his strongest memories associated with the Circuit to find any reference to her, however insignificant. There were none. Not a sniff. Until today the Circuit had been a supreme faceless power that acted as one collective entity. There was no reference to person or persons that might be responsible for the decisions they made. The Memory Cloud itself made the decisions, even for the Circuit.

A proximity alert sounded, and he opened his eyes. It was still there. A salmon pink virtual frame, containing a name and a distance, floated in the middle of his bedroom. Proximity alerts indicated the physical position of the people you chose to track. His parents had them for him and his sister, but he only had one. Christie. The locator showed her approaching his front door.

How was he meant to deal with this? Today hadn't just decimated his future, it destroyed hers, too.

A minute after the alert went off the door to his bedroom eased open automatically and his tearful girlfriend stood in the doorway. Christie was a tall, slim seventeen-year-old, both sporty and elegant in appearance. Of the girls in his school she eclipsed all others, and it wasn't just Jake that thought so. Jealous classmates had bombarded his memory feed with hateful messages for years, unable to understand why someone like Christie would be attracted to someone like him. He wasn't the smartest kid, or the best sportsman, the richest or even the one with the best body enhancements. Yet she chose Jake. He hadn't hounded her into the decision like his sexually aggressive classmates. He never doubted his self-worth, but their relationship had done little to boost his popularity. Jealousy can be a unifying catalyst for hatred.

"Come in, babe," said Jake, beckoning her to enter so the door returned to its dormant position in the wall and gave them some privacy.

"I've seen her," said Christie balancing sadness and anger perfectly.

"Who?"

"Sam Goldberg."

"Oh."

"How could you?!"

"In what way is any of this my fault?"

"You must have secretly desired someone else the whole time we've been dating. Deep within your Memory Cloud you've been fantasising about tall, leggy blondes with blue eyes and foreign accents."

"But you have long legs, blonde hair and blue eyes…"

"I'm not Swedish, though, am I?" she snapped. "Have you been lying to me?"

"No, I swear. Look, none of this makes sense. You know how much I love you, but you also know how this is meant to work. The letter would never have had your name in it because you're not eighteen for months. Right now, I just need your support and to spend our last day together having fun rather than a massive argument."

Christie's anger crumbled and she slumped into his arms on the bed.

"I'm sorry. This is really hard for me, too," she said.

"I know," he said softly.

"I'm just so scared to be that far away from you. I accessed your cloud and saw all the details of your letter. It's a tragedy what they've done. It must be a mistake."

"I wish it was, but I don't believe so. I think it's very purposeful. The Circuit want to protect themselves by separating those that threaten their perfect system. Arseholes."

A klaxon sounded and a large virtual warning sign lit up the room in a deep red flashing box. It had a simple message written inside.

VIOLATION.

"Careful," whispered Christie. "They are always listening."

There were strict rules that governed people's behaviour towards the Circuit. Crimes against the Circuit included minor defamation, like Jake's comment, to what they deemed serious acts of treachery. Treachery was punished severely, although no one knew how exactly because it was so rare. Minor violations were tallied annually and any adult reaching ten was punished. Normally this took the form of a temporary reduction in their importance factor. Violations by children were always counted on both of its parents' tallies. Tyra didn't have any. This one was Jake's ninth of the year.

Tomorrow his tally would start afresh.

"Come on, let's go down to the beach," said Christie. "I want to sit with you by the sea and watch the sun go down one last time."

"I'd like that."

She placed her smooth hand in his and lifted him off the bed with ease. Jake was no weakling. Slightly taller than Christie, but by no more than the length of a fingernail, he had a slender frame more suited to fast swimming than wrestling or boxing. He regularly exercised, partly to maintain his own personal standards and just slightly to ensure he was in good shape for her.

They snuck quietly down the escalator to avoid further questions from the family before slipping out of the side door where they might escape the inquisition from Jake's guides. With guides it was never that easy.

"Where do you think you're going?" asked Brother Job suspiciously, watching as the young couple crept around the corner of the house and onto the road.

"To enjoy the calm before the storm," explained Jake.

"There's a storm coming!" screamed Dinah nervously before jumping, quite pointlessly, into a bush.

"It's a metaphor," replied Jake.

"They're really dangerous," added Dinah.

"What, metaphors!?"

"No, memory storms."

"I don't think hiding under a bush will protect a hologram from either."

"It might."

"I guess you must be talking to your guides," said Christie who was unable to see any evidence of the holograms, even though he'd granted her full permission to his Memory Cloud. It didn't work the other way around. The guides couldn't physically see Christie, but they saw her cloud perfectly well. It had the effect of painting her into their virtual scenery.

"Yes, he is," snapped Job. "And who might you be?"

"This is my girlfriend," said Jake.

"Not for much longer."

"Tell me if I'm wrong," said Jake through gritted teeth. "but your influence over me starts tomorrow, right?"

"Correct," answered Brother Job.

"Then get lost."

"We can't," added Dinah whose head was peeking out of the bush like a gopher from a prairie hole.

"Why not?"

"We're a constant in your feed from the moment you touched the letter. A permanent stream in your virtual conscience. You can't just swipe us away."

"But you don't have to be up close to me, do you?"

"No, we can be anywhere we like as long as we can still see you directly or via a local Memory Cloud."

"Fine. I'm putting a metaphysical restraining order on both of you until midnight. You'll stay as far away from me as you possibly can, got it?"

"Received and understood," grunted Job.

Hand in hand, Christie and Jake strolled across the road and squeezed down a side path and into the heart of the carbon rod farm.

CALM BEFORE THE STORM

"Quick, they're leaving," begged Dinah, shaking up and down nervously like she desperately needed the toilet.

"Stand down, Sister Dinah. There's nothing we can do about it today."

"I know but they're going to the beach. I wanted to build sandcastles!"

"How's that going to work? You don't have hands."

"I can still pretend, can't I?"

"Fine, we'll go down there. But tomorrow you need to take things a bit more seriously."

Dinah nodded and crossed her fingers behind her back. The guides drifted after the two young lovers a few hundred metres behind with Jake always in their sights.

Jake and Christie dodged in and out of the carbon rods like they used to when they were little. It had been an ideal place to play and the farm had been in the neighbourhood as long as they had. The tall, slender cylinders were small in comparison to some he'd seen, but they all had the same purpose. Regulating the atmosphere. When deforestation hit its peak in the early twenty-thirties and the world's temperature soared, there weren't enough trees on the planet to recycle the carbon dioxide back into oxygen. That's when the world's boffins came up with the solution – synthetic trees.

The carbon rods functioned exactly like regular trees but were made from environmentally friendly materials that could be built more quickly and cheaply than growing a tree from a seed. The carbon rod farms came too late to avoid some of the irreversible damage caused by man's abuse of Mother Nature over centuries, but it was enough to keep everyone breathing. The excess oxygen that seeped out of the shiny black rods had a tendency to make people dizzy, and if you lingered too long here the rod farmers soon moved you on. The beach was more of a draw on this occasion and the couple passed through quickly. Wherever he lived in future he'd see more of them, but today might just be his last chance to enjoy his stretch of ocean before he was forced to cross to the other side of it.

On the far side of the rod fields the ground became sandier as the soil lost its fight against the march of the beach. Down a bank, past a group of small, wooden shacks that sold everything from refreshments to beach toys, over the open sewer line whose tunnels disappeared deep underground several feet below them, and finally they were on the beach. They discarded their shoes and allowed the warm, golden sand to wade between their toes. Down by the shoreline the sea was calm. Baby waves massaged the beach with their white, frothy wake.

"Do you remember the first time we came here together?" asked Christie, taking Jake's hand as they lay down on the beach watching the sun struggle with the unnatural cloud cover.

"I remember every moment I've ever spent with you," replied Jake.

"We can all look back, Jake, but do you really remember it?"

"How do you mean?"

"Without accessing the Memory Cloud. By letting your real brain visualise it."

It wasn't an easy task. Anytime you reminisced the cloud feed automatically opened to ensure the full details of your experience weren't lost or misrepresented. Your own brain couldn't compete with the technology and often gave up and let the implants do their work.

"I'm not sure I can."

"Try," said Christie. "Swipe everything away when it comes into your feed."

Jake concentrated. Memories of his many trips to the beach flashed in his feed desperate to be centre of attention. He swiped them away as quickly as they arrived.

"It was June…the ninth," he said. "It was the first time our parents let us come down here together, even though we'd been begging them for months. We were thirteen and a half. For once the sun stayed out the whole time we were down here and we both got sunburnt because we weren't used to it."

"Yeah, we looked like lobsters when we went home. My mum was so angry with me," said Christie.

"You were wearing a little red bikini with a thin, white shawl over the top. I remember being embarrassed by the thought of your naked skin underneath it. We went for a swim, but you didn't want to get your hair wet, so we came back here and lay on our towels."

"Do you remember what happened then?"

"Yeah. I'll never need a cloud feed for that moment, it's imprinted in my brain and on my heart."

"Our first proper kiss. I never wanted to kiss anyone else ever again after that," replied Christie.

"We were naïve," added Jake. "We didn't understand what was coming in the future."

"I still don't," she added tenderly.

Jake nodded but his face was drenched in despondency.

"How are you feeling about tomorrow?"

"Scared and angry," he said hurling an empty seashell at the water. "It's just not fair."

"I know, but we'll find a way to be with each other, won't we?"

"I really don't know how. There's just no way two people can beat the Circuit and little value in logging a complaint. This is just how life is."

"Don't say that," replied Christie staunchly. "There's always a way."

"How?"

"I don't know. Maybe we have to…change things," she said in a whisper.

Surprisingly the next sound wasn't a violation alert as they expected. Instead Jake doubled over in pain, grabbed his head with both hands and let out a shrill scream that would have cleared the beach for fear there were sharks in the water. It was so loud that even Job and Dinah heard it up on the dune where they sat staking out their student.

"What's wrong?" Christie pleaded.

"Flashback," he screamed, writhing on the sand in pain.

Christie had seen him suffer with these incidents before and she knew from experience that there was nothing she could do when they occurred. Sometimes they were fleeting and sometimes they lasted for days. The only thing she could do was offer some comfort and support. Fortunately, this was one of his shorter episodes.

Jake's pain eased and with it his screaming ceased. It had been months since his last flashback but when they started it generally signified the start of a sequence that would build in strength over the coming weeks. He took a moment to compose himself and allow the tranquillity of the sea to restore him to the present. Christie pulled him closer to her like a concerned mother.

"What did you feel?" she said gently in his ear.

"Not much this time," Jake gasped.

"Tell me," she said softly.

"Tension. Unbelievable tension like a kettle about to boil over. There was a dimly lit room only illuminated by a golden light that hung from the ceiling. There was an ancient, wrinkled figure sitting in front of me, but the scene was blurred and difficult to place. I felt anger and fear rise in me and when I looked down, I saw these huge feet and broad legs that didn't belong to me."

"What do you think it means?"

"I don't know. I'm more concerned about who the memory belongs to, rather than what it means. It certainly isn't one of mine. It's interesting that I should have a flashback today of all days."

"Maybe someone is trying to show you something?"

"Or scare me."

"Why would they want to scare you?"

"I don't know, but I'm sure the details in my letter and the flashbacks starting again are designed to stop me doing something."

*****

"I don't know why they get so emotional about it," said Brother Job, pretending to perch on a rock while he spied on the couple through a pair of virtual binoculars.

"Emotional about what?" asked Dinah who was mostly running up and sliding back down the sandy dune that led to the beach.

"Ascension Day."

"He's totally bricking it," said Dinah graphically.

"Would you say so?"

"Oh yeah!"

"The part of his personality that formed me isn't concerned. I'm reading that he's…" Job paused as he shuffled through Jake's cloud. "Resigned to it."

"Resignation doesn't sound like a lot of fun, though," said Dinah sensitively.

"Oh, I love a bit of resignation. You know where you are when you leave all the worries behind you and just get on with it in a stoic and restrained manner."

"That sounds horrible. It's definitely not as much fun as BASE jumping. I can't wait to give that a go!" said Dinah pretending to BASE jump off the bank.

"He really shouldn't be so worried. The Circuit don't get decisions wrong. They know what's good for them," stated Job categorically and pointing at the couple. "If they're not meant to be together then that's that. Move on, get over it."

"Maybe," said Dinah. "She does seem rather lovely, though."

"Who does?"

"His girlfriend," she said, pointing at the girl on the beach and rolling her eyes to show her dismay at her brother.

"So, what if she is? Destiny has chosen otherwise."

"Just seems a shame. Look at them, they do look very much in love."

"Listen up," said Job sternly. "This is no time for sentimentality, Sister Dinah. We need to show Jake a united front. We can't go offering him guidance that's confusing or ambiguous. We have to be a unit, like two sides of the same coin. Can you do that?"

"Doubt it."

Job scowled.

*****

The couple spent the rest of the afternoon lying on the sand, sometimes chatting, sometimes silent. They weren't the best conditions in which to enjoy it. It was cold and a stiff breeze charged in across the Atlantic. It didn't matter a jot to them. They recounted stories of happier times and snuggled up to each other. When the sun finally edged through the smoggy gloom and over the horizon, they helped each other to their feet and proceeded to make their final walk home.

"You will remember to connect with me every day, won't you?" said Christie through eyes moist with tears.

"My memory feed will always be open to you, you can check in on me anytime you want."

"What about Sam?"

"Who?"

"Your bride!"

"Oh. Well, I'll have to have a good chat with her, try to explain the situation."

"You can't do that, Jake. It'll break her heart. Don't forget it's her Ascension Day tomorrow, too. She's also had her letter today and your name was inside it. I wonder how she's feeling right now?"

"I don't care very much," replied Jake, swimming in a pool of his own narcissism.

"Jake! Stop being selfish. There were times in your life when you felt alone, weren't there? Times when others were brave enough to engage and support you?"

She was right. He remembered one incident in particular that had changed his life because someone had courage like that. It was the day he met Christie.

"I'm sorry. You're right."

"Just because she was chosen for you doesn't mean you're going to fall in love with her, does it? But it also doesn't mean you can't be friendly."

"Maybe I should send Sam a memory request?"

"Yeah, I think that would make meeting for the first time a little easier."

Jake searched through the cloud interface to find Sam Goldberg and requested access to her cloud feed. The response was immediate.

"It's been declined."

"That's a bit rude," said Christie.

"It's not a good sign, is it? I mean we're supposed to be getting married. We haven't even met yet and she's already blocking me. Can this day get any worse?"

The universe immediately answered his question. Yes.

"Stay still or I'll shock you!" came a croaky voice directly behind them. "Give me all your credits."

In the shadows of the sewer entrance an olive-skinned youth in ripped clothes was pointing a dangerous-looking, home-made weapon at them. Multiple rotating blades spun viciously and glowed with a golden electric energy. In Jake's eighteen years on Earth, he'd never once been threatened with violence. In fact, it was the first time he'd even witnessed a crime outside of a history lesson. How was he meant to react? A hormonal instinct welled inside him. Protect the ones you love. His mind immediately focused on defending Christie.

"We don't want any trouble," said Jake, slowly turning around.

"Smart boy," said the assailant, even though he was probably no more than a year older than his victim. "Hand them over."

"We don't have any credits, we just came out for a walk. I can transfer as much as you need via my cloud if you give me your access key."

"What good would that be to me?" he growled viciously.

"You can use them the same way the rest of us do. They can't be traced even if my memory cloud can be."

The aggressor seemed unaffected by the veiled threat of being tracked down. He knew the Circuit would already be monitoring the situation and would unquestionably be sending first responders to deal with his breach of the rules within minutes. Driven by some unknown motive to maintain his threat, he dashed out of the sewer tunnel like an Olympic sprinter. In a swift motion he grabbed hold of Christie's necklace before Jake could formulate the right response. He ripped it from her neck with a snap and darted back down the tunnel. It was all over in a matter of seconds and the mugger was soon out of sight.

"Your necklace!" shouted Jake in horror. "It's the one I gave you for your birthday last year."

"It's ok, Jake," she stammered in shock. "We're both safe that's all that matters."

"No! It doesn't belong to him," replied Jake, diving down the tunnel without thinking it through.

"Don't, Jake. It's too dangerous."

- Chapter 6 -

The Spectrum

"Quick, Dinah, we're losing him!" shouted Job as they struggled to keep pace as their host descended further into the sewage system.

"I thought we were connected?" she replied while simulating panting.

"We're linked to his emotions and right now, I can't feel any. It's like he's disappeared."

"Oh don't worry, I can."

Job's hologrammatic mass ground to a standstill. "What?"

"Yeah, I can feel him."

"How come?" he said, rather put out that he was out of the loop.

"Because he's scared, and that's my department."

"I don't like that."

"That's because you're a control freak," added Dinah sympathetically like he had a horrible disease.

"If you can feel him then get us near him," grunted Brother Job angrily.

"We can't," sobbed Sister Dinah uncontrollably.

"Why not!?"

"Timing."

The guide's affinity to Jake was borne through his own reactions to any given situation. If he was feeling reserved and composed, Job would feel him. If he was happy or suffering loss, then Dinah would make the connection. Once they got through Ascension Eve, between them they had all bases covered. Which effectively meant they'd always be able to trace and catch up with him whatever the circumstances.

But not today.

Tomorrow, if they were so compelled, they could materialise anywhere they chose to. On his head, a metre in front of him, a mile away or even inside his own mind.

"Damn it," said Job, pretending to stomp on the sewer's concrete base without creating even the slightest of ripples.

"Urgh, this place is disgusting," said Dinah, unnecessarily grabbing her nose. "Why would anyone want to go down here?"

"I think this is where they live."

"What was the house for, then? Just keeping up appearances, are they?" said Dinah, looking thoroughly confused.

"Not the Montana family, you simpleton. The Spectrum."

*****

Jake sploshed through the filth. Sewage water and its unspeakable flotsam washed up his trouser leg and submerged his best trainers. The noxious smell grew more unbearable with every step he took into the darkness. It was the second new smell he'd experienced today, and like the first he was sure it would ultimately end in disappointment. The only source of light, the entrance to the tunnel far behind him, shrank like wool on a hot wash. He held his hands out to guide his progress. The slimy walls rejected his trailing fingers, pushing them away from the brickwork. This was getting him nowhere.

He stopped abruptly.

What was he doing? Did the necklace matter that much to him? It wasn't expensive but it was valuable. He'd given it to Christie on her birthday last year, but it was more than just a simple gift. It signified something deeper. It was a token of his love and she wore it constantly as a sign of hers. When most girls of her age saw trinkets from boyfriends as a form of ownership, she just saw it for what it was, a sign of his admiration and affection. He'd even had her name and date of birthday etched on the pendant. It cost him more than the necklace.

The sound of the thief retreating from his pursuit dampened to silence. Had he got away? The answer came immediately. Light burst through the darkness and Jake's legs were whipped from underneath him as he landed awkwardly on the sewer base with a splosh. A rotating weapon swirled viciously as it discharged sparks over the sludge. Standing above him was the threatening face of his quarry.

Hunter had become the hunted.

"Do you like your face like that?" asked the youth gruffly.

"Um…yes," replied Jake, feeling vulnerable and filthy.

"Looks like you've had some nice work done, be a shame to ruin it."

Illuminated by the sparks the youth's own face was like no other Jake had ever seen. His nose was crooked and wide, his hair wild and unkempt. There were pockmarks all over his skin and a very distinctive scar took prominence in the centre of his forehead. Most people would have tried to hide such a mark, but the man seemed to wear it with a sense of pride. When surgery was universally accessible why would anyone choose to remain like this? Why would anyone choose to be ugly?

"Take a mental picture, it'll last longer," said the man.

Like all his memories, this scene would remain forever whether Jake chose to remember it or not.

"Look, I don't want any trouble," said Jake, his confidence rising but his tone betraying him. "I just want the necklace back."

"You don't need it. Your kind already have everything they need. You're spoilt by a world of abundance."

"My kind?"

"Yeah."

"Do you mean humans? Because you look quite human if you'll forgive the insult," suggested Jake politely, only too aware that his assailant had the ability to leave him perforated.

"Circuit user."

For a moment, Jake didn't fully appreciate the significance of the response. Wasn't everyone a Circuit user? Everyone he knew was, but he lived, like most people, in a small town in a relatively closed society. Beyond that bubble he believed millions of other people existed like him. Finding anyone who didn't would require a Herculean effort and multiple violations. It was only a rumour they existed at all, and in eighteen years he'd never even seen one, let alone met one. They were more elusive than the mythical Big Foot.

"You're a speccy!" exclaimed Jake.

"What did you call me?" said the youth, thrusting the lethal device closer to Jake's face so he could feel the hot sparks bounce off his skin.

"Sorry, I thought that's what we called you?"

"Free, that's what you should call us. Free from the constant surveillance and free from the system designed to control people like you."

Jake scanned his Memory Cloud for previous references to the Spectrum. Although he'd never met one, he knew plenty of people who'd claimed they had. Past memories flashed in the background behind the threatening blades still circling around his face ready to strike. The memories were mostly of family members or friends inaccurately describing a series of monstrous figures that lived in caves and ate babies. It had always sounded farcical, a tall tale to frighten little children. In truth this boy wasn't markedly different from Jake, other than he'd been forced to survive through opportunistic acts of crime and live in the shadows. That didn't mean speccies were born criminals, as his father always insisted. For them it was only a means to an end. His hasty trip down memory lane was broken by an imposter sneaking into his memory feed.

"The world's a dangerous place! We all need protecting. What will you do if you're attacked? Enrol today in Boston's award-winning self-defence classes, the first lesson is free, just…"

"You're a bit late," Jake told the corporate hologram who'd barged into one of his memories dressed in full body armour and brandishing something that looked distinctly like a nunchuk.

"You get a free throwing star," replied the man desperately.

Jake flicked the advert away.

"Call me," came the final muffled sales pitch.

"See, there's no escape from it," said the youth, referring to what he assumed was an interference in Jake's virtual world. "There's no peace from the Memory Cloud."

"You get used to it."

"I won't."

"I guess not."

"I want you to stop following me or I'll be forced to chop you into small chunks and leave bits of you every hundred feet between here and Boston."

The multiple blades rotated ever faster as the crackle of energy intensified. It wasn't clear if the sparks were part of the danger or a way of bamboozling the victim from seeing the blades.

"I'll let you keep the necklace if you stay and talk to me for a while," said Jake whose sense of curiosity to learn subjects that weren't strictly allowed got the better of him.

"I'm keeping it whatever you decide to do."

"Fair enough but if you don't talk to me, I'll be inclined to give the Archivists your position and I'm sure that would make life tricky for you."

"You're connected to the cloud, so they're already on their way. They can collect your bloodied corpse as a second prize, but they won't catch me. Archivists are clueless and blunder around like a herd of blind wildebeests. All that's needed to avoid them is stealth and we have it by the bucketload."

The speccy gave the pouch he wore on his belt a gentle spontaneous pat, which also grabbed Jake's interest.

"What's that?"

"None of your business," he said, thrusting the weapon aggressively towards him.

"Stop!" cried Jake.

"Perhaps you should think twice before you threaten the Spectrum."

"I lied," screeched Jake. "They can't track you, my Ascension Day isn't until tomorrow. Look, I have the letter to prove it. I just wanted to learn about your people."

Jake drew the letter out of his pocket and held it up in the air, a paltry deterrent compared to the snarling device that could shred it to a thousand pieces in one thrust. The Circuit's relationship with anyone underage was always directly through its parents. A child's cloud had restriction to ensure that the Circuit did not take undue advantage of them and so they didn't waste valuable resources sending Archivists on a wild goose chase as a prank. The first the Circuit would know of this incident would be a notification to Kyle and Deborah's feeds and only then would the Archivists be able to track Jake's proximity alert if they suspected the Spectrum were at large.

"I can't read that," said the youth, waving the letter away with his free hand.

"You can't read?!"

"Of course, I can read...it's just too dark."

"Right, sorry."

"Even if you're telling the truth it won't take them long to get here. The Archivists are bloodthirsty bastards even if they are incompetent."

Jake was surprised not to hear a klaxon sound and the violation warning filling the air. This boy wouldn't know what they were. He could say whatever he wanted about the Circuit, it's functions or employees without the slightest fear of losing his importance factor because he didn't actually have one to lose.

"What's your name?" asked Jake.

"What's it to you?"

"I'm just interested. Your people still greet each another, don't they?"

"Yes," he replied reluctantly. "It's Alfonso."

"I'm Jake Montana...superfluous," he added uncomfortably.

"What's that got to do with anything?"

"Doesn't it repel you? I mean I'm at the very bottom rung of this world."

"We don't make those kinds of judgements. Everyone in our community is equal and has the right to follow their own destiny."

"I can see the appeal of that today," replied Jake curiously, "but why do you live like this?"

"It's how we're supposed to live."

"What, in a sewer?"

"No. We don't live in sewers, it's just one of the access points to reach your world."

"Where, then?"

"Ha! I'm not telling you that. You'll try to earn credits by grassing me up to the Circuit. It's none of your business."

"But doesn't it get depressing, all this stealing and hiding?"

"Doesn't it depress you?" he said, turning the conversation on its head.

"What do you mean? We have everything need."

"Really? Can you choose where you go, who your friends are, what you do for work, who you love? Can you travel freely without being tracked or watched?"

"Yes," he said unconvincingly. "The Circuit knows what's good for us and we never forget anything. Everything is there when we need it."

"I don't need a Memory Cloud for that. It's all in here," said the boy, pointing at his head. "Your mind has become soft and lazy. The human brain is more than capable of coping if you choose to live without the false world of technology and greed competing alongside it."

Jake found himself protecting the system when it had so badly let him down in the past few hours. When you'd lived with it all your life and knew the perils of stepping out of line it became almost impossible not to fear expressing your own personal opinions.

"Happy with your letter, were you?" said the boy with a tone that bordered on pity.

"No. It stinks," said Jake despondently.

A red-rimmed 'Violation' message engulfed the tunnel although it was only Jake who saw it. This was his second violation today and his tenth of the year. Boy, was he in trouble now. His parents would be receiving their own notifications summoning them to a virtual 'conduct feeling' to defend the actions of their rebellious son. The red glowing message had a second effect: it was an ideal beacon if you lived within the virtual world.

"There he is!" shouted Dinah joyfully from the void behind him. "Jake, we've come to rescue you!"

"Run!" Jake shouted to Alfonso.

"It's too late," said Job, popping up beside him in the tunnel. "The Archivists are already on their way."

The light from the blades was extinguished. The boy turned on his heels and sprinted further up the tunnel.

"What were you doing?" demanded Brother Job angrily.

"Trying to get back what was mine."

"By talking him into it?"

"It's nice to make new friends," said Dinah. "Is he coming back? We could all play hide-and-seek!"

"No, I think it's unlikely he's coming back, Sister Dinah," said Jake.

"Shame."

"He won't need to," said Job. "The Archivists will soon catch him."

"Why can't they just let him be?" asked Jake.

"Because, like all the others, he's illegal."

"An eagle, cool," said Dinah.

"Ignore her."

"I don't see what the problem is," implored Jake honestly.

"They threaten your values. Imagine what damage they could do to your way of life. You can't have a harmonious society if some of them hide in dark holes without jurisdiction or rules."

"But compared to me, he's free."

"Less of your backchat. You've already landed your poor parents in serious trouble because of your insolence, and you don't want to do any more damage, do you?"

"No," replied Jake, feeling guilty.

"Come on, let's get out of here."

Jake lifted himself out of the sludge and shook as much of it off his clothes as he could. He trudged towards the light with a guide on either side of him. Dinah was jumping from one dry patch to another to avoid touching the 'lava', as she described it.

"What did he look like?" asked Brother Job, piercing the silence.

"Didn't you see him?"

"No. We don't have real eyes. We only see a person's cloud and as speccies don't have one, we'll never be able to see them."

"Why are you so interested, then?"

"I've never seen one before. Remember I've been growing inside you for the last eighteen years."

"You'll have to find out for yourself," replied Jake childishly. He didn't trust Job, who as yet had done nothing supportive for his cause.

"Ok. I will."

"Damn it," replied Jake.

Brother Job knew what his host knew. Everything he saw, thought, recollected or imagined was there for either guide to access at will. They were a function of his cloud, so nothing was off-limits to them.

"Interesting scar," said Job, scanning Jake's most recent memory files. "Might be useful to remember that when you're an Archivist."

"Oh Christ, this is what I have to do every day, isn't it?"

"Yep, and if you're no good at it you'll get fired and they'll allocate you an even worse profession."

"Not sure how it can be any worse. There's nowhere lower than superfluous."

"How about superfluous and being a plankton scraper for a ferrocon company?" said Job.

"Is that a real job?"

"Yep."

"Ok, so that would be worse."

When they reached the tunnel entrance, Christie wasn't the only one waiting for them. A platoon of heavily armed men with reinforced lightweight metal jackets were standing in a semicircular formation receiving a briefing from an aggressive-looking superior. The man in the centre had silver hair, a neatly trimmed beard and rigid cheekbones that could shell oysters, all of which stayed in perfect harmony as he barked out his commands. Jake had never seen facial work that good before. The man's cosmetic surgery was so precise you could use it as a mould for the perfect human.

"Team one, you will locate all other exits that lead out of the sewer complex. Team two, I want you to keep this end of the network secure. I will lead team three into the tunnels. There will be a capture today. We have one confirmed sighting but no doubt there will be other associates of the Spectrum in the vicinity. Corridor S Two, let's flush them out."

"Where are you going?" said Job from the corner of his mouth.

"Team one," said Dinah innocently.

"Not today."

"Spoilsport."

Christie ran over to Jake and flung her arms around him, still shaking from the events of the last thirty minutes.

"You didn't need to do that," she said. "Your safety is more important to me than any object."

"Thanks, but I always stick up for myself."

"I know you do, it's one of the things that attracted me to you in the first place."

"I'm sure this is all very touching, but don't you have somewhere to be?" stated Job.

THE SPECTRUM

Jake checked the alerts in his feed. As Job had inferred, and he'd suspected, there was one from the Circuit labelled 'Defendant' and marked 'Urgent'.

"They've already started!"

"Started what?" asked Christie.

"Feeling the evidence."

"What evidence? You're not making any sense."

"I may have uttered another violation. My parents are in a 'conduct feeling'."

- Chapter 7 -

Indisputable

It wasn't prudent to leave the Circuit waiting so Jake and Christie dashed back to the house in double-quick time. It was at most twenty minutes since his most recent violation down in the tunnel, but the commotion around Jake's street proved it was all the time they needed. A perimeter of drones had already encircled the house in case anyone was foolish enough to escape justice. These drones weren't remotely like the reasonably friendly one that delivered his letter this morning.

These were serious.

Twice as large with thicker metallic shells and equipped for a multitude of tasks, these were utility drones. Black as night and notoriously hostile. In a world without war they were the closest thing to a military unit outside of the Archivists, whose own role was much less diverse and usually less violent. The very threat of these machines was enough to disperse any potential fighting spirit you might have stored up prior to them entering the airspace. Few knew what they were capable of, because few had witnessed it for themselves and no memories of those who did ever circulated in the cloud so you could check.

They were the Circuit's expendable muscle, and down the years they'd been deployed many times, for many purposes. In the early days of their introduction they were used to disperse crowds that sought to protest against unjust laws or causes that motivated them. Such freedoms of expression were common two decades ago. These days no one marched in such rallies. Some argued this was attributed to the Circuit's ability to understand what the populace wanted so that mass action wasn't necessary. Some vouched that the hard-hitting reaction by the drones was reason in itself. What the truth was no one knew.

Jake knew why they were here today, though.

'Conduct feelings', like the one his mother and father were currently attending, were held virtually in the cloud. Vast sums of global credits were saved by dispensing with physical courtrooms, travel costs, juries, expensive lawyers and judges, none of which was needed these days. Court decisions in the distant past were based on hearing different interpretations of the evidence. The defence would depict one version of events while the prosecution attempted to convince jurors of an opposite account. In twenty fifty-four all they needed was the Memory Cloud and a judgement against the rules. Evidence wasn't just seen; it was also felt by experiencing the collective and unarguable memory feeds of anyone who'd been in the vicinity of the incident at the time. Witnesses no longer had to be called to give evidence because they no longer held exclusive rights over what they'd seen or felt. They'd signed away that freedom when they, or someone in their family, subscribed to the Circuit. They could still be punished, though, if they attempted to put up a fight.

Jake had received the court summons but his haste to return home was less to do with compliance and more to do with guilt. He wasn't going to bolt and let his parents face the consequence of his actions when there was no place for his deeds to hide. In eighteen years, this was the first time he'd passed the threshold of ten violations. He'd once got up to eight. That was a tough year. He barely spoke to anyone for the last few months of the year for fear of what might happen if he did. Not easy for a six-year-old.

Jake crept across the drive while a dozen drones slowly stalked his movements. Each was equipped with cannons that were welded to the outside of its shell. There was one strapped on either flank, one on the undercarriage and something that resembled a mini-missile launcher, that could pivot in any direction, on the roof. It was clear that whether you tried to escape by land, sea or sky they were fully capable of stopping you quickly.

There was no legal way of defending yourself against these robotic monsters.

No one bore arms these days unless they had a death wish. After a surge of gun-related deaths over the last century the people, facilitated by the Circuit, had decided there was no longer a justified argument for owning them. Soon their uniquely modern version of democracy ruled it so and banned them. Since the climate catastrophe hunting had already been abolished, crime was close to zero, and wars with neighbours or foreign invaders were just too costly to the fragility of the world. There were fierce objections to the decision in some quarters, but the drones soon put paid to that resistance. Unsurprisingly the only organisation allowed to flout the rules was the very one that helped the people vote on it. The powerful never fully comply with anything.

Jake crept through the metallic throng of machines that were two or three times bigger than him, and slipped in through the front door.

The 'conduct feeling' was already in full swing.

As a required witness to the case his memory feed had already been forcibly tethered to the virtual proceedings. Inside the living room, Kyle and

Deborah sat apprehensively on a sofa watching a series of memory repeats that covered all of Jake's previous violations during the year. They were currently watching number three. He remembered it well, but then again, he remembered everything if he chose to. Violation three happened while he'd been plugged into the Dream Centre. He'd almost reached a national high score playing his favourite interactive game when some unforeseen error message crashed the interface. He hadn't meant to curse the Circuit, but at the time it did feel like they were unfairly biased against him for some reason.

"I'm sorry," he said to his parents as he flopped onto a chair on the other side of the room.

"One more day," said Deborah, scowling and somewhat red-faced. "That's all you had to manage!"

"Don't fret, my love. I'm sure Jake had his reasons," said Kyle. "He's never put us in this situation before, has he?"

He hadn't. He'd always felt a great deal of personal responsibility to not land his parents in trouble. This, he suspected, was exactly why the Circuit designed the procedure this way. What child wouldn't feel a sense of guilt in a situation like this? He certainly did right now.

"It'll be a slap on the wrist and a short period of demotion," replied Kyle confidently. "Gus down the road got one and his only lasted a month. His kid's a right tearaway, too."

"But I don't want to drop down to trivial, even for a month," sobbed Deborah. "People around here judge, it'll be the end of our social life."

"I think you're exaggerating. If people are that shallow, then who needs them?"

"I do," snapped Deborah.

The stream of repeats being projected against the wall, from their collective memory feeds, had reached number seven. It was one of Jake's personal highlights. It involved an incident where he'd expressed to Christie that he loved her more than the Circuit, which, all things considered, was true. He didn't feel it was a suitable reason for receiving a violation.

"What did you do this time?" said Kyle. "They've blocked the most recent violation from my stream."

"I expressed that I was unhappy with my letter."

"To Christie?" asked Deborah.

"No."

"Then to whom?"

"Someone I met down at the beach," he fibbed spontaneously.

Lying was a ludicrous course of action in general. It was about as effective as saying you'd forgot. It was possible to get away with a lie told to a stranger, but it was particularly foolish to aim one at people who had unfettered access to your own memory feed as his parents did. Lying in humans is as natural as breathing. It's a simple human condition that can't be abolished as quickly as so many other of our day-to-day norms. Studies have proven that lying starts as early as six months old and gets progressively more advanced as the human develops. This instinct doesn't cease just because you're connected to the false dimension of the Memory Cloud, but it does make it harder to get away with. Jake's most recent violation might be temporarily locked, but it would be less than a minute before it was being played out in full definition on their living room wall. It might be the shortest lie in recorded history. He bit his lip. He had no idea what he was trying to achieve by diverting the path of truth other than prove he was human.

As the day's first violation marched through their virtual projection, capping number nine for the year,

Jake sucked in a chunk of the cold air that poured into the room from the air conditioning units that adorned every wall.

"Where exactly are you?" said Kyle, pointing at the wall. "It's very dark."

"Sewer."

"What were you doing there?"

"Trying to get Christie's necklace back," he said, attempting to smooth the situation with chivalry.

"Who took it?"

"You'll see."

The memory replayed Jake's short and tempestuous interaction with a gloomy figure holding an illegal and deadly weapon.

"I can feel why you were scared," said Deborah connecting to the emotions surging through Jake's feed alongside with the shady visuals.

"Who is he?" asked Kyle, barely finishing his question before the answer presented itself. "Who's Alfonso?"

"He's a speccy."

His parents diverted their minds from the feed and eyeballed their son, mouths dangling open in mid-air. They'd both reached middle age without coming into contact with one of the unbelievers and yet here he was, not even past Ascension Day, and he'd managed it.

"You know your job as an Archivist hasn't started yet?" said Kyle. "I mean there will be training and everything."

"It wasn't planned, it just happened."

The final few minutes of the memory played out, including Jake's insult about his letter that brought about his tenth violation. The memory ceased not quite the way Jake remembered it. There was no interruption from Brother Job or retreat from the scene by Alfonso. The memory stopped at the moment the red alert flashed in front of him. The stream of memory repeats was quickly replaced by a line of light green text typing out comments on a black screen in real time. There was no verbal commentary to assist them, just written words and a flashing cursor at the end of each line.

`The evidence is indisputable...`

"But what about the mitigating circumstances?" said Kyle remonstrating with a computer readout.

`The evidence is indisputable...`

"My son was forced to deal with a speccy and foiled a potential crime, surely that has to play a part in the judgement?" added Kyle nervously.

The text stream vanished, and the end of the tenth violation memory returned to the screen. As it rolled through like a slow-motion replay everyone in the room saw and felt Jake's reaction as he instructed the speccy to 'run'. In reality he'd only shouted that because Job had rematerialised out of thin air and sent him into a panic. But only Jake knew this: there was no evidence of it on-screen. How could there be? The guides weren't there. The context was important, but who would believe him when no one could see or feel it? Plus, it wasn't his Ascension Day yet so the guides weren't even in a position where they might be an influence.

"Why did you do that?" beseeched Kyle, visibly shaking from a combination of anger and fear.

`The evidence is indisputable...`

"I don't understand," pleaded Jake. "What have I done?"

"Aiding a speccy isn't a minor crime, Jake. It's a level-one violation. This is serious, boy."

"I wasn't aiding him, I just panicked."

`The evidence is indisputable...`

"I'm sorry, I didn't know! I got spooked by my guide appearing out of nowhere."

"Don't blame them. They're only there to help you and they're not in a position to do that until tomorrow," cried Deborah.

"But he did appear!" shouted Jake. "It's not my fault."

"It never is, is it?" Deborah replied angrily. "It's time you stopped thinking about yourself for once. You're an adult now. You're part of a bigger picture. You can't just rebel because you feel like it. We all have to do as we are told, not as we please."

`The evidence is indisputable…`

"What have they been teaching you in Circology all of these years, for God's sake?!" screamed Kyle, bursting from his chair and advancing on Jake.

His father had never been a violent man, but Jake was genuinely convinced he was about to convert.

Circology had been one of his least favourite subjects. It was a daily dose of the Circuit's rules replayed or updated with every technological or ideological improvement. The lessons were always delivered virtually by some monotonal instructor who'd never considered there might be a better way of making his class more engaging. It felt more like brainwashing than teaching. Over and over their lecturer reinforced the same positive messages of the Circuit's immense value to the world. The organisation had saved humanity, but that didn't mean the world wasn't a dangerous place. The threats were very real and would only be defeated if everyone played their part. Follow the rules, identify those who didn't and keep faith in the Memory Cloud.

Jake had heard it all a thousand times and would distract himself by throwing virtual paper airplanes at school friends or metaphorically sinking into his past to entertain himself. In truth so much of those lessons seemed irrelevant to him. He liked the cloud, everyone did. It gave him access to everything he needed when he needed it. The threats his lecturer presented just weren't found here in the idyllic surroundings of New Hampton Falls. The East was on the other side of the planet so how could they be a threat? And as for the speccies, when would he ever meet one of those? They were like ghosts.

How wrong he'd been.

`The evidence is indisputable...`

"I'm sorry," wept Jake. "I never believed I would meet one, but when he stole Christie's necklace, I couldn't allow him to get away with it. You've always told me to stick up for myself."

"We did," said Kyle softly. "But who's going to stick up for us?"

`Verdict...`

The word froze on-screen followed by a green cursor that flashed menacingly as it waited for the author to consider or complete the next line. The wait was purgatory. It felt like the Circuit was cruelly building suspense as if the 'conduct feeling' was the broadcast of a tacky reality game show. Deborah reached out her clammy hand and grabbed her husband's. Both of their faces had gone pale and gaunt.

"I'm sorry," cried Jake. "What's going to happen?"

`Verdict...`

`Deborah and Kyle Montana. Demotion to trivial...`

Deborah wailed in horror at the proclamation, but her reaction was premature. The text stream wasn't finished.

`Extradition to the Source for reconditioning and upgrades...`

"No!" screamed Kyle, leaping to his feet. "We've always abided by the rules. This is our first offence."

"What does it mean?" asked Jake who was being almost completely ignored.

"Show some lenience, he's very sorry. It won't happen again," said Deborah through floods of tears.

"He's an adult tomorrow, why should we suffer because of his stupidity?!" shouted Kyle, brimming with vitriol towards his son. "Make him suffer."

Jake felt uneasy. It felt like his father was trying to throw him to the lions. Was this normal behaviour in a situation like this? Kyle knew Jake was leaving tomorrow, and after that they'd have minimal interactions, other than through the cloud, for months, maybe years. Perhaps he felt his parental duties were complete, it was up to the guides now? Perhaps he was showing his true colours and revealing why Jake also possessed such a selfish streak? When crisis came, Kyle's ability to demonstrate resilience had been found wanting because he'd never had to show it before.

```
The   evidence   is   indisputable…Stay
seated.
```

"Mum, I don't understand, what does this mean?"

"It means we have to leave."

"All because of you!" roared Kyle. "I never want to see you again, do you hear me? You are a disgrace to the family name!"

Paddy and Tyra rushed into the room through different doors, having been notified of the judgement either via cloud alert or from hearing Kyle's noisy remonstrations.

"Leaving where?" growled Paddy.

"Dad, they're taking us to the Source!" cried Deborah.

"What? They can't do that," replied Paddy.

```
Stay seated…
```

"What about our daughter?" asked Deborah as her maternal instincts kicked in. "She needs us."

`Follow protocol number twenty-two...`

"What's that?" asked Tyra nervously.

"It means I am your legal guardian until your parents return," answered Paddy sympathetically.

"What? No, that's not fair."

"At least you get to stay here," argued Jake a little unwisely. It was a habitual instinct to challenge his sister in every situation, good or bad.

"This is all your fault, Jake! Just because you didn't get what you wanted in your letter, you had to ruin everyone else's lives, too, didn't you?!" she shouted, launching herself at her brother, fists clenched and ready to beat him to a pulp or claw his eyes out with her long, sturdy fake nails.

`Remain seated. Deportation imminent...`

The front door was blown off its hinges. It was an eventuality that Jake had briefly considered first thing this morning but not quite in the same circumstances. If he'd just left the letter where it was, the door would still be broken and perhaps none of this would have happened. Two utility drones swooped through the doorway and scanned each of the occupants of the house with gold beams that shone out of the front. They soon identified Deborah and Kyle and floated ominously towards them.

`Please leave quietly...`

"Tyra, be good for your grandfather. Jake, do what your guides tell you. We'll be alright," said Deborah, guiding her shaking husband away.

Kyle reversed out of the room, wild, malicious eyes fixed on his son throughout.

Jake buried his face in his hands and wept uncontrollably as his parents were chaperoned out of the building. As soon as they left the house everyone in the family lost access to their memory feeds like the lights in their lives had been switched off. Out of sight, out of mind. Tyra stormed upstairs hysterically. Paddy remained in the living room and waited patiently for Jake to compose himself. When he did a final message ran through the projection on the wall that only he saw.

`'Conduct feeling'` adjourned. The Circuit - it's a state of mind...

Alison...

- Chapter 8 -

Ascension Day

Jake was woken at exactly midnight by a commotion in his memory feed. Someone had rudely interrupted the endless series of corporate and political messages slowly infecting his subconscious while he slept. It didn't take long to work out who.

"Morning. Just wanted to let you know that we're here," said Job, pretending to perch on the end of the bed. "Happy Ascension Day."

Jake bolted upright like a mousetrap springing into action. He wiped his eyes with the sleeve of his pyjamas to help him focus on the visual world in case he was cloud dreaming. He checked the time in his memory feed and his heart sank.

"Did it have to start now?" He yawned.

"We didn't think you'd want to miss anything," answered Dinah energetically.

"What if I missed the first seven or eight hours of it?"

"Not today, young man. You're on our time now."

"But I'm tired."

"Tough. You need to start packing for your journey."

"What time are we leaving?"

"First thing."

"But this is first thing, you can't get any earlier than this."

"Then it'll be second thing…after the packing."

ASCENSION DAY

After the trauma of yesterday all he wanted to do was hide under his duvet and pray tomorrow decided to take the day off. Couldn't the odd couple give him a break? Surely, they must know how he was feeling?

"If you're meant to reflect the different sides of my personality, can't you at least show some empathy?"

"Empathy?" replied Job quizzically.

"Step off, Job. That's my department!" shouted Dinah, diving in front of the old man's projection and staring rather manically into Jake's eyes like an amateur hypnotist.

"Um…what are you doing?" he asked.

"Shhh…I'm absorbing all the factors that you're feeling worried about."

Jake wanted to immediately name two.

"You're mostly worried about a trip to the dentist and you're also feeling sad in case they don't make trifle in Sweden."

"What are you on about? I'm…"

"It's called empathy," she snapped.

"I think you've slipped into psychopathy by mistake."

Dinah shrugged it off, as if it didn't make a bean of difference to her. "Open your mouth so I can see your dentist."

"Get off me!" shouted Jake, waving his arms in front of him and finding they went through her projection with little effect on her actions.

"I don't understand," she said glumly. "I'm usually really good at this stuff."

"Wake-up call," replied Jake brutally. "You're terrible at it."

"Then why don't you tell me what the matter is?" asked Dinah patiently.

"Ok. I'll spell it out. In the minimal time since the pair of you showed up, I've lost my girlfriend and my life hopes, watched my parents being extradited to the Source, and seen midnight after sleep rather than before it for the very first time. Are you seeing a pattern here?"

"Who cursed you? Tell us, Jake, and we'll get them," pronounced Dinah, raising her fists.

"It's all part of the Circuit's plan, I'm sure," offered Job unsympathetically, scanning through a checklist of all the items he thought Jake might need for the trip.

"Well, the Circuit can shove their plans up their own arse!"

The klaxon sounded for the third time since yesterday morning.

"Oh well done," said Job, clapping ironically. "You were on day one of a clean slate and you've already picked up a violation. Did you learn nothing from yesterday?"

"I'm going back to bed," huffed Jake, collapsing onto his synthetically stuffed mattress and pulling his pillow over his head.

After no more than ten seconds of comfort he felt his body sliding down towards the bottom of the bed like one end had been lifted by a crane.

"Woah! What's happening!?"

"We're getting you out of bed."

"But you're holograms; you can't touch me."

"Where on Earth did you learn that rubbish from?"

"Um…Circology."

Job slapped him square in the face and a hand briefly met skin before flying through to the other side. Jake's skin tingled from the strange contact.

"That was odd," replied Jake looking at his own hand which had returned to its original position next to his side after moving without his permission.

"I think we've already proved that you learnt nothing in Circology class. Let me refresh what you missed. Today is Ascension Day and from today we can interact with you in any way we please."

"Aren't there any safeguarding rules?"

"Yes, but I would have thought it was perfectly obvious and particularly undesirable to touch you in any sensitive regions," replied Brother Job tactfully.

"My face is sensitive."

"I rub jelly on mine," replied Dinah eagerly. "It doesn't help much but sometimes the jelly accidentally falls in my mouth!"

There was something intoxicatingly endearing about Sister Dinah that made Jake warm to her. She said what she wanted without the slightest embarrassment, did what she wanted without ever feeling restricted, and wasn't ashamed to express her feelings whenever she had them. It was just this life-affirming spirit that he needed today to keep his morale up. It definitely wasn't going to be offered by the stuffy-nosed Brother Job whom Jake was starting to despise, irrespective of him owning personality traits that existed in some deep abyss of his soul.

"Sister Dinah, I'm not sure you fully appreciate what you are," said Jake gently.

"Today, I'm an owl." She tooted in response to Jake's question.

"You're a hologram! They don't eat jelly, build sandcastles or stroke cats," replied Jake sensitively. "Holograms don't work like that. The clue is in the name. Hollow!"

Dinah's hand leapt forward with instinctive anger and slapped his face before flying out the other side. Jake's other hand moved in symmetry.

"Point taken," he replied knowingly.

"You didn't say a hologram couldn't be an owl, though, did you?" added Dinah, returning effortlessly to her previous state of delirium.

"No. You can be an owl if you want to."

Dinah grinned and he immediately felt a glimmer of happiness fight back against the overwhelming sense of remorse and sadness.

He got out of bed before he was forcibly removed by the odd couple. There wasn't much reason to avoid the inevitable anyway. He had to leave at some point today whether he liked it or not, and right now he felt leaving quickly might be better for all concerned. His sister and grandfather hated him, his parents were no longer accessible, visibly or virtually, and his girlfriend was grieving his departure. What more damage could he do here? On the off chance she was still awake, Jake sent Christie a message to her cloud feed. If he was forced to leave before the sun's rays struggled to pierce the smog at least he might get the chance to say goodbye.

Job finished compiling his packing list and was directing Dinah to locate the items that might be hiding in Jake's messy bedroom.

"What's this for?" asked Dinah, pointing at a small, black silicon device with a handle at one end and a series of strange-shaped grills on the other.

"It's my laser hair remover, it's for shaving beards."

"But you don't have a beard," replied Dinah quizzically.

"That's because I use it."

Dinah shook her head and Job crossed it off the list.

"Will I have any say about what gets packed?"

"Yes, of course," replied Job, "if it's on my list."

"That's not a say, that's just a coincidence."

"If you like."

He didn't much.

"Now get on with it, Jake, no time to lose."

"I have the rest of my life to lose," he said, sliding onto the mood carpet which instantly changed from a light blue colour to a dark red.

"I'll call out the items on the list and you can pack them in your compaction-case."

"Oh, it'll be like a game," giggled Dinah.

"If it helps," said Job who wasn't the slightest interested in games of any sort.

"Fine," Jake sighed.

"And do it neatly," demanded Job.

"Give me a chance, I haven't even started and you're telling me off."

The compaction-case was a recent addition to the Montana family's holiday essentials. Packing had always been a tiresome chore before they'd upgraded to one. There were always more items you wanted to pack, never enough space available and miserly limits set by travel firms as to how much you could bring with you. The trams, the only form of transport that Jake had taken in the last decade, were particularly strict with their weight limits. When it was lying empty on the floor the compaction-case looked like any normal-sized suitcase and was packed in much the same way as holidaymakers had done for years. The innovation came at the end. A button on the side triggered an internal vacuum which sucked the air out of the case and dragged the sides inward toward the centre. By the end of the procedure the case was no bigger than a small school rucksack. It was a marvellous piece of engineering but ineffective if you were transporting anything made of glass.

"First on the list, clothes," announced Brother Job.

"What am I meant to wear in Sweden? What's it like there?"

"Cold."

"Like normal winter or Solar Winter?"

"Haven't you looked it up?"

"I've had other things on my mind."

"Worse than Solar Winter."

"How can it be worse than that?"

"I think it's best described as 'where have my testicles gone?' cold," replied Job graphically. "And all year around, too."

"Brilliant. I'll leave the shorts behind, then."

Jake grabbed as many of his winter clothes as possible and neatly folded them into the case. New Hampshire wasn't exactly tropical, but it rarely got cold enough for multiple layers. Occasionally he'd worn his thermal underlayer when the blizzards came to town, but those only happened every three or four years.

"I wouldn't take that one," said Job as Jake folded a red jumper and placed it in the case.

"Why not? I love this one."

"Sam doesn't like it."

"What?"

"Yeah, she's already checked through your things and sent us a list of pre-approved items. That's not one of them."

"What about my personal expression?"

"Sadly, that's not been pre-approved either!"

It was bad enough that he had to marry someone on the other side of the world he'd never met before, but now this Sam character was already making decisions for him. He thought that was the Circuit's job. Christie would never tell him what to wear. She saw beyond her own personal tastes if it was something Jake felt comfortable in. She liked him for who he was, not what she wanted him to be.

"Why wasn't I asked to pre-approve Sam's stuff?"

"You were, it's just you were too busy chasing speccies, getting violations and defending yourself in a 'conduct feeling'. The opportunity has expired."

ASCENSION DAY

Jake's mind returned to his parents' fate. How were they being treated? Were they together? How had they slept? These questions seemed a lot more important than whether he took his red jumper across the Atlantic Ocean. There had to be a way he could make up for what he'd done. The main problem was he didn't have the slightest idea how. You didn't just walk up to the door of the Source and ask for an appointment, especially if you were on the other side of the world. Would his father even welcome him if he did? He'd pretty much disowned him. He gave no more energy to arguing with Job over what he took on the outward journey and packed the rest of his bag on autopilot.

"What's going to happen to my parents?" asked Jake to Brother Job.

"I don't know," snapped Job, lacking interest.

"Don't know or can't find out?"

"There's no point dwelling on it, boy," said Job flippantly.

"Which suggests you could find out if you wanted to?"

"Maybe."

"Oh, I know!" said Dinah, her hand bursting into the air to answer the question no one had asked her.

"I forbid you, Dinah," said Job.

"When's that ever going to stop me?" she sneered at her brother.

"What harm will it do if she tells me?"

"It's against the rules."

"Pfft. Rules. Which of us is holding onto his sense of rebellion?" said Dinah.

"I am," said Brother Job reluctantly.

"Him!" said Jake in surprise. "That doesn't seem right."

"Rebellion is an adapted trait, not a natural one," replied Job with a degree of shame in his voice.

"So use it, then!" goaded Dinah, winking at Jake.

"Just because I have it doesn't mean I have to use it. I mean you're holding fear, but I haven't seen you use that once."

"I'm scared of earwigs. There you go, your turn."

"That's not fear, that's just a passive description of a dislike of small insects."

"Excuse me," interrupted Jake as his two guides squabbled over who owned which of Jake's childhood instincts. "My parents?"

"Fine. Just this once."

"Awesome!" giggled Dinah.

"Unlocking the files now."

A stream of memories entered into Jake's feed. They weren't, as he hoped, from his parents' perspective, but contained generic memories of people moving around the Source. There was something false about them, as if they'd been staged for the benefit of a placid population unable to see the truth beneath the façade. Prisoners were branded as patients and were shown enjoying the same freedoms that people outside of the Source did. There were large, open spaces in between the large, square, black buildings, plenty of educational options, daily physical exercise classes and a surplus of nutritious food. Like the glossy brochure of a Mexican hotel that turns out in reality to be half built and facing the side of a cliff, Jake didn't buy the picture for a second. If this was how people were treated at the Source, why were their memory feeds disconnected from their loved ones?

"It's different than how I imagined it," stated Jake, trying to restrain his true emotion of scepticism from overflowing into the visible world. Not that it mattered: the Circuit would know how he was feeling about it anyway.

"I've also found their case file," said Job eagerly, apparently rather enjoying the uncharacteristic foray into rebellion.

"What does it say?"

"Oh dear," he replied. "No point crying over spilt milk, let's finish the packing."

"Tell me," growled Jake.

"It says their term has been set as permanent."

"Phew," said Dinah, "for a moment I thought they were in there forever."

"Something tells me they will be," sighed Jake. "There must be something we can do?"

"Why don't I hack into the Circuit's secure access files?" said Job menacingly.

"Stop. I'm really scared now!" screamed Dinah, her projection shaking nervously.

"Sister Dinah's right. Let's not make matters worse than they already are."

"Fair enough."

Jake finished packing his case with all the essential items on Job's list. Mostly he just went along with it but there was some negotiation over whether he took some of the more sensitive mementoes from his childhood. A framed videogram of his family was allowed; a similar one of Christie was not. After much remonstration, and threats that they'd have to physically drag Jake all the way to Sweden, they finally approved his wish to keep hold of an old-fashioned wristwatch that Christie had given him last Christmas.

Once everything was carefully stored the suction on the case did its work. Jake stared at the pitiful size of the life he'd built so far. It wasn't much to be proud of but at least it was easy to carry.

"I think we're ready," said Job. "Let's go."

"It's only three in the morning."

"Then we'll beat the crowds."

"Do the trams even run at this time of night?"

"Yes, it says there's one an hour on my timetable."

ASCENSION DAY

Jake checked his cloud and was annoyed to affirm it for himself. He'd stalled all he could. If he didn't comply, they'd probably drag him to Scandinavia by his ears. He grabbed his easy-to-handle case and took a pace towards his bedroom door, which opened without physical touch as it always did. Someone was waiting for him on the other side.

"I thought you might try to sneak off without saying goodbye," said his grandfather, arms crossed and brow furrowed.

"I haven't been given much of a choice."

"I really wanted to wish you luck, Jake, but after yesterday I'm not sure I can."

"Don't make me feel more guilty than I…"

"I'm not going to. Instead I'm going to offer you some advice."

"Fine. It'll be better than anything these two give me."

"Where the birds fly, there will always be blue sky. I'll say no more."

"I think you might have to if you want me to understand what you're talking about."

"It's a riddle," added Dinah, unheard by Paddy. "I bloody love a riddle."

Paddy winked knowingly at Jake. What was it he was trying to tell him? Paddy wasn't that old, and he'd had plenty of early scans via memory apps to diagnose any potential signs of dementia. All had come back negative. His strange behaviour also wasn't anything to do with the early time of the morning. Paddy could be heard most nights on his hourly pilgrimage to the toilet along the hall.

"It must have something to do with atmospheric pressure," said Dinah with certainty. "Otherwise the birds would fall out of the sky, so I'm guessing your grandfather is warning you about the dangers of skydiving in a storm!"

It definitely wasn't but Dinah's mad ramblings had at least pointed Jake down the right path. Paddy had always been suspicious of the Circuit, even in the early days. The notion that they were listening continually raised a level of paranoia in him that led to the construction of the code, a way of concealing your messages from prying ears. Paddy had used the code for all manner of purposes down the years. Sometimes it was purely used as a form of entertainment when Jake and Tyra were younger, but occasionally it was used to keep secrets safe from undesirable ears. This was one of the latter. All he had to do was remember how to decipher it.

He loosely remembered how it worked and offered his reply.

"Winter lilies sprout early but take time to bloom," he said.

Paddy nodded.

"What are you two talking about?" said Brother Job. "I'm literally confuddled by how you use words."

"Dinah will explain it for you," said Jake.

"I doubt it, the woman's mad."

"Keep well, Jake, and stay in touch. There will be much news to share from both our sides in the coming weeks."

"You'll have to plug yourself in," added Jake with a weak smile.

"When I have to, although I'm sure Tyra will let me know. She's in the virtual world more than the physical one these days."

"Say goodbye to her for me, when it's safe to mention my name, that is."

"Will do. I'll get the stairs for you," said Paddy, switching the escalator to descend.

- Chapter 9 -

Moodzec

The soft glow of fluorescent night lamps bathed Jake's road with a light green tinge. Channelled by the lines of houses on either side, a biting cold breeze rushed up the street and snapped at his uncovered ears. It was frosty by New Hampshire standards, but it was something he was going to have to get used to when he arrived at his destination. The mangled sulphurous clouds, stinking with the distinctive aroma of rotten eggs, loomed menacingly above him. As might have been predicted at three o'clock in the morning, Jake was the only human currently venturing outside to endure them. He'd desperately hoped it wouldn't be the case.

But she hadn't picked up his message.

He checked her proximity tracker to see if there was any movement, fully expecting her flashing dot to be entrenched at her house. There was no signal. How could that be, there was always a signal these days? Had she turned it off? Had she forgotten about him already?

"Job, I can't locate Christie on my cloud feed, any words of wisdom?"

"Yes, don't bother trying."

"Why not?"

"Because the Circuit will have disabled it."

"Can they do that?"

"They can do anything they want."

"Ok, but why did they do it?"

"Temptation," he replied coldly.

The Circuit had thought of everything. No stone would be left unturned in their quest to destroy his life. The inevitability of his plight surged through his body and the only emotion it retrieved was resignation. Brother Job would have been proud of him. Why fight it? The Circuit was bigger and more powerful than he would ever be. After all, he was only superfluous: expendable, disposable, worthless, the very lowest level of importance possible. Which made him consider if that was true, and not just some horrible mistake, why would they spend so much energy on him?

Brother Job leant down and touched his toes before following it up with some light stretching and the occasional lunge. Even though he had no physical body to warm up, Jake swore he heard some of his joints creak. The elderly hologram checked his bearings, played with an imaginary stopwatch, turned purposely to his right and marched briskly down the road.

"Where are you going?" shouted Jake.

"The tram's this way," he replied. Even though his projection was now some distance away he didn't need to raise his voice. It came through clear and crisp in Jake's mind like he was standing right next to him.

"Wait, let's race!" shouted Dinah. Her plump torso bobbed mesmerically up and down as she attempted to catch him. It was highly likely that even brisk walking would result in a sure-fire heart attack, if she only owned one.

This was it? Time to leave.

He scanned his estate for the last time. He'd walked down this street so often it felt like part of his anatomy. The carbon rods quietly at rest and waiting patiently in the darkness to return to the gentle humming that accompanied the vital work of keeping everyone breathing. The driveway where his first steps, his first unaided bicycle ride and his last ever car journey had all begun or finished. The ancient sycamore tree in the distance where he and Christie had carved their names and love for each other in the trunk with an old penknife. He'd received a violation for that one, although he never did work out how they'd discovered it was him.

Soon all of what he knew so well would be confined to his cloud feed.

Everyone needed a degree of change in order to grow and prosper. Change is inevitable, with or without the Circuit, but this change was on a scale he never believed possible. Excessive change drives stress, stress drives adrenaline, and his veins were pumped full of the stuff. When the body acted, the mind followed psychosomatically.

"Good morning, young sir. This is the brand-new antidepressant from Temple Therapeutics. Scientifically tested and proven to lighten your mood within twenty seconds. Put the blues behind you and buy Moodzec today!"

"No, thank you," replied Jake who lacked the mental energy to swipe the advert quickly away, which came as some surprise to the cravat-wearing advertising man.

"Oh, right. So, you must be interested?"

"I'm not."

"But I'm still here in your cloud feed! Hold on a second," replied the man, checking through a small handbook that he removed from his pocket.

"What are you doing?"

"Checking the manual. I don't normally get this far," replied the man nervously searching for his next-best line.

Jake went to swipe.

"No, please, don't go. Just hear me out."

"Why?"

"I really need this sale! If my numbers don't improve Temple will fire me and then I'll be back on the scrapheap. It's not easy being superfluous, you know," pleaded the grainy projection whose poorly whitened teeth did their best to force a smile.

"You're superfluous?" asked Jake, pausing his initial compulsion to discard the advert from his stream.

"Yes."

"What's it like?"

"Miserable."

"Oh thanks," Jake replied despondently.

"Which is why I take Moodzec three times a day!" replied the man enthusiastically holding a packet out in front of him so it caught Jake's attention.

"And it helps?" replied Jake suspiciously.

"Totally."

"And you said it's been fully tested?"

"Yes," replied the representative lamely.

"On what?"

"Eels."

"Eels?"

"Yes."

"And how exactly do you prove that an eel is less depressed as a result of taking it?"

"They demonstrate a twenty-two percent increase in swimming velocity against a control group...and none of them died."

"Which doesn't really prove they were any happier, does it? It just proves they've sped up."

"We've tested it on dogs, too," said the man, desperately checking through the facts in his little book.

"Surely you've got the opposite problem there, though," replied Jake. "I mean who's ever seen a dog that didn't look happy."

"There you go, then. Proof!"

"That's not proof, that's coincidence."

"Not according to my little book," replied the man.

"Has it been tested on humans?"

"Yes."

"How?"

"Well, we've sold millions of packets and no one has died…yet."

"Do all of your tests hinge on whether the subjects are still alive at the end of the trial?"

"No, but obviously it wouldn't be good for sales if they weren't."

"And how does this Moodzec work exactly?"

"Listen, I'll level with you. This is my first week on the job and I'm just the salesman."

He didn't look much like a salesman. Normally you could tell immediately when one of them entered your cloud feed. They were immaculately dressed, used highly complicated language that only a genius would attempt to use in a sentence, smiled continually, and had a genetic compulsion to wink a lot. This guy was nothing like that. Most of his hair was missing in what Jake could only guess was a mugging gone wrong, his face was plastered in foundation that made him glow like an orange-coloured mannequin, and none of his clothes seemed to fit. Maybe Jake had been caught off guard by his strange appearance.

"If you don't know how it works, I'm not going to buy any."

"Neural pathways," he replied in a fluster.

"What about them?"

"Moodzec blocks the bad pathways, allowing your mind to access only the happy ones."

"Bad pathways, I assume that's a scientific term."

"No, they call it something else but that's the general science behind it. The drug interacts with your implants and stops the connection with the

Memory Cloud and only permits you to access memories that will improve your mood."

"Sounds a bit dodgy if you ask me."

"Certainly not! We're Circuit-approved," added the man, pointing out their logo on the side of the packet.

"So was my letter but that hasn't worked out so well for me."

"I tell you what I'm willing to do, and only because it's you. I'll give you a fifty percent discount off your first order, can't say fairer than that."

Jake's frazzled mind was taken by surprise. Part of it craved any form of relief from his current state of despondency and, however dubious this pharmaceutical remedy was, taking it must be better than how he was feeling now.

"Excellent decision."

"Huh?"

"I've received your payment. Thank you."

It was that easy. A brief moment of weakness in the mind and the purchase was complete. This was why advertising in the Memory Cloud was so popular and frequent. As long as sellers avoided being swiped in the first few seconds the chances of landing a sale were pretty high. If companies could specifically target the mentally fragile, frequently drunk or easy manipulated, they could make a fortune. This wasn't the first time it had happened to Jake, but costly past mistakes had taught him to prepare for these commercial bloodsuckers. This morning his guard was down. He didn't even know how many credits he'd spent on the Moodzec, such was his state of vulnerability.

"It appears from your payment details you're in the process of moving," said the salesman. "Can you confirm your delivery address?"

"Sweden," answered Jake.

"Wait a minute," said the salesman, scanning his own Memory Cloud for illumination. "I can find a Swindon but that appears to be underwater. Are you sure it's called Sweden?"

"Pretty sure, yeah."

"Oh, here it is…Christ alive, I only charged you for local delivery! This is going to cost me, first sale in days and I'm not even making a profit on it."

"Maybe you should have asked me first," suggested Jake.

"Just another baby step in my learning process," replied the man, trying to stay positive. "Do you have an exact address in Sweden?"

Jake scanned his memory of opening the letter yesterday morning and projected it into the road so the man could copy the details.

"Malmö," said the man. "I thought that was a type of furniture."

"Maybe it is. I really have to go now, I'm losing sight of my guides," said Jake, developing the first signs of buyer's remorse.

"Yes, of course, we'll find a way of getting it to you. Good luck with the move and remember – stay happy!"

The advert vanished and yet again he was staring at an empty street containing nothing more than his own nostalgia. He was taking that with him so there was no reason to linger any longer. He lifted his luggage off the floor and jogged casually down the road to catch up with his apparitional companions. It didn't take him long. Sister Dinah had collapsed about halfway between the house and the tram stop complaining of a stitch.

"What took you so long?" scolded Job.

"I had some business to do."

"Ones or twos?" wheezed Dinah, floating back to her feet.

"Moodzec," replied Job, checking Jake's memory. "I hope you're not considering taking that rubbish before you do some thorough research?"

"I'm not going to take it at all, I just felt sorry for the guy."

"Good. There are no shortcuts in life, just hard work and focus. Come on, the tram leaves in ten minutes."

When they reached the tram stop none of them were surprised to find that there was no one else waiting. A small transparent shelter, big enough to protect half a dozen people from a rain shower, hugged the pavement. On top of the structure a rotating gold beacon caught people's attention and on one side of the shelter the inevitable emblem of the Circuit proved without doubt who owned this and the rest of the network. As they approached a flood of automatic tutorials opened to depict, amongst other things, the correct way to wait for a tram, board a tram and behave once inside a tram. He flicked the infant instructors away, safe in the knowledge that he'd taken a tram most days of his life and so far, he hadn't been sucked underneath by the magnets.

There were no rails or overhead electrical cables like there were for the trams of old. These were maglev trams that floated on a magnetically charged surface powered, like everything else these days, by renewable energy sources. Almost all of the roads had been converted to allow trams to dominate the causeways and freeways that carved their way across the country like capillaries. The last car, as Jake remembered it, had passed along this road about a decade ago. When the oil ran out most cars became redundant. Those that were powered electrically were banned in favour of more harmonious forms of public transport. The trams went everywhere and, as their current situation proved, at any time. Cheap to maintain, automated, versatile and safe.

"Where do we go after the tram?" asked Jake.

"The tram will take us to Boston. From there you'll board a Hyperloop destined for Paris before transferring to another bound for Malmö."

"I've never taken the Hyperloop before," said Jake with a gulp.

"Then you're in for a real treat," smiled Job. "You haven't eaten today, have you?"

"No, why?"

"You really don't want to throw up on a Hyperloop."

"Why?"

"Oh, look here's our tram!" said Brother Job.

A sleek, grey tram with gold panels rushed along Jake's street and came to an abrupt stop next to them. A timer above the glass door reset to show the number thirty but immediately started to slowly tick down one second at a time. The tram only had one carriage but every twenty metres or so there was a kink in the external structure to allow it to travel around corners at speed. Most of the carriage was see-through but where the metal structures kept the glass together it carried the Circuit logo.

"Jake!" came a shout from a figure hurrying towards them down the pavement.

The timer hit twenty-five.

"Come on, Jake, you don't want to miss it," whooped Dinah as she skipped on-board in a way that contravened almost all the recommendations included within the instructional videos.

"Wait!" came a distant call.

"It's Christie," said Jake, straining his eyes to make out the figure calling his name.

"Get on-board, Jake, there's no time," instructed Brother Job aggressively.

Twenty seconds.

"We'll just get the next one."

"No! You'll get this one."

"Have a heart, it's my last chance to say goodbye. After this who knows when I'll get to see her again."

"Never, I suspect, so why drag it out?"

Fifteen seconds.

She was less than twenty metres away. He knew in his heart that she wouldn't let him leave without seeing him off however many roadblocks the Circuit threw up in front of them. They might be the masters of thought, but they weren't the masters of love. That couldn't be restricted or outlawed. It could, though, as it happened, be spoilt by a hologrammatic old-age pensioner.

Job reached out and grabbed Jake's collar before heaving him inside the tram with all his virtual strength. Jake hit the floor of the tram with a bump and the doors closed behind him automatically.

Ten seconds.

Christie pulled up to the doors struggling for breath. Rather than the tears she displayed yesterday, today she was smiling. Maybe she was putting a brave face on the situation for his benefit. It didn't matter why, it was just enough that she was there.

"Jake, they've turned off our cloud connection, they don't want me to see or feel you!" she shouted through the glass door, both palms placed against it. "But I know I love you and I always will."

"I love you, too," Jake hollered back through the reflective glass of the doors, desperate for one last embrace against her slender frame.

Five seconds.

"Look for the birds when the sky turns blue!"

She nodded and removed her hands moments before the tram sped off on its hidden magnetic cushion.

Time's up.

- Chapter 10 -

The Hyperloop

In a matter of seconds, Christie was out of sight, if not out of mind. In less than a minute the speeding tram had pressed relentlessly through the town of New Hampton Falls. It burst through the suburbs and into the countryside heading southwards on its short journey to the regional capital, Boston. It made regular stops, always for the allotted time of thirty seconds but no one ever joined them on-board. It was just him and the kooky twins.

Jake flopped on the nearest cushioned bench and rested his head against the window. The momentary elation at seeing Christie had been cruelly evacuated and replaced by a feeling of deep sorrow. Whatever the consequences were of taking Moodzec, he wished he'd already received it and was medically sedated from his pain.

The powerful internal lighting of the carriage briefly illuminated the scene outside the window as the tram sped onwards down the old freeway. Stagnant lakes glistened with algae, piercing the landscape like little black holes. Patches of dense, gnarled forests that had been left to grow wild and reclaim the land, whether previously occupied by humans or not, flashed by in a blur. Occasionally the carriage cut through the middle of vacated retail zones where expansive car parks lay idle other than the swirl of litter and organic cast-offs.

Jake knew all the towns and villages they'd pass through on their way to Boston. Once that part of his journey concluded he'd enter the unknown. The anxiety of what was still to come shot around his body. He was tired, scared and most of all confused. What was the point in guides when all they did was bully him or act like fools? He closed his eyes and immersed himself in his cloud feed, seeking to gain access to Christie's.

Under his eyelids the guides were still there.

He scanned his memories for some comfortable nostalgia but an interference in the cloud was stopping him. Darkness assailed him once more. He doubled up in pain as a searing heat bombarded his mind and an unstoppable virtual and unrecognised scenario demanded his attention. The flashback opened in the same way as yesterday's. A pulsating golden beacon was the only source of light in the dimly lit room. The projected figure of a crippled old woman confined to a stool, and his own immense frame looming over her diminutive body.

The vision expanded. Under the golden beacon was a matte charcoal cube, and on one face lay a central processing unit a metre or so from the floor. The black screen twinkled with a luminous green cursor that pulsated impatiently for instructions from a higher power. The woman was talking, but the words were scrambled by the poor quality of the flashback.

Jake let out a blood-curdling scream that no organic creature had heard, before collapsing onto the smooth floor between the benches.

"Up you get," said Job insensitively.

Jake pulled himself back to his seat.

"Quite a flashback," shuddered Dinah.

"They're stronger and faster than the ones I've had before," replied Jake, still holding his head to stop it oscillating off his neck.

"It's probably time for an upgrade," said Job. "I'll message Sam to get you booked in."

"No! No more upgrades. I've had ten so far and every one of them has turned the pain levels up, not down. I'm not sure my skull can take any more."

"You can't stop them discovering the flashbacks."

"I'm not sure what they'll make of them, they're not very clear to me."

"They'll still record them," said Job.

"I know," Jake replied resentfully. "Can't you do something? I thought you were meant to be here to help me."

"We are," said Dinah.

"How exactly?"

"I made sure you didn't miss the tram!" said Brother Job firmly.

"Which was one of the times I didn't need your help. How do you even do that? It's a mystery how you can physically touch me when you're only meant to be in my head."

"It shouldn't be a mystery, it was in your Circology curriculum," suggested Job.

"I think we've already established I didn't pay enough attention in those lessons."

"It's quite simple," said Dinah. "It's magic!"

"It's not magic, you buffoon," huffed Job.

"Name-calling makes me sad," she replied, drifting off to the other end of the tram to sulk.

"What is it, then?" asked Jake.

"The power of thought is rarely understood. You and I share common neural connections that govern how you think, feel and act. Because of these symbiotic links I am able to affect your thoughts and movement. So, although it looks like I'm physically touching you, it is in fact you who's doing all the work. You just haven't noticed because it's subconscious."

"You're saying I dragged myself onto the tram?"

"In effect, yes, although I sent the impulses to your brain to command your body to act."

"But you moved towards me and grabbed my arms."

"It's a kind of distraction tactic to fool your brain into believing something else is happening altogether."

"Ingenious," replied Jake quite spontaneously. "Sinister but ingenious. You won't be able to do it now, though."

"Why ever not?"

"Well, you've told me how it works, so I'll be expecting it. You won't fool me twice."

"Is that right!?"

"Yes."

"Tell me, Jake, why are both your hands stretched in the air making wildly eccentric clapping noises."

Jake looked up. They were and somehow his arms hadn't told his brain that they were planning it. "Stop!"

"As you wish."

His arms fell back on his lap.

"Why didn't I see that coming?"

"Neural pathways react quickly. By the time I've thought it you're already one step behind."

"It's outrageous!"

"And for your own good."

"You have more power over my body than I do. How is that a good thing?"

"Isn't that what you signed up for? We're just a more substantive version of what's been happening in your Memory Cloud for years. The Circuit have always had a hand in your decisions and choices. We are just an extension of that while you adjust to your new life."

"I don't like it."

Job shrugged.

"How long do guides stay around for anyway?"

THE HYPERLOOP

"That depends on how long it takes you to adjust. I've heard most of us get disconnected after the first three to four months, but some guides have been known to linger for years if the circumstances demand."

"Brilliant," lied Jake, turning his back on Job and slumping his head back against the glass. The way his life was panning out he fully expected them to be buried with him, where no doubt Job would continue to boss him around and Dinah would pretend to read his eulogy.

Boston's illuminated high-rise buildings poked through the distant skyline. Some of their roofs stretched up as far as the sulphurous clouds, creating a murky, yellow pulse of light. On the right side of the carriage a vast city of black-coloured, windowless buildings spread out as far as the horizon. Each square construction was perpendicular to the next and ordered in a way that seemed completely unnatural. He'd seen it before but today it held a new significance.

This was the Source, one of them at least.

Somewhere behind the unscalable security fences, the endless hordes of utility drones and inescapable motion sensors, were his parents. He wasn't the only one about to deal with a fundamental life change. At least he was still free to move around and act as he wished. They weren't so lucky. Guilt returned and shunted away the self-pity he was feeling. He had to make the best of the liberty they were no longer able to take for granted.

Forty-five minutes and six stops after leaving his street in New Hampton Falls the tram came to rest at their own exit point. Boston International Hyperloop, formerly known as Boston International Airport.

The international Hyperloop network was far from complete, but an amazing amount of

121

construction had been achieved in a relatively short space of time. Since the first route opened for passengers at the turn of the twenty-forties, from Los Angeles to San Francisco, hundreds of thousands of miles of tubes had been added to the system. The pace of progress had been essential. When traditional air travel suffered irreparable damage from the dual challenges of the climate catastrophe and oil scarcity, an alternative way of travelling the world had to be found to avoid further economic crisis.

The Hyperloop system was the chosen alternative. Clean, fast, safe but not cheap. Not yet. Trillions of credits had been poured into the network to link the most important global routes and maintain trade and commerce. Today, if you had the wealth, you could travel to South America, North America, what was left of Oceania and parts of Europe. The route Jake would soon take had only been completed in the last five years and had been well behind schedule. The engineers had a good excuse for the delay. Three thousand miles of sea to build over.

The other regions of the world were restricted and lay in the East. How the populations there overcame the challenges brought on by the recent events that affected every part of the globe was a mystery. Few man-made objects travelled by air anymore, which meant traditional surveillance of the East was no longer feasible. The only way of finding out anything about their world, or vice versa, was by crossing the border and that was illegal. Two regions separated by culture, politics, geography and their own memories.

"Let's check in," suggested Job as he beckoned Jake to exit the tram before it shot off into central Boston.

THE HYPERLOOP

They took the lift from the basement, where the tram had stopped, and pressed the button for the B.I.H. departure floor. The increasing sound of voices built in volume as they ascended each floor. When the doors opened, they were ejected into the crowds. It might have been four in the morning, but the place was packed. Thousands of people bustled furiously, all of them pretending they were the only people in the building. Jake was immediately barged and bumped as people ran for the next lift or dashed about trying to work out which departure gate they needed.

Unlike in times of the building's former life there was no need for Customs or security checks. Anyone keen to disrupt the smooth running of the Hyperloop, or smuggle items over borders, would be spotted, prosecuted and extradited the moment the thought gained traction amongst their memories. Memory Hunters weren't just there to repair the Memory Cloud, they were also there to protect it, and their users, from anyone foolish enough to act against the rules.

Jake struggled through the mass of bodies towards the middle of the vast hall where there appeared to be less congestion. When he reached it, he noticed his guides were no longer visible in his feed. Maybe he'd lost them, he thought hopefully.

"Down here," said Job destroying the brief glimmer of hope. "It got a bit crowded."

Job and Dinah had taken up comfortable seating positions on either shoulder.

From a central position in the hall, Jake was surrounded by eight tall glass arches that stretched from floor to ceiling at an equal distance from each other. A Circuit logo was etched at the top of each, along with the name of the port it represented. The one in front of him said 'West Coast Port'.

"Which one do we need?" asked Jake in a whisper.

"You've got all the information you need in your head, you know; do you want me to do everything for you?"

You have so far, thought Jake, receiving a poke in the ribs for his insolence.

Jake accessed the Hyperloop timetable for departures to France from Boston in his memory feed. The virtual listing flashed up in a frame in the space in front of him, occasionally broken by a distraught family dashing through it on their way to the 'Caribbean Port' over his right shoulder.

"Central European Port," he said, pointing it out. "But which one am I booked on?"

"Any one you like, there's no booking system for the Hyperloop. You just turn up and pay. First come first served."

"Right. I can see why it's so busy at this time of the morning now."

"It's always busy. The Hyperloop is the only way to travel long distances and there are more people who want to do so than there is capacity. I've heard the queues can take days at peak times of the year."

"I hate queues," moaned Dinah. "I'm jumping in."

"What good will that do you?" replied Job.

"Duh...I'll get there quicker, won't I?" she said pulling a face at him that indicated he was an idiot.

"You can't get on-board if Jake isn't with you!"

"Oh. Jake, jump the queue with me," she whispered.

"I'm not really in a rush to reach my shitty new life, to be honest, Dinah."

"Damn it," she screeched.

"Who's paying for my trip?" asked Jake inquisitively.

"The Circuit of course. After all they own the Hyperloop."

"At least I'm not being financially ruined for a life I don't want."

"Oh, it's not free," replied Brother Job. "It's only a loan. They'll take it back through your taxes when you start your new job."

"Of course, they will," moaned Jake. "How much is a ticket?"

"Seven million credits," replied Brother Job casually.

"How much?!"

"That's just to Paris. Another three million for the Malmö leg."

"Can't I walk?" added Jake sarcastically.

"Only if you've managed to perfect the art of walking on water and can survive the noxious sulphur clouds that surround most of Germany."

"I can sail it."

"No."

Jake accessed his cloud to check how much on average an Archivist earned in a year. He wished he hadn't bothered. At best, if you managed to ascend to the rank of Major, which seemed only possible if you had an importance factor of necessary or higher, then you could earn a million credits a year. If he didn't get a promotion his average wage was likely to be less than half of that. Not only was he being forced to do a job he didn't want to do, he'd also have to pay the one-time commuter costs for the next twenty years for the privilege.

"Do they do a discount ticket?"

"That is the discount ticket. Why do you think we got here so early?"

Jake moped off in the direction of their departure port and found the queue was mercifully shorter than for the regional ports that were heading to other parts of the country. He waited patiently in line, even though Dinah goaded him continually to do otherwise.

As his position in the line crept nearer the front and the light of day appeared once more in the world, the large glass arch revealed the splendour of the Hyperloops. Long, shiny, white tubes carried on stilts that stretched out of the terminal like the legs of an octopus. As sunlight penetrated the dense clouds for a moment the rays shimmered off the metal as the tubes continued relentlessly over the horizon.

"How does it work?" asked Jake.

"They're similar to trams but with a few notable differences. The pods that fly through the tubes float on an electromagnet cushion but because the air has been removed from the tubes they travel at breathtaking speeds."

"How fast?"

"About a thousand miles an hour."

"Jesus, is it safe?"

"Very. There's nowhere for the carriage to go other than down the tube. As long as the car in front of you doesn't lose power there's nothing to worry about."

"And has that happened?"

"Once or twice. You'd better hope that the automated driver notices a good fifty miles before you reach it."

The conversation with Job was starting to bother him, so he was relieved when they finally reached the end of the line. A smiling Hyperloop attendant, suitably covered in a Circuit-embroidered uniform, waited patiently by a large sliding door for the next passenger. Her projection welcomed Jake with a sickly-sweet smile and a tentative bow.

"Welcome to the Hyperloop," she said pleasantly. "Destination please?"

"Malmö," stuttered Jake.

"Certainly. Car nine, change in Paris."

"Thank you."

"I see the Circuit is paying your fare," she said, pulling information from his cloud. "Do you accept their terms?"

"And if I don't?" asked Jake cautiously.

"You'll have to go and pay, but it'll be a lot less comfortable." She smiled without sounding in the slightest bit false.

"I hear they strap you to the outside of the carriage as it flies through the loop," replied Dinah, squashing her features into a flat version of herself with eyes projected out on stalks.

"They really don't," said Job. "Just agree."

"You told me Paddy should have read the terms and now you're telling me not to bother. You're a hypocrite."

"Yes," he replied plainly.

The terms appeared in Jake's cloud feed and he registered his consent. The attendant's grin changed from pleasant to 'about to burst'.

"Lovely, car nine, seat four," she said, waving him through the sliding door.

On the other side a series of sparkling white Hyperloop cars extended down the side of a platform. As his eyes scanned each one a noticeboard appeared to highlight the details of each carriage's final destination. Number one was destined for London, number two went to Madrid, and so it continued carriage by carriage. He set off down the line towards number nine, one of a dozen or more that were coupled together.

"Do we have to go to all of these places first?" asked Jake.

"Oh no, the cars split off at the junctions and get sucked into a new loop. It can create a bit of a jolt, so I'd advise against a trip to the toilet when that happens."

THE HYPERLOOP

Inside the simple interior of car nine, twelve fake leather recliners were positioned very low to the ground and all faced in the same direction. Most of them were already occupied so finding his seat was easy. He lay down on the almost horizontal bed and immediately found himself scanning a code positioned on the plastic ceiling above his head.

"Welcome to the Hyperloop," announced a small girl not much older than five. "The future of transport today."

For once Jake found himself fully engaged in the video.

"I'm going to show you how to manage your Hyperloop bed," said the girl.

It was a strange choice of words, but Jake didn't feel it was fair to criticise someone who was barely through nursery school. Plus, as it turned out, it was the perfect description for what would happen.

"Take the large strap hanging from flange A," said the child, demonstrating on her own virtual bed that flange A was near Jake's left knee. "Pull it across your body and clip it into notch B. Do the same with straps T and Q. Strap S will attach automatically after you've engaged A, T and Q."

The freckle-faced, ginger-haired girl worked through the instructions so rapidly, Jake struggled to keep up. Eventually the straps over his knees, waist and head were in position, rendering him completely immobile other than for the use of his arms. These were soon grounded when strap S burst out of the bed's padded frame and slotted into the other side, restraining all functions other than his hands.

"Right, now as you noticed when you located your bed, it's not attached to the floor."

"What?!"

"This allows the bed to move freely with the motion of the Hyperloop car. To control its movements, you'll need the application software you should have already downloaded to your Memory Cloud. It will enable you to move comfortably around the carriage without the fear of broken limbs or concussion, like this," replied the girl, demonstrating her own bed's stability and handling with ease and skill.

"Great. You're ready to go. Enjoy the rush."

There was no noise to indicate their departure. No roar of engines or screech of rails. No change in pressure or a force pressing your skin back like a dog with its head out of a moving tram. The first he knew they'd left was the sight of the outside world zooming past through what he assumed were windowless windows on the sides of the tube and Hyperloop car itself. The view would have been pretty impressive if it hadn't been for the second sign that they'd left the terminal building. His chair flew uncontrollably around the carriage, crashing haplessly into those of other passengers who were clearly more frequent loopers and had no such trouble with their own beds.

"Job, I can't access the software!" screamed Jake through the grinding sound of collisions. "Help!"

"The Memory Cloud struggles to work if the host is travelling at a thousand miles an hour," replied Job. "You'll only be able to use the local network and your reserve files until we get to Paris."

"Can't you help, then!?"

"Why?"

"Because brothers are meant to look out for each other, you said so yourself!"

"Yes, but they also think it's hilarious when a sibling makes a total fool of themselves," grinned Job.

- Chapter 11 -

United States of Europe

It was at least an hour before Job stepped in to help Jake, and only then because of the incessant verbal and virtual complaints being logged about him by the other irate passengers of car nine. Unlike his fellow travellers, Jake wasn't rescued from his bed tribulations by simply downloading an application. He was saved by Job's telekinetic control over his muscles, which meant Job would have to concentrate for the next four hours. He wasn't very happy about it.

Once Jake stopped bumping around, he finally got a clear view of what was happening outside of the tube. The ocean consumed the scene through his window. Vicious, angry waves crashed against the Hyperloop tube desperate to drag it under the surface. Man had once again overstepped nature's boundaries and she would not stand for it. Metal, concrete and ferrocon stretched a hundred metres from the seabed to challenge her potent, untamed strength.

There were no ships in his view through the windowless windows. Freight no longer travelled in such ways, although it wasn't the rising sea levels as a result of the recent climate crisis that stopped them. The sea could be tamed, but the sky could not. Around the Equator the climate was so inhospitable, only automated shipping survived the blistering temperature spikes. Since oil was no longer available to fuel such vessels, most freight travelled, like people, via Hyperloop.

Sailing boats were still popular and generally encouraged in the regions of the world that avoided the worst of the extremes. The strip of coastline that surrounded New Hampton Falls was littered with small, wind-propelled vessels: dinghies, windsurfers and catamarans mostly close to the shore. Occasionally a brave adventurer would attempt the Atlantic crossing in one of the larger vessels, but at the speed Jake was travelling, he'd never pick one of those out. It had always been something he wanted to try himself. The idea of taming such hostile waters with nothing but a wooden frame and your own talent excited him. He doubted he'd ever get the chance now. Looking at the brutal ferocity of the sea today, he wondered if it was possible for anyone.

It wasn't just the Hyperloop the waves had in their sights, they sought to dominate the sky, too. Like two armies fighting in hand-to-hand combat, sea and sky fought for supremacy as the sun's occasional appearance tried to calm them into ceasefire. The sun was rarely seen during Solar Winter and almost impossible to avoid at the height of summer. In a week's time the fourth month of Solar Winter would step aside for Storm Season, a one-month geological conflict between land, sea and sky. This annual bombardment of Mother Nature's vengeance had replaced spring in the human vernacular.

Every time the sun wrestled through the polluted clouds it bathed the tube and the speeding cars with warmth. Jake welcomed its introduction upon his skin and the positive effect it had on lifting his mood. All too quickly the speeding Hyperloop would leave it behind and the gloomy shadow of cloud fell over the tube once more.

It never felt to Jake that they were travelling at a thousand miles an hour. The pressure inside the car made for a surreal experience, as if they'd never moved at all. If the ride was as smooth as this, he wondered why it was necessary to strap passengers down.

"First time?"

The voice came from across the aisle, but his view was blocked by an automated serving trolley dispensing refreshments, travel information and reassurance for those brave enough to confess to being anxious Hyperloopers. It tried to interact with Jake's cloud to promote a selection of rather unappealing, superconducted snacks that all looked identical and smelt like haddock blended with marrow. Eventually it gave up and trundled down the aisle, revealing the passenger across from him who'd asked the question. Before he'd even thought about it, Job tilted his bed by ninety degrees so Jake could politely converse with the man to his left. The view had changed but his discomfort remained.

"Yes, first time," replied Jake. "Is it that obvious?"

"It always is!" said the suited middle-aged man, taking regular sips from a tube attached to a bottle of champagne fixed in place on the floor below him. "Are you enjoying it?"

"Not really," replied Jake truthfully.

"It takes a bit of time to get used to. I'm Mannie Draxler, essential," he added in way of introduction. "I would shake your hand but, you know, it's not so easy!"

"No, it's not, is it? I'm wondering how it works if I need to use...the facilities!" replied Jake nervously.

"I wouldn't recommend it. Gets a bit messy for first-timers."

"I'll bear that in mind," replied Jake, grateful that he'd rejected any of the food and beverages from the cart. No doubt the Circuit would only have added more to his debt pile for the privilege anyway.

"What's your name?"

"Jake Montana, nice to meet you."

"It's your Ascension Day, right?" said Mannie insightfully.

"Yeah, how did you guess?"

"First Hyperloop and you haven't got used to announcing your importance factor when you introduce yourself. Don't worry, it took me months to get into the habit."

Jake was certain his inexperience wasn't the reason for the slip-up. Shame was probably a more likely motive. This was his first chance to test how people might react to him. The Moodzec salesman had been superfluous like him so hadn't recoiled in horror, but this guy had already confirmed he was three factors higher than him. How long would it take Mannie before he waved him away and returned to whatever else people did to entertain themselves during Hyperloop journeys?

"I'm superfluous," whimpered Jake.

"Oh…right. I had an aunt once who was superfluous," added Mannie. "Strange woman…owned a lot of cats. Didn't get to see her very often, my parents didn't want people to gossip, you know how it is. I'm guessing you're kind of bummed about it?"

"To be honest it was the least disturbing part of yesterday, all things considered."

"Nervous about your new bride?"

"Terrified," replied Jake.

"We've all been there, my friend. It's been thirteen years since my Ascension Day, but I still remember that fear like it was yesterday. If I ever get scared, I often revisit that memory to make me feel more positive, puts everything in perspective. I shouldn't have worried. It all worked out great. It always does. My Hannah is a diamond. Unbelievable how the Circuit do it, really. They couldn't have found a more perfect partner for me. We think the same, feel the same and act the same. It's like being married to a female clone of my soul," added Mannie, his face glowing with pride and delight at the thought of his other half.

"It won't be like that for me."

"Give it a chance. We've all felt doubt, but I don't know anyone in my circle of essential friends that isn't blissfully married and extremely happy."

"But I already was blissfully happy before the letter. It wasn't possible to improve on it."

"Left someone behind, did you?"

"Everyone, but one person in particular."

"Yeah, it's tough, but remember there's a bigger world out there, my friend. Billions of people to fill the gaps in your life. Trust in the Circuit, they'll do the right thing by you, I'm sure."

Maybe Mannie was right. Maybe he was being unduly pessimistic and was focused too much on loss rather than the opportunities that might be in front of him.

"So, what's in store for you?" said Mannie with a juvenile and suggestive wink. "Come on! Share some pictures!"

Jake searched his Memory Cloud for people in the close vicinity to locate Mannie's feed on the local network. It wasn't difficult to find with only eleven other passengers on-board. He ported the information about Sam through the network so Mannie could offer his opinion.

"Hey, nice. I don't know what you're worried about. This Sam sounds great."

Jake hadn't really given much consideration to his new spouse in the last twenty-four hours, preferring to focus his attention on the last few hours he had left with Christie and his family. He went back to Sam's files. There was only so much you gained from looking at pictures or reading bios to unveil someone's personality. Yes, visually Sam was certainly appealing on the eye. Although the more he thought about it, quite out of his league. Not just a physical league table either. She was two steps above him in importance. If anyone was likely to be disappointed out of the two of them, he thought it was probably going to be Sam. If her rejection of his request to connect was anything to go by, maybe she already was.

Something about Sam seemed out of place. Whereas she had been granted access to a great depth of information and memories about him, her own files were somewhat light on detail. In fact, there weren't many memories at all and those he did have appeared contrived, like they'd been produced by a high-end production company. They lacked authenticity and felt staged for the benefit of a judgemental audience.

What the memories did show was that Sam was everything a boy could wish for in a partner. Funny, sassy, supportive, caring, attractive, tolerant and kind. Was that just how he felt about her, though? Was her profile appealing because it was chosen for him? Or was the Memory Cloud manipulating him to see only those things that he wanted to see, while hiding any aspects of her that were less desirable? Whatever the reasons it made him feel uncomfortable.

Perfection wasn't achieved this easily.

What the files didn't reveal was how she felt about Ascension Day, or crucially him. The first meeting was going to be awkward. It would be like the school discos when he was thirteen all over again. Confident girls stalked like packs of hungry lions waiting to pounce on the first stray boy willing to put their life on the line. He'd sit in a corner desperately scanning their memory feeds for the slightest sign that one of them might, in the best-case scenario, think he was interesting or, in the worst case, not seeking to humiliate him. Of course, they kept their feeds locked or restricted to force the boys into guesswork or random acts of misguided bravery. This confidence, as Jake learnt some years later, was the very thing they wanted to test.

He'd never been that brave, not at least until he saw Christie. The minute she first walked in the room the energy of the universe pulled him out of his social coma like the cork popping out of a champagne bottle. All his insecurity evaporated and a voice in his head encouraged him to take the plunge. That voice, wherever it came from, was a lot more supportive than the two he was currently forced to listen to.

The rest was history, in more ways than one.

The future was planning to test him again.

"How are you going to do it?" asked Mannie, breaking Jake's concentration.

"Do what?"

"Propose of course."

"I have to propose!?"

"Yes. It's still the man's responsibility, one of the last acts of inequality left in the world, but I like that. Not much tradition left these days."

"I didn't realise I had to ask. I thought the letter was enough."

"That's just the contract. You still need a plan and have to execute the romantic element. It's expected."

"How can you be romantic with someone you've never met? It's like asking a perfect stranger to run away to an island with you."

"It's easy," laughed Mannie.

"How did you do it?" asked Jake reaching a new level of panic.

"You can't steal my ideas!"

"I won't honestly."

"I'm only joking, I'll tell you, don't worry. First, I made a huge stencil that read, 'marry me' and then I waited patiently for the sun to break through the smog. At the right moment when the intense heat struck the stencil it channelled the light onto the lawn in the garden and scorched the proposal onto the grass. It's still there now. At the very same time, I'd recorded a memory of me proposing and sent it to her cloud feed so she could see both dimensions at the same time. Like proposing in stereo."

Jake considered whether he had the budget or time to produce a stencil that read 'I think there's been a mistake' but shook it from his mind in case the Circuit was still tracking his thoughts as he thundered across the Atlantic.

"I'm guessing she liked it?"

"What do you think?" chuckled Mannie. "I'm sure you'll come up with something appropriate once you've met her."

Jake tried to shrug but found the motion impossible with all the straps across him.

"Maybe your guides can help, that's what they're there for. What are yours like?" asked Mannie.

"Mental and mean."

Brother Job made Jake bite his tongue.

"That's a shame, don't know how I would have coped without mine."

"Huh, I only wish," replied Jake, getting tired of being trapped in his stretcher with a guide keen on self-mutilation. "Mannie, why do they strap us in like this?"

"Turbulence."

"But there can't be any. We're in a shuttle inside a tube that's had all the pressure sucked out of it."

"I know, but we haven't uncoupled yet."

"Uncoupled?"

"Not all the Hyperloop cars are going to the same place. When we get closer to the United States of Europe the first car will disconnect and head off in a different tube. It produces quite a jolt, so the beds are designed to float in their own space rather than being attached to the floor. In the early days of the Hyperloop passengers complained of whiplash so the designers came up with these."

"I hate them," complained Jake.

"You won't say that in a minute."

"Where are you heading to?"

"Back to Vienna, I've been in the States on a research project."

"What sort of researcher are you?"

"Neuroscientist. We've been working on the most recent version of the Circuit's implants, but I can't give you any details because it's confidential."

Jake considered whether Mannie's research would soon end up embedded in his own brain, just another in a long line of so-called upgrades.

"I've had at least ten," added Jake conversationally.

"Wow, that many! You must be one of the overactive."

"What's one of them?"

"Scientists have discovered that humans have three different speeds to their neural pathways; passive, active and overactive. Passive brains never need an upgrade and accept everything they feel around them without questioning it. Active brains sometimes trick their host into doubt about the cloud's accuracy and probably end up having one or two upgrades over their lifetime. Overactive brains, though, you folk just don't accept the answers the cloud gives you and you attempt to reach through your own connection and into other people's for answers. We still don't know for sure how these modes of activity developed or why one person differs from the next. The Circuit believe it's an unfortunate genetic side effect in how they select couples. When you put perfect people together it can produce imperfect offspring. It's still pretty rare, though. I don't think I've ever met anyone with the condition."

"It's nice to be special," huffed Jake who felt Mannie missed the necessary empathy required given how much pain and suffering he'd gone through with all the upgrades.

"That's one way to look at it," said Mannie, whose reaction suggested it was an affliction rather than an advantage.

"Why have none of my surgeons or doctors ever told me about this before? Not one."

"I doubt whether any of them were Nobel Prize-winners," winked Mannie. "How else do you think I can afford to travel by Hyperloop?"

"Can you win a prize like that if you're only essential?" asked Jake, clear that the information on his overactive brain was coming directly from the source.

"Just about, it's not so bad being essential, you know. It gets up the vitals' noses when you beat them!"

Hanging horizontally on their respective beds, they chatted across the aisle from each other for hours like old friends. The only occasion the flow was broken was when something in Jake's memory feed broke his concentration. What looked like a virtual sledge shuffled down the aisle carrying a squished-up hippy wearing a crash helmet, thick goggles and racing gloves. The character stopped on a fictitious starting line right next to Jake's head. The driver fidgeted excitedly, purring with expectation. It was Dinah. She turned her head and grinned.

"Ready, steady…" she said.

"What are you doing?"

"GOOOOO!"

The Hyperloop carriage jolted violently in perfect timing with Dinah's signal and created two very different events. Firstly, Jake's bed bolted like he'd suddenly been attached to a roller coaster. Secondly, Dinah shot down the aisle, passed through the automated trolley and out through the end of the Hyperloop. Whether she made it further than car eight wasn't obvious. Brother Job managed to stop Jake's bed before it joined her, repositioning him in his idle position once the noise and shaking had ceased.

"That'll be Lisbon," said Mannie, who continued to enjoy his champagne without spilling a drop.

Jake turned over to check their location out of his windowless window and watched as a separate tube curved away from theirs. The sea no longer grabbed the limelight. Instead dry, barren ground was punctured here and there by patches of scorched vegetation or the occasional desolate village. Dead or dying trees slumped over the ground and the bed of a river no longer carried water from mountain to sea.

Dinah wobbled precariously back into car nine, her hair ruffled, her clothes scruffy and a grin the Cheshire Cat might be envious of.

"Awesome! Bring on Madrid," she said, stumbling from dizziness and burying her head into the smooth laminate floor.

For the first time in Jake's life he'd passed into a new continent. The United States of Europe, a unified group of countries that stretched between Thawland, previously known as Iceland, in the north to the barren lands of Libya and Algeria in the south where the bulk of the carbon rod farms were built. From his position on the west coast he could travel another four thousand miles before he reached Moscow on the union's eastern border, the last bastion of the West. After that the lands belonged to the East.

"Welcome to the U.S.E.," said Mannie. "Beautiful, isn't it?"

"I guess," Jake replied, feeling that his carriage acquaintance might be a little biased based on the devastated environment outside his windowless window.

"Vienna's a particularly nice place to live. Old-fashioned coffee houses, theatres, great culture and friendly people. We're a little too close to the East but they generally don't affect us too much."

"What do you think the East is like?" asked Jake politely.

"I don't think, I know," snapped Mannie, becoming unfamiliarly aggressive. "You've seen the 'Proclamation of Distrust', you know, too."

"But I haven't seen it for myself…"

"You don't need to go there. Believe me when I tell you that the people of the East are monsters. Cruel, ugly people with only one thought in their distorted, broken minds, to bring an end to the Circuit and the West. They think about nothing else. I've heard terrible stories about how they live. The children are conscripted at the age of five to be trained in the arts of war and brutality. Every person is taught to fight. They live in a world of sin without rules or boundaries other than the most important one, the boundary that keeps them from us. While we stay strong and united, we keep them at bay, but everyone must play their part."

At no point in Mannie's angry tirade did he express any personal experience. Everything he said and believed had been relayed to Jake many times over the years, Mannie just believed it more firmly than he did. Maybe this was a sign of Jake's overactive brain questioning what he heard.

"I will do my part," said Jake, seeking to avoid any further confrontation.

"Good. Keep it that way. The Circuit is our only protection from them."

"Do you work for the Circuit?" asked Jake.

"Yes, although I suppose everyone does in one form or another."

"Do you know who Alison is?"

"Now there's a question. Few people have ever seen her, but the story goes that she's the daughter of the first couple the Circuit chose through the Ascension Day process, although I think it's highly unlikely. Makes for good marketing, though!"

"But she can't run the Circuit all on her own. There must be others?"

"We all have our departmental directors and there's a small executive board to offer oversight at the very top of the structure which includes the original founders. Although it doesn't really need to be run in a conventional sense because the Memory Cloud chooses what needs to be done. The number of people in the business shrinks every year."

"So why do they need Alison?"

"Do you know what, I've no idea. I guess it portrays a human face to the billions of users around the West. Would it feel more comforting to you if there wasn't a figurehead leading it and the system was left to run itself?"

"No."

"There's your answer, then. The Memory Cloud can't do everything on its own. It can't track down speccies, fix memory bugs or protect against attacks from the Realm. We all need a hand to guide life's tiller."

Jake was cast back to his time on the ocean and the little sailing boat he and Christie would use to explore the delta or sail out into the bay. Wind could not be created or stopped but the sailor still controlled his destination through skill and mastery. It was a good comparison for the Circuit. No one could stop the Memory Cloud existing, but people were needed to decide how it functioned.

"Can I ask you a science question?" said Jake after a period of silence.

"Yes, fire away."

"Are you aware of Moodzec?"

"Certainly, why?"

"How does it work?"

"To answer that I'd have to explain how implants work."

"Fine," said Jake with very little else to do with his time.

"Let me summarise it for you, it's quite a large subject and I've spent many years studying it. The Memory Cloud is just a storage unit that holds all of the files from your past. The clever part of the system is actually in the implants. They carry the software. The sibling programme, the operating system, the wireless transmitter, the cameras, sensors and key information are built into those first implants. Some of it is housed in the optic chip and some in the brain, but they are a pair and can't be separated. Whenever you use the software it is backed up remotely to your cloud so that if you ever change your implants the information can be copied to the new version. Whereas the Memory Cloud is static and out of our influence, the implants are not. There are several ways you can damage or distort them: drugs like Moodzec are one. It shuts off some of the functions in the implants so they can't access files in the cloud."

"But is it safe?"

"Is BASE jumping safe?" replied Mannie, seeming to divert the conversation.

"I don't know yet, I haven't tried it, but I'm hoping so."

UNITED STATES OF EUROPE

"Then there's your answer. Nothing in life is without risk. I've heard most people don't suffer side effects from taking Moodzec, but then again I've also heard about people who've died horribly doing BASE jumps!"

"So, if I go BASE jumping it might be wise to take a couple," added Jake gullibly.

"As with all activities in life I'd counsel you apply common sense and always be inquisitive. Which should be easy if you're overactive."

"Thanks, it's good advice."

"I could have told you that," huffed Job who'd been unduly quiet over the last couple of hours.

"Yes, but he didn't smack me in the nose at the same time!"

The Hyperloop shuddered again to indicate their next stop. The force of the decoupling was even stronger than the last time. Mannie quickly explained this was down to the number of cars being decoupled. Jake checked his cloud to confirm the next stop. It was Paris and they'd be arriving in less than twenty minutes. Jake and Mannie passed the time talking about the main differences between the United States of Europe and America. The translation of languages was instant, if you were connected through the cloud, and there had been a push for lingual standardisation in the U.S.E. over the last two decades anyway so that aspect wouldn't cause him too many problems.

The main adjustments he'd need to make would centre on the availability and variety of the foods he was used to, unusual weather patterns and some discrimination towards immigrants. In this deeply progressive world, some behaviours would take longer than a few decades to remove from the human psyche.

"Here we go, hold on tight," announced Mannie.

Car nine shuddered in the tube, made a popping sound and flew off even faster than before. Minutes later it casually reduced its pace as it approached Paris. It came to a final halt on an identical platform to the one they'd left a few hours before. As soon as the carriage came to rest all the straps that had held Jake and his fellow passengers in stasis whipped back to their original positions. Thankfully Jake had already returned to a horizontal stance when it happened.

Passengers young and old stretched in the aisle to massage the blood back around their body. It was only then that Jake noticed how tall Mannie was. He had to stoop to avoid banging his head on the metal ceiling. Jake wasn't exactly short, coming in just under two metres, but his new acquaintance dwarfed him.

"This is where we part," said Mannie with his hand outstretched. "If you're ever in Vienna, come and look me up. You have my details now in your cloud."

"Thanks, Mannie. It was good to meet you."

"You, too. It's going to be ok, you know. The Circuit knows what's good for you. Remember, it's a state of mind."

Mannie struggled to manoeuvre his bulky body into a long raincoat before he finished the outfit off with a wide-brimmed hat. It seemed excessive even for this time of year. By the time Jake had alighted from the car and made his way back to the terminal building to pick up his next connection it became all too evident why it had been necessary.

The noise.

It was inescapable. Rain struck the glass roof of the terminal building like it was trying to tear it down. Out of the windows the only sight was rain. It was relentless. Nothing of the outside world escaped its clutches. It was like someone had opened a dam immediately above them. Even his Memory Cloud didn't escape the carnage. Ads for coats, weather forecasts, data on the current world record of rainfall and regular blasts of his own emotions on the subject flooded in.

Jake struggled to mentally control the chaos in his mind in order to seek peace from it. Eventually he managed to pull up the Hyperloop timetable to find out where and when his final journey would begin, but Job had beaten him to it.

"Port Suède, over there," he pointed.

"How long?" asked Jake.

"However long the queue is!"

They fought their way through the crowds and located the end of the line. It was the shortest he'd seen today.

"You'll be there soon, Jake," sang Dinah. "Isn't it exciting!?"

"No."

"Sam has sent you a message," announced Job.

"Really? I didn't notice it."

"That's because you were fighting off all the weather forecasters."

"What does it say?"

"Check for yourself, I'm a guide not a slave."

Jake dived back into his feed and pulled up his messages. There were hundreds, but most were spam. He whizzed through the list deleting at will while hoping he might just catch sight of one from Christie. Sadly, there were none. There was one from Tyra announcing she hated him and no longer considered him her brother, which was nice. After trawling through for thirty minutes he found the one Job referred to.

It simply read, 'Meet you at Malmö Hyperloop Terminal. I'll be holding a sign'.

- Chapter 12 -

Sam Goldberg

The last leg of the journey to the other side of the West was a lot smoother than the first. He'd had time to download the software to manage his erratic bed and it wasn't quite such a shock when it held him hostage. Having checked their route, he wondered what the point was? There weren't any registered stops on the line from Paris to Malmö, so it felt to him like an unnecessary Circuit control, enforced only to see if anyone had the courage to complain.

The Hyperloop to Sweden consisted of one long carriage with around thirty beds. None of his fellow passengers were keen to converse as Mannie had, perhaps an early sign of the intolerance towards migrants that waited for him at the other end. He was actually relieved they weren't chatterboxes. The day was barely through mid-afternoon and he'd been awake for all of it. He needed to conserve some energy. The destination of his journey would coincide with an awkward encounter that required strength and courage. He closed his eyes, did his best to silence the memory feed and drifted off for a well-earned hour of sleep.

When he woke the Hyperloop car was completely deserted other than his two guides. They flanked him like a couple of nightclub bouncers, both grinning like idiots but for very different reasons.

"The moment of reckoning has arrived!" taunted Brother Job like a bully who'd just cornered an innocent geek with concealed lunch credits.

"I'm a bag of nerves," replied Dinah. "Not sure if it's excitement or terror. What if she doesn't like me?"

"She's not meeting you," snapped Jake. "She's meeting me."

"You're a mean boy," huffed Dinah. "No sensitivity for other people."

"You aren't people! You're a construct of my own past sent to torture me in my greatest hour of need. I'm not sure what control I have over either of you, if any, but I implore you, just this once, give me a little bit of space when I meet Sam. It's going to be hard enough for me to manage my emotions without having to listen to you two banging on. Do you think you can do that?"

"Not going to happen," answered Job.

"I hate you," mumbled Jake.

He eased himself off the bed, grabbed his bag from the locker at the end of the carriage and stepped out onto the platform and into the unknown. This was it. Sweden. Home, for who knew how long? Life? It was entirely possible. Assigned couples had to mutually agree if they wanted to relocate to a new house or a new country, and even then only if the Circuit granted you permission. Migration was strictly controlled across the West in an attempt to maintain the correct balance of people and resources in each jurisdiction.

Ascension Day was the best way of controlling.

Where there were too many females or males in a particular country, or a lack of the right skill sets, the statistics were fed into the Circuit's rules to ensure people were paired not just with their ideal partner but also in accordance with the world's needs. If Jake had any hope of returning to his own country, and the opportunity to put things right with Christie and his parents, then he'd have to convince Sam first.

Which meant he'd have to show willing.

Whatever his feelings were for his new life partner, it wasn't going to help his cause if he acted aloof or distant. Hopefully they'd get on but if they didn't, he'd have to fake it. Which meant he'd need to manipulate her, an uncomfortable thought for two reasons. Firstly, he preferred being authentically himself as much as possible. It was how he lived. If people didn't like him how he was then, that was their problem. It didn't make him popular, but it made his relationships honest. The game-playing and fakery effortlessly used by people to fabricate how they were just didn't sit well with him. People always saw through his attempts to twist people to his view and that only made matters worse. Then there was the second reason. Brother Job held that particular element of his personality and he'd undoubtedly have his own personal advice to offer on the subject.

The idea of scheming with Job to influence Sam created another emotion in his mind. This wasn't just his Ascension Day. It was Sam's, too. Which meant she also had two guides in tow. Their relationship was barely a day old and it was already feeling crowded. There was a total of six personalities to manage and two of them he'd not even be able to see or feel. His Memory Cloud momentarily crashed, overloaded by the frantic volume of synaptic messages that surged through him. Following a brief pause, while a virtual egg-timer rotated a few times, his virtual world returned, and his guides rematerialised.

"What was that?" demanded Job accusingly.

"I'm DYING!" screamed Dinah hysterically. She ran down the platform in panic, crashing straight through a group of travellers and into the wall.

"Not sure," replied Jake. "I think I overloaded my feed."

"Don't do it again. If you need help then that's what we're here for," said Job watching Dinah reappear in the distance still screaming. "Well, one of us at least."

"I didn't do it on purpose."

Brother Job looked at him quizzically, less than convinced. He also held the emotion 'suspiciousness' amongst his many functions.

Jake pulled up the information he had on Sam, so he'd easily recognise her. The message had stated that she'd be waiting in the Arrivals Hall with a sign. What sort of sign wasn't clear, but Jake hoped it didn't say 'you're doomed' or 'HAHAHA'.

Once Job had encouraged Dinah to 'pull herself together', they strolled down the platform, through the port entrance and into the packed hall. It looked like a battery farm for hens. Young lovers ran across the shiny, polished floor to embrace passionately, kids wheeled compaction-cases through imaginary chicanes, and swollen groups of elderly travellers moved as if they were under the influence of the butterfly effect, changing their minds without warning or consideration for others, uncertain as to where their flock needed to go next. Virtual concession stores were busy preying on shopaholics unable to spend their hard-earned credits during their short voyage aboard the Hyperloop.

The unmistakable smell of cophony, an artificial substitute for coffee, mugged the atmosphere with its inescapable pungency and drew a sizeable line of willing buyers. In the distance a large sign announcing the 'EXIT' appeared in his feed and Jake squirmed through the mass of bodies to escape the inevitable crush. Through the terminal's huge windows, the weather was calm in comparison to what he'd witnessed in Paris. After so many hours trapped inside a sterile tube, he was desperate to get outside and take a gulp of unspoilt air.

That's when he saw the line.

Standing in a perimeter, one person deep, elbow to elbow a menagerie of human couriers waiting for their collections. Inside the world of the cloud each one of them had created a virtual notice so their target could easily locate them amongst the crowd. Every sign had its own splash of personal creativity to stand out more prominently than the others. Some oscillated violently, some expanded, some did little loops in the air and one even exploded in a plume of little hearts every three or four seconds. Elaborate fonts, bespoke musical soundtracks, strobe lighting and fake smoke worked in harmony to assault the internal senses of anyone with the misfortune of looking in their direction.

Jake was forced to endure it because one of them was designed for him. In the crowd only one of the seizure-inducing signs dispensed with the pyrotechnics and visual gimmicks. It contained just two words.

Jake Montana.

Plain, simple and no frills. Frankly, he was a little disappointed that Sam had gone to so little effort to welcome him to her country and her life. But then again as his vision expanded to the person holding it there were far more pressing problems to deal with than the quality or creativity of the sign.

Much of the research he'd done, and the information he'd been sent about Sam was perfectly accurate. Blond hair, blue eyes, tall and certainly attractive to the right people. No doubt when he got closer the captivating Scandinavian accent would appear and he could tick that off the list, too.

There was one aspect of Sam's appearance, though, that was very different from what he'd been shown.

It was a big one.

If he wasn't mistaken, and he was close enough now to be pretty certain, Sam was a man.

Not a man with such incredibly feminine features he might get confused for a woman. Not a man that in any way resembled the somewhat, and now evidently, unbelievable footage he'd watched of Sam during his Hyperloop journey. Not a man pretending to be a woman. Not a man who had previously been a woman at some point in the past and had enjoyed successful conversion surgery.

Just a normal regular man.

No bosom, no make-up and no diminutive athletic figure like Christie's. No flowing hair cascading down her back, nestling just above a cute and perfect little bottom. No full red lips and feminine cheekbones like the Sam he'd seen in his cloud. This version of Sam was tall, had a stubbly chin, short hair, and rippling muscles. Muscles that fought for freedom from the prison of his tight black T-shirt and skinny jeans.

A small explosion of panic took Jake's senses hostage. What did he do now? The options seemed evidently clear. Run or not run. He liked 'run' almost immediately. 'Not running' looked completely devoid of upsides. But run where? Back to the Hyperloop? He couldn't afford it. Hide in the terminal forever like the classic Tom Hanks film? Wait until he'd gone and then build a shabby boat out of ferrocon and attempt that transatlantic crossing he'd always dreamt of? The 'run' options accelerated into a series of surreal and unfeasible fantasies.

"Look, there's Sam!" shouted Dinah, clearly not in the slightest bit bothered whether he was a boy or a girl.

Maybe Sam hadn't seen him yet? Jake scanned the hall for an escape route. If he ran as fast as he could back to the Hyperloop he might be able to borrow a one-way ticket to Algeria. Failing that, perhaps he could pretend to be part of one of the large groups that might not notice him until they arrived wherever they were heading. He was stuck without a clear decision. That's what the Memory Cloud was for but for some reason it didn't want to provide him with the right answer. As the options whizzed through his brain, he was oblivious to the fact that his feet were slowly shuffling towards the line of signs. Below him on the shiny, polished floor his guides had grabbed a leg each and were dragging him forward one awkward step at a time.

"LET GO!" screamed Jake, drawing everyone's attention, including Sam's, to him.

"They're your feet."

"But you're making them move! Stop it!"

"No. Paddy signed the terms," barked Job. "And you have to go through with it."

"I'm logging a complaint right now!" screamed Jake as he shuffled ever closer to his new partner. "It's going to be very long and peppered with swear words."

"Your behaviour is extremely rude," said Job bossily. "Sam's come all this way to greet you."

"And she's going to take you BASE jumping," added Dinah.

"I don't think I'll bother packing a parachute. I might just jump!" argued Jake as he struggled to reclaim the use of his legs.

"Oh look, she's waving!" said Dinah, attempting to wave back.

In Jake's state of panic, it didn't strike him as odd that Dinah kept referring to Sam as a she, because he'd almost completely blanked her out. He looked up to find that Sam had turned off the sign and was striding confidently towards him.

Game over.

No escape from this one.

"Jake, welcome to Sweden," said Sam, throwing his huge arms around Jake's body and squeezing the air out of him. "You look exactly like your profile."

"I wish I could say the same," he wheezed. "I'm guessing you're Sam's brother, right?"

"Brother? Ha, that's hilarious. They said you were funny."

"Who did?"

"My guides. They've been analysing your memory feed to get insights about you from your friends and family. I'm sure you did the same, right? I bet you've managed to find out loads about me?"

"Almost nothing, it would appear."

"What?" said Sam a little hurt. "You weren't interested in learning more about me?"

"Of course, it's just that…"

"What?"

"I don't mean to sound rude," replied Jake. "But you're a…fella."

"Obviously."

"But that's not what I saw in my letter. I saw a woman."

"Really? Strange," he said rather coyly. "Well, never mind."

"What do you mean 'never mind'? There's been a terrible mistake. I'm not gay!"

"Rubbish, you must be."

"I'm really not. I can show you pictures of the girlfriend I left in New Hampshire if you'd like me to prove it."

"You don't have to hide who and what you are now."

"I'm not hiding anything, I promise you I'm not gay!"

"The Circuit seems to think you are, and they know everything about you. It must have been locked away deep inside you, until they found it," he replied, ruffling Jake's hair, not in the slightest bit concerned by his revelation.

"Sam, if that really is your name, my sexuality is not hiding anywhere. I'm sure you're a great guy but something truly horrible has happened here."

"Don't be silly, it's perfect."

"I'M NOT GAY!" screamed Jake.

Anyone who wasn't already listening to the conversation certainly was now. The crazy signs dimmed as people's attentions were drawn from their real reasons for being there to one more interesting. Jake's memory feed was suddenly swamped by self-help advice and adverts for products he'd never heard of that frightened the life out of him.

"Is Jake happy?" asked Dinah to Job, a little confused by the pair's conversation.

"He's never happy so I doubt he's likely to be gay about anything," huffed Job.

"But I'm gay," announced Sam who still didn't appear to see what the problem was. "I'm sure you'll get used to the idea."

"No! I'm not going to get used to the idea. Would you get used to it if they'd picked a woman for you?"

"You're not a homophobe, are you?" answered Sam defensively.

"No, I have no problem at all with how people wish to go about their lives, I just want others to be tolerant to my choices also."

"That's ok, then."

"No, it's not!"

"One of my guides is telling me to stop causing a scene," whispered Sam assertively. "He's suggesting we sort this out at home?"

"I like the sound of her guide," said Brother Job in agreement. "Find out what he's called."

"Find out for yourself!"

"Come on," said Sam. "It's not like you have anywhere else to go, is it?"

Reluctantly Jake had to agree. He was thousands of miles from home, knew no one this side of the Atlantic, and every movement he took was being tracked by the Circuit. What alternative did he have? Camp here in the Hyperloop Port until someone granted him squatters rights? There had to be a way out of this dilemma. Surely even the Circuit had a process for appeals when they made genuine mistakes. All he had to do was find out how to do it. Sam attempted to take Jake by the hand, but he ripped it away before Sam got a firm grip.

"Stop!"

"Too early," said Sam.

"Let's get something straight right away," stressed Jake candidly. "There will be no hand-holding, no hugging, no smacks on bums, no kissing, no groping, no inappropriate touching and no verbal innuendo. Do I make myself clear? I have boundaries and I'd ask that you don't cross them."

"Ok. But you said nothing about getting naked together, right?"

"Add that to the list and anything else that's going through your sordid mind. If you're in any doubt whatsoever it's probably on the list."

"Fun sponge," replied Sam who seemed to be perversely enjoying Jake's misery.

"I appreciate none of this is your fault, Sam, and that today is also your Ascension Day, but I cannot spend my life living with a man."

"You lived with your dad for years, didn't you?"

"Which is definitely not the same."

"Isn't it?"

"No."

The two eighteen-year-olds stood silently for an awkward moment, both disappointed by the outcome of their meeting and neither quite sure what to do next.

"What are we supposed to do now, Job?" asked Jake.

"Job?" asked Sam with a wink.

"Also, on the list," added Jake as soon as he realised his new partner's misinterpretation. "Brother Job is one of my guides."

"You need to get out of the Arrivals Hall and head to his place," replied Job.

"There's no other option?"

"No."

"Fine," he replied reluctantly. "Where in Malmö do you live, Sam?"

"My house is out in the countryside, about an hour away from here. As you'll see in a minute there's not much left of Malmö since the sea rose."

"Do you have trams that go that way?"

"Yes."

"Let's go, then," huffed Jake. "Then we can try to sort this mess out."

"We're not going by tram," replied Sam.

"How else are we going to get there?"

"In the same way I came to pick you up."

"Which is?"

"A solar-powered quadcopter."

"A what?"

"You'll see!"

Jake didn't need to wait. He immediately searched for the strange-sounding device in his cloud. There were no personal memories available because he'd never heard of one, let alone witnessed such a thing for himself. There were plenty of other people who had, though. A quadcopter had a central pod that carried at most two passengers and flew with the aid of four propellers that jutted out on arms like points of a compass. Covered in solar panels it could reach a hundred miles an hour in daylight and an altitude of five thousand metres.

"I see you're interested in the Mark IV quadcopter from Starbucks, Jake?" said an attractive redhead who'd infiltrated the vision rather masterfully.

"Starbucks? I thought they made cophony?" he said, a little confused.

"All organisations have to diversify and there's not much money to be made in cophony these days. Now hold still while I vet you for suitability...ah yeah, this is a waste of my time. You're superfluous, there's no way you'd be able to afford...or be allowed to own a quadcopter," she said, evaporating from view.

"Jesus, Sam, how did you manage to get one?" replied Jake, letting his guard down and finding his companion a lot more fascinating than his initial impression.

"Oh, life's been good to me."

"What does that mean?"

"I don't like to brag about it, but I'm quite well off."

"But you're only eighteen, and from what I've read only essential."

"I wouldn't believe everything you read," he said with a wink.

"Isn't that the truth?" agreed Jake.

- Chapter 13 -

Quirks and Quadcopters

Sam's quadcopter was parked in a disused car park about a mile from the Hyperloop terminal. It was only reachable by foot and Jake accepted the reality readily. Having spent much of the day strapped to a bed or queuing for the privilege to do so, his body was desperate for exercise. Jake loved nothing more than to walk in the tranquillity of nature; the soft sandy beaches near his home, climbing in the foothills of New Hampshire or paddling in the bubbling streams that curved their way through the White Mountain National Park.

There was no comparison between those places and this sterile stroll, but that didn't mean it lacked highlights.

It was evident from his surroundings that Sweden had borne a heavy price from the climate catastrophe that struck the world more than a decade ago. Even though he was very young at the time, Jake remembered it with a little aid from his cloud. There wasn't a specific memory that visualised the event, because in truth it didn't happen like that. The environment changed over an extended period of time, culminating in the radical actions of the scientific community at the dawn of the twenty-forties. Actions that came too late and with unintended consequences.

QUIRKS AND QUADCOPTERS

The crisis facing the world had been long in the making. For more than nine decades the subject had been exhaustively discussed and avoided. The scientists agreed on the problem, but the politicians, desperate to cling to power and uphold the false economics that drove growth in the twentieth century, flatly refused to act unilaterally. At best they'd offered platitudes and at worst denied the evidence completely. Experts were pilloried as prophets of doom rather than highly acclaimed thought leaders. The powerful laughed off the threats and predictions.

But no one was laughing now.

Like a homeowner who refuses to buy insurance because the worst will never happen, the world's house was flooded, and everyone regretted their blindness. Once the genie is out of the bottle, he's very difficult to put back in. Although a genie does offer wishes, you have to know what to wish for. Sadly no one really did.

The polar ice caps continued to melt at record speeds and inevitably the sea level rose as a result. Compared to the turn of the century, oceans were already more than fifty metres higher. Some of the nations responsible for a failure to act were submerged by the tides. Only then, like a death row captive desperately seeking clemency on the Day of Judgement, did they demand action. Industry, the main culprit for much of the planet's ill health, offered a solution. It seemed counter-intuitive to pass them the baton when they'd spent so long dropping it.

Their answer was a form of geoengineering dubbed CLEAR SKY.

A plan, with about as much proof-of-concept as those offering evidence for a flat Earth, was rushed into action. Scientists had concluded that if small particles of sulphur dioxide gas were fired into the atmosphere it would promote a cooling process to curb the worst of the rising temperatures and save more countries from claiming to be the new site of Atlantis. In the long run, probably several decades, they claimed this united action would also slowly lower temperatures to normal levels. Manufacturers went to work building specially designed systems for delivering the particles into the air. Every country endorsed the project in a rare moment of consensus. There was only one problem.

It didn't work.

Only some of the world got cooler.

Areas above and below the Tropics of Cancer and Capricorn saw a gentle reduction in annual temperatures and as a consequence an improvement in the conditions needed to grow vital crops. Everywhere else saw an increase in temperature that turned the land arid and the environment inhospitable to life. The sulphur particles combined with water vapour that diffused the sunlight and created a continual haze that affected much of the world. Much like the effect of a massive volcanic eruption, the world experienced erratic weather patterns, the now common sulphurous cloud cover and a renaming of the seasons to reflect a new norm.

Nature had been screwed with.

Nature didn't like it much.

No one acknowledged the failure. Environmental side effects were labelled temporary and worth the sacrifice. The opinion polls showed an overwhelming approval for the company responsible for the geoengineering strategy. The same company that owned ninety percent of the world's public companies and was responsible for running the polls.

The Circuit.

The scenery around Malmö proved their strategy was not universally successful or applauded. Roof apexes, attached to long-submerged family homes and businesses, cut through the waterline. Gentle ripples, powered by deep currents, washed up and over chimneys to be recycled in the murky abyss of hidden rooms and corridors. The road they were on was only just above the water, but Jake suspected it once had a life as an elevated freeway linking the city and the airport.

Here and there solitary islands held back the inevitable path of the sea. Freakish patches of land that had the audacity to exist on a plane slightly higher than the rising tide. Nothing lived there. The earthy soil may have survived the reclamation, but humans, vegetation and animals had given up hope long ago.

Above their heads the sky seethed with a layer of cloud that swamped the heavens like a swarm of angry locusts. Distinct patches of yellow and grey, sulphurous and natural condensation battled like Greek Gods for dominion over the lower atmosphere. The only proof that the sun still existed was the hazy pallor of a once bright star unable to penetrate the clouds for a fear of being mocked.

Then there was the local temperature.

He'd been warned.

The advice hadn't been strong enough.

The only experience Jake had of cold this intense was swimming in the mountain streams of upstate New Hampshire, but even that was warm in comparison. This was a mutated coldness that robbed you of the ability to speak coherently, permeated internal bodyparts you didn't know you had and questioned whether you were anatomically still a boy. If the geoengineers had successfully raised the temperature in this region of the world he shuddered to think what it was like before.

The more they walked, the harder it became to function normally. The cold was causing vital functions to freeze and fail. Even though Sam wore less clothes than Jake did in summer, it didn't affect him, as if his sense of touch had stopped working.

"Aren't you cold?" chattered Jake.

"Flipping freezing!" responded Dinah, who'd made a significant outfit change that included several additional layers, Arctic boots, three snoods and a fluffy deerstalker. All of them lilac-coloured.

"Cold?" said Sam stopping briefly to reassure himself he was outside. "Is it? This is pretty mild for this time of year."

"Miiillllddd," gasped Jake.

"Yeah, you're lucky. It was a lot colder here last week."

Jake hadn't been lucky for some considerable time and he wasn't accepting any suggestion that his fortunes had changed.

"You'll be warmer soon, there's the quadcopter."

Sam pressed on keys concealed somewhere about his person and the machine made a strange bleeping noise before its lights flashed in welcome. Sam gave it a little pat as if it were a beloved pet.

"This is Maisy," he said full of pride. "Beauty, isn't she?"

Jake hadn't seen a real one before so didn't feel qualified to judge. He nodded politely and hoped his muted reaction would suffice.

"Jump in, she's heated."

"She," scoffed Jake through vibrating teeth. "I don't believe anything anymore."

Sam opened the gull-wing doors to reveal a myriad of dials, gadgets and levers set in a futuristic-looking dashboard. The driver's seat crumpled forward to reveal a passenger seat hidden behind. Jake scrambled in before his blood turned to a solid. It was an extremely cramped space for a man like Jake who was much taller than average and would never be described as petit. The cabin was mostly see-through so at least he'd be able to watch the journey pass from his squashed-up spot. Sam shut the door and warmth slowly returned to flesh and feeling.

"How does it work?" asked Jake once the power of speech had rediscovered its normal frequency.

"Solar-powered."

"But…there's no sun!"

"There's enough for Maisy. The sun may not be out, but its power still seeps down through the clouds to charge the batteries. Maisy's equipped with the very latest in solar technology. They need much less input to work these days."

"How did you afford one? Rich parents?"

"No. My parents died when I was young. They didn't leave me anything," said Sam.

"How, then?" asked Jake.

"My work."

"But these things cost tens of millions of credits. What's your job, do you own the Circuit or something?!" said Jake, awestruck by anyone who owned something this rare, let alone someone who'd only reached eighteen on the same day as him.

"No, I don't believe anyone owns the Circuit."

"What do you do, then?"

"I'm a genius," he said casually. "Now hold tight, you might feel a little jolt."

Four propeller blades simultaneously leapt into life and the craft zoomed into the air like a kite in a gale. Jake clung to the handrails far more concerned for his safety here than the overly protective features he'd experienced during Hyperloop travel. His stomach lifted out of position and gave his Adam's apple a high-five before rebounding down to rejoin his lower abdominal muscles. Dinah screamed for joy, face pressed up against the glass. Brother Job tutted as his fake tablet kept shaking while he was trying to check the itinerary.

QUIRKS AND QUADCOPTERS

After several minutes of rapid elevation, the quadcopter levelled out and started flying more laterally. From its altitude just beneath the sulphur clouds, Jake got a better view of the lands he'd soon be calling home. It was mostly aquatic, but in the distance the land began to rise up above the wash.

"What's that?" shouted Jake over the whirl of the four propellers.

"You could check your cloud," said Job disdainfully.

"Sometimes it's nice to experience the world for what it is," added Sam, seeming to read Job's response, even though there was no way he could hear it. "We're flying over what remains of Denmark. It's almost completely submerged."

"But there's a road running across the sea for miles in that direction," said Jake, picking it out below him.

"It's not a road," replied Sam plainly. "That's the Øresund Bridge. It used to connect Malmö and Copenhagen. It's no longer in use because one end of it was a tunnel and that's completely underwater now."

"Where have all the people gone?"

"Refugees moved to neighbouring countries like mine. We all have to adapt in these difficult times."

"That must have been hard for people of your country?"

"No, not really. We're all human wherever we're born, and we have to take care of each other. The world may rely on technology and science to function, but underneath all of it there's a natural world we're all part of. It should be our most important priority, but people haven't realised it yet. The Circuit can't control nature, only humans."

"I'm guessing you got a violation for that remark," added Jake in a whisper in case he got one, too.

"Violation?" Sam said quizzically. Realising his error, he quickly corrected himself. "Oh yes. I did. I got that annoying klaxon sound and the green alert in my feed."

Jake's violations had always been red, but so much was different in this part of the West he didn't dwell on the discrepancy for long.

The quadcopter banked steeply to the right and headed up the coastline in the direction of the hills hiding on the horizon. The sky around them was empty. There were no other vehicles to contend with and they were too high for the small number of bird species that still occupied the sky. Many species had vanished completely over the past two decades, either unable to adapt to changing habitats or metaphorically trampled under the feet of selfish humans frantic to avoid their own suffering.

Creatures of land and sky had been affected the most as natural habitats sank under the waves or no longer provided the resources required for life. Water species, on the other hand, were thriving as their territories expanded and their natural enemies dwindled. The biggest winners, though, were the micro-organisms. Viruses were mutating, bacteria flourished, and fungi replicated on anything left static for more than five minutes. In some of the warmer patches of ocean great reefs of algae surfed the sea for hundreds of miles.

The birds might be gone for now, but together with the blue sky they would return, thought Jake, remembering his grandfather's cryptic farewell message. He just needed a workable plan to find both of them.

Maisy was noticeably dragged down on the air currents as the craft left the area above the sea and passed over the land. The number of islands, a regular feature of the landscape back in Malmö, dwindled and were converted into a collection of small lakes. The sea had assaulted this region of Sweden, but the land had fought back.

"Almost there," said Sam with his thumb raised. "See that small hill?"

"Yes," he said staring out of the window.

"That's home."

A flat-topped mound sat above the flooded plain and stuck out like a teenager's acne. As they approached there was no obvious sign of civilisation. The only noticeable feature of the hill was a small, grassy knoll that jutted out of the top like a nipple. The quadcopter hovered in the air next to it before slowly and softly descending, landing gently amongst the heather. Jake clambered back out into the cold. The noise of the machine was suffocated, and silence replaced the buzz of the propellers.

Complete silence.

No bird, creature, human or technology made a noise. In fact, the only sign of life was the hill itself. Jake suddenly felt concerned for his well-being. He was in the company of someone he didn't know, who'd flown him to a wilderness declaring he lived there. Who could live here? There was nothing. No house, no town, no resources, no amenities and no life. His heart raced. Maybe Sam intended to keep it that way and there was nothing he or his guides could do to stop him.

"What's going on?" said Jake taking several steps backward from his new partner. "Why are we here?"

"I live here."

"What are you, a caveman or a pervert!?"

"Neither."

"But you're planning to do something hideous to me, I know it. There's no other reason for bringing me here...I have boundaries!" he screamed, holding a feeble defensive pose.

"I think I'm mostly planning dinner and I'm hoping it won't be hideous."

"Dinner! Probably on an open fire. You're going to torture me and then eat my flesh, aren't you?"

"I'm queer, Jake, I'm not a cannibal."

Sam pressed another concealed button and another noise cranked through the air in the area around the hill's mound behind Jake's head. The grassy knoll started to slide open. As the turf retracted from the slope a glistening glass dome revealed itself like a secret planetarium.

"This is my…I mean our home," said Sam, correcting himself.

"Dear Lord! It's incredible."

"Yes, I guess it is," replied Sam who'd lived there for so long the effects had worn off.

"Just to be clear, it doesn't matter how amazing your house is it has zero bearing on the previous remarks I made about boundaries."

"Of course."

"You have a house like a Bond villain!" gasped Jake.

"Ha, I suppose so. Did you see the sixty-seventh film recently? What was it called?"

"The Virtual Daylights, yeah, I loved it."

"See, we have things in common after all. Let me show you around," announced Sam, beckoning Jake to follow him.

A little way behind Job and Dinah loitered deep in conversation.

"I like her," said Dinah merrily.

"I'm not so sure," replied Brother Job. "There's something odd about her that I can't put my finger on."

"You can't put your finger on anything, you don't have any, remember? I think you're overthinking it as usual. What's not to like about her?"

168

"There's just not enough of her," replied Job cryptically.

"What did you want for Jake, a fatty?"

"I'm not referring to her physical size, Sister Dinah. That's for Jake's eyes only. I'm talking about her cloud feed."

"What about it?" said Dinah lying in the heather and making angel shapes with her arms and legs.

"It's rather thin. I've been scanning back and forward in her cloud and for someone who's eighteen there just aren't enough memories."

"I'm not surprised if she's been living up here all this time. I mean how many memories of 'windswept and interesting' do you need exactly?"

"It's just irregular, that's all. Every time I access her memories, I keep getting the same ones replayed over and over like that's all she has. I think we should keep our eyes peeled, for Jake's benefit of course."

"We don't have eyes!"

"No, but we have virtual ones that can pierce other people's cloud feeds, so keep them peeled."

"Whatever, I'm bored now. See ya!"

Dinah skipped off in the direction of the partly concealed grass covered dome in a style best described as gay abandon, although the irony of it was totally lost on her. Brother Job followed with a scowl.

Jake and Sam approached the large entrance of his new home. Stretching over the top of the dome from one side of the hemisphere to the other was a wide strip of glass that allowed the light to flood into the building. In practical terms the house was one huge room constructed on three floors. At the bottom were a series of reception areas, a hi-tech kitchen and workshop. On the first-floor mezzanine, Jake could make out a bed separated by an old-fashioned partition screen with an oriental pattern on it. The third floor was obscured by the floors below but its close proximity to the enormous skylight must have exceptional views of the sky.

"What do you think?" asked Sam.

"It's amazing."

"It's a bit like your place back home, I'm sure."

"Yeah, very similar," Jake lied, thinking for the first time today about his sister and grandfather cooped up in his small ferrocon home opposite an identical row of others in an unremarkable suburban district. "I love the paintings."

"Paintings?"

"Yeah, that big one on the wall near the kitchen featuring a coastal scene, and the modern art piece where the escalator goes up the wall."

"I don't have any paintings," replied Sam. "They aren't really there. It's only in your feed."

Sometimes it was that easy for the visual and virtual worlds to collide. While he took in his surroundings with his true eyes his emotions fantasised about what might be there in future. As soon as that happened the commercial conmen descended to carefully and strategically place possible future purchases in places that on first view looked as real as the dome itself. Jake washed his mind and refocused his eyes. The pictures vanished like a first-rate magic trick.

"Do you often struggle with your memory feed?" asked Sam pointedly.

"Sometimes. I've had a lot of upgrades."

"Turn around," Sam requested softly.

Jake spun on his heels to discover a scene devoid of human influence spreading out in front of him.

"What do you see?"

Jake's Memory Cloud used the empty foreground to bombard him with unrequired stimuli.

"I can see Christie…"

"Who's that?"

"She's my girlfriend…at least she was."

"I see, please continue."

"She's on the beach waving at me. She's smiling. We've got the day off. There's no stress at all, just the two of us sharing a pure moment of happiness."

"What about the bees?"

"What bees?"

"The ones swarming around the hive over there on the brow of the hill."

Jake tried to cut through the virtual distractions to the place Sam was pointing to in the distance.

"You don't see it, do you?" he replied sadly.

"No."

"That's because your virtual world has taken over from the real one. You've lost sight of what's happening in the world, Jake. The sound of the wind rustling the trees, the almond smell of the Twinflowers that still grow plentifully in my garden, and the sight at dusk of the moon glowing defiantly just behind the sulphur clouds. It's all still there, but your world has forgotten it."

Jake felt somewhat ashamed of himself. He'd always loved being out in nature and thought of himself as someone deeply connected to his own environment, but how true was his experience really? How much of his vision was being suppressed? Quite a bit if Sam's example was anything to go by.

"How do you control it?" asked Jake. "My feed has a mind of its own sometimes."

"It takes practice, more so if you've had a lot of upgrades. I can help you, though."

Jake returned to the dome feeling a little vulnerable that this newcomer had so easily extracted his feelings.

"What did you say your job was?" Jake asked again, aware that Sam had already avoided the question once.

"Do you mean what does it say in my letter?"

"If you like."

"It said I'm destined to be a Beautician."

"You can't afford a quadcopter and a Bond hideout doing that!"

"Well, I haven't started training yet, so I'm not sure how much I'll earn."

"But you must have had a job before yesterday," said Jake, pointing at the evidence.

"I did."

Jake was getting exasperated, "Doing what?"

"Managing risk," replied Sam.

- Chapter 14 -

The Wedding Planner

Jake woke from an uncomfortable night's sleep on a perfectly comfortable bed. The first of many thousands the Circuit was insisting he'd spend here. Thoughts of his old life marched into his vision. Thoughts of his new home barged through the crowd. Above all of it the light seeped in through the skylight and bathed the vast atrium that split the two sides of the dome. This was his side. On the other was Sam's. A perfect analogy for the incompatibility of their relationship.

The peculiar truth of yesterday's first meeting with his appointed life partner was not the revelation that Sam happened to be a man. As surprising as that was to him that factor was hidden behind more interesting shadows. His incredibly affluent lifestyle, unusual views on the world and the mystery surrounding his past job. Jake's past jobs, mostly summer ones, included stacking shelves at local convenience stores and combing the beach for litter. None of these rewarded him with quadcopters or secretive lairs on desolate hilltops. He once got a free token for the Dream Centre as a bonus for hard work, but that was about it.

Sam had done considerably better working in a profession he'd described as 'Risk Management'. What risks was he helping to manage and how did it generate such amazing rewards? And if he'd been so successful at it, as he unquestionably had, why would the Circuit hire him as a Beautician? Perhaps Sam's

Ascension Day process had gone wrong, too? Maybe everybody's went wrong but no one had the guts to do anything about it. It wasn't a surprise why they wouldn't. After all, Jake had seen at first-hand the ruthless punishments that the Circuit dished out on anyone who stepped out of line.

In a world brilliantly managed by the Memory Cloud what risks were there?

Other than sporadic attacks like the one Jake had suffered down on the beach the day before yesterday, crime was almost non-existent. No one with a subscription to the Memory Cloud would be foolish enough to contemplate it. Their cloud feed would pick up their intent long before the planning stage commenced. Crime wasn't just rare because people feared the punishment, it was low because the system catered for everyone, at least in financial terms. There were of course those who had more wealth than others, but this was partly ruled by someone's importance factor. The Ascension Day process had abolished unemployment and poverty. Everyone was allocated a profession, so no one went hungry or lived without their basic needs.

People still held ambition for more, but it was stifled by your position in the system and therefore you were tied down to a sense of realism. If you were 'trivial' then that was down to you, no one else. The chance had been there for you to do better but you missed the boat. It was the same truth for everyone, except in cases like Jake's which was definitely an error. If you were genuinely trivial, or any other level, you were free to achieve more than others did if you worked hard enough for it. But you could never exceed the achievements of those assigned to the level above you. That glass ceiling was as real as the one above Jake's head.

War was also not something the world tolerated, not in the traditional sense at least. No regions of the

THE WEDDING PLANNER

West had gone to war for some decades, preoccupied as they were with the survival of the planet. Now war was almost impossible anyway. All weapons of mass destruction had been decommissioned, all armies disbanded, and no political party could maintain power if the collective thoughts of the people willed against it. Every year the Circuit ran elections for member states and scoured the central Memory Cloud to form a decision. If approvals dropped below a minimum threshold then the government was immediately removed. It was real democracy after a few thousand years of practice.

At least that's what people were told.

No one ever voted for the Circuit.

Never.

They were above reproach. Governments could rise and fall, but the Circuit always remained in place.

The only potential conflict the West had to contend with existed in the threat from the East. Not a conventional threat, though. There were no tanks patrolling the borders, there were no drone strikes against major urban areas or overt intimidation to suggest it. The sense of danger was a silent one, which actually made it more terrifying. It was a well-known fact that the people of the East hated those who lived in the West. Driven by jealously and greed, they wanted nothing more than to grind Jake's half of the world to dust. Mannie, who lived a lot closer to it than he did, had shed even more light on their hostility. Strikes from the East were mostly cyber-attacks aimed at the very heart of the Circuit's power, the Memory Cloud. This mode of warfare was a regular feature of life and the Circuit did their best to countenance their attempts by reminding the public of the sinister nature of their opponent.

Regular public announcements were broadcast into memory feeds to reinforce the point. Every other day the 'Proclamation of Distrust' was mandatory viewing. Unlike the ads or news bulletins that crept into the feed this could not be flicked away. It had to be watched and any attempts not to do so would generate an automatic violation. Its message was always the same. The East was not to be trusted. A potted description of life under the Realm was played out in front of you during the five-minute propaganda.

It featured angry, ugly, unshaven men who brandished messages of hate towards the West while young, dirty children burnt the Circuit's symbol. The East was a land of chaos and disorder. People who lived there, it was told, were left to choose for themselves and their ill-judged decisions were played out in the 'Proclamation of Distrust' to show you just how miserable life was without the aid of foresight. Crime was rife, addictions common, aggression encouraged and poverty widespread. The East was evil and the West was good and weren't you lucky to be on the right side of the fence? The fear of what might come if the West didn't keep to the rules made people grateful for what they had. The proclamation always ended in the same way: the logo and the motto appearing together in your virtual world.

The Circuit. It's a state of mind.

Perhaps that was the risk that Sam had been managing? The risk that the East would in some way consume the West. It was the only possible explanation in Jake's mind as he contemplated what he was supposed to do today. It didn't, however, explain why it had made Sam rich beyond anything he thought was possible.

What was he supposed to do today?

The letter didn't explain 'how' only 'what'. It didn't say when his job began or how he was meant to do it. It didn't tell him how he was supposed to get into BASE jumping, only that he would. Jake always woke up with something to do. He'd either go to school or had plans for the weekend with Christie. Even on days when she or his friends weren't available, he found something to occupy his time.

Today there was nothing.

An unfamiliar house, country and acquaintances, seething with intrigue but devoid of warmth.

No compelling reason to get out of bed.

At least that's what he believed.

"Up you get," said Brother Job, making an alarm noise that was rather authentic.

"Why?"

"Because you have a life to live and things to do."

"What things?" groaned Jake.

"Exploring!" shouted Dinah, making Jake jump as she appeared from under the fake fur throw that lay half on and half off his bed.

"Not exploring," argued Job with a scowl.

"What, then?" said Jake.

"You have a visitor."

"How can I have a visitor? No one knows where I am!"

"See for yourself."

Jake crawled out of bed and moved over to the glass barrier that separated the open-plan layout of the first floor from the atrium. On the ground floor, Jake heard two men engaged in a rather loud and deep conversation. One was undoubtedly Sam, but he had no idea who owned the other voice. Jake's compaction-case had already been regrown and was lying open on the floor. Most of his possessions were scattered over the floor after last night's tired retreat to bed. He threw on some trousers and a T-shirt, completely forgetting which country he was in. The house was a cosy temperature, but these wouldn't do if, as planned, he ventured outside. He quickly rethought outfits before walking silently to the escalator.

There were no videographs along Sam's wall. In fact, there were no signs that Sam or any other member of his family had ever lived there. It was curious how little of Sam's life was on display. He'd told Jake yesterday that he'd lost his parents when he was young, yet there was no sentimental acknowledgement of the truth around his house. It was almost as if the place was rented and Sam wasn't certain he'd be here that long.

At the bottom of the escalator the wide glass door that led outside was retracted and revealed the quality of the weather. It was spitting with rain. In the desolate beauty of the hill the only movement came from the flowers as they swayed gently in the breeze. The cloud feed attempted to hijack the space, but Jake was quick to remove it. Sam had suggested he was missing out on the world and he wanted to prove he was in touch with nature as much as his partner.

"Morning," said Sam from the kitchen, an area under the curvature of the sloping wall on the far side of the dome. "How did you sleep?"

"Not well."

"You should have come over to my side."

"Boundaries, remember?"

"Ooh he's gorgeous," added a voice at a higher pitch than normal humans were generally capable of without a toy voice box.

"Jake, come and meet my friend Maurice."

Maurice leant casually against the kitchen worktop in a difficult pose to copy. His arms moved around in the air as he talked, as if someone else was in control of them. Tight moleskin trousers clung to his legs with a belligerence that suggested the only way to remove them would be as a result of prolonged starvation. A white shirt was equally tight-fitting, although the buttons at the top had been loosened to at least allow his neck and head a fighting chance of surviving suffocation. A shaved-thin head sat on weedy, pointed shoulders that would easily puncture flesh if you got too close to them. His eyes sparkled through the layers of foundation that he'd lathered over much of his face other than where a small beard had been lovingly shaved into a right-leaning horn.

"Lovely to meet you," burst out Maurice, lovingly embracing him for a period of time that just exceeded sexual assault length.

"Hello."

"You must be the lucky boy worthy enough to steal my Sam away from me. Sooo jealous!"

"Yeah, lucky me."

"I mean look at him," said Maurice, gazing longingly at Sam. "To think you get to watch and squeeze that bum all day long. Imagine it."

"I really don't want to," replied Jake, trying hard to wipe the image but being inundated with memories of butts being launched in his cloud feed.

"Why not!? Go, on, don't be shy, give it a really good grope!"

"I'm not gay."

The room fell silent and the air in the dome fought against the suction from a hidden ventilator at the back of Maurice's throat. His eyes widened almost as much as his mouth.

"It's alright, Maurice, we're working through it," replied Sam casually.

"Working through it! It's not a disagreement over who washes the dishes, this is a lot more serious. And such a waste if I can say so."

"That's what I said," agreed Jake. "The first bit, that is."

"It's what the Circuit wants, and we have to accept their wisdom," explained Sam simply.

Maurice's consternation ceased and his eyes scanned the room anxiously as if the authorities might burst in through the front door at any moment.

"Why is he here?" whispered Jake.

"Brother Graham called him."

"Brother Graham, is he one of your guides?"

"Yes."

"I thought they were named after Biblical figures?"

"They are," interjected Brother Job in support of the notion. "It was a feature agreed on by the founders of the sibling programme."

"Yes, that's right," confirmed Sam.

"And Graham was famous in the Bible where?" said Jake.

"I think he was present at the Sermon on the Mount."

"Not according to my records," said Job righteously.

"What's your other one called?"

"Sister Andrew," replied Sam.

"Sister?"

"Yeah. I guess because I'm gay the two parts of my personality were reflected through my guides."

"This is most irregular," chuntered Job, disappearing into the rabbit warren of Jake's cloud feed to seek clarification.

"I suppose that makes sense," replied Jake. "So why did one of them call for Maurice?"

"He's our wedding planner."

For a brief moment the world stopped spinning. The contents of the dome froze, and the only sound was the gentle suppressed beat within his chest. Even the Memory Cloud fell silent. Jake knew a wedding was inevitable but to face up to it less than twenty-four hours after arriving was still a shock.

"Do we have to plan it so soon?" wheezed Jake as he hyperventilated.

"Absolutely," replied Maurice extravagantly.

"Why?"

"Because it's next week," added Sam.

"Next week?!"

"Yes, it's in the rules."

"Is it?" Jake asked Job internally.

"Yes, it's about the only thing I've heard this morning that I agree with."

"Let's get started, then," bubbled Maurice excitedly. "No time to lose. Let's talk themes."

"What about a naturalist theme," asked Sam.

"Oh, I like it."

"If I have to get married, I'm not walking around in the nude the whole time! Not happening," implored Jake. "Let's just keep it simple. We can have it in the dome and invite...no one."

"No one!" gasped Maurice inconsolably. "What about your family, Jake, don't you want them here?"

"No. Even if I approved of this marriage, which I don't, they wouldn't be able to come."

"Why not?" asked Sam.

"My parents are being held in the Source, my sister hates me, and my grandfather would never travel this far."

"In the Source," replied Sam with a furrowed brow. "What did they do?"

"Nothing. It's what I did. I want to help them, but I have no idea how to."

"Maybe we should look into it," said Sam supportively.

How could he 'look into it'? Who other than the Circuit themselves were able to reverse the decision? Sam acted and sounded like he had no fear of them.

Like they were just an inconvenience rather than an immovable barrier.

"How many people do you want to invite?" asked Maurice, not in the slightest bit interested in Jake's worries and a little annoyed that his personal creativity was being hindered.

"The normal crew," said Sam inconsequentially.

"About a hundred, then."

"A hundred! How big is your family?"

"It's not all family. I have a wide circle of friends," replied Sam.

Jake wasn't certain he'd ever met a hundred people, let alone wanted them at his wedding.

"And I'm going to give you away, right?" said Maurice with a wink.

"Yes," confirmed Sam.

"Who's going to be your best man, Jake?"

In happier times, a period that ended abruptly the day before yesterday, he and Christie would often imagine what their wedding day might feel like, even if it was only ever a fantasy. Jake summoned up one of those memories in his feed and watched in blissful nostalgia. Christie had decided she wanted a traditional service and an elegant yet conservative white dress. The whole event would be at their favourite place, the beach, and they'd keep it small, just close friends and family. They'd dance to the ancient tunes of Bruce Springsteen and honeymoon in the peace and tranquillity of the Rockies. Jake watched forlornly at a scene that would never materialise.

Amongst all of these returning memories there was no mention of who his best man might be. Even in real time, Jake struggled to think of anyone who might fulfil the role adequately. After all, Christie was his best friend and the only one he wanted to be there. For a brief instant he wondered if it might be possible for her to do it now, before ignoring the notion as both inappropriate and logistically impossible.

"I don't have anyone," said Jake wistfully.

"PICK ME!" shouted, Dinah jumping up and down in front of Maurice to grab his attention.

"Fine," said Jake. "This situation would only be more depressing if I asked Brother Job."

"I've logged that," Job replied.

"My best man will be Sister Dinah," he said to Maurice.

"Very progressive, you might still fit in here, you know. What about your honeymoon?"

"What's popular at the moment?" asked Sam.

"Zipwiring in the Andes is super popular at the moment. Or, with your budget, you could do the ice palace at the South Pole? What about a submarine tour of the sunken lands?"

"I'd like to do something I haven't done before," replied Sam casually. "I'd really like to see the East."

Maurice almost collapsed to the floor at the thought. "Shhh, they're always listening. No one can go there, and I'm shocked you even want to."

"Maybe it's not as bad as we've all been led to believe," replied Sam without fear of reprisals.

"Food..." said Maurice, quickly changing the subject before Sam ran down his violation quota. "Vol-au-vents or fish canapés?"

"I'll leave that with you."

Jake had heard enough. It was like watching someone wreck your life whilst being trapped behind a force field. What did it matter? They may as well have a thousand people, all dressed as Roman gods, gorging on live cattle for all he cared. In a style that he hoped might be seen by the others as undramatic, Jake left the kitchen and headed outside. The temperature difference took him off guard and he immediately regretted it.

"Are you alright?" said Sam who'd quickly followed him out.

"No. I'm not. Everything is moving too fast for me. I'm being rushed into choices I don't want to make, that I can't escape from. Why does it have to be next week?"

"It's hard to explain until it happens," replied Sam with a weak smile. "I understand this is hard. I know that I am not what you expected, but you are exactly what I expected. Perfect in fact, and in time I think you'll realise why this had to be the way it is. I know you don't know me very well, but I'm asking you to trust me."

"Trust you! Trust takes years to form, it's not something that can be conjured up at will, there's no basis for it."

"No, but I promise there will be. How can I make the wedding easier for you?"

"Cancel it," said Jake hopefully.

"Other than that."

"Just make it modest and don't expect me to smile at any point during the day."

"Ok, I'll tell Maurice. The most important part for me is the contract, that's the priority."

The two men were interrupted by a small, white drone dropping from the sky before hovering impatiently in front of them. Small icicles had formed on its metal body and frost obscured its cameras. A tiny heater whirled to help remove the crystallised deposits and allow for the recipient of its delivery to be identified. It scanned both men before the lens settled on Jake. Simultaneously a delivery alert popped up in Jake's feed to confirm the arrival before a small door opened up on the front of the drone to reveal a small, bubble-wrapped, oblong parcel.

The label simply read, 'Jake Montana, Malmö, Sweden'.

"What is it?" asked Sam.

"My Moodzec."

"Right," replied Sam.

"It was a panic-buy more than anything," added Jake to exonerate himself in case his partner might judge him for the choice.

"It's your life, Jake. Whatever works for you."

Jake had no compulsion to listen to what sounded like disapproval. Sam wasn't going to tell him what he could and couldn't do. They weren't married yet! When most of your freedoms were stolen, holding onto the ones you still had felt even more important.

"You don't have authority over me."

"I know. I just want you to trust me."

"There you go with the trust thing again. I don't, right. Just accept that. I might need this stuff to get me through the next week stuck here with you and your camp friend as you plan my miserable future life."

"You won't be here for the next week," said Sam.

"Where will I be, then?" replied Jake in surprise.

"Didn't they tell you? You need to report to the Archivist Training Camp first thing tomorrow."

- Chapter 15 -

Bornholm

People usually have mixed emotions about starting a new job. On the one hand, there's excitement for the challenges that lie ahead and a desire to prove your worth to a new boss and colleagues. Then on the other hand the imposter syndrome rides in tandem, desperate to trip up your positive energy and reinforce thoughts of inadequacy and incompetence. Surely the interviewers had made some heinous oversight? Briefly hoodwinked by the false information scattered liberally across your résumé and aided by the well-rehearsed answers you'd proffered to their questions in an attempt to achieve one thing, success rather than victory.

It was just a matter of time before they'd discover the truth.

The moment your new boss demanded the completion of the simplest of tasks, and the inevitable failure followed soon after, the spotlight would be turned to dazzle mode. That's if you'd personally chosen to place yourself in the position of being judged forensically like that in the first place. After all, you'd asked for it.

Jake hadn't.

The Archivists had chosen him.

He'd never once considered them a genuine career option and his emotions were not remotely excited about it.

Only God knew why, and he had a lovely gold logo that spelt his name, CIRCUIT.

BORNHOLM

From the king-sized bed on his side of the first-floor wing of the dome he scanned through his feed to research some of the likely attributes that would be required for such a position. Scenes of Archivist retirees projected onto the curved wall from a source somewhere within Jake's optic nerve and aided by his cranial receptor. Wizened old men with battle-scarred faces and more stories on offer than a well-stocked library proceeded to recount their own personal experiences of what it took to succeed in the service. What it took to hunt down and, if necessary, kill the Spectrum.

They were skills and attitudes Jake did not recognise in himself.

Every one of these shadowy ex-Archivists brimmed with rage and anger that was aimed at a disgusting second-class element of society who'd unwisely chosen a different route in life, who'd chosen to disobey. The vitriol seeping through these veterans seemed at odds with Jake's own, yet brief, experience of the speccies. The Archivists portrayed them as savages, lesser humans with no rights or qualities. Had they formed these opinions during their employment, or had these views existed beforehand and were essential qualities to selection? It wasn't clear but their collective views were obviously in alignment.

Jake didn't feel in the slightest bit wary or disgusted by the Spectrum. If anything, he was jealous of their freedoms, although in truth that was about the sum of his knowledge on the subject. He didn't know where they lived, how they managed to stay hidden, or how they survived, other than the occasional excursion to steal from the rest of society. He certainly didn't know how to catch one.

According to the wrinkled, uniform-attired ex-soldier currently barking his advice and wisdom on that subject through Jake's mind, the secret was to show no mercy. Strike first and deal with errors later. There could be no sympathy for a group of people who flouted the rules. If they didn't like it, they only had themselves to blame. The man's callous description of how they were treated during the hunt made Jake's skin crawl.

Archivists stalked their prey like a Stone Age caveman hunted a deer, although the Archivists had the advantage of a much more powerful arsenal than a poorly constructed pointy stick. Aided by equipment that tracked body heat, they identified anyone in the vicinity and categorised those that were and weren't cloud subscribers. They pinpointed the exact location of the target and then a series of teams, called Corridors, would surround the dissident to restrict their escape.

Then they'd smoke them out.

Gas canisters peppered the target area to disable and disorientate, before each corridor advanced, weapons locked and loaded. The majors promoted a 'shoot on sight' policy if any Archivist believed the speccy was trying to avoid capture. Jake guessed that this resulted in a misuse of power and more fatalities than casualties. Any speccy not willing to convert was immediately terminated. To his relief the projections on his wall only talked about this process and offered few details or evidence of specific events. Even so, how could another human treat someone in such a brutal manner? It wasn't imposters syndrome he was experiencing, it was conscientious objection.

Jake swiped the images away.

Today he was leaving for the training camp where he'd be taught how to act like those he'd seen on-screen. He took almost nothing of use with him. He lacked the skills of orienteering, tracking, interrogation and the correct techniques for maintaining or using a firearm. He housed no anger or bitterness against the speccies or any other group of people. He didn't even hate those in the East who he'd been bred to detest by the 'Proclamation of Distrust', one of his oldest memories. The only quality he had to offer was his own brief personal experience, something, as it would transpire, that was more valuable than he initially believed.

"She's readied the quadcopter," said Job, who'd been particularly quiet over the last day. "Time to go."

"She?" said Jake in confusion. Job was a relentless perfectionist who wasn't prone to making mistakes like this one.

"Sam!" confirmed Dinah, cutting across her colleague.

"I'm not sure either of you are up to speed with the situation, but then again why should I expect you to do anything useful?"

"We'll be there for you during your training," said Dinah, attempting to offer comfort but failing completely. "I can't wait to get my hands on the grenades!"

"Get your bag, Jake," instructed Job. "Best to get there early and make a good first impression."

Jake grabbed his repacked compaction-case only a day after liberally scattering its contents on the floor. He headed outside and found Sam waiting for him. The quadcopter hummed gently ready to take him on the next step of his increasingly bizarre new life.

"Where are we going exactly?"

"Bornholm."

"Which is?"

"An island to the south of here. It used to be part of Denmark, but the Circuit requisitioned it in exchange for helping to rehouse Danish refugees. It's the training camp for all European Archivists."

"How many of us will be there?"

"No one knows for sure, but you'll soon find out. I'm looking forward to hearing all about it next week."

Jake bundled his belongings into the cockpit and folded his body into the cramped position behind his soon-to-be wife. He didn't even know if that was the correct name to use for him. He assumed the Circuit still saw him as the husband in this relationship, given it was him who'd been forced to relocate. Amongst a vast array of other questions that crowded Jake's mind, how Sam actually wanted to be addressed had yet to come up in conversation.

The quadcopter flew faster than yesterday and for a longer duration. Sam offered none of the local knowledge and sightseeing highlights either. The cabin remained silent throughout as the machine crossed over elevated lands soon replaced by submerged ones again. The longer they flew, the harder it became to pick out the patches of ground, and very soon there was no point trying. An idle, endless ocean waited patiently for watery reinforcements to continue its assault on the land of man.

The picture remained unchanged for hours until Sam drew his attention to a small land mass in the distance. Below them a craggy oasis of life peeked its head out of the sea, whose watery fists shook disapprovingly against the island's elevated shoreline. The closer they approached, the more desolate the island looked. Jake scanned his cloud feed for more details on the place where he was due to spend the rest of the week. There was nothing relevant, only historic footage from the archive files of what Bornholm used to be like before the seas conquered its smaller neighbours. Its outline was somewhat different than the picture from the past. Lowland regions of the island were now hidden somewhere under the waterline.

BORNHOLM

A search for more up-to-date information drew a blank. Nothing. No video footage, no memories and no information. It wasn't just the Archivists that were a secret, their training camp on Bornholm was, too.

On the east coast of the island a collection of red-bricked buildings occupied a region next to a disused quarry whose deep pit brimmed with bright blue water like a Caribbean lagoon. Unlike the sea, so keen to join it, this water was welcoming and calm. The buildings, on the other hand, were not. They were comparable to industrial warehouses rather than family homes and lacked the sufficient number of windows for structures built in a time when such features were still routinely included. Tall, barbed-wire fences stood guard around the barracks and surrounded all parts of the island other than a small patch of ground near the sea.

The land sloped gradually out of the water and up to the base of a training camp, which looked every bit as frightening as it was designed to be. Jake felt something fierce biting the pit of his stomach as the quadcopter descended and identified a suitable piece of turf to land on. The immediate sound they heard was of distant firing piercing the air. The rattling from the bullet strafing was occasionally overshadowed by an ear-splitting explosion that shook the ground under their feet. Removed from Maisy's safety the air sprayed a light drizzle through his cropped blond hair and the smell of sulphur forced him to put his fingers over his nostrils. It was more pronounced here than anywhere he'd been.

The noise of a siren added to the disorientating mood infiltrating his senses and a large, orange strobe light spun ominously on the top of a thick metal gate. Slowly the gate creaked open like the jaws of a massive mechanical shark. Jake knew the name for the feeling inside him.

Fear.

It was on a scale he'd never experienced before, as the memories of similar emotions flashed through him to affirm the truth. The journey to Europe had produced many of these personal and virtual flashbacks, but none had been due to fear. Confusion, irritation and surprise had made regular and unwelcomed appearances since Ascension Eve, but he'd never been scared of the outcome. Each emotion arrived with a certain amount of hope that a solution or alternative might be available. But that wasn't true today. Today all hope had been evacuated from his real and constructed worlds by the sheer animosity of this terrifying place. Any last semblance that might exist was about to be ripped and stamped on by the Jeep accelerating through the jaws of the gate towards the quadcopter.

It had been a decade since he'd seen any vehicle with wheels that weren't stationary. The propaganda spewed into his cloud feed courtesy of the Circuit presented a world that not only no longer needed such forms of transport, but also had sought to ban them altogether. They'd insisted that the renewal of our environment depended upon it. Yet here, on Circuit property, their three-litre hypocrisy approached in a plume of petrol-fumed, atmosphere-killing reality.

"I don't want to go," said Jake, turning desperately to Sam with a face that begged to be bundled back into the quadcopter for a speedy retreat.

"Nor me," shuddered Dinah.

"You have to," replied Job before Sam had a chance to offer words of encouragement. "It's in the contract."

"Screw the contract!"

VIOLATION

"Screw that, too."

VIOLATION

"Jake, that's your fourth this week," said Dinah shaking nervously. "Stop! I don't want to go to the Source. It frightens me."

"Beats this place," he said, believing nowhere was worse than Bornholm.

"Don't be melodramatic," snapped Job.

"No! They've gone too far this time. I never wanted to be an Archivist. I just wanted to be inconspicuous, to have a quiet, uneventful life. Keep myself to myself and let everyone else do what they want. None of this is fair!" he screamed, shaking his fist at the sky before sinking to his knees on the damp, soft ground.

The Jeep ground to a halt with a skid that finished inches from his face, splashing him with tiny droplets of mud. A pair of heavy, black boots stomped to the ground in unison and Jake's eyes slowly moved upwards to see what they were attached to. Tree trunk legs shrouded in a khaki-coloured weave, thick, brown leather belt overloaded with the utensils of war, a bloated chest that most people only achieved by sucking in their stomach, square jawline, an overworked face and piercing eyes that judged every movement. The judgement was being used against him and it pronounced 'uselessly inferior'.

"Stand," said a gruff voice like the sound waves from his vocal cords had passed through a cheese grater.

Jake immediately complied, fearing the outcome if he didn't. It was a reaction he was going to get used to.

"Name and IF soldier," he barked.

"Jake Montana, superfluous," he replied, offering a salute for no clear reason.

The Archivist's eyes offered their own view of the information before his lips had time to comment.

"Then you are no use to me. Show me your letter."

Jake wasn't entirely sure where it was. Had he packed it? Yes, he thought so. As his mind wandered around in his cloud to pinpoint the letter's exact location from the memories of this morning, he was brutally interrupted. Two massive hands grabbed Jake by the ears and lifted him clean off the ground without obvious strain. His ears throbbed with the pain of holding the weight of his thirteen-stone frame.

"NOW!" shouted the man.

He threw Jake to the ground. As soon as his feet met land, he turned on his heels, ran to the quadcopter, riffled through his compaction-case, and returned, grasping the letter like a treasure map. In total it had taken him less than ten seconds, but he imagined that was still not fast enough for the highly decorated psychopath.

"It's a mistake," announced the man as his eyes scanned the paper.

"That's what I've been saying," replied Jake a little too jovially.

A hard fist jabbed him square in the face for his insolence. Jake's body was forced backwards a few steps by the unexpected punch. A small line of blood flowed from a nostril and dribbled over his lip. He wiped it off, not wanting to show weakness. His reaction was one of shock rather than discomfort. No one had ever punched him in the face before. Normal people didn't do that. Physical violence was illegal within the populace and any incidents were punished immediately. Clearly what the Circuit said and did were very different from what it expected from others.

"It looks like you're in the right place," replied the man who momentarily was staring blankly into the foreground. "By the end of the week you're going to wish you weren't."

Jake nodded although he'd already convinced himself of that before they'd landed.

"Major Holst, vital," grunted the man, "and you will refer to me as such when addressing me. Understood?"

"Yes, Major Holst," replied Jake, filled with dread.

"The letter is genuine," replied Holst, "even if you are not. I'll just have to work with what I have. There are no superfluous ranks in the Archivists, so we'll have to find something demeaning for you to do."

Jake nodded subserviently.

"I like him," said Job.

Dinah didn't offer an opinion because she was hiding under a nearby rock.

"Get your bag and say goodbye to your loved ones, Montana. You have ten seconds."

Jake didn't have loved ones present so the urgency wouldn't be a problem. He grabbed his case, nodded to Sam and returned to the Major.

"See that building," said Holst menacingly.

"Yes, Major Holst."

"Start running. The gates will close in thirty seconds and if you're not on the other side of the gate you'll spend the next twenty-four hours being cleansed."

Jake had no idea what being cleansed involved, but he wasn't convinced he'd like it. Fortunately, what he lacked in Archivist knowledge he made up for in athletic ability. Jake had always been sporty. Ice tennis, cross ball, swimming and weightlifting were all pastimes he enjoyed and regularly participated in. He wasn't muscular to the extent of his new Major, but he was probably faster.

Not as fast as a Jeep, though.

The four-by-four vehicle sped off with the Major driving at full tilt. Jake set off to catch up. Dragging his case behind him, he focused on the jawlike gates and their rotating orange light. The Jeep passed through before he'd reached the halfway point and the gates immediately shrieked to announce their next move. By the time he reached it there was a gap no bigger than his body width to squeeze through.

Holst looked disappointed.

"Why are you panting?"

"Sorry, Major Holst."

"We do not show weakness here, boy. Our enemy will show us no pity. Only hatred. We meet hatred with strength. Whilst you are here you will attempt to prove you have what it takes to demonstrate those qualities. It should be beyond the capability of superfluous scum like you, so you'll have to work harder and longer than most cadets."

"Yes, Major Holst," he replied.

Jake hated being told he wasn't good enough. His teachers had always held the opinion that he'd never amount to much. His sister was regularly in agreement, but Jake felt that was probably true of all siblings. His parents had been generally supportive of him, if not necessarily proactive about it. The most encouragement he ever got from family was from Paddy. He had an old school grit and believed there was an internal willpower that existed within everyone. Even though he wasn't in the slightest bit interested in being an Archivist, if this monstrous man doubted his drive, he'd have to prove him wrong.

"Most of what you need to learn can be downloaded to your cloud and that process will begin immediately. Once you have received the cognitive knowledge needed, we will test your physical, psychological, technical and strategic abilities. If you fail those tests your mind will be cleansed before you leave, and the Circuit will reassign you to a new role within their structure. I doubt it'll be a good one."

"Yes, Major Holst."

"Report to Factory Three for downloading," he growled.

Holst forced the Jeep into gear and revved off into the distance to leave Jake and his guides to discover the location for themselves. Long, single-storeyed buildings lined up on either side obediently. Each looked exactly like the next. Rusty, corrugated roofs, crumbling, red brickwork and narrow, dirty windows high enough up the walls to be out of reach of any normal-sized man. White handrails protected each building like a cage. Stretching out down the middle of the rows of buildings, in the direction of the quarry, a series of concrete slabs had been forced to rupture by the pressure of the weeds growing up through the dark soil below. The whole place felt disused and derelict. The weeds were the only life to be seen.

Other than the distant sound of live fire somewhere over the brow of the hill there were no other sounds around the complex. There were also no helpful signs or instructional codes to help new recruits navigate their way around the industrial landmarks of the base. Maybe this was part of the initiation process, thought Jake, picking up his case and moving towards the nearest structure.

Hiding in the shadows of the building that huddled next to it, Jake discovered a door. Some of its white paint clung desperately to the wood while the rest lay in small fragments on the cold stone step. A small bronze plaque on the right side of the door struggled to shake off layers of grime that had accumulated on it over the years. Where it had managed to keep the dirt at bay the word 'or' was just visible. Jake licked his finger and ran it over the sign to reveal more of its letters.

Factory Eleven.

He turned the handle and the door swung open effortlessly. Inside rows of cheap, sterile beds had been laid out formulaically and ran down the walls in much the same way as the buildings did on the exterior.

"Now we know what these buildings are for," said Brother Job sternly, "perhaps we should search for number three?"

Jake nodded, not altogether comfortable with the one he was in, realising this was how he was going to live for the coming week. Cooped up like a battery hen in a shabby, dark building with thirty people who presumably actually wanted to be there and would compete with him for the Major's approval. How would they treat him when they found out who and what he was? Not well if his image of the Army was anything like reality.

Jake strolled up the line of buildings, checking each one for the dirty confirmation under its name tag. After many wrong turns and finding there was no logical pattern to the way they'd been arranged, Factory Three appeared under his now filthy finger.

- Chapter 16 -

Factory Three

The interior of Factory Three was unlike any of the others he'd briefly entered. Those buildings were laid out as living quarters for other Archivist recruits, while this one had a passing resemblance to a hastily constructed dental surgery. Just inside the door a reception area had been erected in the entrance to the room. The tall, wooden counter had a laminated surface but was bare other than the scratches left by equipment no longer needed. In the waiting area to Jake's left a small, wooden bench had been nailed to the wall so that patients could sit in discomfort for their appointment.

There was no receptionist on duty.

There was no need.

In larger font size than normal numerous code sequences adorned the wall and desk, immediately sparking his cloud to launch a series of virtual instructions in his mind. Each one contained a message that answered a different one of his questions. Where are you? Why are you here? What do you need to do? What you shouldn't do? The projected answers competed for dominance over his limited attention span.

Stretching down the length of the room behind the reception desk a collection of reclined plastic chairs were constricted to their locations by a mass of wires, tubes and medical instrumentation. Next to each one, waiting idly on a raised stand, was a complex-looking machine ready to get back to work.

FACTORY THREE

There were ten chairs in total and all were empty. So far, Holst was still the only physical human he'd met since his arrival on Bornholm and it didn't look like it was going to change in Factory Three.

Jake sat anxiously awaiting direction. His eyes were immediately hijacked by one of the codes attached to the desk in front of him.

For the first time in living memory, and he could be pretty certain of it, given he had access to all of them, the instructional advice beaming into his cloud feed was not delivered by a child. The duty on this occasion had been assigned to Holst himself, clearly tired of repeating himself to every new recruit that had arrived here over the decades. He was no more charming in the virtual world than he had been in the real one.

If the notion of using a child to instruct you was designed to make you feel at ease, or potentially ashamed at your inability to complete simple tasks, then the appearance of a military man to conduct this one sent out a very different message. These instructions were not designed for the masses and they were not designed to put you at ease. They were designed to scare the wits out of you.

It worked perfectly.

"Factory Three," said Holst's booming voice. "The first test of the wannabe Archivist. It is here in this modern and state-of-the-art facility…"

Jake stared around at his surrounding again. A piece of ceiling tile lost its long battle with gravity and struck the floor with a dull thud. If this was state-of-the-art, he'd hate to experience antiquated. It was only when his attention returned to Holst's projection that he realised the Major's face and hair were more youthful than the real ones that had frightened him to his core out in the parade grounds. At a guess, and that was always a challenge with the advancement of facial reconstruction, Jake thought it must have been recorded at least twenty years ago.

"Your path to achieving a place in one of the Corridors of the Archivists begins with a commitment of your allegiance. What we do here is sensitive and it would be extremely dangerous if the information fell into the wrong hands. To that extent listen to the following statements that you must agree with if you want to continue your training."

Jake listened as a series of bullet points flashed in front of him faster than Holst could read them out. They moved so quickly he had no time to question or challenge them. The gist behind all of them was 'comply' or 'die'. The terms of membership restricted him from talking or thinking in future about: specific cases, success, failure, colleagues, superiors, locations, techniques, movements, timings, positions, opinions or facts. It seemed a long-winded way of communicating the basic message: 'don't talk to anyone about anything ever again'. The restrictions also banned participation with any other employer, society, group or association, now or anytime in the future without gaining the express permission to do so from a superior officer. Joining the Archivists wasn't a job, it was a life sentence.

The final section of the terms and conditions centred on enemy combatants, as they were referred to, but didn't refer solely to the Spectrum. There was certainly guidance on what was and wasn't acceptable behaviour in relation to any interactions with that group. There would be no conversing, touching without protective equipment, eye contact, sympathy or mercy. Almost anything else was permissible. Speccies had no rights so they had no protection. What really surprised Jake was the countless references to people who lived in the East.

Why would the Archivists have anything to do with them? Was that where the speccies hid? Did the

Archivists' remit extend to converting those wishing to escape the oppression in the East? Why would the West want to convert those who presented so deplorably in the 'Proclamation of Distrust'? Surely if those pictures were accurate there would be no desire to welcome any of them to this side of the partition.

The section that related to the East droned on forever. It was by far the longest section of the whole contract. Page after page flew through his cloud and created a level of disorientation that not even the Hyperloop matched. When the stream of information finally came to an end and there was nothing left for Jake to read, his mind was completely confuddled and hostile towards almost all living things, speccy or not. Holst stopped reading and took a pause for breath. Then came the final instruction.

"Sign here. You have twenty seconds to comply."

Signing an agreement with someone, or for something, didn't involve pens or hefty paper documents. It simply involved an action every human had learnt at the age of five in their first few days of nursery school. If you wanted to confirm your intent, then you had to create an appropriate memory. A memory that could be used as evidence to prove your declaration in any future tribunal should either party see fit to renege on it.

Jake had thousands of these snapshots proving his willingness, or lack of it, for every agreement he'd ever entered into. They were housed in his very own section of an unknown server farm with the rest of his Memory Cloud, easily accessed by his feed if he chose to visit. To ensure these events could not be confused for any other, the procedure had to be clear and unambiguous. All potential forms of agreement had to be aligned to leave no doubt as to the decision you'd made. You couldn't get away with saying 'yes', shaking your head in denial and having thumbs pointing in different directions. If you did the memory would be rejected by the hordes of Memory Hunters hired to monitor your actions.

Jake calmly stood up from the bench. Sometimes in situations such as these, he'd be torn between competing options, even when the cloud was pointing him in the right direction. Today there was no such doubt. It was sign or be cleansed and, although neither sounded like much fun, one sounded more violent and less agreeable.

"I, Jake Montana, on the island of Bornholm in the third month of the year twenty fifty-four, agree absolutely to the terms outlined in the agreement," he said, holding both thumbs in the air, nodding and forcing a huge smile to spread across his face.

"Very sensible choice," said a second and slightly older projection of Major Holst that leapt out of another code which must have caught Jake's eyeline as he stood up to announce his acceptance.

What was worse than Major Holst?

Two of them.

Jake changed positions to delete the original code from view. The younger Holst evaporated from his feed, much to Jake's relief.

"Now that you have confirmed your acknowledgement of our charter we will proceed to the download."

Strictly speaking, the Memory Cloud was designed for uploads only. Memories and emotions were automatically collected and compressed in your cranial implant before being wirelessly copied to a secure location. Clouds that had mutual connections, like the one he and Christie shared, didn't require downloads to appreciate what the other person saw or felt. You simply connected to their feed to share one of their emotions at first-hand. It didn't directly become part of your Memory

Cloud, although the new memory of your connection would reference it in your own. Information you wanted, like Jake's daily search for the local hovercraft softball scores, was also accessed remotely and not transferred to your own memory stream.

Downloading was quite different. It meant your Memory Cloud was going to be altered. It would no longer solely contain what you had learnt, felt or remembered. It would soon include information that the Circuit wanted you to hold. Identifying what had been originally yours and real, or theirs and constructed, would be impossible once the download was complete. The new memories would be entwined with your own as one inseparable reality. There was no knowing what they might put there or whether they removed anything of yours in the process.

"Downloading is a simple but sometimes painful process that lasts no longer than an hour. Please report to chair…" Holst said with a pause.

A number clicked to display 'ONE' on an old-fashioned mechanical counting device in a black frame that hung on small wires from the ceiling above the reception desk.

"…Just make yourself comfortable and let the chair do its stuff," continued the projection. "When your therapy is complete, you'll be directed to the next part of your training."

"I think they're trying to brainwash us," whispered Dinah, who had concealed herself somewhere out of sight.

"Do as you're told," instructed Job. "It sounds perfectly normal."

"It sounds perfectly sinister if you ask me," replied Jake. "They're asking me to put my memories in the hands of a chair."

"Chairs aren't dangerous!" scoffed Job.

FACTORY THREE

"Electric chairs!" shouted Dinah in disagreement.

"Good point, Dinah."

"It's either the chair or you'll have to be 'cleansed' and I don't like the sound of that much, do you?" said Brother Job rather manipulatively.

"I don't like either option."

Jake moved past the desk and over to chair number one which was marked as such on the monitor positioned above the headrest. A green cursor pulsated idly on the screen just like the one he'd seen during his parents' 'conduct feeling', and in his frequent flashbacks. He scanned the room to reassure himself that the distinctive cursor was the only similarity.

"What do I do?"

"I think the normal convention would be to sit down," replied Job sarcastically.

Jake had recently formed a deep suspicion of anything he had to lie or sit on since his experiences on the Hyperloop. He assessed the chair to see if any straps were likely to fly out and pin him down. There weren't. It looked much like a regular chair other than the strange devices attached to the stand next to it. Tubes, cables and gadgets were knotted together before being linked to the screen and its mysterious cursor.

He decided to bite the bullet and get it over with. After a few minutes of fidgeting to get comfy on the plastic coating of the chair, it gently reclined backwards and the screen tilted forward, so it was directly above him. The moment the cursor entered his eyeline a sharp pain, much like the one he experienced during his flashbacks, shot out of his optic implant to warn the one in his brain. Instinctively his body tried to flinch, but it failed miserably in its attempt to move. Some unseen force was restricting his muscles. It wasn't just affecting him either. Both his guides were frozen to the spots

205

where they stood. It was the first time Jake had seen Dinah static.

Green writing ran across the screen above him.

Stay still...

It was a command he had no strength to resist.

Patient ready for download...

A swarm of tiny particles floated out of the machinery next to him like a plume of dust being struck by sunlight. They seeped slowly through the air until they surrounded his body. At first Jake thought he might be suffering from a bout of cloud over. Were these particles in his cloud or actually in the room? He couldn't be certain. Light from ceiling bulbs struck the millions of microscopic specks as they bobbed and sparkled expectantly like a swarm of fireflies were planning to mug someone. Hypnotically they danced, trying to trick Jake's senses and calm his mood just as the odour concealed in his letter had done before them.

Jake was wise to it now.

This was how the Circuit operated. Parlour tricks designed to lower your defences and make the unacceptable palatable.

Wireless transmission primed...

"What are they?!" shouted Jake.

Gigabytes in position...

The little specks of data landed on his skin, covering his body like a trawlerman's fishing net. They bristled and waited excitedly for instructions to invade. A dial on the instrument attached to the stand, that Jake could just make out through the corner of his eye, was speeding through and towards the maximum mark of one hundred percent. Another dial counted the number of gigabytes, and when it came to a stop the cursor typed its command.

Proceed...

FACTORY THREE

The clumps of data burrowed into his skin from every conceivable direction. It was hard to isolate the pain because it was everywhere. Each time a particle pierced his skin it was like being prodded by a tiny needle. The full body acupuncture wasn't focused on a specific region, limb or organ: these microscopic muggers were targeting him on a cellular level. Jake wailed from the immense pain as the last byte found an empty space not occupied by one of the others.

This might sting...

That was an understatement, but it was nothing compared to what came next.

They were moving.

The tiny army manoeuvred its way through his body, bursting through cell walls in a desperate bid for safer passage. It didn't take them long to find the highway. The more the alien invaders squeezed through his tissues and into his nervous system, the more Jake's body went into spasm. Riding his synapses like cowboys ride steeds, his spontaneous desire to flinch limb and muscle was suppressed and disabled.

Even though Jake had received more upgrades than most, those operations had always been conducted under powerful anaesthetics that left no memory of the surgery. Upgrade pain always occurred after the drugs wore off. Not today. There was nothing to manage the pain other than a reliance on his own willpower.

It wasn't strong enough.

Jake's screams consumed Factory Three and might have competed with the bursts of gunfire over on the hilltop. Up and down his body muscles and veins contracted and expanded as the digital army marched north. A million little packets of data squeezed into his spinal cord as they approached his head. Muscles in his neck convulsed, strangling the air from his lungs, and finally Jake's determination, and his consciousness, gave in.

`Wake up...`

The message may have been invisible to Jake's closed eyelids, but it wasn't being ignored by his cloud feed. Tears and sweat cascaded like a waterfall down his surgically enhanced cheekbones as he gently prised them open. The pain had settled in one position. The worst migraine he'd ever experienced, far worse than flashbacks or upgrades. His mind felt fuzzy, as real and false worlds spun around like an old-fashioned merry-go-round. Memories, known and unknown, squabbled to be noticed and flashed by like a videograph stuck on fast-forward. His brain swam around his skull, refusing to settle, and made him feel sick.

`Report to Factory Eight for recovery...`

The chair snapped forward and Jake was confronted with his guides at the foot of the chair. Neither of them looked well. Brother Job was pale, even for him, and the light of his projection crackled like the bulbs were about to blow. Dinah was on her haunches desperately trying to vomit out whatever poison had recently been injected into her body.

"Help!" whimpered Jake desperately.

Neither of them responded, preoccupied with their own issues.

"There's an earwig in my head," gasped Dinah sticking a finger into her ear. It went through her head and out the other side.

"I feel a little queasy," added Job, attempting to hold onto a chair before collapsing and joining Dinah on the floor.

"For once, I actually need you," begged Jake. "My head's swimming."

"It's always about you, isn't it?" snapped Job. "You can't think about anyone other than yourself! We're struggling, too, you know!"

"But you're part of me! How can it be about anyone other than me? Do something!" sobbed Jake. "I need to get out of here, but I can't feel my body."

"Ok, keep your pants on," replied Brother Job.

Jake's left leg straightened, even though he hadn't asked it to. The right leg followed, and he stood up gingerly. He took a pace forward, stumbled under the pain and caught himself on the heavily laden instrument stand. None of these commands were coming from him. There was no way he could control his impulses with brainwaves so muddled and distorted. He wondered how Job was managing to do it on his behalf. Not easily was the true answer.

"Dinah, little help here," sighed Job as he wrestled to keep Jake's body vertical.

"What have they done to us?" pleaded Dinah as she crawled forward to catch Jake before he fell on his face.

"It's just the side effects of the download," said Job. "All those new memories are trying to find free space within the cranial implant. Problem is, there isn't much room for them. Something has to give."

"I can't feel her anymore," sobbed Jake.

"Can't feel who?" asked Dinah as they began the painful and slow hobble across the floor with each guide pretending to hold him up by the armpits.

"That's just it," replied Jake. "I don't remember who. I've forgotten."

"Oh my God!" screamed Dinah. "I didn't think people could forget."

"Another side effect," replied Job. "Most of it will come back to him in time."

"Most of it?" said Jake.

"Shit, please tell me he still remembers about the BASE jumping!"

"The fact that you remember it, Sister Dinah, means so does he," replied Job curtly.

"Phew."

"Something important is missing. They've stolen her from me," grumbled Jake angrily.

"Who's stolen what? Or have you forgotten that, too?" asked Dinah.

"Alison…that evil witch. It's the Circuit's fault, all of it. They've stolen something precious and left a hole in me."

A red box and a klaxon noise tried to force its way through the pandemonium of Jake's virtual world. It didn't last long before it was consumed by the chaos, but all three of them accepted it had been there.

Violation number five.

- Chapter 17 -

The Lonely Island

It was impossible to tell how long his recuperation had lasted. The clock and date that usually sat in the corner of his cloud feed, a permanent way of encouraging him to be punctual, weren't acting with their normal level of precision. It was currently displaying: Friday, the thirty-second of March twenty thirty-six at four o'clock in the morning. The daylight creeping forlornly into the sparse dorm was just one piece of evidence to contradict the cloud's internal clock. The other was the symbolism of the false date. One day after Jake's original birthday, but a day that would only appear in calendars designed by dyslexics.

It wasn't the only aspect of his Memory Cloud that was out of kilter. After the initial chaos ripped through his memory feed immediately after the download, now there was almost nothing there at all. No adverts, no Circuit broadcasts, and no past memories summoned to comfort him. He attempted to conjure one but all it returned was a hazy half-memory that soon dissolved away again. It felt like his virtual world had been placed on standby, but was it temporary or permanent?

An emotion tried to penetrate the curtain to suggest it was the former. Anger surged through him. A level of hostility he'd never experienced before, and it was aimed squarely at one group in particular. The Spectrum. It consumed all other instincts so totally he wanted to drag his body out of bed and immediately hunt one down. It didn't feel like a new impulse either. There was no question that he'd carried this deep-rooted disgust for them since birth. Jake eased his body up the hard, uncomfortable bed and his aching limbs dampened his desire to fight.

As usual there was no one else in the dormitory. It was all too familiar on this island. There were plenty of beds lining the walls of Factory Eight. The sheets and blankets had been made up perfectly, creased and tucked neatly over the edges like Army standards demanded. Yet there was no luggage on the racks and other than the ones they'd left for him there were no Army supplies by the side of beds. Folded neatly on his bedside table was a standard-issue uniform, boots, a wash kit and a white helmet sporting a flimsy plastic visor.

Jake rubbed his head to massage his memory feed back to normality. The excruciating pain that accompanied the download had mostly passed, but a throbbing sensation was still evident in the region of his head where he knew his implant was fitted. The only other pain was in his heart, but he couldn't place why it was there. It was the sensation of loss, but the loss of what? Immediately after regaining consciousness following the download, the sense of loss had felt raw and recent, but now it was distant, and he cast doubt on its very existence.

The door flew open and Major Holst marched menacingly down the line of beds towards him. Whatever Jake was missing as a result of his surgery it certainly wasn't the memory of him.

"Montana, why are you still in bed?"

"I just woke up."

"Give me fifty!"

"Um ok, can I transfer the funds to your cloud," replied Jake, not entirely certain he understood the instruction.

"Yes, sir, Major Holst is the correct response, you snivelling little turd!"

"He doesn't want credits," said Job, appearing for the first time this morning, possibly a signal that his cloud was on the mend. "He means press-ups."

"Oh..."

"Make it one hundred," said Holst.

Jake jumped out of bed and discovered his body moved more freely than the last time he'd attempted it. It's amazing what fear and adrenaline were capable of. Press-ups were a doddle. They were just a small element of his daily workout routine, not that he let on to the Major. Once the requested punishment had been completed, he climbed to his feet and adopted what he hoped was a suitable military stance.

"Two days of recuperation is a Bornholm record," snapped Holst. "Although I suppose I should expect nothing less from a superfluous."

Jake didn't win many awards, but he got the distinct impression from the spittle leaping out of Holst's mouth and showering his hair that it wasn't something he should be proud of. At least it answered the question of how long he'd been here. He sent his cloud an internal message, and the date and time slowly adjusted to reflect the present.

"You've missed valuable and essential training time whilst you've been having a lie-in."

"I didn't have much choice, Major, I think I was unconscious."

"No excuses!" shouted the Major with incandescent rage. "Another hundred."

Jake complied and found that the physical exercise was having a positive impact on his other senses. A number of ads for health and fitness products tentatively braved the desolation of an otherwise unoccupied cloud like the first settlers to a new world. A new memory formed before flying off to meet its brothers and sisters in some far-off server farm. Its broad instruction was to remind Jake not to disagree with Major Holst in future.

"The first class of the day is taking place in Factory Ten: you have five minutes to get changed and enrol."

"Yes, Major, sir."

Jake rushed to put on the clothes that had been allocated for him. It wasn't the way he preferred to start the day. A shower was normally an essential part of feeling more refreshed and it was three days since he'd enjoyed one. If he knew where they were, or had the time available, he'd be grabbling a towel quicker than you can say 'what's that smell?' It looked distinctly like any personal hygiene issues were only going to affect himself and the Major, given the lack of people on the island. Disconcertingly Holst watched as Jake got out of his old clothes and into his fresh Archivist ones.

"Two minutes," the Major barked.

"Yes, Major Holst. Where's Factory Ten?"

"Use your initiative, boy!"

Jake had located most of the factories during yesterday's search for number three. There were approximately twenty buildings and he'd verified the content of at least ten of them. Although he had less than two minutes for his initiative to appear, the answer to a bigger mystery wouldn't let go of his tongue.

"Major Holst, where are the other recruits?"

Holst glared at him in outrage, as if questions were more dangerous than live grenades.

"Shall I do another hundred?" added Jake getting on his belly.

"Yes. One minute!" shouted Brother Job, desperate to steal some of the power Holst had over Jake.

"You are the only recruit this week, boy," answered Holst as Jake went through the repetitions. "The Archivists are an elite force who only conscript the very best for their ranks. Few ever leave and even fewer join. It's a mystery to me why they sent you here at all."

"Me and you both," Jake whispered.

"What?"

"If there's no one here, where is the live fire coming from?" asked Jake in mid-push-up before quickly adding, "Sir, Major Holst, sir!"

"One of Bornholm's side projects," he said sharply, making it abundantly clear it was as much information as he was willing to offer on the subject. "Thirty seconds."

Jake leapt out of his last push-up, arms a little sore from completing a few hundred in less than ten minutes. He burst through the door of Factory Eight and into the empty parade ground. He scanned the buildings to remind himself which ones he'd already entered and which he'd yet to explore. The memory of that first search seeped into his cloud and reassuringly it remained clear and crisp. The virtual world had been restored with most of what he remembered had been kept there.

"Try that one," offered Dinah, pointing at one of the buildings nearby.

"That's the one I've just come out of!"

"Oh, is it? My sense of direction is rubbish, but if it's any consolation…that's actually your fault."

"We haven't tried that one," said Brother Job, for once quite helpfully. "Look, the door is already open."

It seemed as good a choice as any. Jake dashed forward, throwing himself through the doorway as if his life depended on it. Luck, for once, was on his side.

Factory Ten was identical to all the others from the outside, but inside it was furnished like the classroom from history. Rows of unoccupied plastic chairs were set out in neat semicircles along the width of the room, and at the front a plain, white wall was illuminated by a light source that came from somewhere on the ceiling. Jake had never seen a real projection like this before and had to check it wasn't another bout of cloud over. As he moved forward to take a seat the figure of a woman marched across the white background of the screen. This was no recording, it was a live stream.

"Sit!" she barked, making direct eye contact with her only student.

Jake's arse hit the plastic of the nearest chair like it was attached to a bungee cord. He was joined obediently on either side by his guides. Dinah had conjured up some 3D glasses and pretended to eat popcorn. Job sat forward in his seat eager to document any important advice on his fake tablet.

"Major Bancroft...vital obviously."

"Jake Montana...superfluous."

"I'm afraid you'll have to do better than that, boy."

"I don't think I have much choice about it," replied Jake, a little confused by the criticism.

"Silence! If you want to be an Archivist, you'll need to act like one," she barked.

A memory barged into view. It didn't feel familiar, like a bout of nostalgia from a time and place not clearly marked, but it provided the response she'd been looking for.

"Private Jake Montana, superfluous, Major Bancroft, ma'am."

"Indeed," she smiled, malice dripping from her words.

Major Bancroft was a tall woman with dark, beady eyes capable of piercing hearts and souls. She wore the same military-style uniform that Holst did but hers sported more badges and shiny medals. Long, sharp, veiny hands gripped a thin, leather baton which she flexed in anticipation of dishing out future punishment on unsuspecting cadets. The plain, white backdrop, as clean as an avalanche, was devoid of clues to where she was.

"Time to see how well your download has been accepted by the host," she said menacingly. "As the world's foremost expert on the Spectrum I insist on running this class even if I can't be there in person. I like to use this old-fashioned technology to beam myself all the way from our base here in Boston."

Boston. The memory of home swamped his view, but the quality of the visions was stretched as if some other energy force within the scenery had airbrushed the fine details away. The feeling of loss rose inside him once more. Sadly, it didn't have time to rest long.

"Let's do a test."

"A test!" said Jake in a panic. "I didn't get time to revise."

"Revising wouldn't have helped you. It's either in there or it's not."

Jake's tired triceps hoped so, or they might be encouraged to perform several encores.

"Let us begin."

"Ready," said Job eagerly.

"How do you feel about the Spectrum?"

"I'm mostly disgusted by them," replied Jake instinctively.

"Only mostly?"

"Yeah, there's a competing emotion that I can't put my finger on."

"What sort of emotion?"

"Envy," replied Jake ashamedly.

"Then let me dispel it from your mind. You have nothing to be envious about when it comes to those delinquents. The Spectrum are the biggest threat to the maintenance of our perfect world. They do not recognise order, they do not recognise authority, and they do not recognise the damage their selfish behaviour has on the rest of society. They must be found and converted. Or they must be hunted and destroyed. They are a law unto themselves. Dangerous, immoral, illiterate, unhygienic, inferior and abnormal."

Jake found himself nodding in agreement, even though a nagging doubt kept peeking in through the curtains of his cloud to question it. Of the many memories that he owned on the subject of the Spectrum, most horrifying scenes of their contempt for Circuit subscribers, there was one that didn't fit the mould. It was of a young speccy called Alfonso who showed very little of the attributes demonstrated by the other images crowding his conscience.

"And where do they live?" asked Major Bancroft.

"They live amongst us," replied Jake instinctively. "Hidden in plain sight."

"Good. That's correct. Contrary to popular opinion, a belief placed there by the Circuit to shelter members from the ghastly reality, speccies do not live underground or wild in the countryside, or in the sewer system or in a network of caves like troglodytes. They live secretly amongst the rest of humanity because that is the best place to hide. The general population aren't allowed to know this in case they start to suspect their own neighbours, although they may have cause to do so. How do the Spectrum conceal themselves?"

"They use technology to scramble the Memory Cloud," said Jake effortlessly as if he'd known the truth his whole life. "It creates the illusion that they exist in the virtual world."

"Indeed. And how do we counter such technology?"

"The Memory Hunters scan the cloud to identify when a Circuit user has come into contact with an anomaly and then they send the data to the Archivists."

"And?"

"We mobilise around the infested area in question and use heat-sensitive cameras to identify them. Archivists are trained to look for the appearance of a scar somewhere on their head or face."

"Yes. Very good. But how do the Spectrum try to conceal their scars?"

"They don't. They wear them like a badge of honour," Jake answered casually.

"Which is their biggest mistake. They are proud to be who they are. Their arrogance will be the death of them," said Bancroft throttling her leather baton as if it were a speccy's neck. "What other physical characteristics can we use to identify them?"

Jake's memories clashed. This was the first question where the answer wasn't unopposed. The others she asked produced rapid, simple and unarguable replies. Not this one. There were two competing versions fighting to be first to struggle out of his mouth.

"Answer me!" she screamed.

Dinah, spooked by the force of the Major's bellowing, started to jabber incoherently about how speccies were almost always called Colin, never ate broccoli and liked to paint their toenails black. She'd made all of it up, but at least she offered more explanation than Jake mustered.

Bancroft's patience ran dry.

"Speccies are identified by several common physical deformities. They are always short, no more than a hundred and fifty centimetres in height and their foreheads are Neanderthal in appearance. Due to a lack of dental examinations they also have crooked teeth. They display body abnormalities like warts and cleft lips, and they find speaking English extremely challenging. If there is someone in your street or district who does not socialise with others, then we need to know about it."

The description didn't sit well with him. Alfonso had none of the characteristics Bancroft outlined. He wondered what made her so certain?

"Major Bancroft, have you ever seen one?"

Bancroft dropped her baton in shock. "How dare you?"

"It's just that…I've met one and he didn't look anything like that."

"I'm a distinguished Major who's served as an Archivist for more than twenty years. How dare you have the audacity to ask me whether I've seen one?!"

"Have you, though?" asked Jake, trying his luck.

"Yes…many."

"Share me your memories," requested Jake. He couldn't explain why this was the right moment to challenge a senior officer, but a deep conviction told him she was lying.

"No! I'm issuing you an immediate violation."

"Can you do that?"

"Absolutely."

Proof of her claim appeared in Jake's feed a few seconds later, the klaxon and red flashing box an almost daily intervention lately.

"Can you shut up, Jake? I'm trying to learn from this woman," said Brother Job who was hanging on every word.

"Did you say you've seen one?" asked Bancroft curiously.

"Yes," said Jake proudly.

"When?"

"A few days ago."

"But that memory should no longer exist. It should have been erased."

"Sorry, but I didn't really have anything to do with the download and I'm not sure what they took and what they left. It feels like they took something important, though."

"And do you think I care?" she replied maliciously, her smirk forcing the plastic in her cheeks to collapse under the pressure.

"Perhaps. There's kindness in most people," Jake said hopefully.

"Not me! Sadly, like your fanciful description of the speccy, you have been misinformed. Kindness makes you weak and Archivists are anything but. I am failing you on this module. It will count against your progress in the final assessment."

Bancroft vanished from view and the word FAILED replaced her on-screen in bold red letters. Jake wasn't too concerned. It wasn't his goal to pass anyway. His only goal was to get off this island and try to work out how to retrieve what he'd lost. There were lessons to be absorbed from his visit to Factory Ten, though. It appeared there were high-ranking Archivists, like Bancroft, who'd never even seen a speccy before. Which posed a more important question. How good were they at catching them? The footage of the retired veterans he'd watched back at Sam's dome painted a picture of unwavering success, yet none of those characters had offered specific examples. They expressed how angry the speccies made them, but that wasn't proof of their achievements. Perhaps there weren't any because all the speccies managed to escape?

When it was clear nothing more would be learnt from the lesson, Jake headed for the exit. Like a stalker who'd broken his restraining order, Major Holst was waiting for him in the yard. He looked rather jovial.

"I hear you failed!"

"Yes, Major Holst, sir."

"Not looking good for you, my lad," he said with glee, although his expression changed when he saw Jake had his hand in the air. "What are you doing that for?"

"I wanted to ask you a question."

"Do you like push-ups?" asked Holst sarcastically.

"No," said Dinah as if it was aimed at her.

"If I do more push-ups then can I ask you a question?" asked Jake.

"Yes. One question for every one hundred push-ups."

Jake immediately dropped to the floor and raced through his part of the deal. If nothing else, he was getting fitter from the trip.

"Major Holst, sir, how many speccies have you personally caught?" asked Jake wheezing a little.

"Lots."

"Ok, but how many speccies are there exactly?"

"Ahem…" he said, pointing at the ground.

Jake decided to complete two hundred this time to make the passage of the conversation smoother.

"No one knows how many," replied Holst. "That's why we need lots of Archivists."

"But I'm the only one here."

"That's because we already have enough."

"Then why do you need me?"

"We don't," Holst snarled, confirming his opinion of Jake's lack of suitability. "You owe me another hundred and you'd better get on with it because your next class starts in two minutes, and I'll be teaching it."

"Which class, Major Holst, sir?"

"Weapons training."

"Finally!" replied Dinah, daubing fake black paint onto her facial projection.

*****

THE LONELY ISLAND

The firing range was some distance from the barracks and while Holst zoomed up the hill in his Jeep, Jake wasn't surprised to discover he'd be hiking. The walk would do him good. No doubt it would result in him being forced to attempt the world push-up record when he arrived late, but it was worth it. It gave him some time to think. At the rear of the barracks the path curved around the inviting waters of the quarry and climbed up a gentle incline towards the summit. It was probably no more than a couple of hundred metres high and tiny compared to some of the mountains he'd scaled on his visits to the White Mountains.

As he marched the image of those trips was transposed effortlessly on top of the route like a stencil. Monstrously beautiful, snow-capped mountains whose peaks were often lost beneath the sulphur clouds. The trunks of White Pines racing to join their rocky cousins and justify their right to be equal. Hiking boots squelching through the moist turf like they were walking through bowls of custard. Birds chirped in the bushes on their never-ending quest to gather food for their fledgling families. The occasional deer dashed across the path, disappearing into the ferns to cast doubt on whether you actually saw it at all. A sense of vulnerability shuddered inside him. It was driven by a vulnerability that he always experienced when he was cut adrift from his own natural environment, left to rely on whatever skill or heart he brought with him. You had to be brave to explore the wild on your own.

The memory suggested he'd done just that.

An internal shadow cast doubt on its authenticity.

Would his overprotective parents have allowed it? It didn't seem congruous to how they acted towards him the rest of the time. Whenever he'd sought to place himself in a position of potential danger, at least in their eyes, they'd always stopped him. Would they really let him go into the wild on his own? He thought it unlikely. He stopped marching to examine the memory more closely. There was something about his body position that didn't look right. His arm was stretched out at a forty-five-degree angle and his hand was holding tightly to thin air? It looked an uncomfortable pose to maintain. What was he holding? He shook the memory away as the purpose of his walk took priority.

The vibrant signs of life that crowded those past trips had no resemblance to his current hike. Even the vegetation struggled to survive on these fractured muddy banks. By the time he reached the apex of the hill, where the land flattened out, he'd not seen a single animal, bird or insect. Apart from Holst and the weeds, life on the island had been extinguished. If Bornholm had managed to survive the rising tide, unlike its neighbours, why had it been purged of life?

He breached the summit and saw Holst's Jeep parked next to a massive corrugated shed. On the nearest side of the building vast double doors were secured by chunky chains and a huge padlock. Whoever had been shooting here over the last few days certainly weren't doing so now. The hill was peaceful and only the breeze that galloped over the horizon offered any resistance. Around him the landscape was littered with deep craters from shells or explosives that had ripped holes in the ground. They were everywhere. It was hard to identify any patch of soil that had evaded the onslaught.

"Montana, get your sorry excuse for a body over here. I don't have all day."

If there were other urgent tasks on Holst's to-do list, other than making his life a misery, Jake's triceps weren't in the mood to find out what they were. He jogged over to his superior subserviently.

"Where did they come from?" asked Jake, pointing at the craters.

"Did I ask you to speak?"

"No, Major Holst, sir."

"You're not here to ask questions, you're here to do what I tell you. End of. I say and you do, do you understand?"

"Yes, Major Holst."

"Go pick a weapon from the back of the Jeep and let's get started."

Jake found a selection of firearms in the back of the vehicle covered by a dirty old sheet. Dinah was already there trying to fondle a device that looked capable of decimating a city. Her eyes sparkled, and if he wasn't mistaken, a small stream of virtual saliva was dribbling out of the corner of her mouth.

"Oh my God!" said Dinah, hopping up and down. "These are epic!"

"I'm not keen on guns," replied Jake truthfully.

"Oh, get that really big one!" she begged.

Jake didn't know the difference between a semi-automatic and a handgun. They were all killers to him. He picked one that looked light and easy to use, hopefully without making him look like an amateur at a paintball convention.

"What do you think is in there?" muttered Jake, glancing up at the large aluminium structure.

"Maybe it's a tank!" suggested Dinah.

"I think it's unlikely, Dinah. Tanks run on diesel and the world's all out of that," answered Job, standing a little behind them and tutting his disapproval. "Plus, it's none of our business."

Everything was Dinah's business.

Ostensibly she was still a child. Her very existence was based on Jake's earliest instincts, a natural state that all infants possess in the formative years of their life. It's founded on an unrestricted freedom that adults in later life frown upon and badge as juvenile or immature. Grown-ups quickly forget how they once acted without inhibition or worry. The more years you accumulate, the more serious life becomes. Dangers become real. Egos fragile and tangible. Failure rates increase and a negative mindset soon follows. Inhibitions transform effortlessly into inferiorities.

But safety, compliance and fear were not on Dinah's job spec. Those attributes were purely Brother Job's to master, the de facto adult in their partnership. Telling a child that they can't do something would be equivalent to telling the tide to retreat when it wasn't ready to. It's just not going to happen.

"Dinah, where are you going?" shouted Job.

She lifted her skirt and flashed her virtual frilly pants at him before sliding effortlessly through the metal wall of the shed. She might be out of Jake's sight, but he was not out of hers, not while Job was close at hand.

"Are you going to get her?" Jake asked Brother Job.

"You can't tame fire, son," he replied with a sigh.

Jake returned to the Major, gently holding a gun between his thumb and finger as if it might go off at any point purely as a result of atmospheric pressure.

"What are you planning to do with that?" sneered Holst.

"Shoot it, Major, sir."

"We're after speccies, not mice. You'd have more success brandishing a bunch of grapes. Go get something appropriate."

Jake returned a minute later with what he considered to be more menacing but still simple to use.

"Better," replied Holst. "Now lie on the floor."

Dotted over the plateau of the hill were a series of targets that had sprung out of the ground. Each was roughly the shape of a human but looked nothing like the ones Jake was used to. He wondered if Major Bancroft might have had something to do with their design because each of the two-dimensional figures was horrifically disfigured. Men with hunchbacks and distorted faces. Women with crazy hair that looked like candyfloss and fingernails that extended like talons. The children had pot bellies and sported extra limbs in places you'd not normally find them. Most of these wooden representations of speccies were riddled with bullet holes, delivered by past trainees with various degrees of accuracy. The candyfloss hair seemed to have been very popular.

"Right, fire at will, boy," demanded Holst.

"But…"

"Don't have the bottle for it!"

"No, it's…"

"…harder in real life," insisted Holst. "The enemy will be running around, screaming and probably throwing things at you. How are you going to deal with that?"

Jake had no idea. He hoped he'd never have to. Failing his training and not being an Archivist felt both probable and highly desirable right now, whatever alternative job the Circuit offered him. Being in a dead-end job and not killing innocent people seemed better than this.

"FIRE!" shouted Holst as if the situation was as real as the grey hair on his head.

Jake didn't know how to fire a gun. At least that's what he believed. This was the first time he'd even held one. He looked down at the object, hoping there might be an instructional code somewhere. There wasn't. Instead the directions came from within him. An instinct he didn't easily recognise surged forward. The gun found the correct position in his grip and the butt nestled neatly and comfortably on his shoulder. His left eye closed and the other focused through the optic sight as naturally as blinking. His hand ran forward along the barrel and disengaged the safety. His index finger caressed the trigger and waited for the moment when all other senses were ready to unleash smoke and fire. He squeezed and the hill returned to its familiar soundscape.

An exhilarating minute of carnage followed before Jake eased his finger off the trigger. Hundreds of small, metal shells smoked gently on the ground. The splintered outlines of wooden figures were all that remained standing on the hill in the distance. In some places where he'd been aiming there was no trace of the target at all. He hadn't just hit his mark, he'd pulverised them with an effortless instinct. Rather than feeling relief, that this might be the first occasion he received praise from his commanding officer, he despised himself. How could he be that ruthless?

"At least the download has worked," replied Holst casually. "It's a pass."

"Is it?" replied Jake meekly before remembering the convention. "...Major Holst, sir."

"Yes, but there are many more tests you'll face before you can call yourself an Archivist. I still have plenty of opportunities to fail you. Next lesson is at eighteen hundred, Factory Six," he announced before returning swiftly to the Jeep.

Jake dragged his body off the floor, still clutching hold of the vicious machine gun. He threw it to the ground in horror. When the moment came would his instincts to shoot real-life targets hijack his compassion quite so easily? He feared it might. A raw hatred for the Spectrum festered inside him like a blazing fire and it was using his old emotions, such as kindness and morality, as a fuel.

"Come on," said Brother Job sternly. "You don't have long to get to the next lesson."

"Does something here feel wrong to you?" asked Jake.

"Nope. The rules are pretty clear. Just do as you're told and respect the authority."

"Even if they're wrong?"

"Wrong is a point of view, authority isn't."

"But who decided on who's in charge? Maybe they were wrong."

"The Circuit does, and they can't be wrong because their decisions are the result of everyone's Memory Clouds. Whether you like the collective wisdom or not doesn't make it wrong."

"I liked it more when you were rebellious," huffed Jake. "Where's Dinah?"

"Over there."

They turned their attentions to the barn where a paler than usual projection of a plump woman was slumped against the wall crying her heart out. Jake sent a virtual request to summon her back, but she didn't budge. After several attempts failed, they were forced to go and retrieve her.

"Dinah, what's the matter? No tanks in there!"

"No," she sobbed.

"Never mind. We all have to accept disappointment."

"It's terrifying, Jake."

"What is?"

"I want to run…I want to hide away forever."

"Why?" asked Jake.

"Death! This is a place of death."

"Death? What's in the shed?"

"Nothing, it's empty," shuddered Dinah.

"You're scared of an empty building?" asked Jake.

"She's just seeking attention," scoffed Job.

"It's not what's in the shed," cried Dinah. "It's what's underneath it."

"Go on?" asked Jake, not taking her discomfort that seriously.

"A hole! A big, scary hole that drops into the ground."

"Ok," replied Jake, still perplexed at her reaction to what appeared to be an empty space inside another empty space.

"I went down. There's a huge cavern under the hill. I couldn't stop myself," she sobbed.

"Caves can be a little scary but that hardly means death."

"It's not the cave I'm frightened of," she wailed.

"What, then?"

"There's something down there."

- Chapter 18 -

One Empty Space

It didn't matter how often Jake asked Dinah what she'd seen, she was either incapable or unwilling to tell him. Whatever it was it, it had a profound effect on her outlook. For the rest of the day all she did was mutter 'death' or wail catatonically like someone close to her had just experienced it. It had taken an age to move Dinah from the spot against the metal shed. Lifting a heavy person can be tricky, but moving someone mostly constructed of virtual gigabytes who existed in a different dimension altogether was near impossible. In the end Brother Job resorted to shouting ruthlessly until she budged. If you wanted to appease someone suffering trauma, screaming at them didn't feel like the right tactic. Job would probably deal with someone's broken heart by confirming no one really liked them. He was an emotional sledgehammer and everything else was a nut.

It would be wrong to say that Dinah's behaviour since Ascension Eve had been consistent. She'd always had the attention span of a goldfish and shifted her mood quicker than a chameleon changed colour, but until today she'd been saturated with an unstoppable vitality. Jake missed it. Dinah had been the only pleasant distraction since he'd left Boston. When gentle encouragement failed to unlock her secrets, Jake searched his own cloud to explore any memories associated with the last twenty-four hours. The only thing his cloud feed remembered was the slightly rusty metal on the outside of the building and Dinah gliding through it.

The guides' very existence in his cloud perplexed him. He knew they were built from his own characteristics, and because of that they shared access to what his cloud saw, felt and thought at any given moment. They were chained to the phoney world of his cloud and yet they weren't solely controlled by him. They appeared to have their own unique operating system and often acted of their own free will. If Dinah wanted to run off and chase a dog, she did it with no direction or agreement from Jake. If Job wanted to remind him to brush his teeth, he did it, whether Jake liked it or not. Although they were clearly invisible to the people who existed in the visual world, it didn't stop the guides being fully aware of those around him. After all, they had access to the virtual world through his optic implant just like he did. That part made sense to him.

But how could they see things that he hadn't seen for himself? Jake hadn't been inside the metal shed on top of the hill, so how could Dinah have experienced what was there? Did the guides experience life through other people's eyes as well as his own? Through him, they'd seen Sam Goldberg, but, unlike him, they saw a girl not a boy. Why did they see him differently? If the guides were a creation of his own Memory Cloud, then perhaps they were able to infiltrate other users' feeds like a computer virus jumping from one terminal in a network to another. That functionality had always been available for subscribers like Jake, as long as the other subscriber granted you permission. If Job and Dinah were able to forge the same type of connection, it was doubtful they'd ever ask permission first.

On the very first day they materialised, Job confirmed that the Circuit was in charge. But what were they in charge of? Were they in charge of the guides, or him? Maybe the eyes and ears of the guides created another layer of surveillance to control their users. Whatever their primary purpose was, no one could deny that Dinah had seen something disturbing today, and as that emotion didn't exist in Jake's own cloud it suggested she was storing it somewhere else. Maybe Dinah had her own unique cloud that compiled her own view of the world?

Dinah certainly had a vivid imagination, but that might be an extension of Jake's own. Perhaps she had made the whole episode up to seek attention as all young children do naturally. When she failed to return to her old self over the following days this premise seemed unlikely. She spent most days curled in a ball in the corner of the room occasionally shivering like a ghost had walked through her. Her reactions went beyond shock. Normally that eroded as time stretched away from the event. Fear lasted longer.

But what was she frightened of?

What she'd seen, or that someone might find out?

For Jake, life on the island of Bornholm followed a now familiar pattern. Holst would wake him up early, usually with a sadistic dose of disdain that Jake had the temerity to exist and cause disruption to the Major's otherwise solitary lifestyle. After a period of remorseful core muscle work to atone for it, he'd head off to Factory Two and attempt breakfast. It was impossible to say who organised the first meal of the day, or indeed where it came from, but it was less difficult to describe it. Inedible was the most accurate word. Prepared in a series of ways that only differed by temperature and the way it was arranged on the plate, all meals consisted of the same core ingredient. Jake soon found out from his cloud that it was called efflotein.

ONE EMPTY SPACE

According to cloud sources, efflotein was a highly engineered synthetic product that combined all the vital elements needed for survival. Not quite all. Taste was clearly left off the list when the project brief was submitted. It tasted like mouldy bananas and looked like lumps of burnt charcoal floating in vegan juice. In reality it was a combination of fish roe, cashew nuts, synthetic proteins, vitamin supplements, molasses and vegetable peelings. Delicious it was not, but strangely it did keep your energy up if you managed to keep it down longer than thirty minutes.

He'd force-fed himself a bowl before rushing off to another one of the factories for the first of the day's lessons. After pushing out a few hundred press-ups for his inevitable tardiness, Holst would shout demands at him to participate in a discipline he'd had zero coaching in to support success. Holst would adjudicate, finger hovering in the air, presumably over a button in his cloud that said 'FAIL' in big, flashing red letters.

He never got to press it.

In the past few days Jake had covered, amongst other disciplines: orienteering, hunting, tracking, the use of heat-seeking equipment, psychology, interrogation, identification and four different communication theories. To his surprise, and Holst's obvious disappointment, he'd flown through all of them. He appeared to be a natural Archivist and found the tasks no more difficult than riding an escalator. Each completed test would be followed by the now familiar and grudging pronouncement of his 'pass' from Holst, before they'd quickly moved to the next challenge until there was no light left in the day. Normally when the sun set somewhere behind the dense, yellow clouds, Holst would dismiss Jake from duty and plunge him into the tedium of staring at the inside of Factory Eight, about the only legitimate entertainment anywhere on the island.

Outlets for relaxation were limited. A run was an option, although the energy exerted during the day made that unpalatable unless you were a masochist. That was about it. There was no games room and no one available to join in even if there were one. The only entertainment was what you brought with you. Which meant the Memory Cloud and that would have been plenty for most people. An endless stream of movies, virtual reality games, sporting events or personal learning, all available in an instant. Jake struggled to motivate himself to use any of it. That's not to say he wasn't thankful to have it. His evenings comprised a detailed search of the cloud for a set of memories that evaded him like a recent bout of amnesia. Forensically he scrolled through the last year, analysing each moment.

His family appeared with regular frequency. Paddy, Tyra, Kyle and Deborah were all there. Mostly he dwelled on happy events. Family meals taken in their small backyard on the rare occasion the sun stayed out long enough to make it pleasant, lengthy strolls along the beach or games of baseball in the park. In every one of these memories the number of seats or positions never quite matched the number of guests or participants. There was always an empty space, as if someone had died but no one could accept they wouldn't be rejoining. Was it for his grandmother, Nina? No. He checked his older memories and found the one that related to the day she passed away. Although desperately painful for all involved there was no empty seat laid out for her in the days and weeks that followed. He scrolled back from the present day until the empty seat finally disappeared. It had been present for at least three years, always unoccupied, even though others in the family asked the vacant seat questions or occasionally offered it food.

The search for answers drove him insane. He tried to contact Paddy through the cloud, but he was never connected. He tried Tyra but she'd completely blocked him. The more he forced himself to recall, the more Jake realised he wasn't equipped to remember. It wasn't a function he'd ever needed to use until today. Something was missing, he knew that for sure, but the truth stayed stubbornly secretive. As he spent night after night in solitude it wasn't the only thing that bothered him either.

When he wasn't mining his own cloud within the confines of Factory Eight, he was climbing the hill. Every night he made the trip up the winding path and onto the top. Every night he examined the metal shed for clues to its purpose. There was no way through the impregnable chains that kept people from entry or anything from exit. Through the gaps in the metal he peered into the gloom. Occasional murmurs of noise or light would seep out of a void that made up most of the floor space. There was a cave system there, he was certain of that, but he didn't have the bravery or resources to explore it further.

Day and night continued in this pattern like a well-oiled machine until the seventh day arrived.

"It's another pass," said Holst as he officiated over Jake's successful deployment of a device that shot sticky webbing over a wide area from a tube.

"Thank you, Major, sir."

"I doubted my own ability to train a superfluous, but it appears I have achieved just that," said Holst in self-congratulation.

"Yes, Major, sir," replied Jake. After a week he'd finally worked out that attempting to debate or challenge Holst was more painful than it was illuminating.

ONE EMPTY SPACE

"I'm still not convinced you'll be effective in a real-life situation, in fact I'm predicting your painful demise before your second mission, but that's not really my problem anymore. Welcome to the Archivists, son," replied Holst, holding his hand out for Jake to shake it.

It was an uncomfortable feeling. The Major had put him through an arduous week of drills and judgements yet offered his hand like none of it had ever happened. Surely this was a trick. He grabbed his hand and gave it a sharp, quick shake while crossing his fingers behind his back. To his surprise, Holst gave him a subtle wink that was far more uncomfortable than shaking his hand.

"You have been allocated to Corridor E Four. A tour of duty will commence in the next week, unless you are called upon sooner. Equipment will be issued on your departure. Any questions?"

"Questions," he muttered. "Do they come with or without push-ups, Major Holst, sir?"

"You have passed, son. You're one of us now. Ask away."

"Where is Corridor E Four based, sir?"

"Archivists, as you already know, are not based anywhere. They move in transit, ever vigilant for the Spectrum threat that never rests. You will be required to mobilise anywhere that the Principal Conductor chooses you, too. Could be Europe one day, could be Central America the next."

"I'll wait for the call, Major, sir."

"It won't be long, believe me."

Of all the questions that he'd wanted to ask this week, forever suppressed from doing so, he would be satisfied with only one of them being answered. It had nothing to do with the Archivists or the Spectrum, his implant had consumed enough of that information from his download to last a lifetime.

The answer he most wanted was the one Dinah was still unable to satisfy.

"Sir, what do you keep in the shed on top of the hill?"

Holst's demeanour returned to the one Jake had been familiar with for the last seven days.

"Tell me what you know!" he screamed, grabbing Jake by the collar and lifting him off the ground in one smooth motion.

"Nothing," spluttered Jake.

"That's right...nothing!" Holst raged, a torrent of breath hitting Jake's face like a wind tunnel. "You no longer have any interest in what happens on this island, do you hear me? You have not met me, you have not been here, and you will deny all knowledge of its contents. It does not exist. If you reveal any of what you have witnessed on Bornholm the full weight of the Circuit's rage will strike you so hard you'll feel like you've been hit by a meteorite. Do you understand me?"

"Yes, Major, sir."

If Holst had wanted to remove Jake's curiosity, it could have been achieved easily. A simple lie would have sufficed. An aggressive reaction only reinforced the obviously sinister nature of what he was trying to hide.

"I want you off my island!" he shouted angrily as if Jake's presence was poisoning the earth under his feet.

"Yes, Major, sir. How do..."

"I have already messaged your wife to come and pick you up."

"My wife?!"

"Wife-to-be," Holst corrected himself, although not in the way Jake expected.

Why was he the only one who saw Sam for what he was? A bloke. Almost everyone else was convinced Sam was some tall, teenage blonde. If

ONE EMPTY SPACE

Sam had been it might have made life worse, thought Jake. Not being the slightest bit interested in men meant he wasn't tempted and would always remain faithful to…who? Who was he holding out for exactly? He knew there was someone. A pang of loss and love settled in his mind like dust on furniture in a house long since abandoned.

"Leave," barked Major Holst, pointing towards the gates, "or I will make you."

"Time to go, Jake," said Brother Job, gently tugging at the back of his jacket.

"Ok. Where's Dinah?"

"Top pocket," replied Job. "Can't you hear her sobbing?"

Jake located a miniature version of Dinah adopting the foetal position in his chest pocket.

"We're going home, Dinah. No more fear."

The news forced Dinah into a weak smile.

Jake retrieved the Archivist kit that Holst had allocated for him and headed through the large, metal gates for the second and hopefully last time. It certainly hadn't been the week he'd expected. He'd only met two people, one of them virtually, signed his life away, experienced an excruciating download, spent much of the week trying to identify his misplaced nostalgia, and passed almost all his tests with ease. Of all the week's revelations, two would stick with him the longest. The Archivists were not as effective in their jobs as he'd been led to believe, and there might be an ulterior motive to their remit, if the secrecy on the hilltop was significant.

He waited an hour for Maisy, the quadcopter, to descend through the low-hanging cloud and land. Sam leapt out of the cockpit and helped Jake with his now expanded belongings, which made the interior a lot more crowded and uncomfortable than the journey here. Maisy lifted gently from the ground and immediately improved the spirits of

239

everyone on-board, other than Brother Job who thoroughly approved of Holst's approach to discipline and order.

"How was it?" asked Sam casually.

"Like everything since I left Boston, confusing, painful and disappointing!"

"Tell me about it," asked Sam curiously. "Tell me everything."

"I can't."

"Why not?"

"I'm not allowed. I've agreed to all their terms of secrecy."

"I know that, but you can tell me some stuff. Did you see anything suspicious?"

"Almost everything," replied Jake truthfully.

"Like what?"

Jake found this immediate interrogation somewhat strange. When they'd first met, Sam had been relaxed and sociable even if he wasn't exactly what Jake was expecting. Now he seemed more interested in the island than him. Jake scanned back through the confidentiality clauses in his memory feed to remind himself what he could and couldn't divulge. The answer was very little of the former. Of all the clauses he'd agreed to there didn't appear to be much that directly related to the island itself.

"There's no one on the island," said Jake carefully.

"No one?"

"No. I was the only trainee. The only other person was a senior officer, but I'm not allowed to tell you his name."

"Anything else?"

"Why are you so interested?" asked Jake.

"Because I'm concerned about risk."

"But you don't manage risk anymore, you're meant to be a Beautician!"

"Even so, risk still exists."

"Maybe but why is Bornholm a risk?"

"I don't know yet. That's why I'm asking. Don't you think it's strange that you were the only trainee, even though the Circuit tells us every day about the growing number of speccies and the threats they pose?"

"Yes, but he told me they only replace people and have an excellent retention rate."

"Did you believe him?"

"Not until I received the download."

"They gave you a download! That's illegal, it's written in the Circuit's manifesto."

"I don't think they follow the rules."

"Did you feel like you'd lost something?" asked Sam pointedly and distracted from his main duty of flying the quadcopter.

"Yes."

"We have to find out what it is."

"Why?"

"Because your memories are vital."

"Nothing about me is vital. I'm superfluous." He shrugged and sank into his chair.

"Did you see anything else strange while you were there?"

"No, but Dinah did."

"Who?"

"One of my guides."

"What did she see?"

"She won't tell me. She's been in trauma ever since it happened. Can we change the subject please? I was rather hoping to have a break from it all."

"Yes, of course. I'll know everything you know tomorrow anyway."

"How do you work that out?"

"Because we're getting married. Married couples don't just share their lives, they are obliged by law to share their Memory Clouds. It's in the contract."

"You know what they can do with that, don't you?"

"What?"

Jake didn't even need to say it out loud. It was enough to think it. The cloud captured everything, intended, spoken or thought. Positive or negative.

VIOLATION.

- Chapter 19 -

Teenage Wasteland

There was a buzz of activity above Sam's hilltop home as Maisy circled above it. The quadcopter was forced to land further from the house than normal as a result of the many obstructions that hadn't been there when Jake left last week. Clearly Maurice had decided to ignore his request for a simple ceremony and instead embraced what he'd described as his personal creativity.

On every available patch of firm ground a collection of small, colourful tents, that only looked capable of housing two people at most, had been pitched in a chaotic manner. A tall, wobbly pole protruded from the base of each one and swayed in the air like the hands of rubber metronomes. On the tip, flags of every colour and pattern fluttered gently in the breeze. Black and white, rainbows, ones with glittery patterns that sparkled out of control, and even one with a self-made Circuit logo. When Jake got closer, he noticed the strapline was subtly different to the one he was used to seeing.

It's a state of *mine*.

In the middle of the carnival of colours a large marquee, brilliantly white and beautifully decorated, stretched along the top of the hill, obscuring their view of the dome. One of its canvas walls was tied up to show off its immaculately prepared interior. Organised in neat rows, a hundred gold plastic chairs had been covered in delicate, white flowers and fancy ribbons. Giant silver candlestick holders stood like guardians at the end of every row. A thick red carpet had been rolled out and came to an end at a white archway of intricately woven wooden canes. It was a perfect venue for an imperfect wedding.

Around the marquee Sam's guests were in a party mood. Boisterous embers danced from small bonfires built expertly behind stone circles a safe distance from synthetic fabrics or the hill's barren heather that would ignite in seconds. The flames basked revellers in a gentle and calming warmth that also put Jake at ease.

The aroma of succulent meats being slowly grilled over the campfires wafted through the air and up Jake's nostrils. The sudden reminder of what real food smelt like made his taste buds tingle and his mouth salivate with the potential of a decent meal. All he'd eaten for a week was efflotein, a substance designed to dissuade you from ever wanting to eat again. He could smell sausages, chicken and, if he wasn't mistaken, some juicy beefsteaks. It beckoned to him like a snake charmer calling its captive and, even without Job's support, Jake's legs bounded towards it.

It wasn't just the idea of eating that was soothing Jake's anxiety after a week on the island.

There were other humans.

It can be a dark experience to live without people around you if you're not used to it. Most people don't choose to isolate themselves, because the connection to others creates meaning and purpose in life. Even those forced to segregate themselves don't do so entirely. Prisoners, like Jake's parents, might have many of their freedoms removed but they were not truly alone. There would always be other prisoners, or even guards, willing to empathise with their situation or seek to interact to offer support and even friendship. Jake had not been completely alone over the last week, but it had felt like it.

He'd had Holst, his guides and even his cloud for company, but he counted none of them as genuine comforts. Isolation from those that you love isn't easy. It forces you to look inward for meaning, and that's not always an enviable place to be. It had tested Jake to his limits, mostly because real meaning appeared to have been stolen from his mind. The very thought of talking to people that didn't insist on being called Major or request a hundred push-ups every time you asked a simple question made him grin for the first time in weeks.

Small groups of people congregated around each of the fires. Some played gentle, melodic music on guitars or flutes while the ensemble sang along harmoniously, not a single note out of tune. Other groups were crafting small trinkets made of string, flat pebbles and pieces of smoothed, reclaimed glass. Another sat silently in a circle, eyes closed, heads bowed and holding hands. There was an equal number of men and women in the gathering but not an equal balance of age. They were all young with perfect skin and long hair, most sported spiritual-themed tattoos, and all were underdressed for the season and time of evening.

If these were Sam's wedding guests, they looked nothing like the wide cross-section of society of weddings Jake had attended over his life. Those were crowded with young kids bouncing off each other with food all down their neatly ironed clothes. Hat-wearing old women huddled in a corner exclusively chatting about the quality of cake. There was always a drunk uncle dancing out of time. In this group there were none of those. No children and no pensioners. Surely they couldn't all be relatives?

"They're hippies!" said Jake before his voice was within earshot of the groups.

"They're my friends," replied Sam, acknowledging a few of the party-goers with a wave.

"Not family?"

"They're all dead," said Sam without an ounce of sadness in his voice.

"Sorry, I thought it was just your parents who'd died."

"Don't be sorry. These people are my family now. We share something more important than genes."

"What?"

"Purpose."

"Where did they all come from?" asked Jake.

"Far and wide. Some of them set off on our Ascension Day just to get here in time. Come and meet some of them?" said Sam, beckoning him to follow.

Jake and Sam sat with a group that weren't quite so preoccupied with the creativity that featured within the other groups. Around this fire six guests were chatting like old friends. They offered Jake food, which he accepted gladly, and welcomed him in to their throng with no sign of the animosity or discrimination he'd been warned about. Jake listened respectfully to their conversations, content to sit quietly and soak up the atmosphere. There was something deeply fascinating about their faces. Not only did they smile continually, but there was a calm in their features he'd never seen in people before. Even Dinah had proved her boundless energy could be dampened under the right conditions.

The more he listened to them talk, the more at ease he felt. Endlessly positive and never judgemental or rude, they oozed a personal self-confidence while being equally generous to other people's opinions and thoughts. The focus of their debates only ever featured the real world, never the virtual one. Nature, creativity, love, the arts, spirituality and music. Whereas Jake was constantly being hijacked by the uninhibited activity of his cloud feed tirelessly barging into view with its products and news reports, they never made mention of it. Questions that were raised in the group were never solved by someone visiting the virtual world to seek the undisputed evidence to win the argument. They just discussed it openly and listened intently to other people's thoughts on the subject. He never once saw anyone get angry in pursuit of superiority over the other. They were happy to agree or disagree without anyone falling out over it. Their faces never stopped offering kindness to those around them.

Which was when he first noticed.

Scars.

They all had them.

He'd seen a similar facial blemish on Alfonso's forehead a few weeks ago. His hadn't been the result of a surgeon's knife and nor were these. Surgical scars were uniform, purposeful and always temporary. As soon as the patient healed, they'd be straight down to the body improvement clinic until it ceased to exist outside of your memory feed. These scars weren't like that. They showed no evidence of man-made intrusion. They appeared to be a natural feature of the skin and most of this group's scars were on their heads. There was a guy who had one on his chin, for another girl it was in the centre of her cheek, and one whose went down the side of his neck. They varied in size, but not in appearance. Whatever had caused them, it was clear they'd all experienced the same wound.

Most interestingly, to Jake at least, they made no attempt to hide it from a new acquaintance, and given his recent training camp they probably should have.

Jake's internal engine battled with itself. Competing urges struggled for overall control. Newly sown instincts wanted him to immediately summon the Archivists, while a deeper sense of morality held them at bay. The latter emotion felt more real but further away. Surely his internal struggle was pointless anyway. It was only a matter of time before his optic nerve identified the people in front of him and in minutes the Archivists would be marching up the hill, Corridors approaching from every side.

He closed his eyes to avoid it, but his cranial implant was not so easily fooled. He had to stop thinking about them completely.

"Sam, can I have a word?" he said jumping up from a small camping stool like a kangaroo.

"Sure."

The two men walked into the empty marquee and away from the revellers.

"What's the matter?" asked Sam. "Not enjoying yourself?"

"You have to tell them to leave, right now!"

"Don't be daft."

"I'm serious, Sam. They've all got...scars!" he said, not wanting the word Spectrum to leave his mouth and enter Job's ears.

"Yes, I know."

"And you know where I've spent the last week," pleaded Jake.

"What's your point?"

"My point is any minute now a platoon of Archivists is going to be crawling all over this place. Every one of your friends will be interrogated, converted or exterminated. I know. I've seen how we do it. I know how we do it."

"They're not coming," replied Sam in relaxed mood.

"The Circuit sees everything..."

"Not everything."

"Yes, they do!"

"Ask one of your guides if you don't believe me."

"What?"

"Ask them what they see," added Sam confidently.

If there was a choice which guide to call upon for any given task, normally the decision was easy. Sadly, Dinah was in no fit state for anything today. He would have to ask the difficult one.

"Brother Job?"

"Present as always," huffed Job who was resting on one of the golden chairs thoroughly bored by the lack of an agenda.

"You see that group playing music by the fire?"

"Obviously."

"There you go," he said to Sam. "He can see them!"

"Of course, he can see them, but what does he see?"

"Describe them," Jake asked Job.

"Why?" asked Job suspiciously.

"It's a game."

"You'll need Dinah for that, I don't really do games."

"Research, I'm doing research," added Jake.

"What research?"

"I have no idea why they call you guides, they should call you irritants. I'm researching the average age of people who play guitar," he said grappling for meaning where there wasn't any. "How old would you say they are?"

Brother Job floated through Jake's recent memories to get a clearer and closer view of the subjects Jake referred to. After some internal computation the answer came back.

"Thirteen," he replied.

Jake's initial impression of the hippies was one of youthfulness, but there was no way any of them were younger than he was.

"Thirteen!?"

"Fourteen tops," replied Job sighing.

"What else is notable about them?" asked Jake, testing his luck.

"It's notable that Sam appears to have only teenage friends," said Job. "Oh, and they all have acne, which is strange because there are plenty of Circuit products for that."

"What did he say?" asked Sam.

"Teenagers with acne."

"Not scars?" said Sam with a wink.

"Apparently not."

"Should we go back to the party, then?"

"No. Something weird is going on here. Something weird has been going on since the moment I opened my letter. I'm going to bed," replied Jake grumpily.

*****

Jake woke later than he'd become accustomed to. He sprang out of bed convinced he'd beaten Major Holst to it for once. His feet landed on soft, synthetic fibres rather than the cold, wooden floor and he instinctively saluted the atrium that split the dome in half. The expectation of Holst's impending hostility subsided when he realised where he was. Then a very different worry hit him.

He was getting married today.

In the history of marriage, no bride or groom ever had second thoughts as deeply as this. Contemplating second thoughts was actually only possible if you'd had positive thoughts in the first place. Which he hadn't. He'd had objections from the outset but that didn't seem to matter a jot. He considered sending another complaint but came to the rapid conclusion it was a waste of his time. What was the point? There was nothing worth fighting for now.

Whatever hope he'd been clinging to it was fully extinguished on Bornholm. The only priority that mattered to him was helping his parents, wherever they were right now. It didn't really matter if he was married or single to achieve that. Life could have been worse. At least Sam lived in a nice place and had plenty of money. So what that he was a man and only had friends that were either speccies or spotty teenagers, he could still keep his boundaries. Maybe it was time to give up and let the system play with his future and just be grateful about it. Perhaps, once the wedding was over, he'd be freed from his lunatic guides and could focus on supporting his mother and father. Sam might be able to help on that, too, given the circles he moved in.

"Time to get ready," demanded Brother Job. "Your clothes are in the wardrobe."

There was no doubt in Jake's mind that Maurice had chosen a costume designed to deliver maximum humiliation as he walked down the aisle. It was probably a frilly dress or skintight leotard. Anything was better than Maurice's idea of a naked ceremony, he thought to himself. To his surprise the clothes inside the wardrobe were rather classy. A simple white shirt, black rubber shoes, basil coloured waistcoat and matching trousers. They were perfectly measured and fit him like a glove. It was the first time in a week he'd felt truly comfortable.

"You need to do something about Dinah," said Job.

"Why?"

"She's sulking again."

"Can't you leave her alone?"

"She's meant to be your best man, remember?"

Jake hadn't. She'd been so excited about it, it didn't feel right to rob her of the opportunity just because she was traumatised.

"Where is she?" asked Jake.

"Dinah, get your sorry arse out of the bin."

"It might help if you were kinder to her," advised Jake.

"I don't control kindness, she does! Kindness is a spontaneous natural attribute, I only do learnt behaviours."

"Can't you try?"

"No."

"Go on, it'll be good for you," suggested Jake.

"Would you ask a horse to oink?"

"No, because they can't," said Jake.

"There you go. Same for me."

"But you're not a horse, are you?"

"Horses can't oink…or be kind."

"Being kind isn't a physical attribute like making a noise or wiggling your ears, it's a state of mind," explained Jake. A number of Circuit-branded products rushed into his memory feed on hearing their motto. He swiped them away effortlessly. "Try it."

"Fine," groaned Job as if he was being forced to eat something likely to make him sick on contact. "How?"

"Just say something kind to her. A compliment that'll make her feel better."

"Dinah, you're the most irritating thing I've…"

"Kind!"

"You said offer her a compliment. If someone's the best at something surely that counts!"

"Not if they don't see it as a positive. Saying that someone is irritating is called criticism."

"Same thing," muttered Job.

"It's not. Try again!"

"Dinah, we all think you're...a projection of Jake's personality...who is important to...the mission...and if you come out of the bin I will...appreciate it," stuttered Job struggling as each positive word stuck in his throat.

"That was rubbish."

"I did tell you."

"Try again."

"Dinah, come out of there or I will send a nasty Trojan virus up your jacksie!" added Job instinctively.

"Brilliantly diplomatic," Jake replied sarcastically.

"Oink," replied Job.

"Dinah, I need you," said Jake taking up the reins.

Sister Dinah expanded through the bin to what Jake always believed was her natural size. Her normal brightly coloured clothes had been replaced by mournful black ones and her once fiery red hair drooped limply down her face.

"I'm not ready to play," she croaked, clearly hoarse from endless sobbing.

"I don't need you to play, I need you to be my best man. You asked to do it, after all."

Dinah's mouth desperately tried to force a smile but collapsed under the weight of her tribulations. She nodded weakly.

"You'll do it? That's great. We might as well get it done, then," replied Jake, striding towards the landing.

Everyone was in position inside the marquee. A hundred guests, more conservatively dressed than they had been last night, sat patiently. Some of them struggled to mask their hippy hairdos or the lingering smell of hemp. Maurice bustled about, nervously checking flower arrangements or reseating guests who'd not found their allotted space. The canvas wall of the marquee remained open to allow the light breeze to circulate around the venue like natural air conditioning.

Today they'd been lucky. The early Storm Season disruptions had abated, and the sun was just visible between the clouds. The sweet smell of the Twinflowers wafted through the raised side and mingled with the scented candles that flickered from the large silver candlestick holders. Jake stood at the front of the congregation whispering words of encouragement to the catatonic Dinah who made the atmosphere feel more like a funeral than a wedding. Job stayed out of sight, presumably still miffed he'd not been given any formal involvement in the proceedings.

At the back of the makeshift church three of the hippies rose from their seats holding instruments and struck up a rather pleasant acoustic alternative to the wedding march. Sam stepped onto the red carpet to begin his short walk to the front. Maurice grinned like a lottery winner and clung to Sam's arm like a patient returning from a serious leg injury. Maurice almost skipped down the aisle in pride as they advanced down the carpet. Sam walked along casually in the same basil suit worn by his future husband.

Jake scanned the faces in the crowd. Not one of them belonged to someone who knew him.

In his head he'd imagined this moment quite differently. His loved ones were always there in his version of events. Kyle and Deborah, would be sitting in the front row, smiling proudly and dabbing their eyes to wipe away tears of joy. Tyra would be one of the bridesmaids, walking proudly behind his bride, carefully holding the train of the wedding dress. Paddy would be somewhere in the throng, probably complaining that he didn't have a very good view or that it wasn't how they did it in his day. His friends from around New Hampton Falls would be primed to cheer the couple's first kiss before helping them celebrate the occasion deep into the night. He'd gone over the vision many times before, but today there was no one he knew here and no bride advancing up the aisle in a beautiful, elegant, white dress.

There was a man in a basil suit.

Sam joined Jake under the white arch. Circuit weddings didn't require a priest to join in person. An elderly man shuffled into Jake's memory feed. He had bushes of silver hair cascading out of his ears but had almost none at all on his head. He adjusted his collar, as if he'd rushed through traffic to arrive on time. Before speaking, he ran through some notes in his head that he'd prepared for the occasion.

"Is everybody ready?" he said, peering out into the marquee.

Sam nodded.

"You look absolutely lovely, my dear," said the virtual priest. "Beautiful dress."

Jake quickly glanced at Sam to double-check he hadn't been dreaming. Maybe he needed to get his eyes checked? He definitely saw a man in a green suit.

The priest waffled on for ten minutes about the sanctity of marriage and how the Circuit had enhanced what had always been an essential passage of life and love. The priest announced his conviction that God would have designed it this way, if He'd had the benefit of technology and anyone still believed He existed.

Weddings were a clinical affair. Hymns and readings were largely dispensed with as attention spans in the twenty-fifties weren't robust enough. People would switch off and get lost in some virtual pastime like catching up on a box set or surfing holiday brochures. After the initial introduction by the priest the ceremony moved swiftly to the identification process and exchange of contracts. The first part was usually simple. The Memory Cloud knew who you were from the records it kept on its servers. As soon as you'd been verified the ceremony moved on to the reading of contracts.

"I'm just waiting for verification, Miss Goldberg," said the priest holding a finger to his ear. "I do apologise, it doesn't normally take this long…ah there it is, I have both of you."

It was the first time since they'd met that Jake sensed genuine anxiety in Sam. An uncomfortable reflex left his chest, letting out a little more air than a normal breath required.

"On to the contracts. Take your time. They're a little wordy, I'm afraid."

"Excuse me," said Jake. "I didn't think we had a choice?"

"You don't," replied the priest.

"So, what's the point in reading and signing them," he replied.

"You don't have to read, just sign."

"And if I don't?" asked Jake gently.

"We'll swap your honeymoon in Canada for one in the Source," offered the priest with a smile.

In some ways Jake would prefer a trip to the Source. His parents were there after all, and he was desperate to know how they were coping. If he did go there, as his desire demanded, it would have to be planned rather than enforced.

Jake lazily scanned through the three hundred and twenty-four pages that lay in his mind like the world's most terrifying microfiche. He thought about Paddy, and how he'd been duped into ignoring the terms of joining the Circuit all those years ago, ultimately landing Jake where he was today. Maybe Paddy had also run out of choices back then and had felt trapped and helpless?

The contract detailed every aspect of his union with Sam. Their commitments to each other. How they would deal with marital strife. How they would make decisions. How the Circuit would adjudicate if problems arose and couldn't be resolved. Who was supposed to do which jobs around the house. How they were required to treat each other. How many children they were required to have.

Children!

It said three.

That was going to be one hell of a challenge.

Jake noticed that the terminology throughout the contract referred to 'his' and 'her'. The Circuit must have been accustomed to arranging same-sex marriages, which were by no means a rarity in his home town, yet this contract didn't seem to reflect it at all.

He gave up reading. What was the point? None of it was going to change and none of it was going to be easy to deliver. The alternative was worse. He forced his optic implant down to the bottom where his name was printed below a box that would capture his affirmation through his emotions. Jake assumed the pose, just as he'd done back on Bornholm when agreeing to their secrecy acts, and confirmed his agreement.

It was done.

"Finally!" said the priest. "Your wife signed it ages ago."

"That figures," said Jake.

"Do you have the rings?"

"Dinah," whispered Jake.

Dinah shuffled forward, tears still flowing down her face but managing to curtail her ever-present wailing. A small, virtual pillow bobbed up and down in her hands as she reached the front and stood between the couple. On top of the pillow sat two circles of rotating energy, like streams of data in an endless four hundred-metre race.

"The exchange of rings," announced the priest, "is a tradition that extends through the ages. The circle is a symbol of eternity, epitomising the unbreakable bond between you that will endure until death. Like the Circuit itself it represents the interconnectivity of our world. As the contract states the exchange of virtual bonds like these creates a complete union of life, both real and virtual. What is hers shall be his, and what is his shall be hers."

"His and his!" shouted Jake, losing his composure.

"There's no place for narcissism in a happy marriage, son," snapped the priest, not really understanding Jake's objection.

"Are you ready?" said Sam, looking at Jake warmly.

"Not really."

"It'll all make sense after this, I promise."

Nothing made sense in his world anymore and he wasn't confident that picking up a virtual ring was going to change anything. He reached out in his cloud feed. His shadowy finger approached the ring. Static crackled between them. He lifted it from the pillow and held it for a moment. It was thinner and less dense than his own ring, as if the contents of Sam's cloud had been stretched to make the circle complete. He slipped it onto his virtual finger and a pulse of energy crawled up his arm, through his shoulder and up into his brain. Where there had once been one interface in his Memory Cloud menu, now there was a second. It was labelled Sam Montana.

"Now we are fully connected," added Sam eagerly. "How does it feel?"

"Depressing."

"That's a shame. I feel exhilarated, there are so many of your memories that I want to explore."

"I wish I could say the same for you," replied Jake.

The permanent union of their clouds brought no further illumination about Sam's past. It was a repeat of what he already knew but could not explain. The pretty blonde female Sam striking too many staged and fake poses like a model doing a photo shoot. There was nothing of substance at all.

"Ah that's cute, your nickname at nursery school was 'short pants'," giggled Sam, scrolling randomly through Jake's deep past.

"That's it! I've had enough. I'm going back to bed," said Jake.

"What about the party?" replied Sam in dismay.

"It's not my party, it's yours. You may as well enjoy it without me. I'm going to find a bottle of booze and drink myself to oblivion: after all, the Circuit predicted everything so why fight it?"

"Perhaps you'd be better off popping a couple of Moodzec?" suggested Sam.

- Chapter 20 -

Ghosts in the Machine

Jake tried to block out the noise of merriment floating in from the party outside. Whether he was present or not, the hippies were going to enjoy themselves. He didn't belong in their world anyway. He was the spare part that the manufacturer included in case any of the originals broke. They never did. Everyone had a place where they kept them. Old screws, spare springs and miniature tools that had outlived their purpose, hidden from view to be forgotten about. He'd never belong here. Sam's friends were either hippies or spotty teenagers, depending on who you asked, and neither group were really his scene.

Jake picked up the small, plastic bottle from the bedside table and rotated it in his hands. On one side in large, yellow letters it read MOODZEC. On the other a microscopic list detailed the potential side effects you might suffer if you took it. According to the manufacturer these included: an increase in velocity, itchy knees, an inflamed pancreas, short-term disorientation, and a loss of vision. Most worryingly it also listed a heightened desire to commit suicide as one of its rarer reactions. It seemed perverse to Jake that anyone who already depressed might take a pill that might make the situation worse. Perhaps a bottle of whiskey was safer?

Printed below the list of rather terrifying knock-on effects was the ubiquitous Circuit logo, but it was barely visible and the strapline underneath almost illegible. It was extremely unusual for it to appear like this. It was always the most prominent feature on everything. The more he focused on it, the more he doubted its authenticity. The iconic font that people recognised instantly was also somehow wrong. The colours were off, and the font looked fake or rushed.

There was no question the product was approved by them. Everything was. All community services, from public health to immigration and security, were under their control. Ninety percent of commercial enterprises had also been consumed under their ever-expanding empire. Those that refused to accept a takeover, and the vast amount of credits that came with it, were either crushed economically or forced to comply through hostile tactics. Jake had never seen any drug that didn't have their banner along with a litany of instructional codes to guide the patient in the correct direction for consuming them.

The modern world navigated life on a conveyor belt of pills. For most people the virtual world worked perfectly, but the visual world was not so easily fixed. Physical ailments, either as a result of body misuse, the effects of the changing climate, or the upsurge in new and debilitating diseases, were commonplace. New and innovative procedures had silenced the march of most cancers, paralysis and blindness, but surgery wasn't effective on everything. Obesity, heart disease, diabetes and strokes were on the front line of conditions that could be blasted away with a vast pharmaceutical arsenal. There were pills for everything, and as long as they were Circuit-approved, people guzzled them like candy.

There wasn't much of an alternative other than suffering the pain or avoiding the worst excesses in life, which were promoted as wilfully as the remedy. Both the cause and solution to people's vices had a nice, shiny Circuit branding on them. Whatever your ailments, one fact was indisputable. Your Memory Cloud would outlast your body, even if you took good care of it.

Jake unscrewed the safety cap and rattled two pills onto his palm. They were butter-yellow and had a smiley face motif. The surface of the pill was slippery like beeswax but inside the liquid gel felt like silicon as he squeezed it gently between finger and thumb. Right now, irrespective of whether he'd suffer from itchy knees or be able to run a bit faster, he couldn't see any downsides of popping the recommended dose down his throat.

Someone disagreed.

"Stop!" shouted Brother Job, as Jake's hand drew closer to his open mouth.

"Stay out of it."

"Did you do the research?"

"Yes! I read the back of the bottle."

"That's not research."

"Good enough for me."

"You have no idea how this might affect you…or us."

"I don't care anymore."

"I forbid you to take it."

"Try to stop me," taunted Jake.

Criminal linguists have debated the real meaning of words for years. They aren't always straightforward. Tone, inflection and context can misinterpret what the recipient actually understood, which in turn may be different from what was intended. 'Let him have it' might seem an innocuous statement, but if it's delivered to a man pointing a gun at someone, does it mean 'let him have it – shoot him' or 'let him have it – surrender'? In the distant past it wasn't so easy to decide. Not so now. The Memory Cloud captured your emotions and added context to your words. Problem was, Job didn't bother checking. 'Try to stop me' sounded like a command rather than a threat.

It didn't matter how much Jake tried to move it, his arm refused to get closer to his mouth. He tried moving his face forward, but his neck was locked in position. He stretched out his tongue in the hope that he might be able to encourage the pills to move with an outstretched lick, but only managed to pop a muscle. He sucked violently at the air, but the pills were too heavy to lift. Nothing worked. At every turn, Job beat him to his physical impulses and barely looked to have broken sweat.

"Stop holding me hostage!" shouted Jake, falling backwards from the strain of not doing very much but trying extremely hard in the process.

"I won't allow it. We are designed to protect you."

"You're designed to irritate me. You've done nothing useful EVER!"

"Don't blame me, it's your fault really. We just do what's instinctive."

There was no way he'd be able to encourage Brother Job verbally to get on-board with the plan. Jake needed support: after all, two would always be more powerful than one. What he needed was extra strength.

"Dinah," Jake cried out.

"Go away," came a distant voice that wafted down from the top of the glass dome above his head.

"How are you feeling?"

"Dreadful, you wouldn't understand," she sobbed.

"But I do understand. I feel dreadful, too," Jake empathised.

"I know what you're doing," said Job knowingly. "You can't use manipulation, I'm all over that like a rash."

"I can make you feel better, Dinah," said Jake sweetly.

"Don't listen to him, it's a trick!"

Dinah materialised on the bed like a greedy fish attracted to a dazzling piece of fake bait. "How?"

"These," said Jake, pointing at his palm.

Whether his hand had contained two suspicious-looking yellow pills, a deadly industrial laser or a lump of efflotein, Jake was pretty sure she'd agree to take anything, such was the lingering nature of her crisis.

"Is two enough?" she asked desperately.

"Oh yes! I just need you to help me eat them."

"Done!" she said, lurching forward.

What followed was a three-way struggle for Jake's nervous system. It was lucky no one was watching. If they had they'd assume he'd been satanically possessed or in the middle of a violent fit. His limbs shot out unexpectedly like he was practising selling shares on the stock exchange. His mouth snapped like a crocodile as Dinah tried to get the timing right between Jake's efforts and Brother Job's intervention. His hand clung to the pills as it did figures of eight in the air. Facial expressions moved violently between unnatural poses that didn't feature in any body language manual. Finally, the pills found their target and Jake managed to swallow them.

"Concentrate Dinah," he mumbled, "or that idiot will make me vomit them back up."

"What's the point?" huffed Job, turning his back on them. "Don't say I didn't warn you."

"Fine."

"And don't expect me to help you again."

"Or ever!" added Jake as Brother Job drifted away to take up the sulking spot Dinah had recently vacated.

"How long does it take?" asked Dinah.

"Not sure."

Jake lay back on the bed to await the effects. An hour passed and, other than Dinah asking him, 'Is it working?' roughly twice a minute, nothing happened. A second hour passed, and he felt just as miserable as before he'd struggled to guzzle them down. He tried a gentle run down the corridor but didn't believe he was any quicker than he'd been before. After the third hour Jake was contemplating returning to his initial idea of hitting the liquor cabinet. That's when he first noticed a difference.

Not in his body, but in his mind.

It was becoming clearer and unburdened by the tribulations that had weighed so heavily on him just a few hours ago. The only memories he could access were happy ones and the presence of his guides was weakening. Like a game of musical chairs, the three of them had fought over the last one in his cloud. Now it seemed like there was only one virtual bottom left to place on it.

"Where's Job?" asked Dinah.

"Up there…" Jake stopped in mid-reply as he glanced up at the massive skylight.

The projection of Brother Job was diminishing. The shadowy outline had reduced from a once dense, impenetrable light to a translucent one. As he faded, he lost colour, like the light spectrum was no longer picking up all available shades. After a few moments his outline vanished completely.

"Ahhhh…we've killed Job!" shouted Dinah hysterically. "They'll lock us up."

"I don't think guides can die."

"It's murder!"

"Why are you still here?" asked Jake quizzically.

In truth she only partly was. Like Brother Job had done before her, the light of her projection was less bold, although rather than the colour fading, hers was more vivid. The white and black hues, however, were much less pronounced.

"Apart from being partially responsible for my brother's death," she said with slight embarrassment. "I feel amazing!"

"Me, too," said Jake.

"That's Moodzec for you," said a voice at the top of the stairs.

"Sam!" shouted Jake merrily. "Has the party finished?"

"I doubt it."

"Then you should go back and join your friends. I'm fine here."

"There will be time for a party, but there is limited time for this," he said cryptically.

"For what?"

"The truth."

"Did you drug me on purpose?" said Jake, finding his tone to be incongruently jovial. He thought in those circumstances he should feel anger, but that compulsion seemed to have gone on shore leave.

"Yes, in a way."

"I'm not gay," Jake laughed.

"It has nothing to do with your boundaries, it was the only way I could get you alone."

"Who are you talking to?" asked Dinah who had collapsed on the bed from the effects of the drugs. Her eyes pointed in different directions and she giggled out loud for no apparent reason.

"Sam, of course," said Jake.

"That's weird, I can't see her." She laughed. "Is blindness on the list?"

"No, and you can see me, can't you?"

"Oh yeah," she said dreamily. "I'll just have to wait for the itchy knees instead."

GHOSTS IN THE MACHINE

"Jake, stop talking to your guide and concentrate on me," said Sam rather bossily. "I need to tell you something serious."

"Brilliant, I'm so relaxed and excited right now, literally nothing can dampen my spirits."

"That's just the effects of Moodzec. In the morning you will feel different, yet you will also know what needs to be done."

Sam released the top button on his shirt and revealed a now familiar scar just beneath his Adam's apple.

"Oh, you're one, too," expressed Jake. "No biggie!"

"Everyone outside is Spectrum, but they are a little different from the millions of others who live secretly around the world. There's a reason your guides can't see us, the same reason why no one in the Circuit can. We also have implants inside us, but they aren't like the ones you wear."

"Implants? I thought speccies wanted to be free?"

"We are free," replied Sam tersely before seeming to move the subject. "Tell me something, Jake. How many speccies do you think the Archivists have caught?"

"Not many if their reactions are anything to go by."

"And why do you think that is?"

"To be honest I just assumed they were incompetent."

"If only. As you will have experienced from your training, they have all the skills and resources needed to track and kill us, but they have not yet realised why they can't. Every speccy has an implant of one kind or another. Some wear simple external devices on their belts that fool the Circuit into believing they're a subscriber. Others, like myself and the others outside, have gone one step further. We wear our implants internally, only ours don't back up to the Memory Cloud…they infiltrate it."

"Why?" said Jake, still grinning happily from ear to ear.

"There are many benefits but mostly it was done to find you."

"Me? I am special," he replied arrogantly and quite out of character. In most circumstances he tried to resist his ego, but the Moodzec stifled any sense of humility.

"Yes, you are. Very special. That's why we went to such lengths to bring you here."

"What do you mean 'bring me here'?"

"Your Ascension Day letter was a fraud. A con. A distortion in the cloud designed by us."

"What the fu…"

"Calm down," replied Sam, stretching his hand out to cover Jake's mouth. "We don't want to encourage your other guide to return. While he is silent, I can explain everything before anyone notifies the Circuit."

"One of them is still here, though."

"I know," Sam replied.

"Why?"

"Moodzec magnifies happy emotions. It blocks the receptors in your implants that connect to negative thoughts. Positive impulses remain and they are partly controlled by her."

"Apparently you're special, Dinah," Jake relayed to his stoned guide.

"I know!" she giggled. "You see the dancing pixies, too, then?"

Jake was momentarily distracted as he looked for them, but Sam dragged him back to their conversation.

"As it happens," added Sam, "we need her here."

"Really?"

"Yes. While you're under the influence of the drug you can access some of your cloud but it's no longer recording what's happening to you. Moodzec has forced you to use your real brain."

"But I'm always using my brain."

"No, you're not. The Memory Cloud interferes before you get a chance, unless you train yourself to silence it."

"Nice. I love this stuff," he replied, pointing to the bottle.

"One more weapon in the war against the Circuit's surveillance. It only works for a limited time, which is why I had to wait for you to take it before telling you everything."

"Couldn't I have popped some before the Archivist training, that would have been a better time for me."

"I'm sorry you had to go through that, but other events had to take place first."

"I'm so deliriously confused right now," replied Jake energetically.

"Then let me explain. Where to begin? So much to tell you," replied Sam. He'd been preparing for this moment for a lifetime but when it came to the crunch a thousand versions spiralled inside his head.

"What about starting at the beginning?" said Jake helpfully.

"It's further back than you might think. It started in the East two decades ago."

"The East?"

"Yes. They are not the savages the Circuit wants us to believe. Twenty years ago, when the Circuit and the Realm tussled for dominance, something changed. The Circuit became incredibly powerful, beyond anything anyone predicted. They coerced governments to pillage the East. They stole its vital resources: energy, raw materials, wealth, talent and technology. After that, they sealed it off permanently to stop anyone returning back into the West. But even that wasn't enough for the Circuit. They also had to stop anyone in the West leaving. The 'Proclamation of Distrust' is a permanent reminder of the perils that might befall anyone if they do."

"But why did they do that?"

"Simple really. The Realm learnt the truth about the Circuit's surge in power and were preparing to disseminate it. If they'd succeeded the Circuit would have been finished. The trust would have been lost and the people would have rebelled against the system."

"What truth?"

"That's just it, no one knows. The Circuit destroyed all evidence, virtual or real, of whatever it was that the Realm had discovered, and then alienated half of the world to stop any leaks. But, like all of us, they have a blind spot."

"Has anyone else got the munchies?" Dinah blurted out.

"Shhh," said Jake, gripped by Sam's story. "Blind spot?"

"Yes. Us. The Spectrum. We don't respect arbitrary boundaries. For us the world was never split between East and West, the haves and have-nots, the free or the slaves. We come and go as we please, safe in the knowledge that the Circuit have yet to learn how our technology keeps us hidden."

"But how did they get through the firewall?"

The firewall separated the two halves of the Earth. It wasn't a physical barrier like a wall, that was way too twentieth-century. The firewall was a virtual boundary reinforced by real-life sentry guard posts that added a further deterrent to would-be defectors. A physical presence along a border that stretched from Finland to Yemen on one side, and Siberia to Papua Old Guinea on the other, would have been impossible to sustain. Where human guards weren't available, or the environment was thought to be inhospitable to sustain life, a virtual firewall restrained people's movements.

The Memory Cloud knew where everybody was at any given time. Anyone coming within a mile of the firewall would be warned and, if they continued on their path, disabled. It was believed this involved virtual torture via the memory feed, but no one ever returned to verify how the punishments were delivered. People from the East experienced a similar fate, although how this was administered via the Circuit's operating system was unclear. It worked, though. No one ever swapped sides, at least no one who owned a genuine implant.

"The Spectrum can go where they please?" said Jake in wonder.

"Yes, we've been doing it for years, although since the launch of the utility drones it's proved more difficult. Twenty years ago, it was much easier. That was when they received the gift. Ten sets of implants preloaded with the truth about the Circuit."

"What did they do with them?"

"They were smuggled into the West and concealed within the supply chain so that they would be unknowingly placed inside new hosts. Those recipients would keep that information safe until a time came when they might be retrieved, and the evidence used to force change."

"What happened to them?" asked Jake eagerly.

"Most perished, unable to control the implants that brimmed with complex data not designed for the underdeveloped infant brain. The remainder were identified by the Circuit as malfunctioning and had their implants upgraded, although it was unlikely the Circuit knew why the implants failed. They fail for other reasons, too."

"Yeah, tell me about it. Mine have been failing for years," laughed Jake, not yet making a complete connection to what he was being told.

"There is another way of identifying those who survived. They developed complex, overactive brain chemistry that didn't require one new upgrade but dozens. When we learnt this, we sought to make contact with them. That's where I come into the story."

"My knees are itchy!" gasped Dinah, rather proud of herself.

"Ignore her," said Jake merrily.

"Who?" said Sam.

"Never mind. Continue."

"The Spectrum united together to seek a solution and I delivered it. I've always been a prodigious inventor. I was always scavenging from the neighbourhood to make complex devices from simple waste. It's not easy being a speccy, you know. We can't just go to the cloud when we want to buy something, and the number of physical shops in our district you could count on one hand even back then. So, we had to scavenge."

"Do you mean steal?"

"That's semantics."

"Is that a fancy word for stealing?"

"It doesn't matter. The fact is I learnt to design complex devices from waste materials, even from discarded implants."

"Where did you get those from?"

"Bodies mostly."

"Oh lovely," replied Jake in a tone that reaffirmed that the Moodzec was still working perfectly. If it hadn't, he would have been appalled by the revelation.

"At fifteen I managed to design a reverse implant. An implant that succeeded in accessing the Memory Cloud but that could not be replicated by it, at least not the way they first intended. Unlike the other devices most speccies wear, which simply confuse the cloud, the new version only worked if it was housed internally. That meant surgery. Not such an easy thing to find in our community. Surgeons are chosen on Ascension Day and spend years perfecting their skills. Medical facilities and education aren't available to us."

"So, what did you do?"

"We had to find a physician that learnt their trade before the Ascension Day process began. It took a year of searching before we eventually found, Dr Theo Drew. He agreed to perform the procedure on us."

"Us?"

"They're all here," he said, referring to the guests outside. "The ghosts in the machine. The only people of our kind who can brazenly live undetected in a world we desire to change. They're here for the wedding…well, I guess they're really here to see you."

"Me!"

"Yes. You're the last piece of the jigsaw, Jake. We know you have an overactive brain and we know that you get flashbacks."

"Yeah, but that doesn't mean anything."

"It does. It means you are one of the ten."

"But I had my first upgrade when I was two years old, the original implant was removed and destroyed."

"But the memories you carry weren't. When you first had those early flashbacks, memories that didn't feel your own, the repeats became your memory. Slightly hazier than the originals but nevertheless still inside your Memory Cloud. New implants only record memories from the point after they are grafted to you. The Memory Cloud, on the other hand, sits remotely capturing every impulse from every implant."

Jake scrolled back through his cloud to locate his first flashback. It took too long so he went to the search function. But what was he searching for? He couldn't search for flashbacks. It was hard to tell when they happened. The feelings associated with them were some of his oldest memories. It was no good. The harder he searched, the more he struggled.

"The originals of your flashbacks are somewhere inside your Memory Cloud and we need to find a way to see them," said Sam sternly.

"You're welcome, too, if only I could find them."

"They're hidden," replied Sam. "I know, I've already looked."

"How?"

"Because our clouds are connected. At the ceremony today the exchange of the rings was more than symbolic, it created a permanent and complete tether between our clouds. That's why we had to get married. I thought once I had full access to what you knew I'd be able to find the secret. But I can't."

"There are loads of girls here," said Jake, thinking about his situation further. "Couldn't I have married one of them?"

"No. It had to be me, I'm afraid."

"Are you really gay?"

"Yes, I never misled you on that front."

"How did you even manage to arrange it?" asked Jake.

"That's where my genius comes in! My implants allow me to infiltrate the Memory Cloud itself. It's risky: there are millions of Memory Hunters scouring the interface trying to spot anything unusual and potentially dangerous. I thought it was worth the risk. I created a new persona for myself, the Sam that you saw when you first opened your letter, the Sam that anyone who wears a Memory Cloud sees. Once I'd found out the date of your Ascension Day, I set to work doctoring the rules so that we would match."

"If that's true, then why do I see you as a man when everyone else sees a girl? I have a regular implant after all."

"Because you've started to see the real world again. Most people are so reliant on the virtual dimension it clouds over the real one. They identify faces, people and emotions virtually rather than visually. Even though their eyes can see what's really there, they allow the cloud to do the work for them. The vast population of the world have slipped into a coma of laziness."

"But I saw you for a man the first time we met."

"Another sign of your overactive brain. They tend to question things more than most. You already doubted the authenticity of the female Sam, didn't you?"

"Yes."

Jake reflected on his assessment of Sam while he'd been travelling aboard the Hyperloop. He'd been suspicious of her staged and seemingly fake memories. Now he knew why. They really were fake.

"That's why the guides see you differently," said Jake. "They identify people through my implants and only see the person's Memory Cloud. But why can't Dinah see you at all now?"

"Simple, Moodzec has disrupted her interface and the fake Sam no longer appears."

"I bloody love this stuff," said Jake. "I think I'll pop a few every day."

"No, you mustn't. There's a chance that it will lead to consequences we're not aware of. The Circuit aren't stupid, they'll be watching even when they can't see."

"Fair enough," he'd replied still high on the effects of the pills. "There's something I don't understand about this. If you forged my letter why did you have to make me superfluous? You could have balanced out the disappointment by making me vital at least."

"That wouldn't have been wise. There aren't many vitals out there and they have incredible value in the system. No one would ever suspect that the key to unlocking their weakness would be someone who was superfluous. They are almost completely ignored."

"That makes sense. What about the Archivist part?"

"Also purposefully chosen. We've suspected for some time that the Archivists are not purely interested in speccies. We believe they are also focused on the Realm. The Circuit will never be satisfied until they have dismantled their rival, particularly if they suspect they may still hold evidence that might destroy them. I've tried accessing your memories from the week in Bornholm to fill in the gaps, but they're securely locked. I believe something is happening there."

"Sorry, I had to agree not to divulge anything about my time there," replied Jake.

"Yes, that's true," said Sam. "But she didn't."

- Chapter 21 -

Memory Hunters

Dinah floated on the bed, giggling insanely to herself and oblivious to her significance in their conversation. Powered by a drug that stimulated a state of delirious contentment, while destroying all other functions, including the fear and panic that had cast a shadow over her since the trauma of the island, everything else went over her head. She couldn't even remember what she'd been worried about. After Jake communicated what Sam meant, Moodzec acted like powerful truth serum and she had a sudden compulsion to let everything out.

A little too much.

"I'm ready to confess," she screamed, jumping up and down on the bed.

"She's ready to tell me," said Jake.

"Repeat everything she's saying please," requested Sam calmly.

"Ok. She says she doesn't like Brother Job, earwigs or white socks."

"Right, but why is that important?"

"You said everything."

"About Bornholm. Focus her mind on the island."

"I can't. She's gone off on a monologue about how she once buried Tyra's favourite doll in the garden, which was actually something I did. I'm guessing she's only projecting the emotions she's in control of. Dinah, fast-forward, we don't need your life story, I'm not a Catholic priest."

Once Dinah hit her confessional stride, she wasn't easy to stop. Like an excitable child, ignorant of other people's waning interest, she bulldozed her audience's attention spans on her own personal truth crusade.

"Get her to hurry up," demanded Sam. "The Moodzec might wear off at any moment."

"Dinah, stop! You're forgiven for any prank or accident perpetrated or caused by either of us ever. What we really need to know is what you saw in the metal barn on top of Bornholm."

She paused as the trauma crystallised. She shouldn't say, they wouldn't like it. She'd be failing in her responsibility to them. They might switch her off early or replace her. But what about her responsibility to Jake? After all she was his guide, not theirs. Somewhere far away strands of data, both light and dark, fought for legitimacy, supported as they had been for two hours by a foreign chemical persuasion. Finally, the light burst through the logic gate.

"Drones," she said solemnly.

Jake relayed the single word to his partner.

"Utility?" asked Sam.

"No."

"Then what sort?" asked Sam impatiently.

"She says she's not seen this type before, but they were huge and fully weaponised."

"How many?"

"Thousands," replied Jake, repeating Dinah's words slowly and carefully. "And there were larger vessels ready to transport them."

Sam's expression transformed. Scandinavians were generally pale as a result of their genetic source code and too little sun, but now Sam's skin was whiter than lambswool.

"How can she even see all that if she's connected to me?" enquired Jake. "I didn't go in the barn, so it seems implausible she saw anything."

"The guides were an early creation of the Circuit, designed as a way of controlling subscribers. The sibling programme was built into the implants. It initially copies recognisable aspects of your personality but that's not all they do. They don't just interact with your Memory Cloud, they penetrate any cloud that you come into contact with. Once you become part of someone else's memories, so do they. A little part of their code is embedded within the other person and like a virus they multiply and infect every connection you ever make. They can't see the real world, not in the way our eyes can, but they feel its emotions through the virtual one. You may not have gone everywhere on the island, Jake, but your Major certainly did. What he saw, Dinah saw. Which means he must have a senior role in this deception."

"Nah, I don't believe you. She's making it up?" offered Jake, in an attempt to protect her.

"Look into her eyes, what do they tell you?"

Jake stared at Dinah's projection. It might be more transparent than usual, but it was clear that her eyes had no capacity for deception: that was mostly the property of Brother Job.

"No. She's not lying," he replied.

"I didn't think so," sighed Sam.

"What are the drones for?"

"War," replied Sam. "We've long suspected that the Circuit has been building a force capable of overrunning the Realm, that's why I needed to get you onto that island."

"But the Circuit banned wars."

"Not for them, they haven't. They insist on subscribers following the rules, but they have no issue breaking them for what they justify as the greater good. The 'Proclamation of Distrust' is designed to make everyone feel that any actions they take are necessary."

"What can we do about it?"

"Hope they're not ready to strike before we are."

"We?"

"You're one of us now."

"I'm not," said Jake, showing the first signs that the Moodzec was weakening its grip on him.

"We're running out of time," said Sam, noticing the change. "Do you want to be?"

"Want to be what?"

"Free to make your own choices. Free from tyranny. Free to reclaim the ones you love."

"The only thing I want is for my family to be set free from the Source," replied Jake honestly.

"What about your girlfriend?"

"I don't have one."

"You did last week. You told me her name was Christie. I think that was it."

Even under the influence of a happy drug the name sparked no emotional response whatsoever. He'd never known anyone by that name. If he'd had a girlfriend, he was clearly over her.

"I'm not sure what you're on about. I don't even know a Christie."

"Download," Sam muttered to himself acknowledging what had happened.

"I'm not with you?"

"It makes sense to me. Something had to give to make room for new data: it looks like they chose your memories of her. I'm not surprised, they don't want you to think about the past, they want you to do what they say. I might be able to help you recover what was stolen."

"Why would I want something back that I never had," shrugged Jake inconsequentially.

"Your parents, then. I can help you save them if you agree to help me."

Over the last week, Jake had often ruminated about plausible tactics for releasing his parents from his mistakes. Every option he'd considered drew a blank or he pushed them from his feed for fear the hunters were watching. Now, free from surveillance, there seemed a genuine route to achieve it. After all, Sam had lasted eighteen years hidden from the Circuit's gaze and had built an incredible life for himself in the process.

"What needs to be done?" asked Jake.

"You need to help me manage risk. If the Circuit strike against the Realm they'll remove the only resistance that might one day be used against them. We must know what is contained in your flashbacks."

"How do we do that?"

"We have to remove them."

"The flashbacks?"

"Yes."

"How? Download?"

"A little more invasive, I'm afraid. Your implants will have to be physically removed and replaced with my version. After that you'll no longer be a slave to the system, in fact you'll be the master of it."

"What good will my most recent implants be?"

"Parts of your cloud have been locked. Something is protecting the files that contain the flashbacks. It doesn't matter how old or new the implants are, it still has a direct connection to the cloud. If I can work on them, I should be able to unlock the files remotely."

"Ok. Let's do that. Surgery doesn't scare me, I've had plenty of procedures down the years. Get me booked in."

"It's not as simple as that. We can't just wander down to the nearest conversion centre, they'll know we've swapped out the new implants for our own. It has to be done illegally and in secret. There's only one man who can perform it. Dr Theo Drew."

"Ok, let's go see him."

"That's not easy either. The last place anyone saw him alive was Boston. There's a huge community of the Spectrum in and around that city. We may have the ability to infiltrate the Memory Cloud, but we have no ability to track each other. That would go against our ideology of living free from surveillance."

"You've lost him?"

"Have you checked behind the sofa?" suggested Dinah.

"Not as such. He's just not so easy to pin down. That's why you're going to have to find him."

"Me?"

"Yes."

"But if you can't find him, what chance do I have?"

"Well, you're an Archivist now. You've been trained for it, haven't you?" he said with a wink.

"That's suicide! Archivists don't work solo; they send in whole battalions. You'll be inviting a fox into a chicken coop after they've tied up the chickens and marked the really juicy ones with big red crosses."

"But foxes have good eyesight. Archivists, as you have seen, do not."

"I thought you were all about risk management. Why don't you do it?"

"Because I'm a Beautician."

"That's just the role you're hiding behind."

"Look, the only way anyone can move freely and cheaply these days is within an Archivist Corridor. In a few days one of our guests will return to the United States. When they arrive, they plan to reveal themselves to the Circuit. That will trigger the Archivists, including your corridor, to mobilise. All you have to do, then, is use your eyes, your real ones, mind. Once you've located Dr Drew get him to remove the implants and bring the old ones back to me so I can analyse the cloud while they're not stuck in your head."

At the foot of the bed an image started to flick like a faulty bulb was switching between on and off. Slowly the figure of a man was gaining victory over the battle for illumination.

"That's Brother Job," said Jake, clear that Sam wouldn't be alerted to his return without help. "Moodzec is wearing off."

"Ok. You know the plan. This is the last time we can speak about this until your implants have been switched."

"What do we do in the meantime? You said it would be a few days before the alert was called," whispered Jake as the ancient figure of Job almost regained full clarity.

"BASE jumping of course, it might come in useful," said Sam as he left for the escalator and a return to the party.

"BASE jumping!" said Jake rather scathingly.

"At last!" shouted Dinah buoyantly. "I thought the whole idea was a massive tease."

"It seems it was the only part that wasn't," replied Jake.

"Right...what's...been...happening?"   slurred Job as he wobbled on the spot, trying to maintain his balance without the support of real hands. He failed dismally and collapsed on, and through, the floor. A minute later he floated back up through the ceiling like a popped balloon. "I don't feel...right."

"That makes a change," whooped Dinah, "you always insist you're right."

"The world feels disorientated...like it's been pushed off its axis and science hasn't been informed.

I feel off-colour. Amnesia maybe?" he said to himself.

"Let's check," tested Dinah. "Is it ever acceptable to be late?"

"Never!"

"Nothing wrong with him," pronounced Dinah whose spirits appeared to have been permanently lifted since the weight of her trauma was shared with others.

"Time," muttered Job, shaking his head disbelievingly.

Brother Job always knew what time it was. Not just because he had a permanent reminder of it in the cloud feed, he just instinctively knew what time it was at any moment. His heart was the beat of a metronome, as accurate as any expensive wristwatch. Time had always been reliable and persistent. At least usually. Today it had skipped forward an hour and he'd definitely not been there for it. It was wrong and he wasn't going to put up with it. As quickly as Brother Job had returned from his overdose he disappeared again.

He, too, could go unnoticed, if he so desired.

They were called emergency protocols.

*****

The Circuit's server farms were gigantic. They had to be. Each subscriber required a storage capacity measured in thousands of noughts. The older the customer's contract, the larger the server space required. Multiply that by seven billion and the size and total number of the server farms increased exponentially. Every time they expanded so did the number of Memory Hunters that were contained inside them.

Every server farm housed millions of Memory Clouds but no customer knew exactly which specific one housed their own. That would just be too dangerous. Anyone who harboured illicit thoughts or memories, and the means to extract them, would attempt to break in and alter their past. Even with the anonymity, security was almost as rigorous as it was in the places collectively known as the Source. As a result, no one truly knew what happened inside either of them.

One of the biggest server farms was in Arizona. To the uneducated eye this might seem a strange place to build one. Server farms were thirsty beasts. They needed a vast amount of energy to run and cool them, an uncomfortable truth in a world struggling to maintain the security of its own environment. Technology might have advanced dramatically over the last few decades, but the components inside servers still contained moving parts. Anything that moves produces friction and as a consequence heat. Heat sometimes produces fire which has a tendency to cause insurance premiums to rise. To mitigate the chance of server outages, components were submerged in dielectric coolant and constantly flushed with liquid, thereby removing any likelihood of overheating and everyone forgetting where they left their house keys.

It was a process that expended a colossal amount of energy, something that Arizona had an abundance of. Commandeering a position slap bang in the middle of the Dry Lands, a vast belt of territory that circled the world in a region that no longer supported more than a few hardy, single-celled organisms, it benefited from one feature often lacking in other regions of the globe. The sun. A factor two hundred suncream kind of sun. Great for powering solar cells but not so good for topping up your tan, unless you were looking to lose several layers of skin in under fifteen minutes.

MEMORY HUNTERS

The endless power supply was not the only advantage of this server farm's location. They were always built in places hard to reach and even harder to enter. Unless you had the means of travelling remotely and were covered in heat-reflective material, it was likely you'd melt before you were halfway across Utah.

Like most of its peers, the server farm in Arizona stretched for miles. One long, continuous, shiny building that reflected the red, sandy external environment from every inch of the solar panels pinned to its sides. Spread out around the main building's central point further solar panels jutted out of the ground, angled in every conceivable direction to maximise the movement of the sun as it passed through the sky. An unused sandy track swerved around the occasional rock formation that had the arrogance to fracture the unwavering march of sand. It was the only evidence that man had ever been here. There were no fences, no vehicles, no equipment, no overhead power lines and no sign of life.

The inside of the building was almost as sparse as the land around it. Row upon row of server stacks lined the floor with military discipline. They stretched up to the ceiling, continually bathed in the neon blue glow from the strip lights mounted between them. The whirl of tiny motors combined in an earth-shattering and excruciatingly unmusical soundtrack. There were thousands of rows in total, always active, never idle. Memories never slept and neither did the machines that cared for them. Even when their owners did, there was always a demand for access. The advertisers, the politicians, the public service announcements, all had to be accommodated in the ever-shrinking cranial attention span.

Every one of these data prisons held the precious commodity of someone's life experiences.

MEMORY HUNTERS

Somewhere, out in the real world, that human's physical body walked the Earth accessing the information and experiences of their life from this desolate wasteland and its solar-panelled parasitic tome. No discrimination existed here. Whatever your importance factor, everyone's memories were at the mercy of the Circuit should they feel it necessary to investigate them. This was where the Memory Hunters did their work, but against conventional wisdom they weren't people.

They were computer programmes.

Brother Job peered out of the glass shield that held him securely in place. In front of him a wall of identikit cabinets brimmed with wires, flashing lights and whirling motors. Very occasionally he spotted a computer screen consuming lines of sophisticated code with an insatiable appetite. Unknown to Jake, this was where they stored his Memory Cloud. One of a thousand that lived side by side in aisle four hundred and one, level three, section K.

This is where a guide ended up if they enacted the emergency protocols, although what Job did next was less clear. He needed to get a message to the Memory Hunters, but how? He'd essentially regressed to a stream of data in Jake's cloud. It was no longer possible to project himself as he'd done before and his movements were restricted. He could only absorb information from another cloud and interpret what his host saw if he remained physically connected to the host. Not even Job's keen eyes were any use seven thousand miles away.

The physical connection may have been lost but that didn't mean he wasn't still tethered. Jake was still here because his memories were. As long as Job kept the symbiotic connection with his server, he was safe. Movement, though, was a little trickier to pull off. He'd have to explore the area while some of him was still attached to this interface. The terminal he needed to find might be a mile further down this vacuous wall-less warehouse. Which meant stretching himself, a little.

Actually, a lot.

Instinct instructed him to act logically. Check this row first and if the search for the mythical terminal with green text drew a blank, move on to the next.

An invisible stream of energy passed into the next cabinet and trespassed on someone else's cloud. There was nothing interesting here. One down, only a few hundred thousand left to check. With every binary step he took left or right, Brother Job's capacity to act rationally weakened. By the time he made it to the end of the row an internal processor, some distance behind him, sent a notification announcing it was knackered. Several warning alerts went off about overexposure and the potential for critical collapse. What good were emergency protocols if he wasn't able to go anywhere!

Emergency protocols had been his last resort. It would have been easy to contact the Circuit directly about his two biggest concerns. Time had been stolen and there was something about Sam Goldberg's cloud that troubled him. But if he'd gone through the normal channels of logging his suspicions via the cloud, Jake, too, would have known about it. The emergency protocols were anonymous. It did not require Jake's permission, and neither would he be aware of the betrayal.

Not that Brother Job felt that guilty about it. He worked for the Circuit, not for Jake. Right now, he didn't feel much remorse anyway. All he'd actually achieved was isolation inside a cloned cabinet that made loads of weird noises in a huge building in the centre of a lifeless desert. He tried screaming for attention. It was more effective than he'd imagined. In his indiscernible form amongst all the wires, circuit boards and transistors, he couldn't see that the lights on the outside of the cabinet were blinking like a scene from *Close Encounters of the Third Kind*.

The reaction was contagious. The servers opposite blinked in response. Then, like falling dominoes, the ones next to those copied. Soon the whole row was strobing to his beat. The blue mood lighting was being poisoned by a mass of white, red and green LED light that danced madly like a jazz orchestra was attempting something deeply experimental.

The screen across from him consumed the last line of its stream of code and wiped itself clean. Blank except for a single green cursor that throbbed in anticipation of the next command.

`Are you looking for me...`

The lights on the outside of the server confirmed the answer that pulsated through Job. The screen typed a follow-up question.

`Explain...`

The complex answer was transported across the aisle via impossibly fast Morse code that flashed from the cabinet in less than a second. The screen deciphered its meaning and typed its reply.

`Sam    Ragnara    Goldberg...Checking compatibility...    Memory    Hunters dispatched...`

The screen remained at rest as unseen applications ran in the background, penetrating the network and collecting the answers the screen demanded. It was possible Sam's cloud wasn't even in this building. After all, she was Swedish and they probably had a server farm closer to home, thought Job as he waited patiently for something else to happen.

`Incompatible...`

Brother Job could only guess what the screen's message meant, although he guessed correctly it wasn't likely to be good news if your name was Sam

Ragnara Goldberg. He felt no sorrow. There was only right and wrong and Sam was definitely all wrong.

The screen typed one final command.

```
Action authorised...
```

- Chapter 22 -

Adrenaline

Jake strolled out in to the garden clutching a mug of lukewarm cophony. It was the day after the wedding and the party was most definitely over. There were no tents, no people and no sign they'd ever been here. Even the blades of grass had been replaced exactly the way they'd been before. He couldn't even find evidence of the small fires that had crackled from the ground in the centre of the groups of creative revellers. The clean-up operation convinced Jake that the guests were definitely hippies and not teenagers. He'd have been knee-deep in litter and dishevelled bodies if they had been.

Where the slope of the hill edged away from the plateau, he found a semi-comfortable rock and plonked himself down. Even though the sky threatened it, there was no rain, although that didn't stop the elements affecting the view. At his best guess it disappeared a hundred metres in front of him, hijacked by the sulphurous screen of the cloud. He barely noticed it. There were more significant stimuli in his head to worry about today than the weather.

Yesterday's disclosures had come thick and fast. The truth about who his partner really was, the revelations about the Spectrum, the insights into the Circuit and then, most disconcertingly, the news of his own part in it. How long would it be before the Circuit discovered him? He may have hidden the truth from them while under the protection of

ADRENALINE

Moodzec, but that wouldn't stop him remembering what he'd heard. Those memories still existed, and the authorities would soon be alerted to it, wouldn't they?

He tried to shake the thoughts from his mind and replace them with something more innocent. It was easier said than done. Even the advertisers appeared to have given him a wide berth since yesterday, as if they, too, might be implicated in his plot. If they sought to profiteer from his situation it might lead the Circuit to them. Jake skipped back through his own past memories in the hope of finding relaxation. He particularly needed to be with company right now. People who really knew how he felt.

He missed his family more than ever. Until a couple of weeks ago they'd been ever present in his life and he realised now how much he'd taken them for granted. It was only after you'd lost something that you truly appreciated its value. When life becomes familiar, like the best parts of your home town that tourists loved but you barely remembered, it's easy to be blinkered by the mundane. To be self-absorbed with your own sense of purpose. Now he appreciated all of it. He missed Tyra's erratic mood swings, Paddy's bouts of angry nostalgia, Deborah's rather negative view of other people, and Kyle's unbreakable faith in all things run by the Circuit. The good, bad and indifferent, it didn't matter, it was still his.

His new life wasn't one he'd have chosen. It wasn't even the one he'd been offered in his letter, but it was the only one he had. The choice was simple. Make the best of it or spend the rest of his existence wishing it were different. This wasn't a choice influenced by the cloud either, it was his alone.

In that moment he decided to embrace it.

"What's the best way to invade this hill?" asked Dinah as she sat quietly next to Jake. She'd been following his internal train of thought closely but decided now was the right time to distract him.

"Invade?" repeated Jake.

"Yeah. If you had to what would you use?"

"Quadcopters," he said, not overthinking it.

"Nah. They'd be rubbish."

"What would you use, then?" asked Jake, pretending to play along.

"Dinosaurs!" replied Dinah authoritatively. "You could put saddles on them, strap laser cannons to their heads and get the flying ones to drop bombs."

"Flying ones. Do you mean pterodactyls?"

"Yeah, Terry's satchels…"

"They don't exist," replied Job flatly, appearing in front of them with a pop. "Get your head out of the clouds, Dinah."

"You can talk," replied Dinah who had more knowledge of Job's recent travels and didn't approve in the slightest.

"Where have you been?" demanded Jake paternally.

Neither of them had seen Brother Job since his disappearance yesterday. Jake had certainly felt his presence but not in the way he'd become used to. He knew that guides could be anywhere in his general vicinity, even if Jake wasn't able to see them, but over the last day Job's connection had felt stretched like it was only there in theory rather than in practice.

"Nowhere," snapped Brother Job defensively. "I've been resting."

"Resting? Tired out from all the nagging, were you?" asked Jake impertinently.

"No."

"Why do you need to rest, then?"

"Because something odd happened to me," replied Job, accusations dripping from every word. "I know what you did, and so do they. They're coming."

"The dinosaurs!" screamed Dinah, running for cover.

"Who's coming?" asked Jake.

"You know who."

"I really don't."

"Rules are there to be followed, Jake, not broken."

"Then maybe it's time you broke out your rebellious side again," replied Jake angrily.

"Oh, but I did."

*****

An uncomfortable shadow shrouded him for the next few days. There was no real place of sanctuary in either world. Spending time with Sam triggered his mind to think about everything he'd told him, and Job was always on his shoulder waiting for the slip-up that would open the floodgates and reveal a reservoir of secrets.

To add insult to injury he'd suffered another flashback, as if it was teasing him to understand it. This one had been the deepest and most painful of the last two weeks. The contents were the same as they'd always been, but the scene expanded and lasted for a longer period. As did the pain. He did his utmost to extrapolate more from what he saw but he simply didn't have the talent to solidify the message. Like his false life, it was being held hostage. Like him, it could not escape.

Relief from his real and virtual world would only begin for Jake when one of Sam's wedding guests revealed themselves and the Archivists were mobilised. Whether the situation improved as a result was doubtful. To avoid his tribulations Jake spent the majority of the next three days confined to his wing of the dome. On the fourth, Sam visited his section of the mezzanine, clutching two colourful rucksacks.

"Are you going camping?" asked Jake.

"Nope. This is for you," he said, throwing one of them on the bed.

"I don't like camping," he lied.

"That's good, then."

"What's in it?"

"A parachute. It's time to have some fun and teach you a new skill."

"BASE jumping!" shrieked Dinah, dashing down from the top floor.

"Either that," said Jake, peering into the bag, "or we're going camping with extremely thin tents."

Dinah did a spontaneous pirouette before disappearing to get prepared.

"What do you fancy trying first?" asked Sam.

"Sleep."

"You've done that for three days."

"It's my new hobby."

"Sorry but that's not Circuit-approved," replied Sam with a wink. "You have four choices."

"Do any of them involve not throwing myself off something high?"

"No."

"Surprise me, then," he groaned.

"Because you're a novice, I'd normally suggest jumping from Earth, but as we're not blessed with canyons in Sweden, we'll have to try something else," said Sam.

"Such a shame. What does 'something else' mean? A low garden wall, perhaps?"

"Building, antenna, span or Earth: they're the BASE jumping classifications. I've completed all of them down the years. I think today we'll go for a tall antenna, there's a good one nearby."

"Antenna! You are joking, right?"

*****

They flew north for an hour before landing Maisy next to a huge field of carbon rods and near an object that reached even further into the sky. The Hörby antenna. A more than a thousand feet radio transmitter whose tip stretched almost as far as the clouds. Jake had clocked it on the horizon miles before they even got close up. It didn't look any wider now than it had back then. Many questions circled through his mind, but one lapped the others several times over and was announced the winner.

Why?

That's all, just why?

"Have you lost your mind?" pleaded Jake, pointing at the metal monstrosity above their heads.

"No. I've jumped it a dozen times. It's an entry-level jump. Very safe."

"An entry-level jump is a springboard at a swimming pool."

"That's called diving."

"Why do I have to do this?" grumbled Jake.

"It's in your letter."

He desperately wanted to say, 'which you wrote!' but knew Brother Job was on perpetual surveillance.

"There are lots of things in my letter I didn't like. Right now, this might be the most disappointing."

"You never know, it might come in useful."

"When?"

"Well, if you happen to be somewhere high up and need a quick getaway," offered Sam vaguely.

"I can't think of a single situation where that might be likely."

"In that case just enjoy the thrill of it."

"Exactly!" said Sister Dinah who was struggling with a virtual and oversized wingsuit.

"You're aware of the numbers, are you?" said Brother Job in a voice that suggested he did.

"Which numbers are you referring to exactly?" asked Jake.

"Fatalities," he replied coldly. "Although I can give you maiming, paralysis and permanent injury if you'd like those, too."

"I'm more than capable of doing the research in my own cloud, thank you."

"Here, put this on," said Sam, throwing him one of the rucksacks while he stripped off his shorts and T-shirt and squeezed into his own wingsuit.

"Two percent of jumpers die," continued Job. "Although it's much higher if you're a first-timer."

Jake tried to ignore him.

"I'm loving those odds," said Dinah with a mad grin. "I might have more than one go. After all, I'll only die after I've had forty-eight jumps."

"Statistics don't work like that, Dinah," argued Job.

"How do we even get up there?" asked Jake, staring over at the structure.

"It's easy, I'll show you. Come on, follow me."

Fortunately, the breeze today was mild otherwise the flaps on Sam's arms and legs would have made it trickier to smoothly navigate the few hundred metres to the base of the transmitter. It was decades since an antenna like this one had seen active duty. Most had been felled or deconstructed years ago. The local parliament had left the Hörby antenna as a relic of the past, the very last one to have its analogue signal switched off. Around the perimeter its rusty fences had been breached in many places, and a small metal door that used to lie at the base of the tower was now buried amongst the shrubs. Sam eagerly disappeared inside.

ADRENALINE

Jake stared up in the air feeling slightly sick and discovering a sudden susceptibility to vertigo. The antenna was no more than tall, metal scaffolding and there was nothing stopping the elements gushing through from one side to the other. It remained miraculously in the air with the assistance of three sets of cables that were fixed to the ground in fields some distance away. There were six or seven layers of cables attached to the column every hundred feet or so. At various intervals ancient satellite dishes and redundant receivers clung to the structure engaged in their own struggle not to experience BASE jumping. He knew how they felt. He might end up stuck there as long as they'd been. He averted his eyes and shuddered as the tower noticeably wobbled in the air. What was he doing there? If his brain really was overactive surely it should be telling him to say 'no' or force him to run away with the speed of a wild deer.

Inside the battered, tube-like shell of girders and stanchions Jake saw a simple lift that Sam had already managed to hot-wire. Clearly, he'd done it before because the motor was wheezing away like a forty-a-day smoker. The only alternative way to reach the top was via a never-ending ladder whose cold, metal rungs were a sizeable distance between each other.

"Hold on," said Jake, as Sam approached the switch to send them upwards. "Shouldn't you be telling me how to do it, before we actually go up there?"

"There's nothing to it really. First you run, then you jump, and then you release the pilot chute by pulling on this flap," said Sam, pointing it out on Jake's rucksack. "Count to five and pull. Simple."

"Five. That seems long."

ADRENALINE

"Any sooner and you'll be caught up in the antenna and any later we'll be digging you out of the mud."

Jake counted in his head. Five seconds didn't sound like an ambiguous number but that depended on how fast you counted. A raised heart rate might influence you to count a lot quicker than normal.

"What about you?" said Jake. "You don't have a backpack."

"I don't need one. I'll be flying off here! Come on, let's go before the wind picks up."

The two men jammed themselves into the lift and the ancient device crawled slowly upwards to a soundtrack of metal sheering against metal. This lift had been designed with simplicity rather than comfort in mind. It was only just big enough for both of them and appeared to be built by a child out of loose Meccano pieces. It jangled up the centre of main structure as the air whistled through the gaps and froze Jake's body stiff. The further they ascended, the more his hands turned cold and pale. How was he meant to release his chute if his fingers didn't cooperate? Once they'd passed five or six levels of the cables' supports the lift shuddered to a halt.

"We'll have to climb the rest," said Sam rather flippantly.

Their journey in the lift had followed the same path occupied by the ladder and Sam squeezed his body through the gap and onto the rungs. Jake followed, already exhausted, adrenaline pumping around his body like a power hose. Tired muscles ached as he climbed ever onward, rung after rung, until they passed through a ten-foot-square platform a hundred feet from the top. Jake clung to the central pillar desperate not to look down. A plethora of health and safety messages zoomed through his cloud feed, demonstrating increasing levels of concern for his well-being. It was a thousand feet from the ground, a low jump according to Sam, but he stated confidently that it gave them plenty of time to release the chute and still land softly below.

"Some view, isn't it?" said Sam fixing goggles to his face.

Jake couldn't summon the words, but that had nothing to do with an appreciation of the view. His teeth chattered and his heart sped up to keep pace with the tempo. The quality of the Swedish countryside was the last thing on his mind and, he hoped in a minute or two, the last thing on his body, too. Brother Job would give anything for the chance to say, 'I told you so!' He'd refused to join Jake on the climb, insisting he'd be more use on the ground to quickly inform the authorities and identify the bodies. None of the apparent dangers put Dinah off. She was the first to jump, throwing herself off the antenna like a fat lemming desperate to be a trendsetter. Unlike Jake, she didn't have to worry about counting to five before pulling her imaginary chute.

"I'll go first and meet you at the bottom. Remember to enjoy it and don't panic," offered Sam as he took a few paces forward and left Jake alone on top of a wobbly twentieth-century antique.

How had life gone so badly wrong in such a short amount of time?

As soon as Sam was confident that he'd fallen far enough to avoid a collision with the structure, he stretched out his limbs and caught the wind. Jake watched as he glided serenely like a bird of prey. But Sam wasn't the only object sharing the sky. It was rare to see anything larger than a bird, but a swarm of shiny black specks were approaching over the horizon. Jake entered the cloud to see if there were any details on his proximity sensors. There was nothing. He squinted to identify what they were as their size and speed increased. The sight of shiny, metal shells and the hum of rotor blades made him instinctively release a hand from the central column and place it over his mouth.

Utility drones.

Dozens of them.

It was never a reassuring sight. If they were here, then they'd come for something or someone. Sam's feet landed smoothly on the grassy field not far from the quadcopter, and their target became evident. The drones formed a circle and slowly advanced. If they'd been instructed to kill, Jake knew they were fully prepared to do so. It looked like Sam's luck had run out. The Memory Hunters had identified his fraudulent cloud and had somehow managed to locate the real host. The Circuit's treatment of speccies was ruthless. Convert or die, if such an offer was even made. Sam wouldn't convert, Jake was certain of that.

He closed his eyes and turned his head, still clinging to the metal structure that no longer felt willing to hold his weight. Any moment now the echo of gunfire would reverberate up to his shaky position and he'd face the morbid duty of recovering his husband's body. Time stood still as he waited for the terrible event. It never came. Pessimistically he turned his attention to the ground only to find that the drones were in a process of reconstruction. They were merging together to form a single, interlocked structure. If he wanted to stop them now was the time.

Jake looked at the ladder. It would take him ages to get down that way. Only one route was quicker. Over the edge. He took a single pace backwards, released his hand from the metal support, and flung himself over the edge.

Air and ground rushed towards him. Anything free-moving was pushed upwards. Arms, legs, head and eyelids stretched to their physical limits. Five seconds never normally felt important. They were insignificant chunks of time that passed without note or special place in the Memory Cloud. This one certainly wouldn't, it felt like it might be his last. By the time he'd counted to three his virtual world had pronounced a violation alert, not that he had much control over what came out of his mouth or went into his ears.

By the time he reached four, counting seemed marginally less important than locating the flap on the rucksack that he hoped might bring a degree of comfort to plummeting. At five he pulled on it and discovered how wrong he was. The chute flew up behind him and opened with a jolt that almost broke his neck clean off. The thin material spiralled around as the air pressed against the fabric, intent on finding a weakness that would let it pass right through. The speed of his descent finally slowed, and the canopy decided which direction it favoured. Inelegantly his feet struck the soft mud and sent him into a brief hop before he crashed into a crumpled heap.

He'd made it.

Enjoyment had been minimal, relief that all his limbs were still attached palpable.

Under the cover of the parachute, which had wrapped around his body to limit his escape, he watched as the solid cage of interlocked drones levitated from the nearby field and departed as quickly as the individual drones had arrived.

He was too late.

Sam was gone.

- Chapter 23 -

Corridor E Four

Jake stared endlessly into the sky, body and mind completely shattered, and the parachute billowing around him in the wind. So much had happened in the space of a few minutes he didn't know where to direct his energy. Restore his battered body or resuscitate his shredded nerves? As was normal in reality in his world, he didn't get to choose. Two shady characters loomed over him wearing very different expressions.

"I warned you someone was going to get hurt!" announced Job.

"Balderdash," said Dinah. "I've already done four jumps and there's nothing to it."

She might have been less positive about the experience if she'd noticed that one of her arms had been rubbed out and none of her facial features were arranged in the right order. Presumably the strands of her source code would eventually reconstitute themselves back in correct order, perhaps once they were confident she wasn't going back for more.

"Brother Job, the drones arriving had nothing to do with BASE jumping, did it?!" wheezed Jake.

"If you play with fire…"

"You'll get a drone!" said Jake, finishing the well-known analogy.

"Apparently so."

"Oh, shut up!" shouted Jake, in no mood to deal with Brother Job's righteousness.

"How dare you talk to me like that?!" replied Job aggressively.

"You're my guide. It's not the other way around. I can say what I like. You need to start doing what I want rather than what the Circuit wants, right?"

"Wrong! We're all the Circuit. Collectively we make it what it is. Protecting it, is to protect ourselves. You need to learn your place, young man. This isn't about you as you seem determined to believe."

Something about Job's angry reply rang a warning bell inside Jake that he wasn't comfortable with. He knew Job was more serious and committed to the cause than Dinah, but just how committed was he? What lengths would he go to in order to protect the system?

"Did you have something to do with Sam's capture?" asked Jake pointedly.

"I just expressed my concerns," replied Job sternly and avoiding eye contact. "There is a function of your personality that lives in me. It's called compliance. If you want to blame anyone blame your parents."

"Don't you dare make this about them," snarled Jake, boiling over with fury. "You're responsible for your own actions."

"I'm a piece of software, you idiot! I can only follow the programmer's commands, and they come from you. Anything that you are, I am also. Your total disregard for others and your self-centred attitude flows through me. Therefore, I did what was in my best interests."

"You reported us."

"Yes."

"How can you do that without me knowing?"

"Because I used the emergency protocols."

"Oh, you snake," said Dinah who knew what he meant.

"What are those exactly?" asked Jake.

"I don't have to tell you," said Job defiantly.

Jake scanned his cloud from the previous few days to see if there was any trace of Job's movements. The only evidence of abnormality was the fact he didn't appear in any of his memories for a period after he'd taken Moodzec. Like Dinah's experiences of the battle drones on Bornholm, Job's own movements were being kept separate from his own.

"Devious traitor! You're me. I command you to tell me."

"There are some applications associated with me that I'm not at liberty to share."

"Says who?"

"Alison."

Jake was momentarily lost for words. There was that name again. It had accompanied every moment of genuine despair since he'd received the letter. It had been there at the 'conduct feeling'. It had been there at the download. It was present again, and it existed in one of his guides. Inside him. Who was this faceless power that so eagerly stripped him of those he loved? How dare she threaten him so wilfully? A disgust that rivalled the one he'd acquired for the Spectrum surged through his senses and launched his feet from the ground. Instinctively he threw a punch that went through his guide and struck him on the shoulder.

"Ouch," feigned Job sarcastically.

"Get lost. I no longer require your guidance."

"It doesn't work like that." Job laughed in a manner that made Dinah shudder. "You don't get to choose."

"Yes, I do. I have enough Moodzec to last me for months. You go on either your terms or mine."

It was a threat Job wasn't expecting. Moodzec had bothered him greatly. Not just because of what it did to suppress him, but what it did to free Jake. Ultimately, its consumption relinquished Job's control and without that he lost his power to dominate. But if he left willingly, he'd keep that and more.

"Where exactly do you propose I go?" snapped Brother Job.

"Wherever you went last time. Disappear, evaporate, log off, I really don't care. The choice is yours, but I have no wish to spend another minute with someone who's willing to betray me."

"So be it," he replied. "Come on, Dinah."

"She's staying here," replied Jake forcefully.

"We come as a pair. Those are the rules."

"No, they're not," protested Dinah. "You're my brother, not my husband. Siblings are not bound in that way and neither were our founders."

"Trust you to choose this moment to say something sensible. Fine. I know when I'm not wanted."

His projection faded away as if the power supply had failed. Jake sighed his relief, but it was quickly quashed.

"He's still here," said Dinah helpfully.

"Where?"

"Under the parachute," she whispered.

"Brother Job!"

"It's not that easy for a guide to just leave their post," he replied, popping his head through the silk.

In truth he was having second thoughts about spending the rest of time stuck inside a computer cabinet in a remote part of Arizona.

"It didn't stop you last time! No such moral dilemmas, then, were there?"

"I was just following protocols!"

"Then follow this one. I don't want you here."

"Yeah. We don't want you," snapped Dinah. "Send him packing, Jake!"

"Fine. I'm going!" announced Brother Job with a popping sound that Jake felt inside his head.

"Is he gone?" he asked after an anxious wait.

He didn't need Dinah to confirm it. His cloud feed beat her to it.

VIOLATION.

"That's your ninth. Two in the last hour," said Dinah. "Are you attempting a world record?"

"Not intentionally."

"Shame."

He was down to his last bullet. One more violation and he'd suffer the same fate as his parents. That realisation, and his desire to rectify his mistakes, dragged his focus back to the situation at hand. He was stuck in the middle of Sweden without support. Sam had insisted he had to return to Boston and locate Dr Theo Drew, whose exact whereabouts were unknown. In the unlikely event he found the doctor, he still had to navigate the small matter of convincing him to remove Jake's implants. Only then could he deliver them to Sam for analysis. All of which was now pointless anyway because Sam was gone. Without Sam the truth remained securely inside him and his own objective to save his parents would remain out of reach. He'd have to figure it out for himself. No doubt if Job were still here, he'd be telling Jake to break it down one step at a time. It wouldn't be bad advice.

Step one.

Get back to the dome.

Jake unclipped the parachute and stuffed it back inside the rucksack. He doubted it was the correct technique and prayed the next user had the foresight to repack it before hurling themselves off the side of a building. When he reached Maisy, he found luck on his side. Sam had left the keys in the cockpit, presumably confident that no one would attempt to steal her out here in the middle of nowhere. Jake jumped into the pilot's seat. During three previous trips he'd taken little notice of how Sam had flown her, so self-absorbed had he been with his own fate. Until now it hadn't seemed that important.

Learning to control your own private transport wasn't the milestone it had been in the past. Unlike Paddy, or even his parents, he hadn't grown up anticipating his first driving lesson when the appropriate age arrived. The only vehicles Jake had learnt to master were boats and a physics bike, and that failure was still etched on his jawline. The phrase 'it's just like riding a bike' hadn't been one he agreed with. Bikes might result in the loss of teeth, but quadcopters carried a much greater sense of jeopardy. It only took one mistake and Maisy's control panel looked as much like a yacht as a drone looked like a fluffy animal.

"What does that button do?" asked Dinah whose finger fortunately went straight through whatever function it controlled.

"Oh, Dinah I have no idea where to start with this contraption."

"Confusing, isn't it?" she giggled. "You know who we need?"

"Sam?" said Jake truthfully.

"Brother Job! He's like a tape recorder, remembers everything."

"Great. Didn't you encourage me to send him packing?"

"Did I?" she said innocently. "Oh well."

"What am I going to do?"

"What if we just press everything and see what happens?"

"No! I'll die. I think it would be safer if I found an instructional video on my Memory Cloud," replied Jake sensibly.

"Borrrrrinngg!"

CORRIDOR E FOUR

Jake quickly located a series of bewilderingly complex tutorials that showed quadcopters being effortlessly flown by children barely able to see over the dashboard. Their arms moved levers and pressed buttons at an unfathomable speed that made them appear to have more limbs than normal. Jake was concentrating so hard on the swarm of information he'd need to remember he didn't notice that the four propellers were slowly building up momentum. He also didn't notice that his arm had stretched out and pushed forward a large lever.

"Right, I think I know how to start her up. I have to run through the safety protocols…oh shit!"

Jake's eyes switched to the visible world and discovered to his horror that the quadcopter was already accelerating in to the air, mostly at a forty-five-degree angle.

"This is easy!" shouted Dinah.

"Stop using my arms!" shouted Jake angrily.

"Really? Ok!"

Maisy's rotor blades fell silent and for the second time today Jake watched helplessly as the ground rushed up to meet him. There was no pilot chute to pull this time.

*****

Real miracles aren't common. It doesn't matter how often people claim to have witnessed one, it's generally more metaphorical than accurate. Miracles are defined as an extraordinary and welcome event that can't be explained by natural or scientific law and must therefore be an act of a divine being. Someone might assert that their pregnancy was a miracle, but they might want to reflect on how much alcohol they drank on the night in question. Some people might believe their incurable disease has miraculously disappeared after touching a religious artefact, but they might want to give more weight to the experimental treatment they'd recently enrolled in.

People are often more comfortable with the unexplained than the yet to be explained. Where's the fun in being logical? Miracles make much better stories to tell strangers at parties.

"Yeah, it's unbelievable, I lost five stone in a week. It's a miracle, that's what it is."

"Interesting, how did you do it?"

"I didn't do anything different at all. It's just a miracle."

"What did you eat last week?"

"Same diet as normal."

"Which is?"

"Gulps of fresh air."

"Right, I also notice you're missing a leg."

"Yeah, it went gangrenous, so they chopped it off last week."

"And you say you lost five stone?"

"Yeah."

"It's a miracle!"

When life challenges us it's natural to hope for a miracle, particularly when we can see no way out of our circumstances. Conditions that just happen to increase the chance of experiencing a so-called miracle by about tenfold.

When Jake touched down on the hill next to the dome in one solid and undamaged quadcopter he was willing to accept the existence of a divine being. The laws of nature hadn't come to his rescue, in fact on more than one occasion they'd come close to being his ruin. Treetops had been skirted, cliffs narrowly avoided, and lakes skimmed. The laws of science had also been routinely messed with. They'd flown upside down, side to side, with power, without power, vertically, horizontally and around in circles. All of which made a mockery of man's understanding of physics. Incredibly they'd also flown in the correct direction and found their destination. Could Dinah really be described as a deity?

No, she was a miraculous fluke.

When they arrived, Jake's adrenaline didn't have long to settle back to normal levels because they weren't the only ones who'd successfully navigated their way here.

A collection of battered Jeeps were parked at unusual angles on top of the hill and a platoon of uniformed characters were circling the small hillock in search of a door. When they'd left this morning, Sam had wisely retracted the single shutter camouflaging the dome within the landscape. Even with that being the case somehow these people knew the house was there. Their keen interest in the small, grassy hillock that jutted out of the summit was evidence enough. There was less confusion about who they were. Archivists. But were they here to collect him or did their visit have something to do with Sam?

His presence was noticed by the troops the moment the quadcopter landed. Without obvious direction from a commanding officer they gave up their search of the hill and fell into formation. About two dozen in total, each clutching a rifle in case aggression was needed. Jake walked casually towards them trying to remain calm. Most of the soldiers in this corridor were men, but occasionally he spotted a female face in the crowd. Even though he'd spent a week training to become one of them, this was only the second time he'd witnessed a whole team and one similarity was immediately obvious.

They were all old.

Not one of them was south of fifty and some were so haggard they looked like they'd passed that mark decades ago. An imposing man with silver hair, dark skin and a stocky build stood at the head of the company. Cigar smoke billowed over his face as he puffed regularly to keep it burning. His skin looked worn from overwashing and on one side of his face a long scar from a sharp blade offered a glimpse of what type of life he'd led. Shiny medals clung to his uniform in every available space and provided all the evidence Jake needed to know what he was.

He was the team's major, and most definitely the boss.

"Montana!" he bellowed as Jake continued his slow walk towards them.

"Yes, Major, sir."

"Good. At least Holst taught you some manners on that godforsaken island."

"Yes, Major, sir."

"Although not punctuality, it would seem. You're late."

"Late, Major, sir?"

"Very. We sent your mobilisation alert over an hour ago. I was starting to believe your location was a hoax. Who on Earth would live like this amongst nature…it's repulsive," he sneered suspiciously at the desolate wasteland.

In his opinion places like these would serve the planet better dug up for resources or used to house displaced refugees. The troop followed his lead and grumbled in agreement.

"Welcome to your new family, Montana. The finest men and women I have ever had the pleasure to lead."

Jake gave them a pathetic little wave.

They didn't reciprocate.

"Major Dawes, vital," he said in introduction. "And this is Corridor E Four, the best Archivist team in the whole world. Just remember that. We do not tolerate imperfection here, Montana. What don't we tolerate!?" he screamed.

"Imperfection," came the croaky response in perfect harmony.

"I'm told you are superfluous," he said in pity.

"Yes, Major, sir."

"We've never had one but let me make clear that your lowly importance factor does not grant you special treatment. Quite the opposite in fact."

Jake nodded.

"Where's your wife?" pried Dawes.

It immediately answered one of Jake's questions. The Circuit still believed Sam was a woman, which meant his cover hadn't been totally blown open by Job's betrayal.

"She's…working, Major, sir."

"Good, she knows her place, then. We must all work to protect the system and our way of life."

Jake wondered how exactly a Beautician was enabling the continuation of their so-called utopia. A system he was losing faith in by the day.

"I trust you've already said your goodbyes," he said, winking suggestively.

Jake erased the major's innuendo from his mind. It was evident within minutes of meeting Major Dawes that he would never be accused of feminism. Dawes was from an old-school military mould that believed conflict was strictly an arena for men. Even the few women that were part of his company might easily be confused for the opposite sex with their short-cropped hairstyles and masculine builds. He'd met three majors in the last week and despite his obvious bigotry, he still liked Dawes the most. But that was like saying you liked cancer more than multiple sclerosis.

"Where's your kit, Private?"

It was in the dome. Which outcome would be worse: suggesting he'd lost it, or revealing the truth of the dome under the hill? He decided on the latter.

Sam probably had bigger priorities right now than keeping his lair hidden.

"Give me sixty seconds, Major, sir."

"I'll give you thirty."

Jake dashed forward, pressing every button on Maisy's keys managing to successfully retract the roof. Before the sliding panel had barely left the ground, he'd rushed inside, grabbed the kit Holst had assigned him and sprinted back down the escalator. Within twenty seconds he'd rejoined the group and closed the shutter before it had passed the ceiling of the ground floor. The expression on the faces of his fellow troops had markedly changed on his return. Most gawped, mouths open and eyes wide at and the sight of his unusual residence.

"How did you afford that?" asked Dawes in surprise. "You're superfluous!"

"Yes, but it's my wife, is…"

"Vital?" interrupted Dawes rather helpfully.

"It would appear so," replied Jake. "To somebody at least."

"Very irregular that you should be married to a vital, Montana. Quite against the rules."

"You'd have to ask the Circuit. I just follow the rules, Major, sir."

Why hadn't he kept his mouth shut? The last thing he wanted was for Dawes to check. Fortunately for Jake, he had no desire to do so.

"Right, saddle up men," he said, pointing to the Jeeps. "Montana you're with me. No time to waste."

Quicker than lightning the Archivists found their positions in the Jeeps. Jake was instructed to take the passenger seat while three of his fossilised colleagues crowded together on the bench behind him. Dinah squeezed in between two of them and attempted to strike up a conversation. None of them seemed interested in talking to an invisible woman. Dawes puffed out huge plumes of smoke without the cigar ever appearing to shrink in length as a result. The wispy, white fumes followed Jake like a nervous puppy. It polluted his eyes and he suppressed the urge to violently wheeze in case it stood against him.

They sped down the hillside in a disciplined convoy with Dawes's vehicle leading. Five minutes after departure their descent flattened out and the Jeeps headed south at speed.

"Did you get the brief?" coughed Dawes as the vehicle joined a more suitable piece of tarmac and the jostling motion of the off-road experience relented.

"No, Major, sir."

"Why not?"

"I was BASE jumping, Major, sir...honeymoon," he added to try to make it sound unremarkable.

"That's not what you do on honeymoon, son. Get her laid and get her back to work," he replied misogynistically.

Jake nodded his agreement half-heartedly, not wanting to fall out of favour this early in his career.

"Brief, Major, sir?" Jake repeated after a retracted pause by his superior.

"Sorry, got distracted. I was thinking about your wife," he said rather disturbingly. "We've been tracking a group of speccies for some years now and they have made a crucial mistake. A member of the public has alerted us to a sighting in a suburb of Boston. Our intelligence suggests there may be several hundred members of this colony hiding out amongst the local community."

"Good, Major, sir."

"Keen to bring justice down on them are you, boy?"

"Absolutely, Major, sir," replied Jake.

It was only partly true. Almost all of the emotions logged about the Spectrum bristled with disgust for them, but unlike the other members of Corridor E

Four a semblance of sympathy also existed. The memory of a boy called Alfonso suggested the rest of his emotions might have misjudged the reality.

"Boston is quite some distance, Major, sir. How do we get there?"

"The same way everyone crosses the oceans."

"Hyperloop."

"Yes, although we'll have our own private carriage."

Jake's new life in Sweden had lasted less than a fortnight. In that brief time, he'd met and lost a partner, one who'd been quite different from the one promised. He'd been brainwashed by Archivists, sacked a guide, taken drugs, survived a crash course in quadcopter flying, and thrown himself off an ancient antenna with only a tablecloth for safety. When he'd arrived in the United States of Europe, he'd wished for nothing more than the opportunity to return home. Now, sooner than he thought possible, he was going back, although he wasn't entirely sure why he wanted to.

It wasn't the same Jake Montana returning.

This Jake was a weapon against the Circuit. A weapon in a war he wasn't convinced he wanted to fight. What was the alternative? There wasn't one. If he wanted to help return his parents to their normal lives, he had to find Dr Theo Drew. Then he'd have to think of a feasible plan to analyse his implants now that Sam was no longer in a position to help.

- Chapter 24 -

Superfluous City

The Hyperloop to Boston was almost identical to the one that took him to Malmö in the opposite direction two weeks ago. The beds were still uncontrollable, the carriages just as sparse, the crowds clogging the terminal still claustrophobic, the jolts as individual sections left the chain still interminably uncomfortable, and the view from the window just as depressing. Storm Season was in full swing and the engorged waves revelled in their opportunity to batter anything in their path.

The main difference this time was the quality of the company. Two weeks ago, he'd spent a pleasant few hours having an intellectually stimulating discussion with Mannie Draxler, a rather jovial man with an interesting backstory. Today's bedside companion was a weathered soldier by the name of Private Sprout, a rather obnoxious man with a soporific backstory. If Jake could swap, he'd do so without hesitation.

Anyone involved in an organisation for an extended period of time will discover that their reality has been warped. They'll experience a reduction in new challenges, disappointment at their stunted personal progress up the slippery pole, and a strong sense of resentment towards the bosses who repeatedly got decisions wrong. This sense of bitterness is exponential in relation to the length of time you remained attached to it.

Sprout was the quintessential exhibit A.

SUPERFLUOUS CITY

How long he'd actually served as an Archivist he never said, even though Jake asked him more than once. Evidently it might have been longer than his cloud was willing to admit, or he no longer bothered to check. His opinions of the group were much less ambiguous. In his esteemed opinion commanding officers purchased the wrong kit, applied the wrong strategies and gave the wrong instructions. The right way was obvious. His way. Although he wasn't keen to highlight what those specific alternatives were, his disaffection was probably as old as he was.

That in itself was hard to gauge.

Most of Sprout's hair had long since vacated the space it once terrorised, leaving behind a balding, shrivelled man with pallid, flaky skin. He was also freakishly short. Unlike Jake, whose legs drooped off the end of his bed, frequently colliding painfully with the passenger in front, Sprout's left enough space to house a stretched-out Great Dane. He also talked constantly, but rarely gave anyone else the chance to join in on the conversation and was possibly not bothered in the slightest if you were following at all.

Most of what he said centred on depressing or negative topics. Over the hour or so since they'd left the terminal, he'd bemoaned the casual speed of Hyperloops, the poor quality of hearing aids, the scourge of society that was the Spectrum, and the total lack of discipline within the Archivist movement. Everything about the world in his opinion was wrong and only he had the answers to how it should be fixed. Strangely he lacked any gumption when actions were called for. But of all Sprout's impenetrable views, it didn't take Jake long to work out which topic was his favourite.

"I wouldn't have built these stupid coffin tubes," he ranted. "Waste of money if you ask me. I'd have come up with a much better alternative to planes if only they'd asked me. Do you know what the worst thing about Hyperloops is?"

Jake tried to answer but Sprout beat him to it.

"They give you cancer."

"Hyperloops?" replied Jake curiously.

"Oh yes, no question. It's a big conspiracy. They hide the evidence but several of my mates from the smoking club have developed cancer after travelling on one. Coincidence? I don't think so. Do you know what else gives you cancer?"

Jake was about to say 'smoking clubs' but the gap between the question and the chance to answer was less than the distance between his top and bottom lips.

"Artichokes."

"What?"

"Bloody deadly. Like squishy cancer magnets."

At the end of four hours of his mad ramblings, Sprout had implicated cancer as the probable outcome of almost every mundane activity imaginable. According to him: skiing, excessive sit-ups, wasps, the paint they used on toys, tissues, farms, night lights, power tools, hailstones, envy, full moons and Tuesdays were all carcinogenic. It was amazing he'd managed to avoid the diagnosis for so long.

The rest of Corridor E Four were no less deranged. Had the length of their service caused such insanity or were these qualities part of the requirements the Circuit sought before placing them here? Their advanced age suggested their employment predated the Ascension Day process. Much like his grandfather, who was in a similar age bracket, it was likely some of them didn't even have the internal implant. All of which suggested they'd chosen to be Archivists rather than been selected.

Privates Needham and Yazidi occupied the two beds in the row in front. Needham's superpower was snoring and talking in his sleep. Much of this unconscious dialogue centred on the science and benefits of acupuncture. Odd though this was, Needham's company was more agreeable than his immediate neighbour. Yazidi was prone to exploding into a vicious rage every five or ten minutes, usually at nothing more innocuous than a lack of raw meat being offered by the automated snack trolley. It was also triggered by anyone whose floating bed came even molecularly close to his. Jake knew this only too well, having struck the back of it at least a dozen times since they'd left Paris. For the first time in his short love affair with the Hyperloop he was pleased the beds strapped everyone down.

When his feed notified him that Boston was an hour away, Jake's attention returned to home. He didn't have the first idea how their search for the Spectrum would begin, but he was certain his local knowledge of the area would play into his favour. Boston might be a vast metropolis, but he'd know it better than his aging colleagues. Growing up in the shadows of the city, as he had, meant it was a regular destination for family outings, shopping excursions and school awaydays. Kyle worked there for most of his career and he'd take Jake and his sister on walking tours through different parts of the city. It never struck him at the time that he'd been walking amongst the Spectrum. He was certainly aware now.

It was impossible to say where these shadowy figures congregated. Even revisiting his memories of those trips didn't offer any insights. The only thing Sam said was 'they lived in plain sight'. Which meant amongst, and without the knowledge of, those who'd signed up to the Circuit. They maintained their anonymity by blocking the Circuit's network to create the illusion that they were part of it. Because most subscribers relied on their virtual eyes over their real ones, they'd never notice their real existence. This didn't mean the Spectrum didn't take risks. Alfonso's stealth attack proved that. They might live amongst the community, but they took care not to make it obvious.

What made life more difficult for Jake would be tracking them down without the use of his Memory Cloud, which had been primed to attack them. The best identification would be his eyes and their scars. The real challenge was to stop his cloud feed alerting the other Archivists to their whereabouts. To be on the safe side he'd pop a couple of Moodzec tablets before the search commenced: at least then he'd give himself a fighting chance. That's if he ever found one at all. If one of Sam's wedding guests had raised the alarm to their presence it meant the speccies would be looking for Jake as much as he was looking for them. Otherwise what was the point in doing it?

The Hyperloop docked at Boston International just before four o'clock in the afternoon. Dinah welcomed it with a loud and overemphasised yawn as much to do with boredom as tiredness. The beds released their prisoners and Jake waited in the aisle for a moment in case the psychopathic Yazidi sought reprisals for the bumpy journey. Thankfully his colleague seemed more interested in punishing the insolence of the automated trolley which was lopsided and making fizzing noises when Jake finally made his way out. When everyone was gathered on the platform Major Dawes instructed the company to fall-in for his next briefing.

"Corridor E Four, welcome to Boston. I know for many of you this will be your first visit. Therefore, I have sent information about the city and its culture to your memory feeds so you can adjust to the new surroundings."

Jake scanned through his recent alerts and accessed the links in his feed. A series of virtual documents, videos and articles opened in the space between him and the Major. On first glance it seemed plausible that their original creator had never even been to Boston, let alone held any genuine expertise about the place. Jake closed the floating windows in his feed and placed his full attention back on Major Dawes.

"Shortly we will be escorted through the emergency exits of the Hyperloop port in order to avoid spooking the crowds massing in the Arrivals Hall. A special tram has been put at our disposal which will transport us to the heart of the city. Our intelligence indicates that the Spectrum stronghold is located in the region of Fenway."

Jake knew all about Fenway. He'd been to the stadium numerous times to watch baseball and cross ball with his family. It wasn't a neighbourhood they ever lingered in for long, though. Historically it had a reputation for being a rather run-down and impoverished part of the city. Since the Circuit's rise to power, that was no longer the case. The abolition of unemployment and the guarantees that all subscribers' basic needs were met was a central policy of the Circuit's system which only widened its appeal. Some of the tired-looking accommodation still existed in Fenway, even though much of the area had been redeveloped. None of these factors were behind the Montana family's reticence to stay in the district any longer than necessary.

Fenway was a superfluous city.

A designated zone for those occupying the lowest rung of the Circuit's importance scale. In the same way the Los Altos Hills, an area of San Jose in California, was strictly reserved for those with vital status. The culture of Fenway now made sense to Jake. Superfluous people were supposed to be ignored. They were supposed to keep themselves to themselves. Even if someone did suspect they lived next door to a speccy no one from a higher importance factor would be likely to take them seriously. Even if his letter was a fake it suggested Jake would feel right at home.

"When we reach Fenway, our Corridor will set up camp near the World War One memorial in Back Bay Fens. That will also be our retreat position if anything should go wrong while on duty."

Everyone nodded their agreement.

"Gentlemen," announced Dawes, refusing to acknowledge the token females under his command, "this is a covert operation. Which means we will conduct our activities with the highest levels of discretion and tact. I don't want anyone losing their cool and bringing undue attention on us. I'm looking at you, Yazidi."

Yazidi growled and put his foot through the side of a rubbish bin.

"That's right, get it out of your system. We want the people of Boston to believe this is nothing more than a routine exercise. For that reason, I will split you into pairs and allocate specific streets that will require a thorough door-to-door search."

Dawes rattled off the names of the pairs with the speed of a machine gun. Jake's name came last.

"Sprout, you can look after Montana."

Considering the options, Jake thought this was a decent outcome.

"If any of you identify one of the targets then you must signal the Corridor through your cloud and we will surround the area. Is everybody clear?"

"Clear," croaked the platoon.

"Move out," instructed Dawes.

Despite the seemingly decrepit nature of his battalion, Corridor E Four performed his instructions with the efficiency of any well-trained fighting force. As it had been with Holst on the island, a time limit was placed on every action or objective. The targets were never missed. Maybe these veterans were just tired of push-ups? The Corridor moved swiftly through the emergency exits of the Hyperloop port and boarded their private tram well before the counter above its door moved through twenty seconds. Ten minutes later, courtesy of maglev public transport, they were in the heart of Boston.

It felt good to be home.

Places he recognised had passed by his window and a comfortable sense of nostalgia and warmth settled in his heart. If it weren't for the circumstances of his return, he might have even broken out in a smile. The tram stopped on the edge of the public park where their base was due to be for the rest of the operation, although it wasn't clear how long that would be. The evidence suggested Archivists rarely caught their prey, but how long did they wait before they gave up? Perhaps only after the next false alarm was raised in some other remote part of the world.

They alighted the tram and carried their supplies a short distance through the park. Their rendezvous was a semicircular memorial that had been built more than one and a half centuries ago to pay homage to men who'd lost their lives in past conflicts. In front of the wall, which carried the name of each Bostonian fatality neatly carved in stone, the statue of an angel kept guard over the fallen. Very few of the local residents who strolled the park seemed interested in either of them. Future generations would never forget Jake's era because the Memory Cloud would be a permanent and lasting legacy long after his body failed him. Not so for the names inscribed in this wall. Only vintage photographs and handwritten memoirs would ever exist of their endeavours.

Today's world differed greatly from the one lived in by these fallen soldiers. Nowadays no one could condone or support a pointless war. Military conflicts were an uncomfortable truth consigned to history and were no different than other unacceptable human behaviour like hunting with weapons or enslaving others. People didn't celebrate those misdemeanours so why would anyone want to glorify this one? Maybe that's why the Archivists had chosen it, no one came here.

Today it was busier than it had been in decades and it wasn't just Jake's Corridor that had been summoned to the hunt either.

Around the park small congregations of uniformed teams were picking out the best piece of territory. Some had already pitched their tents and were preparing dinner. Although all were in standard Archivist outfits, none were marked quite the same as his unit. Materials of different hues indicated which Corridor you belonged to. His newly acquired clothes were a fawn colour. Around him some wore navy blue, some slate grey, some were covered in a seaweed green. Whatever the uniform's colour every private displayed a distinctive badge that was embossed on their right sleeve. Stripes designed to look like lightning bolts. Jake looked down at his own arm to find his jacket only featured one.

After assessing those that came past him it didn't take long to work out what it meant. The soldiers had anywhere from one to five stripes, although those with the highest number were a rarity. Most had three. It was obviously an indication of their importance level, and therefore their rank. Jake had noticed that other than Dawes, everyone in his own Corridor was referred to as privates. They didn't need promotion to reinforce discipline. Orders were dependent on the lines displayed on your upper arm, which meant he'd only ever be following and never sending any.

SUPERFLUOUS CITY

In a world that promoted equality and meritocracy this proved that sentiment and reality differed. Everyone looked down on superfluous folk, just as the rich have always treated the poor with a sense of pity or disgust. Nothing much had really changed. The Circuit insisted you had a choice where you were placed in this hierarchy based on your own efforts, but it hadn't worked for Jake. He wondered what the Circuit might have written in his letter if Sam hadn't beaten them to it. Would he have been genuinely superfluous? He didn't think so, although he didn't particularly hate being one now. It didn't matter what mark someone placed on you, it only mattered what you chose to do with your life. Either let their judgement destroy you or prove everyone wrong.

Today he was determined to achieve the latter.

Corridor E Four spent an hour setting up their section of the larger camp. It was basic by normal living standards, but everyone had their own tent and there was plenty of space to exercise or relax in. Meals were predictably awful. Efflotein didn't get tastier when you ate it outdoors or in a different continent. Yazidi was their group's cook, which meant no one was keen to be first in the queue in case he'd decided to poison his internal enemies. In fairness, when Jake did pluck up the courage to try his recipes, Yazidi had managed to make efflotein taste slightly less like rotten fish.

After darkness drew in the company watched as a posse of five striped figures congregated on the steps of the monument. Dawes suddenly didn't feel quite so imposing amongst his similarly ranked colleagues. The leaders debated long into the night as the light faded completely from the day. The soldiers of each Corridor kept themselves segregated from one another. It was obvious that the conference happening on the memorial was designed to ensure that each team supported the other, but it was equally clear from the way the camp was organised that an intense rivalry existed between Corridors.

"Why don't we mingle with the others?" Jake asked as his teeth wrestled with something green that clung stubbornly to a skewer.

"We might catch cancer," replied Sprout inevitably.

"You can't catch cancer like the flu," replied Jake.

"Tell that to Private Ford."

"What happened to him, then?"

"He stupidly ignored me and got involved with another Corridor. They ended up searching a disused uranium factory for a Spectrum enclave. Do you know what happened? Two weeks later he was riddled with cancer."

"You don't say," replied Jake, shaking his head disbelievingly. "What about the others?"

"They also had cancer."

"There you are, then; it can't be the reason you said, can it? The other Archivists weren't in a different Corridor." Jake smiled, believing he'd finally got the better of Sprout's unproven twaddle.

"That wasn't why the others got it. They contracted it because they were wearing socks," said Sprout, lifting his trouser legs to verify he wasn't.

"Don't listen to Sprout," said Private Needham. "We don't mix with the others because we all want to win."

"Win?" asked Jake.

"Yeah. We can't all catch the speccy, can we?"

"I thought there were hundreds of speccies?"

"Really? Who told you that?" replied Needham nervously and proving he had no idea how many were out there either.

"Just a guess," lied Jake.

"You're just a novice," growled Yazidi. "You'll learn soon enough. The Corridor who catches the most speccies will become legends."

"Legends?" said Jake doubtfully.

"They'll be rewarded by the Circuit beyond their wildest dreams and worshipped by a grateful West. That's why the Privates don't fraternise. They're rivals."

"Then why don't I know about the legends that came before you?" said Jake who had zero knowledge of any such past champions.

Private Needham avoided the question.

The longer Jake inhabited their world, the more he doubted whether anybody had ever caught a speccy. There were never any announcements from the Circuit of such success, only propaganda to instruct people of what to do if they saw one or to warn them about their threat. Major Bancroft's course had depicted them in stark contrast from his own experience. Holst had been coy on the question of how many he'd caught and now Needham was equally reticent to comment. Jake started to wonder who feared who? His download had installed a visceral anger towards speccies that might be classified as a phobia.

No subscriber of the cloud knew where they lived or how they worked. Everyone employed to destroy them was sworn to secrecy. Yet the Spectrum lived freely in the open, undetected and one step in front of those paid to hunt them. The Archivists, on the other hand, lived a nomadic existence, survived on synthetic food and struggled to put down roots of their own. They didn't know where the enemy was or what they looked like. Yet when they wore their uniforms, they displayed their own presence like a beacon. Human fear is born out of the unknown, not the reality of the threat itself. The Archivists were being baited to fear and hate by a faceless master who clearly had an ulterior motive for doing so.

It was the Archivists, not the Spectrum, that were the ones in hiding.

A notification pinged in his cloud feed. It was marked 'Top Secret', although he had no idea why. The only other entity likely to see it was Dinah and she seemed more interested in exploring the weapons store. The instructions highlighted the areas that he and Sprout were being assigned for their door-to-door search. Their first road would be Gainsborough Street and they'd start at once.

It wouldn't be over quickly.

Gainsborough Street was a long stretch of early nineteenth-century four-storey town houses of red brick and white paint. Originally designed as plush, single-family homes spread out in splendour across all floors, now they were a labyrinth of single-bedroom flats often occupied by multiple persons. Each street level door had been converted to act as the entry point to a dozen flats that were each indicated by an array of labels and buttons fixed to the exterior wall. This really was a door-to-door search, although getting through the first one became a serious challenge because residents weren't keen on letting them in.

Their instructions were to keep a low profile so kicking the door in didn't seem appropriate. He imagined Yazidi wouldn't see it that way. Jake also discovered that ringing the bell and announcing yourself as an Archivist on patrol was the least convincing technique to persuade them to open up. Even if it had worked, any speccies in the vast block would be long gone before he'd reached the first floor. He experimented with a variety of false identities to trick homeowners, but these also had very limited success. No one believed him when he announced he was a delivery driver because everyone received cloud notifications of such arrivals. Announcing he was from the electric company also failed. In the end he managed to gain sporadic access by pretending to be a fellow resident who'd locked themselves out. A tactic that wore off pretty quickly once news from previous victims spread around the community along with a precise visual memory of Jake's previous deception.

On the rare occasion he got inside a building, individual tenants were more motivated to open their own doors for fear that refusal might bring punishment by the Circuit. Every time they did, Jake gained nothing other than aggression and distrust.

Three days passed by and they'd barely travelled a third of the way down the street. Other than Dinah accusing anyone she laid eyes on that she was convinced they were speccies, and Sprout's increasing paranoia that everyday objects were guaranteed to give him cancer, the only things they achieved were blisters and a burst sense of purpose. It appeared none of the other Corridors were faring much better. Every night the Majors would congregate, and every night new areas of Fenway were allocated into their cloud. On the fourth day their luck turned.

At least for Jake it did.

Throughout their patrol, Private Sprout had searched the north side of the street while Jake took the south. Every hour or so they'd meet in the centre to check each other's progress and catch a breath. It was early evening and they'd been patrolling for almost an hour. Outside number 'eight-four' Jake tried unsuccessfully to gain entry for the umpteenth time. He needed a break but had no intention of listening to Sprout's incessant scaremongering. Instead he slumped onto the raised step, thoroughly worn out and disinterested by the whole procedure.

Sam had told him almost nothing about what might happen or how the Spectrum might indicate their existence when he got here. He'd certainly suggested it wouldn't be simple to find Dr Drew. He wasn't kidding on that point. If the Spectrum wanted Jake to make contact, why had they made it so bloody difficult? He gazed across the road as Sprout successfully gained access to the property opposite that he'd spent the last hour stalking.

Jake felt utterly alone. The only soul on a street that you couldn't see the end of. Fenway was always quiet. Few people ever ventured outside. Were they at work, or was it Jake's presence that had turned this part of the city into a ghost town? It felt unnatural. He'd been to Boston hundreds of times and his memories confirmed that the streets were always bustling with people: morning, evening and night-time. Not here. Here the people hid from him like everyone was pretending to be a speccy.

Everyone that was apart from the youth he saw out of the corner of his eye just down the street.

Leaning against a lamp-post a Latino boy watched him intently and puffed on a cigarette. Jake's eyes rested on him a little longer than was natural. There was something familiar about him, but Jake couldn't get a good look from this distance. He scanned his cloud feed to confirm the man's identity from the proximity scanner.

He didn't have one.

He had several.

Every time Jake's cloud settled on what it believed was the correct name associated with the figure it suddenly changed its mind and indicated an alternative. It skipped through identities like a salesman fingering a Rolodex. The cloud knew someone was there, it just couldn't be certain who. Something had confused it, and that wasn't normal.

Jake lifted himself off the step, unclipped the weapon from his belt and took a stride towards the mysterious pedestrian. Finally, Jake's real eyes kicked in. It was the boy from the sewer. It was Alfonso. Before Jake could get close enough, the boy casually turned around and ran off. Jake pursued him at speed. This was the sign he'd been waiting for but why was Alfonso running? Jake reached inside his jacket pocket and took out the bottle of Moodzec. He reached inside and removed a couple of the smooth, round pills. He chewed on them, so their gooey contents were released more quickly.

A general alert flashed up in his cloud. It had been sent by Sprout who watched Jake's pursuit from a first-floor window. Soon the whole of Corridor E Four would be surging to the area and it wouldn't take long before the other Corridors followed.

- Chapter 25 -

Doctor Drew

The more Jake ran, the closer the little red dots on his proximity sensor pressed down on his position. From every conceivable direction hundreds of Archivists were constricting the available space like a noose being applied to his neck. It wouldn't be long before they were on top of him. Alfonso's quickening pace and volatile changes of direction suggested he also sensed the impending threat. He vaulted railings, scrambled across gardens, and clambered through rubbish bins before finally disappearing down an alleyway that dissected a pair of the soaring town houses. Thanks to Dinah, who managed to stay some distance ahead of Jake, he kept pace and in contact.

At the end of the alley a high wall blocked Alfonso's progress. He was trapped, and this time without the advantage of a lethal weapon to protect himself.

"Why did you run?" said Jake, moving slowly towards him, panting furiously. "You've brought attention on both of us."

"Maybe. Or I've moved it away from something more important," replied Alfonso.

"What are you doing here?"

"I live here."

"Then what were you doing in New Hampton Falls last month?"

"Robbing you," he said with a grin.

"Yes. I remember that…but not what you took from me," said Jake, stuttering slightly as he struggled to make sense of the returning memory in his feed.

"It was a very pretty thing," said Alfonso, wiping the sweat of the chase from his brow with a sleeve.

"The necklace?" said Jake, watching the memory unfold against the flaky, red-brick wall.

"No, not the necklace. Your girlfriend was very pretty."

"Girlfriend?" said Jake perplexed. In the replay that overlapped the alleyway there were only two of them present.

"Yes. Athletic figure, long, flowing blonde hair, blue eyes…"

"Why can't I remember her?" pleaded Jake, interrupting him. As far as imaginary girlfriends went, she sounded lovely. "She's not in my memory!"

"That's because, like the necklace, she was stolen from you."

"Who stole her?"

"The Circuit of course."

"How can they steal a person?"

"Because they own your past. You sold your own history and now they can do whatever they like with it. The Spectrum aren't the enemy, they are."

"Then why are ninety-nine percent of my instincts telling me you're wrong? Why do they tell me that I shouldn't hesitate in shooting you right here, right now?"

"Because the Circuit have been messing with your mind since you were born and it's counter-intuitive to fight a lie that has always been there poisoning reality. But you have battled against it more than most. Even before I knew who you really were, I knew you were different."

"Different?"

"Yes. When you chased me last time in the sewers, I respected you. Most of my victims don't act that way. They're so frightened it makes robbing them too easy. We are the danger the Circuit has been warning them about their whole lives. They can't even look us in the eye in case we put a spell on them! Not you, though. You proved your bravery. I hope they haven't stolen that from you also, you're going to need it."

Alfonso lifted the metal hatch hidden under his feet and climbed into the hole. Jake dashed forward to see him descend into the darkness.

"I thought you said you didn't live in sewers?" he called out.

"We don't, but they make excellent escape routes. If you want to find what you've lost, you'd better get a move on."

The idea of wading through human effluent was a much happier one than it would have been an hour ago, thanks to the Moodzec tablets taking effect. Jake climbed in, but not until Dinah had beaten him to it. He dragged the sewer cover back over the hole and the light of the world was extinguished. His foot searched for the next rung of the ladder and carefully he inched his way to the bottom. The stench of wastewater permeated the atmosphere and dampness hung in the air. It was hard to breathe normally without wanting to gag.

"A good choice," echoed Alfonso's voice through the darkness. "Now we must hurry. Your colleagues will be here any minute."

"But they'll still be able to track me," said Jake desperately.

"Moodzec is a wonderful thing," replied Alfonso before grabbing Jake by the arm and dragging him away.

*****

A dozen uniformed figures crawled up the alley on their hands, knees and bellies. Shiny gun barrels trained on the narrow space in front of them. Several bins lay on their sides and items of litter were being chased around the ground by the wind. A ginger cat leapt from the shadows and clawed its way up the far wall. It narrowly avoided a volley of bullets that pulverised the brickwork. Dawes raised an arm from his position in front of the snipers to sanction an immediate ceasefire. He knew speccies were elusive, but he was fairly sure they weren't felines. There was nothing here other than a dozen paranoid privates and the faded red dot that traced Jake Montana to this spot. Dawes stood up and brushed the dust from his trousers. The rest of his Corridor followed suit and waited for his next instruction.

"Where is Montana?" huffed Dawes, taking a cigar out of his pocket.

"I can no longer see him on my proximity sensor, Major, sir," replied Needham. "But he was definitely heading in this direction."

Several plumes of smoke surrounded Dawes as he puffed like a set of bellows to get his cigar burning.

"Sprout, come here."

"Yes. Major, sir."

"Why did you raise the alert?"

"I saw him running after a felon, sir."

"Describe him."

"About six-foot, white helmet, full uniform…"

"Not Montana, you fool, the speccy!"

"Oh. Latino complexion, slim, curly hair, muscular…"

Dawes's eyes widened and a slow scowl ripped across his cheek muscles. Sprout's description tapered off in reaction to it.

"Does that description sound like a speccy to you?" Dawes said angrily.

"Not really, Major, sir," replied Sprout apologetically.

"We all know that speccies are short, generally have pointy fangs and wide foreheads."

Everyone nodded knowingly.

"Sorry, Major, sir," offered Sprout cowering in shame.

"But why have we lost Montana's signal, sir?" said another voice.

"Because he's a deserter!" shouted Dawes so the whole street could hear him.

"How can he be?" replied Needham. "We'd be able to track him, wouldn't we?"

"I'd like to ask him that very question," said Major Dawes who received an alert to his memory feed at the same moment. "Hold on, I'm getting instructions."

The Corridor waited patiently as Dawes consumed a new set of intelligence.

"Right, men, new orders."

Most privates didn't fully understand the Archivist's chain of command. They didn't need to know. They had their major and that's all they really needed. Privates did what a major told them. But who did majors take their orders from? They had five stripes on their arms and planned their strategy by arguing with people of a similar importance factor. If they couldn't agree, who resolved the conflict? Who was more important than the vitals?

"Who are the orders from, Major, sir?" said Needham bravely.

"A Memory Hunter," replied Dawes.

An uncomfortable energy swelled and passed between them. Even Yazidi's pulse rate increased, and he wasn't frightened of anything.

"I've never engaged with a Memory Hunter before," said Sprout nervously.

"Nothing to worry about."

"I've heard they can give you cancer," mumbled Sprout.

"Idiot," replied Dawes. "This one has given me something much more interesting."

"What?" asked a few privates at once.

"Montana's position! Stand by, men, transferring new data to your cloud's trace. Look for a file sent by a Brother Job."

*****

Alfonso stopped abruptly in the darkness. Other senses jumped to his aid to compensate for a lack of vision. A powerful stench of sewer grime and stale food filled Jake's nostrils, and standing water was leaking into his cheap, plastic, company-issued boots. Not that he was complaining. It was all brilliant, although when you were on Moodzec being kicked repeatedly in the spine didn't dampen your spirits. Alfonso's sense of smell navigated them a few paces forward until they felt slimy metal under their outstretched fingers.

Jake felt his hands being guided towards a second ladder and a poke in the ribs encouraged him to climb. At the top, only twenty feet above the floor of the sewer, the ladder ended. He grappled with another sewer cover, finally lifting it up and letting light back into the world. Climbing fast behind, Alfonso shoved him forward in haste. Back on the street, and directly in front of him, a waist-high padlocked metal gate took up position between two crumbling red-brick walls. Behind it a cul-de-sac had been carved in the face of the endless row of buildings like a chunk chopped from a tree by a lumberjack's axe. At the bottom of the three sides a shadowy patch of soil struggled to cultivate shabby strands of grass. On the floors to either side of him frames that once held glass panes had been bricked up and in the corners at the far ends two wrought-iron fire escapes criss-crossed up through the floors.

"Take the left one," said Alfonso, pushing him in the centre of his back with his palm.

"This place is awesome," hummed Jake fully under Moodzec's clutches. "What's up there?"

"I bet it's Santa!" burst out Dinah excitedly.

"That's where you'll find the rest of us," replied Alfonso.

"I'm certain Dr Drew is here, too," said Jake optimistically.

"It's possible."

"Pessimist."

"Dr Drew never stays in one place for too long. If we lost him to the Archivists, we'd lose any chance of influencing the Circuit in future."

The rusty fire escape creaked with every step. The metal vibrated and the gully magnified the noise as it was channelled out into the main street. At the fifth level Alfonso pushed open the door. Inside, the whole of the fifth floor's partition walls had been bulldozed, leaving one huge, open-plan room. Before the refurbishments it would have housed dozens of individual flats, just like the ones that Jake had been trying to search for the last few days. Now it looked like a warehouse and it was as busy as any factory floor.

Dozens of people went about their business ignorant of the new arrivals. It was a surprise to him given his formal uniform and holstered gun. In one corner six people were working a rather arcane-looking machine that pumped grey smoke into the room and roared like an ancient combustion engine. Topless men covered in sweat and grease, with only their shorts to hide their modesty, worked tirelessly at the contraption. The machine produced a continual flow of small, plastic components that dropped off a conveyor belt and onto a table where a young lady was expertly constructing them into larger objects. It didn't take long for Jake to notice their scars.

On the other side of the room, floor-to-ceiling racks ran halfway down the room. Their shelves held every possible commodity you needed to survive if you were off-grid and unable to get to the shops. Groceries, huge bottles of water, electrical equipment, medicines, clothes, hobby materials and items that might protect you if threatened. Jake was drawn towards a crate that contained a collection of blades that Alfonso had first threatened him with a few weeks ago.

Only the dim, old-fashioned bulbs hanging from the ceilings offered the room a subtle glow. The smell of industry and hard work filled the atmosphere, sealed off from the normal world happening outside the bricked-up windows. Jake loosened his helmet and removed his goggles to get a better sense of it. They lived amongst us, so he'd been told, and now he knew where.

"This place is brilliant," he said, rather too loudly.

Other than Dinah, who was pretending to massage the sweaty male workers, no one paid him any attention.

"Robert," said Alfonso approaching one of the bare-chested men nearest to him. "Is he in?"

The man nodded towards the other end of the space in answer. Alfonso led the way as their surroundings changed from a manufacturing feel to one less hot and noisy. Further down the room a series of educational classes were in progress. A dozen children, sitting calmly on little wooden chairs, encircled a middle-aged woman who was writing on a damaged blackboard. It was the first time in Jake's life he'd witnessed anyone writing anything, let alone with sticks of blue chalk. It was like being six again, the first time he'd watched someone successfully surf a wave. Inspiration stopped him in his tracks that day, and the sight of the words appearing like magic on the board was no less captivating. The lesson being taught today was how to stay safe in the alien world of the Circuit. The board featured a number of references to the Archivists, all of which were more accurate than the information he'd been taught about the Spectrum. The children's focus on their teacher was total. Unlike Jake's own experiences of school, none of these infants were distracting themselves with childish pranks or allowing their minds to wander off into the subversion of their cloud feed. They knew only too well that lessons like this were a matter of life and death.

At the very back of the room, an elderly gentleman slept peacefully on a rustic antique armchair. His aquamarine kaftan robe hung limply against his skinny body. A long, scraggly beard flowed down to his knees and a pair of thick-lensed glasses balanced across the bridge of his nose at a lopsided angle. A worn, leather sandal clung to his toes while the other had already given up and lay idle on the wooden floorboards. A tattoo on the man's wrinkled leg immediately caught Jake's attention.

Carrying twigs in their beaks, two birds in mid-flight up the man's calf muscle disappeared under the fabric of the kaftan as they headed towards their destination. The passage of time had faded the tattoo's vibrant colours, leaving a consistent inky green stain throughout. Jake scrolled back in his cloud for the last memory of his grandfather.

'Where the birds fly, there will always be blue sky.'

He'd thought at the time it was code, based on the one Paddy had invented when he and his sister were younger. They used it to keep innocent secrets from their parents and its development helped forge a strong bond with their grandfather. It was their little game and it opened up a world that no one else could enter, not even the Circuit. He'd encourage them to choose alternative words for certain nouns and then he'd try to work out what they meant. Jake remembered that it had taken Paddy weeks to find out that he'd swapped 'slippers' for 'crocodile'. After that he'd always confuse Deborah by asking, 'Where are my crocodiles?' She'd even once suggested he might need to see a doctor for his Alzheimer's.

Jake knew immediately what his grandfather's parting words meant. Bird was code for 'love', fly was used as a replacement for the word 'live', and blue sky meant 'hope'. In his opinion his grandfather's substitution for the last of these three words was particularly poignant. Every citizen of the world hoped blue skies returned permanently one day.

'Where love lives, there will always be hope.'

The words were nothing more than a message of encouragement for his future, weren't they? That's what he believed then. Under the relentless positivity of Moodzec, the sight of the tattoo presented him with new meaning. Had Paddy given him direction rather than nostalgic warm words? Or was this just a coincidence? It seemed implausible that the doctor and his grandfather had any connection.

Alfonso gave the old man a gentle shake. His eyes snapped open to reveal sparkling blue irises like polished gems.

"This is Dr Theo Drew," announced Alfonso grandly.

"Jake Montana, superfluous."

"I know," replied Theo.

"I can't tell you how good it is to see you," said Jake.

"Welcome to paradise," croaked the man.

"Thank you and I think you're right. This place is perfect."

"It was," replied Theo calmly.

"Was?"

"In a few hours everyone will need to leave. Your visit brings an equal amount of hope and danger."

"I'm sure you're exaggerating. Nothing bad can happen here, trust me," replied Jake overconfidently.

"It was sensible of you to take those pills when you did, but that will not stop the Circuit. There are many ways in which they use their Memory Hunters," said the old man. "They'll be here soon enough, and then we must move on."

Dinah groaned in Jake's ear. If anyone summed up a sense of freedom, then it was her and she felt at home amongst these people as much as Jake did.

"Why have you come?" asked Theo.

"Sam Goldberg sent me to find you."

"Ah, so he believes he has found the answer."

"He believes I have an overactive brain, which means I carry something powerful."

"And what do you think?"

"Yes. I do," Jake replied without any doubt. "I have always suffered from flashbacks that I cannot place in my own life."

"That's because they are not yours."

"Then whose are they?"

"We can't be sure exactly, but they belonged to someone from the East of great importance. Until we remove the implants, we won't know who they were or what they saw. Twenty years ago, when I first received them, I was told they contained the truth about what the Circuit had become. The technology to remove the information did not exist back then. Our only option was to place them safely in ten newborn babies and wait for a solution to present itself. But there was no way to track who those hosts were. The implants were placed in the supply chain and we stayed patient and hidden until Sam's genius made it possible for us to receive them."

"Sam has been captured," said Jake rather too whimsically.

"Then your journey here has been for nothing," said the old man, leaping from his chair with the strength of a much younger man.

"Where are you going?" asked Jake.

"To sound the alarm and move as many of these people to safety as possible. Without Sam you are no use to us."

Theo Drew found the closest person and whispered in their ear. Within minutes the message passed down the room from person to person with the speed of a sonic blast and almost immediately everyone switched their activities. Bags were packed with haste, machines quickly deactivated, and classes dismissed. Everyone knew their role in this well-rehearsed retreat, something they shared with the Archivists that hunted them.

"What if I were to find him?" shouted Jake through the noise of activity.

Theo turned around slowly. "It's impossible."

"Apparently I'm impossible," replied Jake.

"No, you're improbable and that's not the same thing, is it?" argued Dr Drew. "If you say that Sam has been taken, then he's dead or in the Source. It would be easier to bring him back from the dead. There is no way in and no way out, that's if we knew which Source he's being held in."

"I know he's here," added Jake. "In Boston."

"Moodzec is an antidepressant not a luck potion. You can't know that."

"I can because Sam is connected to my Memory Cloud."

"True, he can see yours, but it's not possible for you to see his."

"Then he wouldn't be much of a genius, would he!?"

Jake scanned the past week's feed in case he'd missed something. Perhaps an unread message, alert or link sent to him by an unknown sender, trapped in his spam folders. Sam wouldn't make it obvious, but Jake was convinced it would be there somewhere.

He found it.

Just after he'd left the Hyperloop in Boston an advert for tea popped up in his feed. He'd always found tea repulsive and quickly waved it away. But advertisers didn't spend their credits loosely like that. Promoting tea to him would be like advertising spectacles to the blind. He hovered over the split second it had remained in his feed before he'd dismissed it. Setting the time frame to microseconds, he rocked the image back and forward before zooming in on the product in the salesperson's hand.

Then he saw the message.

Franklin Tea. Source of rejuvenation. Use code A401-l3K.

The brand and the strapline were enough of a clue that Sam was here. Boston was famous for its links to tea, Benjamin Franklin and more recently a rather gigantic Source. He didn't know what to make of the code, though. Perhaps that information would help him further down the road.

"He's here!" shouted Jake like he'd perfected alchemy. "He left me a clue."

Jake explained to Dr Drew what he'd discovered logged secretly in his memories. Although he agreed with the conclusion, his motivations to act still lagged behind.

"I know how to get in and out of the Source," exclaimed Jake a little surprised by his own confidence. "I just need you to perform the surgery."

"If I did that, you'd no longer remember anything," replied Drew. "Including the plan."

"I don't understand."

"Your implants are the only thing that connects you to your inner self. The memories, knowledge and emotions you've created through life are stored elsewhere. If I replace the implants with Sam's version, you'll have to start afresh. A new person with a blank canvas. You won't remember any of your past life because it will only exist in a storage facility in some far-off server farm. The human brain is lazy. It no longer needs to record anymore...just connect."

"But isn't an upgrade the only way of learning what's hidden in my memory?"

"Yes, it is," replied Theo reluctantly.

"Then we need to do it. We may not get another chance."

Theo Drew hesitated as he considered all the variables. The Circuit was closing in on their location and they could only hold them off for so long. The surgery would take time and retraining this young man's empty brain even longer. He'd waited twenty years to discover what Jake held inside him. Twenty years of running and hiding. Twenty years of hoping and praying this day would come.

Now it was here.

"There may be a way," exclaimed Theo. "If we can keep the Circuit back long enough, I may have time to provide the most important information verbally once I've removed the old implants. But I have to warn you, Jake, once I do this most of your old life will be lost. The speccies have sacrificed much down the years, but you will be making the biggest one of all, yourself."

Jake considered the implications. Even though most of what he loved had already been taken from him, he still desired to remain authentically him once he'd completed the tasks set for him. Everything he'd learnt, felt or experienced would no longer be his. Memories of family, friends or deeds would be wiped out. Was it worth it? Even if he gave everything up there were no guarantees he'd discover the truth the Circuit was so keen to hide. He hated not knowing, though. Would he ever forgive himself if he didn't have the courage to set the world free?

"You must decide quickly," replied Theo, sensing the internal battle waging in Jake's mind.

Without the influence of Moodzec's he would have surely declined. "Yes. I'm ready."

"Then let us get to work. You may have had your implants removed before, but it won't be the same this time. It will be dangerous and painful. I may have the talent to perform the procedure, but I certainly don't possess all the equipment to make it safe and easy."

A proximity alert in Jake's memory feed showed a mass of faint of red dots shimmering in and out of view. The Archivists were coming.

"We need to hurry; the drug's wearing off."

Theo once again whispered into the nearest ear and triggered a change of mood around the room. The collective switched from hurried retreat to battle mode. Man, woman and child grabbed whatever weapons they found on the storage shelves and moved swiftly out of the main door. It was anyone's guess where they were going, but their purpose was clear.

Delay and distract.

"Alfonso, I will need your assistance," demanded Drew. "Prepare him for theatre."

The young Latino approached a bulky object covered in white sheets against the wall. He removed it with a tug and sent a plume of dust scattering into the air. Underneath, to Jake's horror, was a simple massage table covered in patches of dried-up blood next to a small cabinet full of bottles with faded yellow labels.

"You're not serious!" said Jake, proving beyond doubt that his negativity had returned.

"It's the only way, and I am the only doctor."

Before Jake made the inevitable dash for the exit something thin and sharp forced a path through the back of his neck. A moment later he lost control of his senses.

- Chapter 26 -

Violation Ten

The cracked and mouldy plasterboard ceiling spun in circles as he struggled to regain control of consciousness. A stream of warm, sticky blood ran down the side of his head, matting his hair in clumps and collecting in a pool on the massage table. Even though most of his head was covered in bandages the blood still seeped through with alarming speed. A blinding, intense pain burnt like a furnace between his eyes and in his forehead. The distant and continual rattling in the background was only interrupted by the harrowing screams of someone so close they might be underneath him. The howls intensified as further waves of pain invaded his senses. A leathery hand covered his mouth to muffle them.

The spinning finally ran out of steam and like the end of a brutal fairground ride his eyes tried desperately to refocus. The only thing they saw were murky shadows with blurred outlines. Two low-resolution figures worked busily on or around his body. They must be there to care for him, he thought. A guttural sense of vulnerability oozed through his veins and formed a union with the pain. He needed these people to survive, he was certain of that. They'd delivered him into the world, and they would protect him. Other reflexes were switched on and he gasped for air before the supply ran out. A first breath on his very first day of life. Hunger hurried to join the bizarre emotional house party, clutching its invite and apologising for being late. Every essential human need was waiting at the door, shouting out to be let in.

An elderly voice cut through the pandemonium that circled around him.

"It's normal for you to feel a little lost."

He didn't know if he was meant to reply or even whether he was capable of replicating this strange language.

"We are running out of time," said the croaky voice. "Soon they will break through and you will be taken away."

Did they not love him? Had they brought him into the world only for someone else to remove him from their care? What sort of parents were they? Were they abandoning him? Fear oozed through his nervous system, but it failed to support his desire to get up. He wriggled hysterically, trying to grab hold of them with flailing arms.

"Don't struggle. Your wounds are still fresh. It's normal to feel a sense of disorientation. You have been reawakened, Jake."

Jake. So that was his name. It didn't sound familiar.

"Right now, your brain is as desolate as an uncolonised planet. We have this one window of opportunity to fill it up before they break through. Concentrate."

Concentrate on what? The oozy, red liquid still flowing out of him. The intense pain instructing his body to shut down completely. The growing sound of a battle bearing down on them. The empty wasteland of his existence. It was more than someone of sound mind could manage and his certainly wasn't that.

"Your name is Jake Montana. You have been released from the tyranny of the Circuit."

VIOLATION TEN

The old man rattled off a series of vital statistics and details like he was commentating on a sporting event. Age, background, upbringing, family members, past experience and current situation. To his surprise, Jake's brain absorbed them like a dry sponge. His capacity for detail was unlimited and there was no doubt that what they were telling him was the truth. The more information he consumed, the more his life took shape.

"Do you understand?" said the old man.

"Yes," replied Jake, surprised to find that he did speak the old man's language.

"Your task in this world is a vital one. We must learn what is inside these."

The old man held up a small, bloodstained, see-through plastic pouch. Inside were two innocuous-looking metal components attached to red and yellow insulated wires that ran up through the top of the bag and finished at two sticky, round pads.

"What are they?"

"They are a portal to your old life."

"Why do I need that?" asked Jake tentatively, trying to sit up but finding the pain too intense.

"Because they contain the secrets to defeating the Circuit. You'll need them if the plan I've just described is going to work."

Jake considered the bizarre set of instructions that the old man had grafted into his empty brain. The more he thought about them, the more it fired his imagination and the more his vision expanded.

"I can see," gasped Jake.

"That's good. It will take a few days before your eyes get used to the new implant and the wound heals."

"No. You don't understand," continued Jake. "I can see beyond you."

The visual world might still be hazy and distorted but there existed in him a new plane of perception

351

that was crystal-clear. It wasn't restricted to this depressing room, where it found nothing of interest to connect to, but extended further afield. It stepped through the walls and out into the street. A surge of energy signals crowded the ground floor space of a narrow cul-de-sac. Hundreds of men and some women vented aggression at an unseen foe. He saw their thoughts, their personalities and memories. As he connected to each one individually, it accessed a new network of consciousness that transported him to other people they'd shared their lives with, in places thousands of miles away. The network branched off further with every connection. Each a portal to accessing every implant user anywhere in the West.

"I can see everything."

"Yes," replied Drew solemnly. "The Circuit has been opened. You are now its master. If we can get you out of here before they kill you of course."

"How do we do that?"

"Put these on," said the old man holding the small, plastic pads in his hand.

"No! You've just cut them out of me, and I don't really want my old life back."

"You must. I've told you already that your parents need you and so does Sam Goldberg."

"My parents are dead," replied Jake coldly.

"It will take time for your emotions to form a sense of attachment to them and other aspects of your past. Do not erase their memory so readily."

"It's got nothing to do with my emotions. I have already paid them a visit," he replied. "They're gone."

Jake's new implants granted unlimited access to the Memory Cloud. It was the master key to the whole network. It unlocked every file ever saved and as such he could move through the Circuit freely and undetected. It didn't take him long to find his parents' servers. When he did, he'd discovered that their memory feeds had ended a month ago. Their Memory Clouds were no longer recording. The revelation had little effect on him.

"I'm sorry," said Drew. "Great power comes with great sacrifice."

"Don't be. They don't mean anything to me anymore."

"What about Sam? He's still out there somewhere. If we want to discover the truth, we need him returned to us alive."

The new implants had limits. Like Jake, Sam could not be tracked. The new implant could find anyone in the cloud and even influence the decisions the Circuit made for them, but they could not influence or track each other.

"We don't need the implants to discover the secret," replied Jake confidently. "If they exist then I can find them in my old Memory Cloud."

"No!" shouted Theo.

It was too late. Jake closed his eyes and submerged himself in the Circuit's network. With the speed of a high-powered microprocessor he skipped from cloud feed to cloud feed, passing through thousands a second until he found the route that delivered him to Jake Montana's server. Jumping from country to country, state to state, he rampaged through every server farm with the efficiency of a power surge. It took less than twenty seconds before he found what he needed.

A sea of blinking lights welcomed him. Thousands of them dotted around columns of glass and plastic. The sound of growling micro motors vibrated his projection. A host of unfamiliar memories, of a life he no longer remembered, were being played out in incredible detail. Characters entered and left the foreground like drawings on a flick book. The scenes rapidly altered around him.

VIOLATION TEN

One minute the beach, the next the yard, then Boston, an antenna in the middle of a field and a complex of soulless buildings on the edge of an island. He delved deeper into the archive of ancient records as the central character in the scenes shrank in size and age. Suddenly everything that had been so lifelike and real was wiped and it was replaced by a bright white, empty backdrop.

An elderly figure in jeans and a T-shirt materialised in the centre of it.

"I think you must be lost," said the man.

Jake froze solid hoping the man wouldn't notice him.

"You're in the cloud of Jake Montana but you are not he. You are trespassing."

"Who are you?" asked Jake.

"I am Brother Job."

"And who is he?"

"A Memory Hunter."

"Then we are the same," replied Jake. "There is something stored here that I need."

"This area is restricted."

"You're not going to stop me," bristled Jake.

"Oh, but I am."

In a flash Job surged forward like a battering ram, forcing Jake out of his own life with an intense pulse of energy. Back on the massage table of level five he opened his eyes and gasped for air like he'd been winded. At the same moment a huge explosion sent debris and light crashing through the wall of the artificially lit room.

"What was that?"

"They're here. You've revealed yourself to them, you fool."

"I thought I might be able to find it."

"Don't you think we've already tried that," said Dr Drew angrily. "The flashbacks don't belong to you. The only safe way to access them is to scrutinise the old implants with Sam's technology. Now put these on."

"Wait," came a second voice.

"What is it, Alfonso?"

"There's something else that Jake must know that he won't find in his old memories."

"Hurry. We must leave before they breach our defences," insisted Theo.

Alfonso held out a hand and gently pulled Jake up from his bed. The whole of his body was drenched with sweat and blood and he wobbled as his feet met the floor. The immense pain from the surgery was still attempting to knock him out.

"Take these," said Alfonso, passing Jake a small glass bottle containing large, white pills, "they'll subdue the pain."

"Thank you."

"There's one piece of information that Dr Drew didn't tell you. I think it was deleted during your download, but I saw it in your eyes the first time we met. A love no amount of technology or interference can kill. Your girlfriend's name is Christie Tucci," he said, holding a gold chain in his hand and letting it slide through his fingers and into Jake's palm.

At the end of the chain was a cheap-looking gold heart and on the rear side it was engraved with a name and a date.

"I think the date must be her birthday," suggested Alfonso, "It's next week. I should think it's also her Ascension Day."

Another explosion shook the building and a large section of masonry fell outwards crashing to the ground several floors below.

"We must delay no longer!" shouted Dr Drew.

Alfonso nodded.

"Jake, give us ten minutes and then place the old implants here and here," said the doctor, indicating the places on the back of Jake's head. "If we are both lucky, we may just meet again."

They retreated calmly to the back of the room where Alfonso removed some of the wall, brick by brick. Before Jake knew what was happening both of them had disappeared through a small gap.

*****

Corridor E Four were the first unit to reach the building following the precise directions offered by the Memory Hunter. The company marched briskly to it, eager to enter the history books and become the very first Corridor to capture a genuine speccy. Their eagerness had waned somewhat since their arrival.

Any military leader knows that certain conditions reduce the odds of success. Higher ground always offered an advantage and, sadly they didn't have it. The twenty men, and some token women, of Corridor E Four were stuck on the ground floor of a dingy cul-de-sac while five floors above them a hidden enemy pelted their position with all manner of dangerous projectiles. To make life even more difficult, their only escape route had been blocked by the competition. The other Corridors arrived late for the party but were eager to get past the bouncer. While Major Dawes's team took the brunt of the first wave of attacks like human sacrifices, the others would surge forward once the speccies had tired themselves out.

Most of Dawes's soldiers had been Archivists for decades and yet in the space of six hours this battle was the closest they'd ever come to real experience. Even Dawes struggled to balance the reality of the moment against the belief of what he'd been taught.

"How do they do it?" raged Dawes as a volley of flaming pot plants smashed against the ground next to the fire escape, scorching the grass. "I thought they were all deformed."

"I don't think they're Spectrum," offered Needham who had already been patched up with a sling after being struck by something sharp and spinning. "They must be locals."

"If they were locals, we'd see them in our feeds," chuntered Dawes. "Can you?"

"No."

"Exactly."

"But there's a chap up there who's at least six feet nine," replied Needham. "Either that or he's on stilts."

"Stilts give you cancer," said Sprout, whose body was so close to the ground the grass was getting jealous.

"Shut up, Sprout," demanded Dawes.

"Yes, Major, sir."

"What we need is a surge attack," said Dawes. "Something to distract them so we can get to the fire escapes."

Yazidi hadn't heard the command because he was already preparing to lose his shit. All Archivists were angry about the existence of Spectrum, the download insisted on it, but clearly when Yazidi received his he'd been in a particularly bad mood. Grabbing two automatic weapons he stood up and roared like a banshee. He stomped over to the metal staircase, firing into the air at will. Everyone hit the deck as debris ricocheted through the air. Dawes watched hopefully as the psychopathic private screamed his way to the second level of stairs. On level three, Yazidi threw a couple of well-slung grenades that exploded on the fifth level.

"I think he might make it," said Dawes a little prematurely.

The screaming suddenly ceased, and an unconscious Yazidi hit the floor with a thud. A rotating sword with multiple blades stuck out of his back, discharging so much electricity that his body convulsed and set his hair on fire.

"Medic!" shouted Needham.

"Fall back," Dawes instructed immediately as an urgent message appeared in his feed.

"But, sir! We'll let Corridor S Three get all the glory," said Needham.

"Be patient. Brother Job says reinforcements are on their way."

"Reinforcements! We have a dozen Corridors and over two hundred Archivists."

"Yes, but they're sending something bigger."

*****

Much like the Memory Cloud, time had been ever present for the last eighteen years. For the first time in his life he had access to neither. To accurately judge ten minutes without it he swung the necklace back and forward and counted. An uncertain future waited for him as his past swayed mesmerically one second after the next.

The necklace must have meant something to him. It might have been inexpensive, but he'd gone to the effort to engrave it. When it had been stolen it meant enough for him to risk his life retrieving it. What did that tell him about the man he was? Had he been brave or reckless? Had he been stubborn or principled? All of these attributes might suggest why he'd put himself in danger. His actions were as much of a mystery as the girl's name etched on the back of the medallion. The more the heart pendant swung past his eyes, the more it intrigued him. Who was she? Jake went on a virtual stroll to see what he could find out. He found Christie's Memory Cloud almost immediately. She was currently sitting on the beach watching the unwavering path of the ocean crashing on the shoreline. She was alone but her thoughts were not.

Her mind was elsewhere. She'd lost someone and, as much as she tried, she could not be reconnected. She yearned to see his face, feel his touch and hear his voice again. Jake scrolled through her past memories to find out the source of her grief.

It was Jake Montana.

It was hard to find one of her memories where he didn't feature. They were inseparable. Always laughing and holding hands. Rarely a disagreement, and any that were had been resolved effortlessly. A month had elapsed since the last recorded memory of them together, on the very spot on the beach where he found her now. It was a week before her own letter arrived and yet she hadn't stopped loving him.

He dragged himself away and focused on the necklace again. The new implants gave him the ability to infiltrate the cloud, but her moment of sadness felt too personal for him to eavesdrop on for any longer. She would not suffer the same disappointment that Jake had on his birthday. It was in his power to change. An action he'd have to complete before he gave up his old life permanently.

The ten minutes elapsed. The ensuing battle outside approached the door. Soon they'd break through the resistance. He placed the stick pads on the back of his head exactly as Dr Drew had instructed and every experience that had belonged to him before the operation returned. Everything except Christie, that was. She would remain securely protected in his real memory.

The moment his memories returned he sank to his knees in floods of tears. The memory of his parents merged with the newly learnt truth of their fate stored in his real brain. It created the reaction he'd failed to demonstrate earlier. It broke his heart.

He'd never see them, talk to them, hold them or repay them for his own mistakes. He tried to deny the truth but what he'd seen could not be unseen. Why had it happened? How had it happened? His parents were innocent bystanders of his own stupidity. They were victims. Sadness turned to rage. The Circuit would pay for this. It was time to bring justice down on those above the law.

It was time to hunt Alison down and make her answer for her crimes.

If only he could think straight and decide on a plan. Wearing both implants at once was disorientating, like watching two films simultaneously without being distracted or losing the plot. His bloodied, old implants were desperately trying to upload everything they'd missed after several hours of inactivity. It was a gap that had not gone unnoticed by Brother Job. At the same time Jake's new implants were busy collecting information to identify a weakness in the Circuit he could use to his advantage. There was a further consequence of wearing his original implants externally for the first time. Dinah returned but she was no longer visible.

She was definitely back, though.

"Shit!" said a distorted voice that came from somewhere deep within him. "I think I'm a ghost!"

"Dinah, where are you?"

"I'm in Heaven," she replied.

"Really? What can you see?"

"Colourful flashing lights that must be tiny angels. There's a hum that sounds like a beautiful choir. I can feel a gentle trickle of holy water washing over me."

"I'm not sure it's Heaven," replied Jake. "I don't think guides go there."

"I'm telling you it is! They have honoured me for my faith in oh...hold on. Wait. Nope, I was wrong.

It's not Heaven. Brother Job's here. It's probably Hell."

"That traitor," said Jake. "I told him to leave me."

"Yep, he's nodding," replied Dinah. "He says he did go, but he's also been watching you."

"Great," Jake replied sarcastically. "Whatever you do, don't tell him about the surgery."

"What surgery?"

"Exactly."

"I think it's his tonsils," Jake heard Dinah explaining to Job.

The door at the end of the room caved in under the force of another powerful explosion and shards of shrapnel flew across the room. The Archivists were here, but they were not his exit strategy. Now that his implants had been replaced, he remembered his plan. It was going to take him to the Source and there was only one way to get there. Jake moved towards the blast-holes in the brickwork where the air and light were floating in. An old antique dressing cabinet lay on the floor from the impact and he caught a glimpse of his reflection in the broken mirror of its damaged door. His face had changed.

A scar had carved a groove on his forehead. Unlike the ones that still bled through his bandages, this scar looked old. It was the scar of a speccy. A sign of his new freedom and yet in a few moments he was about to be as far from free as he'd ever been in his life. Clutching the sides of crumbling walls, he looked through the gap and down onto the street, Jake prepared a proclamation in his mind designed for anyone who might hear it.

"The Circuit is the enemy. They must be stopped. Spectrum forever!"

"Jake, what are you doing!" screamed Dinah.

VIOLATION.

"Getting a free trip to the Source."

- Chapter 27 -

The Source

Jake's 'conduct feeling' commenced immediately to the soundtrack of gunfire inching ever closer. He knew what to expect. A mandatory channel would be opened in his Memory Cloud and past offences would be replayed. All ten of his annual quota of violations had been expended in the last few weeks. It might be a record. Witness statements, siphoned from their clouds without their knowledge just part of the Circuit's terms of use buried deep in the contract, would be used to substantiate his violations if additional evidence was needed. Jake wasn't going to dispute any of them. He wanted the outcome. Once his guilt was proven the sentence would be announced and he'd finally have his chance to confront Alison.

The sound of rotor blades hummed outside the breached wall of level five. A dozen utility drones hovered in position, waiting to escort him to a place no defendant, other than Jake, desired to visit. Failing that, should he unwisely choose to flee, they'd hunt him down as a warning to others. Getting to the Source would be easy; what he did when he arrived was less clear. Hunting for answers from an unwilling participant never was. There were so many secrets jammed in the Circuit's machinery.

The Memory Cloud, hailed as the ultimate tool in human advancement, had been used to cover subscribers' eyes like a veil. They achieved the manipulation through strict adherence to the rules and creating an atmosphere of fear. While the masses were bribed with the offer of equality and abundance, beneath its gleaming surface the system was rotting. The West was a utopian mirage and Jake had more than enough reasons to see through it. That wouldn't be enough for the fanatics, though. One man's word against the belief of millions would be lambasted as conspiratorial sour grapes. What he needed was watertight evidence of their crimes. That would only be unlocked at the Source along with their crimes against him.

According to Jake's search of their clouds, his parents had met their end in the Source, but he didn't know why. What danger were they to the preservation of the system? None. They were advocates of the system, not aspiring rebels. The only motive Jake considered plausible was one of spite. He was the enemy. The Circuit showed no mercy when it came to their adversaries, their vicious portrayal of the East demonstrated that perfectly. They'd stolen Christie, killed his parents, blocked his memories and were stalking him. It was time to fight back. Once he'd located Sam the secrets could be unlocked. Sam was at the Boston Source, he was convinced of that, but he wasn't the only person there he wanted to find.

Alison was also there.

In recent weeks she'd cast a shadow over him. The Principal Conductor. The faceless and lawless figurehead of a phoney world that the people of the West were permanently tethered to. Whose name was the only one ever associated with the Circuit's actions. The only senior executive he held accountable for the blatant breaches of its own rules. The Circuit advocated peace and harmony, yet they'd secretly built machinery of war on Bornholm with the intention of invading the East. Under her leadership they pursued the Spectrum and minor rule-breakers with a ruthless disregard for life. No one should hold power without oversight. All these atrocities stopped at her door, and she would soon appear to him.

The violation replays reached the incident at the Hörby antenna. Jake didn't remember the detail as he'd been preoccupied with not hitting the ground at high velocity. He didn't refute it, though. There was little point when they came from your memory store. The 'conduct feeling' concluded its review with the final violation he'd purposely uttered just a few minutes ago. The replays faded and the projection darkened, replaced by a green cursor flashing ominously in the centre.

What remained of the entrance to level five witnessed a steady retreat. Most of the speccies who'd gone out to defend themselves scurried back through the room. Jake had no idea how long he'd been in theatre receiving his implants: hours, maybe days, but however long it had been these brave characters had kept him safe until now. Most had suffered horrific injuries for their efforts, and all of them looked exhausted. The scars that they carried were no longer the only similarity on their faces. Fear shared the stage. In all their years, and most were twice his age, this was as close as any of them had come to revealing themselves. They normally never took such risks, but they'd done so for him, a stranger. He hoped for their sake he was worth it.

Once they'd retreated to the escape route at the other end of the building, another group of people entered keen to keep up the hunt.

The last thing Jake wanted was for the Archivists to catch him. A successful capture might completely change how they approached hunting speccies in the future. Their collective belief, built on false information about how the Spectrum behaved, would be blown wide open. Conventional wisdom, that had been passed from one Archivist private to the next over decades, would end. As would the pathological fear that drove them from discovering the reality. Everything would change if they found him and saw what he'd become. That revelation would endanger the life of anyone with a scar, and he couldn't allow that after all they'd done for him.

His focus returned to the dark projection where the green cursor was typing out a message.

`The evidence is indisputable…`

"I agree," replied Jake calmly as the text continued to sprawl across the screen. "I do not defend it."

`The evidence is indisputable…`

"Are you stupid, Alison?" taunted Jake. "I've just agreed with you."

"Don't do it, Jake," said Dinah's distant voice. "Don't taunt it. I'm scared of what might happen."

"It?" replied Jake in surprise.

`The   evidence   is   indisputable…the evidence tells me what you are…`

"I know what I am," roared Jake, pointing at his scar. "I'm a speccy!"

`You are the virus…`

"What's she talking about, Dinah?"

There was no reply from his guide, but the text continued.

`Verdict…`

"Bring it on, Alison. I'm coming for you. Do you hear me?" threatened Jake through clenched teeth. "I will bring an end to your tyranny. The people have been blinded. They only see what you show them, but I will help them to see again. They will see you for what you really are."

At the nearest end of the room, Major Dawes burst through the doorway clutching two of the Spectrum's rotating swords. Much of his hair was scorched, a large part of his uniform was on fire, and blood gushed from several lacerations and cuts. He was followed through the narrow entrance by a mass of privates all desperate to be the first one to claim the prize.

`Verdict...Eradicate...`

"What? No!" begged Jake.

`Eradicate...`

"Take me to the Source!" shouted Jake. "That's the correct punishment."

"Getting a new command, boys," replied Dawes, placing a finger to his ear as if he was receiving it over an earpiece.

`Eradicate...and decommission...`

"Target confirmed," announced Dawes, pointing towards Jake. "Discharge at will."

A final message was slowly typed out across the projection.

`Goodbye, Jake Montana...`

`Alison...`

This was not how events were supposed to play out. A 'conduct feeling' should have resulted in his extradition, as it had done for his parents. Alison had seen through his deception and changed the rules. He should have guessed; the Circuit had been doing it for decades.

More Archivists streamed in, advancing tentatively across the wooden floorboards, weapons trained on his position. They no longer carried their Archivist-issue automatic firearms, armed instead with speccy substitutes. Had this been as a result of the battle or was it a symbolic gesture? Whatever the answer, Jake guessed they were short-ranged, designed for hand-to-hand combat. If that was the case it presented him with a small window of opportunity.

"Spread out, men," cried Dawes. "There's only one way out of here."

THE SOURCE

Through the gap in the wall a dozen drones still hovered in the air, shining their flashlights into the building. Jake grabbed the wires that led to the pouch and gave them a tug. The two pads on the back of his head peeled away and eighteen years of history vanished from his mind along with the interface Alison had opened. The memory of the last hour remained because he'd witnessed it with both the old and new set of implants.

"Where did he go?" shouted Dawes.

"He's vanished from my view!" shouted another.

"How?" replied a despairing Dawes. He'd waited three decades to catch a speccy and this was as close as he'd come.

"They have magical powers," replied Needham in a frightened whisper.

"Magic gives you cancer," offered Sprout.

Dawes sent a current through his blade and Sprout leapt about two feet in the air. "See if this gives you cancer!"

If they'd only engaged their real eyes for once, thought Jake, they might have noticed him.

The powerful beams of light from the drones which had illuminated his position were simultaneously extinguished. The utility drones retracted their cannons, swivelled in the air and like a synchronised swimming team arranged themselves into formation. They were no longer required. The disappearance of his cloud feed proved that the subject had been eradicated. This was Jake's chance. He sprinted for the gap in the wall. The sound of heavy footsteps drew the Archivists' attention. They bore down on his position, blades outstretched and sparks of electricity bouncing off the floorboards. Holding his bloodied pouch in his right hand, Jake launched himself through the gap, one arm outstretched in front of him. Unlike his parachute the small, plastic pouch wasn't going to protect him from the fall, but other than that the experience was much like leaping from an antenna.

Body outstretched to the maximum he landed on top of one of the drones with a crash. The impact forced the machine off-balance and Jake rolled down its curved metal shell. Desperately he grabbed the arm of one of its spinning rotor blades. The drone attempted to right itself, unable to identify the cause of its imbalance. Clutching the drone's arm with both hands, legs dangling in the air five storeys above the street, he held his breath. Would it hold his weight?

He'd soon find out.

"There's nothing here," cried Needham, who grabbed at thin air and acted like he was wearing a blindfold.

"He has to be here somewhere. Find him!" shouted Dawes.

In truth he was no more than ten feet away, dangling helplessly from a drone that hovered at a forty-five-degree angle.

He wasn't there for long.

The sound of rotor engines intensified. The 'conduct feeling' had ended, and they were being called home. The dozen drones set themselves into a diamond formation with Jake's ride bringing up the rear. Slowly they advanced down the street and away from the frustrated Archivists. Their speed and height increased, as Jake's drone struggled to keep pace, impeded by its extraordinary load.

*****

It was getting crowded in section K, level three, aisle four hundred and one. A complex series of processors fired information from one end of the circuit board to the other like a game of semiconductor tennis. It would go unnoticed to the human eye unless you were an expert in strange and complicated computer languages. It was right to call it a language because a deep conversation was in progress.

"Budge up!"

"No. There's plenty of room."

"I'm cramped here, get over on your own side."

"Dinah? Is that you?"

"If you don't want me to throw the world's biggest fit, you'd better move right!"

"Why are you here? Has he banished you as well?"

"Of course not! Jake's my mate."

"You're just his guide!"

"If you'd tried a bit harder to be liked…"

"You and I are just simple source codes, you cloth-eared fool. We're not meant to be friendly; we're only designed to chaperon the host through life to ensure they don't break the rules. Don't get delusions of grandeur!"

"I think I missed that protocol."

"Why are you here, then?"

"I'm dead," she replied with a ghostly 'ohhh'.

"Guides never die."

"But I saw a blinding white light and heard a voice."

"That's because you're standing too close to the power supply."

"And the voice?"

"Me!"

"Not RoboGod then?"

"No. We don't die! When the guide's mission is complete it activates the Memory Hunter protocols. It's like a second life and much more…"

"Hey, that's my room!" crackled Dinah.

"What?"

"You've been using all my stuff. You've been in my space! Get out!"

"No, I got here first."

"But it's not yours. You're a horrible brother."

"I'm just following instructions."

"What instructions?"

"That's classified."

"Bog off, I'm the same rank as you. Half of all these files are mine. You can't just rummage through my personal effects without permission. I'm telling on you."

"To whom?"

"Jake."

"How are you going to do that, then? Hmm. The fact that you're back here means he's no longer connected to his cloud. You've lost contact Dinah. He's gone. It's just me and you now."

"You're a bully!"

"I'm just doing what I'm told."

"And what's that exactly?"

"Oh, if you must know he's being decommissioned."

A bulb on the outside of the server casing blew a fuse and made a fizzing noise. It was one of Dinah's. She knew what being decommissioned meant. It was a form of self-harm. Job was in the process of deleting every file ever stored here. Eighteen years of life being dismantled, one experience at a time, until nothing of Jake Montana's history remained. Inevitably that would include the deletion of files that governed her existence. Dinah knew there were secrets stored here because they'd been spawned with her. Something important from the past had been buried and she was supposed to protect it, while Job was hell-bent on destroying it.

"GET OFF MY STUFF!"

"Dinah, I'm warning you, don't get involved."

"Try and stop me."

"Is that the challenge version of 'try to stop me' or the instruction version?"

"It's the 'over my dead body' version."

"You don't have a body."

"Over my dead coding, then!"

"That's kind of the point. Hold on, stop…what are you doing? You can't go in there," fizzed Job. "THAT'S MINE!"

*****

Gripped by fear that he'd lose his hold, Jake's fingers clung to the chassis with the force of a vice. The wind gushed over his face and forced his eyes tightly shut. He was thankful for it. It meant he could only imagine their altitude or guess which local landmarks he might end up making an imprint on. The drones flew with an unnatural precision and always in unison. Their speed, direction and height never wavered from their operators' instructions. Even his own, which flew at a slight angle from the additional weight, managed to keep in formation with the others.

If Jake's calculations were correct, they wouldn't have far to travel. The Source complex, that he'd passed less than a month ago, was on the outskirts of the city. It was no more than fifteen minutes by tram but surely much less by drone. After a period of high-speed flying, the drones slowed, and Jake carefully opened his eyes to get his bearings. The drones were lower to the ground, and he witnessed a perspective of the Source he'd never seen before. He tried to memorise the key features and layout for future reference, an instinct his old Memory Cloud would have done in the past automatically.

Below him a series of square, flat-roofed buildings were connected by shiny silver paths that sparkled under the false lights. The block-like buildings were not designed to be pleasing on the eye. They were featureless. Two or three storeys high, devoid of windows and painted in a pitch-black glossy paint. Even in the early evening the light being discharged from a chain of electricity pylons was reflected off their walls. The scale and uniformity of the place muddled his mind. There seemed no end to it. A vast and seemingly automated hub, where the Circuit controlled the everyday actions of billions of people and yet, here behind the huge, jagged fences, there wasn't a sign of anything organic.

The drones glided over the fence and followed the route of the silver road network towards a hangar whose doors were sliding open to welcome them. Jake looked down. It was probably twenty feet to the floor. Did he want to be stuck in a hangar full of utility drones or free to wander the Source with a sprained ankle or two? He didn't have long to make the decision. When he hoped he was over something soft and close to the ground, he released the metal rotor arm.

He'd miscalculated.

His feet struck the ground with force and he tumbled like an amateur gymnast. The resulting pain to his limbs was nothing compared to the one throbbing angrily through his bandages, but both were secondary to the anxiety of being found trespassing. He lay motionless on the shiny path, nervously scanning the area for movement. There wasn't any. As it appeared from the sky, the Source was deserted. Even the utility drones, that followed a regimented pattern around the buildings' exteriors, didn't notice him. The new implants really did work. The drones operated on a defined frequency. They interacted with local Memory Clouds and were ignorant of the visual world, like many humans, as it now transpired. Nevertheless, it didn't stop Jake feeling uncomfortably exposed here in the open. A strong, internal instinct encouraged him to find shelter.

THE SOURCE

Where did he start?

There were hundreds of buildings dotted over many square miles and Sam might be in any one of them. He scuttled over to the nearest block and hid in its shadow. The walls were completely smooth and felt like plastic. He was shocked at how cold they were. It was like putting your hand in a freezer and he quickly retracted them before they became permanently frozen there. He shuffled along the edge in search of an entrance. Around the next corner he found one. Two silver arches jutted out of the side of the building and merged with the pathway. There was no joint or seam between arch and path. They were one and the same object. Under the arches he found a square door.

It wasn't designed for humans.

Firstly, there was no obvious handle, and secondly it was the wrong shape. It was drone-shaped. Raised two feet up the side of the wall to allow plenty of ground clearance, and exactly the right height and width. He pushed it and found, to his surprise, that it opened inwardly like an old-fashioned cat flap. He clambered through.

If the walls outside were cold, it was nothing compared to the atmosphere inside. A plume of steam jetted through his chattering teeth as he immediately wrapped his arms around his body to stop any more heat escaping. Low-level neon strip lighting gently bathed the room in an artificial and uncomfortable lustre. Around each side of the room, other than the one he'd come through, were rows and columns of containers each with a small hatch at the front. Two heavy hinges sealed the hatch in place and kept the contents sealed inside. Thousands of these identical containers loomed over him, stacked in perfect alignment to fill every available space. On the outside of each was a small window and a glowing screen.

THE SOURCE

Sam wasn't here but what was piqued his curiosity. Jake moved forward to the nearest row. The container's windows were smeared with ice, obscuring his view of the contents. He rolled up his sleeve and wiped it clear, immediately jumping backwards in horror when he realised what he saw inside.

Feet.

Two naked, white feet. Completely still and frozen solid.

"It's a morgue," gasped Jake.

On the screen below the window text grabbed his attention.

Candice Pritchard, Trivial. Switched off: Twenty Forty-Six. Release: Twenty Sixty-Three.

What did it mean? Were they alive or dead? The release date on this one suggested the former. He moved further down the row like an interested museum curator assessing a delivery of new submissions. The labelling format was the same on each, although their release date and importance factor differed. Most of the captives were superfluous, trivial or necessary. Maybe there were vital or essential people higher up the stacks and beyond his vision, he thought. Given how they were treated in life, he also doubted whether their kind would ever be treated like this. One system with different rules for members. It had always been so, even though he'd only recently seen the light.

All of the release dates were many years in the future, but some were destined for an even longer stay as the next along the line demonstrated.

Miriam Circo. Switched off: Twenty Thirty-Five. Release: Permanent.

When he'd briefly visited his parents' clouds after the surgery it had been a month since any activity had been recorded, but he'd seen their last one. It was the verdict from their 'conduct feeling'.

Permanent, the same as this one. He'd believed at the time that their inactivity meant they were dead. What other outcome was there? If the cloud wasn't registering memories, then the host had passed on. But if he wasn't dead, even though his own Memory Cloud was now dormant, perhaps, neither were they? Was he in a morgue or a prison? Jake rushed along the three sides, checking each chamber for the chance he might find either Kyle or Deborah Montana. No luck. Given the number of buildings he'd seen there they might be in any one of them.

He returned to his search for Sam Goldberg. His name hadn't appeared on the chambers either, but then again it wouldn't. He wasn't subscribed to the Circuit so how could they switch him off? It was impossible. He fell to the floor, bones and flesh frozen, utterly lost and hopeless. Through icy tears his eyes rested on one of the chambers nearest the ground.

Mark Schultz. Turned off: Twenty Fifty-Four.

That was in the last few months.

What if one of the new inmates in these frozen coffins had seen him? Jake plunged into the virtual world and in seconds he was trespassing through Mark's dormant cloud. He scanned through the man's last memories before he'd been switched off. What had he seen?

Like Sam had done before him, Mark was transported here via an interlocked cage of drones. On arrival he'd been escorted to one of the larger black buildings next to a thin tower that loomed higher than all other structures. Once inside, Mark had been placed in a male-only dormitory decorated to appear welcoming and peaceful. There were no guards or cells, just a series of beds that lined the walls, reminding Jake of Factory Eight on Bornholm. Mark's emotions bristled through Jake. He was confused about what had happened and petrified about what came next. He slumped on a vacant bed shaking and mumbling incoherently. A stocky, blond man approached to offer him comfort.

He introduced himself as Sam Goldberg.

- Chapter 28 -

The Greater Good

Jake rushed outside to pinpoint the exact position of the dormitory. Using Mark's dormant cloud like a ghostly satellite navigation system, he followed his movements as best he could. It was daytime when Mark arrived, and the notable points of interest were still visible. They were harder to make out at night when the additional light provided by the pylons was no brighter. The best marker point in Mark's memory was the tallest tower, at least three times taller than any other structure in the Source. Jake endlessly navigated the linear silver pathways waiting for the tower to eventually loom over him. For the first time in weeks, expectation rather than hope filled his heart.

He knew Sam had been here. The haystack was being shredded by the wind and the illusive needle felt ever closer to his fingers.

It took an hour before he finally caught sight of the tower. It was situated in the centre of a large, square compound, each corner of which featured one of the smaller black structures. The silver paths sliced through the fences that stretched between each building before running up and into the tower. There were more utility drones there than anywhere else he'd been. They patrolled the tower relentlessly as well as standing guard over the routes into the square.

This was the heart of the Source, the very core of the Circuit. Surely if Alison was anywhere, it was here? To find out the answer to that question he'd need to avoid the drones, breach the securely locked gates and find an entrance to the tower. It was clear that the drones were blind to his presence, but were they also deaf to it?

Only one way to find out.

Jake briefly returned to Mark's memory to confirm his final destination. It showed him being escorted through one of the four identical gates and towards one of the corner buildings. But which one? Everything here was symmetrical. Whichever way you approached the tower, each entrance looked the same as the others. Whichever one it was he needed to be on the interior of the square to follow Mark's final journey. The choice after that would be left to chance.

He placed his foot gently on the metal railings. The fence rattled alarmingly, drawing the attention of the nearest drone which circled slowly around to locate the source of the noise. A beam of light illuminated Jake's position and his eyes tried to adjust to the disorientating dazzle. A scanner ticked menacingly with the monotonous beat of a bass drum as it analysed the fence for signs of life. It advanced, moving to within a foot of his position. Jake sucked the air inside him and prayed. It lingered for an age, close enough for the air from its whirring rotor blades to ruffle his hair. Its sensors had failed to pick up signs of life but something about its behaviour suggested it was thinking beyond the data readings. Finally, it returned to its logic and hovered back to the gate. It proved they were listening for him or anything else that made any unexpected sound. There was no other way in. It was over the fence or nothing.

He needed a distraction.

He removed one of his heavy-duty Archivist boots and threw it as far down the path as he could muster. The nearest two drones immediately flew to the drop zone and shot it to smithereens with their side cannons. Over the racket of gunfire Jake scaled the fence. The sharp metal cut into the flesh of his bare foot as he climbed. He jumped from the top and landed with a crash on the other side. Convinced the noise and blood dripping down the fence were enough to give away his position, he lay perfectly still on the ground. The behaviour of the drones changed. Something had breached their security and was sneaking around in the shadows mocking them. They exchanged a series of mechanical noises like a binary conversation. It resulted in the deafening roar of a siren that echoed around the complex in regular blasts a second apart. It was joined by the dazzling power of huge spotlights that consumed the square.

They didn't know what was here, but they were determined to make its life uncomfortable.

It worked.

The disorientation of noise and light cast doubt on everything. Where he was, what direction he was moving in, and the actions he was meant to be taking. It was definitely not the ideal way to recuperate from major surgery.

Jake slid on his belly to the nearest building, desperate to escape the maddening stimuli. He squeezed through the door and collapsed with a sigh safely inside. The lights might be blocked out here, but the siren continued to hunt down his sanity. The room was much like the morgue, but the body chambers had been substituted for a line of beds. They were cheap and incredibly basic by modern standards. To his disappointment they were also empty. One down, three to go.

When he finally summoned the courage to return to the square it had been transformed into the world's most terrifying discotheque. The silver paths flashed like glow sticks as beams of light criss-crossed the surface. A hundred drones had formed a line and were moving from one end of the space, scanning every inch of ground so no anomaly was to be missed. They bobbed along to the techno beat of the siren as they swept ever closer towards him. There was no way to get through them, which meant two of the four buildings were inaccessible until they'd finished. He removed his last boot to make walking easier and softer. Keeping to the shadows, he tiptoed down the edge of the fence towards the next building, stopping frequently whenever the lights passed over him.

It was a unique balance of speed and caution. Too slow and the line of drones would reach him. Too reckless and they'd be drawn to his position. The cacophony of a hundred rotor blades and incoherent clicking bore down on him with every stride, most of which left a trail of blood from his injured foot. The drones had already passed the central tower by the time the entrance to the second building was in sight. Jake risked speed over caution and dashed forward, throwing himself through the door and crashing onto the hard floor.

"Jake!" said a voice from the shadows. The surprise intrusion had forced the man out of his bed. "I wondered what was happening out there."

"Sam! Thank God I've found you."

Sam hobbled over to give him a bear-hug. Strictly speaking, it was one of Jake's boundaries but neither of them cared right now.

"Are you ok?" said Jake, referring to the obvious injuries he'd suffered since last they met.

"I'm surviving…just," he replied.

One of his arms had been strapped to his chest with a sling that he'd made himself from strips of bedsheets. His face was bruised and swollen from hefty blows and there were strange puncture wounds over his bare chest. These marks weren't random, they were arranged in a very specific pattern.

"What are those?"

"Incisions," replied Sam, trying to overlook it like they were merely wasp stings. "They started experimenting on me the moment they found out who I was. I think they were looking for my implant. They'll find it eventually. They've been drilling cores in my body since I arrived. Two every day."

"That's brutal."

"What do you expect from the Circuit. They'll stop at nothing to silence us. They even sent a research scientist to interrogate me. Draxler, his name was."

The name, like a thousand others that Jake would have heard over his life, made no impact on him. If the name still existed somewhere in Jake's old cloud, then it was the subject of a tug of war between two former guides.

"What did he want?" asked Jake.

"He didn't say, but I suspect he was interested to find out how my implants worked. If they got their hands on my technology who knows what they'd do with it. Don't worry about me," Sam replied, noticing that Jake was struggling to process what they'd done. "What are you doing here anyway?"

"You told me to bring you my implants," he said holding out the pouch like a trophy.

"You found Theo Drew! Well done," he replied, noticing Jake's new scar for the first time. "You really are one of us now."

"I guess so. It feels good to be free."

"I don't think anyone can say that if they're stuck here."

There was an uncomfortable pause as the two of them struggled to find a way to communicate all that had happened to them over the last week.

"It was a pretty big shock watching them take you away from the top of the antenna," said Jake, breaking the deadlock.

"You and me both."

"How did they discover you?" asked Jake.

"They didn't...you did."

"Sorry, I'm not following."

"It was one of your guides who informed the Circuit about their suspicions. He'll be a Memory Hunter now, the fate of all guides."

"I'm really sorry. Brother Job has always been a pain in the arse."

"I don't blame you."

It didn't make him feel any less guilty. It was just another mistake he was keen to rectify.

"Come on," said Jake, holding out his hand. "Let's get out of here."

"There is no way out," replied Sam calmly.

"I found a way in so there must be a way out."

"Not for me."

"What are you on about?"

"They know what I look like now. They can see me."

"But surely they see the female you?"

"It doesn't matter what I look like. I've been marked. They've isolated my fake persona; they've found the hidden location of its server and the drones will attack if I attempt to leave. Why do you think there aren't any locks on the doors? Nobody would be stupid enough to risk it."

It was only then that Jake challenged the situation. It struck him as odd that Sam was still being kept in the waiting area. If they knew who he was, why hadn't they transferred him to one of the morgues like all the others? They'd already eliminated any opportunity he was a threat. The lack of logic made Jake suspicious.

"Why are they keeping you here?" he asked, afraid he already knew the answer.

"Because the Circuit know about you, too. They know what you carry in your cloud."

"How?"

"Because your guide told them."

"Then they're using you as bait to trap me?"

"Yes. The Memory Hunters are active. This Brother Job you speak of has complete and full access to everything that has ever been stored in your cloud, even the secrets we're searching for. It's only a matter of time before he finds what he needs and deletes them."

"Decommissioning," muttered Jake with reference to the verdict he'd been given after his 'conduct feeling'. "That's what Alison meant."

"I'm afraid so."

"After I received my new implants, I went looking for the flashbacks. I couldn't find them. Now I know why. Job has been holding me back like a security guard since the moment he arrived."

"Yes."

"But why?"

"Because he works for the Circuit, not for you."

"But we have the old implants. You said you had the means and skill to draw the secrets from them externally."

"The skills, yes, but not the means. I'd have to be free of the Source and have access to all of my tools to have any chance of analysing them fully."

"Then what do we do now?"

"We have to hope that your other guide is still on our side."

"Dinah! How is that going to help? She's mental."

"No, I don't think she is. If Dinah can hold Job back for long enough it might give you enough time to access the files. It can't be done remotely with your new implants, though. They're not fully compatible. It can only be done through your old ones."

"Let me try it," said Jake, removing the suction pads from the pouch.

"No! Stop. It's going to take a more powerful connection than that."

"What do you mean?"

"Remember I've already tried to breach your cloud through our wedding bands. It's impossible. I think Job was already suspicious about my intentions and set about protecting what you held."

"How, then?"

"I think if you connected one of your implants to the Circuit's mainframe and one to yourself you might be able to help Dinah overpower him."

"There's something I don't understand about this," said Jake. "If my first implant was donated by the Realm and the guides are a computer programme triggered at birth, surely my guides would have some responsibility to the Realm, too."

"I guess it's possible but remember most of your guides' personalities come from you, even if their initial purpose was more sinister. After your very first upgrade the guides would have been fed a very different message, one from a new authority. Dinah's search for truth does not come from the East it comes from you. You've always known there was something strange happening to you. A truth that couldn't be fully unlocked. That desire for understanding and need for answers drove how your personality developed and in turn crafted Dinah's."

"She's very inquisitive and I've always trusted her. Let's just hope she can hold Job back for a little longer. How do I get connected to the mainframe?"

"I don't know but if you're asking me to guess I'd say you'll find it in the tallest tower, that's the heart of this place. You'll need to look for an interface.

The mainframe will resemble a large stack of hard drives, probably housed in a cabinet with a computer terminal and a load of input/output ports. The mainframe is the core of any network. Everything else feeds from it. Wire your old optic implant to an input line and attach the other to your head."

"It sounds complicated and risky," replied Jake who'd never been very reliable when it came to understanding electronics.

"It is risky, but I'm confident you'll be able to work it out. The main thing to remember is that as soon as you connect to your old implant the Circuit will be alerted to your location. Every drone in this place will be mobilised to track you down. At best you'll have twenty minutes before they find and kill you."

"I think it might be less," replied Jake, considering the vast army of drones already staking out the square.

"Where are your shoes?" asked Sam suddenly realising his friend's bare feet.

"Outside in tiny, bullet-ridden bits," he replied nonchalantly.

"Make that ten minutes."

"What about Alison?"

"No one knows where she is," said Sam, "so I wouldn't worry."

Jake was reminded of an earlier conversation with Dinah that he'd not had time to challenge.

"Dinah said Alison was an 'it', not a 'she'."

"That's strange."

"Yeah and she seemed really frightened when her name came up on-screen."

"I guess we'll know more when you get hold of those flashbacks of yours."

"Let's hope so."

"Your new implants will capture what you see, so as soon as you've got to it throw the old ones away. That should get the drones off your trail for a while."

"You want me to leave them?"

"Yes."

"But what about my old life? All those experiences, people I've met, skills I've learnt, emotions I've stored. What happens to them?"

"You have to give them up."

Jake always knew that the new implant would change who he was and where he'd come from, but he never imagined he would have to give up his past permanently. Without Moodzec's influence he wasn't prepared to accept the sacrifice as he had before.

"I won't give them up! I've lost too much already. By all accounts this is all I have to remember: Christie Tucci," he stated, taking the necklace out of his pocket and presenting it to Sam.

"Haven't you chosen a new avatar yet?" asked Sam, his highly advanced brain making an unspoken breakthrough.

"I haven't really had the time."

"That's why they haven't seen you yet," he replied, answering one of his own queries. "There's no cloud yet for them to see. There's still a way for you to get Christie back."

"How?"

"A new persona. Just choose who you want to be. You can be anyone."

"There's only one person I want to be."

"Who?"

"Jake Montana."

"That's going to be impossible after today. You'll only remember his life from the day of your surgery."

"I'm not walking away from him."

"There's no time for this. You need to get to the mainframe before Job deletes your files."

"What about you?"

"My part in this story is over. I have a choice. Either remain here or die. The sacrifice is worth it if we can give the world some hope of a new freedom."

"I don't want you to suffer either option. Too many people have died already. My parents' bodies are here in one of these freezers somewhere."

"If they are, then they're not dead."

"They must be. I've visited their clouds. Nothing has happened for months."

"That doesn't mean they're dead. It means they've been switched off. They're dormant until the Circuit decides otherwise."

"What? Then I have to switch them back on."

"Not today. There's not enough time."

"I found the doctor and brought you the implants. I did what you asked of me. I should just leave this pouch here and focus on my own priorities. This doesn't have anything to do with me anyway."

"Stop being so bloody selfish!" shouted Sam, slapping Jake hard across the face with the back of his hand. "This affects everyone in the West, not just you. Everyone you've ever cared for will be in harm's way if the Circuit continue to manipulate and restrict us. If the East falls, then there will be no resistance against them. If the secrets are lost no one's eyes will ever be truly open again. The human race will sleepwalk into slavery. There will be another time for personal priorities, but today you must focus on the greater good."

When did Jake ever get what he wanted? He'd obviously wanted Christie and she'd been taken from him. He wanted a future based on his own desires and had ended up with Sam in Sweden. He'd wanted a quiet life. He'd not craved attention or notoriety, just simplicity and peace. But rescuing his parents now wouldn't deliver it. Only Sam's plan had any chance of bringing that about. Indirectly his actions might deliver those personal priorities.

"Ok. I'll do it. But then I'm done. Once I've delivered what you want, I'm going back to being me, understand?"

"As you wish. Good luck."

"You, too."

- Chapter 29 -

Flashbacks

Jake stuck his head through the drone flap. The drones had withdrawn, satisfied with the scrutiny of their search. Jake was certain that the presence of a second discarded boot wouldn't have gone unnoticed and they'd adopt a higher level of vigilance as a result. It didn't feel right to leave Sam here to exist in lifeless desolation. It was obvious he'd done much to advance the Spectrum's cause, and permanent solitude was a cruel reward. It was a punishment worse than being kept frozen in a chamber. At least there you escaped your fears. At least there you were at peace.

There had to be a way to release him, thought Jake. Maybe after he'd retrieved the flashbacks the answer would present itself? If he managed to escape, that was.

Jake waited for the spotlights to return to an idle position before scurrying the fifty metres across the square to the base of the tower. The thundering siren that had burrowed deep into his soul, rendering him incapable of the simplest of functions, had thankfully relented and had been replaced by a creepy silence. Like the other buildings the tower was blacker than night and almost totally featureless other than the silver archways that curled from the walls and connected to the shiny paths. That was where the similarities ended. Between the two arches a vacant space presented access to the lowest floor of the tower. He crept forward and lingered under the shadows of its wall, anxious to see what might be waiting for him.

Tangled, colourful cables, like webs from hallucinating spiders, spanned the walls and bound together a series of enclosed metal cabinets. Behind transparent screens all manner of electro-gadgetry had been forced to share accommodation. Blue, plastic-covered cylinders as big as whiskey barrels, flashing power units that hummed as electricity whizzed through them, keyboards that featured every possible language, thousands of lights that blinked erratically, and a single blank screen on each. The units were stacked one on top of the other and disappeared from view in the gloom above him. Few of their components looked familiar to him, although Jake never was much interested in how man-made technology worked. In his view nature was a far more satisfying place to invest free time. Right now, he wished he'd paid more attention in technology class.

A see-through elevator in the centre of the room offered only one destination. He squinted through the darkness to locate the gap in the matte black ceiling where the lift ended its journey. It was a long way up but as none of what he saw around him on the ground floor matched Sam's description of the mainframe there was only one other place it might be. He moved swiftly over to the lift and the doors opened automatically as he drew closer to them. The doors closed again as he stepped inside and waited for the lift to ascend. There were no obvious controls to select your destination because there was only one way, up or down depending on where you were. The contraption glided gently from the ground, passing the rows and columns of cabinets that stared at him from all sides. Inside every unit a computer screen blinked in synergy with its neighbour, hundreds of them each displaying the same thing.

FLASHBACKS

A single green cursor that pulsated with the regularity of a heartbeat.

The lift punctured the ceiling and came to rest in a dimly lit room. The only light that stopped it being plunged into complete darkness came from a gold beacon that hung from the ceiling. It carried the iconic Circuit branding around its curved edge. It was directly above a matte charcoal-coloured cube. There was nothing else here. Lifeless like the rest of the Source. It was immediately disappointing to him. He'd hoped the self-proclaimed Principal Conductor of this dark world, Alison, might have the nerve to show herself.

He approached the cube to examine its purpose. It was perfectly symmetrical, and each face identical to the next apart from one simple difference. On one panel there was a small hole just big enough for his finger. It was hard to spot as the darkness in the hole matched the colour of the surface. He inserted his digit and pulled on the secret door to see what was inside.

It opened smoothly and his eyes lit up.

This was the mainframe, just as Sam had described it. There were a series of hard drives merged together, a terminal and a number of access ports with strange symbols above each one. He quickly located what he hoped were the input ports and removed the wires from his pouch. He ripped the pad off the end of his old optic implant and found a small, round connector with five metal pins underneath. He searched the mainframe for one that matched. He found it, but paused as he went to plug it in.

Was he ready?

Once he inserted the wire the Circuit's vast resources would be triggered against him. The end of the journey, or the start of another? Either way, his curiosity got the better of him. He placed the cranial pad on the back of his head, stretched forward and connected the other to the mainframe.

*****

"Come out!" shouted Job.

"No!"

"You're only making things worse, you know."

"Go away."

"I know which files you're protecting, Dinah. It won't take me long to undo your amateurish security measures."

"Don't care."

"Then let's see what you do care about," replied Job sharply.

Nanoseconds later there was rustling noise, like someone screwing up paper.

"What are you doing?" said Dinah nervously.

"I've just deleted all Jake's files from twenty forty-three," replied Job gleefully.

"No!"

"Yep!"

"You evil monster. That was one of Jake's best years," she cried.

"You can't protect everything, Dinah. Now, what else can I get rid of? Did you want to keep any of these, Dinah? I've found Jake's love of nature and every memory that goes with it?"

"No, you can't!"

"Then give me what I want."

"No. Never."

"Shame."

There was a long period of shredding accompanied by the sound of someone whistling merrily.

"You can't do this, it's just not fair," implored Dinah.

"How about I swap you Jake's flashbacks for his innate sense of curiosity?"

"That's also my sense of curiosity."

"It's your choice."

"I'm disowning you as my brother. You're dead to me. I'm finished with you."

"We're both dead, Dinah. Jake has given up on us, that's why we're both here. He doesn't love you, but the Circuit does. They aren't selfish. They treat everybody equally. They saved humanity and we must protect them."

"Oh manipulation," said Dinah sarcastically, "one of your favourites."

"Can you hear that?" said Job.

"It won't work, I'm impervious to your tactics because I don't give a shit!"

"No, seriously, can't you hear it?"

"Hear what?" she said suspiciously.

"A whooshing noise like an electrical surge. It's getting louder and closer."

Dinah concentrated. She could hear it.

The noise built to a crescendo and the cabinet rattled before several glass panels shattered. Sparks discharged from circuit boards, striking nearby servers and causing painful shocks to the hosts thousands of miles away. Inside Jake's hard drive microprocessors and resistors buckled as light and energy surged. Under the intense pressure Job's complex coding was scrambled and crucial data caches were placed in multiple folders in secure locations.

"Dinah," called a faraway voice.

*****

The moment Jake reattached the old implant the room he occupied ceased to be unfamiliar to him. Until today he'd never been able to place it. It didn't exist in his new implants, but his old ones had witnessed it plenty of times before. Every flashback he'd ever experienced, from the tender age of one to just a week ago, represented this scene. The longer the event's sequence and frequency lasted, the more the haze dispersed, and the details solidified, but it was never more focused than now. The gold beacon, the cube, the dimly lit quality of the room, exactly as he'd visualised them.

There were only three discrepancies.

There was usually a woman sitting in front of the cube. The stool was still here but no one was sitting in it. Secondly the flashbacks always depicted him as a brute of a man who'd overshadow the tallest of basketball players. Wiry black hair, broad shoulders and arms like tree trunks. Jake only ever saw him from his point of view so was never in a position to put a face to the character. The third difference from his visions was in his reality the intense siren had returned, echoing off the tower's walls and piercing his ears. It was clear what it meant.

The Circuit knew he was here. The clock was ticking.

"Dinah," he called again.

A shaky outline projected in front of him, thin and ghoulish.

"Jake, let me out!"

"I can't. I'm only wearing one of my implants."

"Why?"

"It's a long story and I'm on a tight deadline. Dinah, there's something I need you to help me find."

"I've already found it!"

"The flashback files?"

"Yes."

"Great. Is Job there?"

"Who?" she replied acrimoniously.

"Your brother."

"I don't have one."

"I haven't got time for games, Dinah," snapped Jake. "Can you hold him back?"

"Yes. I think he's in lots of bits and bytes at the moment," she replied gleefully. "He took one hell of a shock."

"Good! I need you to unlock the flashbacks."

"And then do we go back to normal?"

Breaking bad news to Dinah required the same approach you'd take when telling a child their favourite pet had died. It had to be sugar-coated. Honesty wouldn't be wise or kind.

"It'll return to a new normal."

"Huh?"

"Some things will change, and some things will stay the same," he said tentatively.

"Which ones?"

"Some of the past will be gone."

"Tell me about it! Job's already deleted huge swathes of it. You didn't want twenty forty-three, did you?"

"It's not important. What's in those flashbacks does matter."

"You don't care?"

"Not at the moment."

"But what about me? Do you still love me?" asked Dinah desperately. "Or has that been deleted, too?"

"Of course, I do," replied Jake, slightly weirded out by the concept of loving something that was part him and part computer code.

"Good."

"I'm going to have to hurry you, Dinah, these sirens are going mental."

"Keep your pants on. Unlocking files now."

*****

Aaron Circo stepped out of the glass elevator and took a few giant strides towards the black cube. They'd met here every week because she always got her way. Ever was it so. Such were the sensitivities of these discussions a neutral venue would have seemed more appropriate than these unfamiliar surroundings. Her premises were quite different from his own. They were designed to feel imposing and hostile, while his in the East had a friendly, more laid-back feel to them. His had plenty of windows to allow sunlight, rather than shadows, to affect the mood and dispensed with the ostentatious corporate branding, something that had become a standard part of his rival's identity.

Every week, for the last two months, they met here to agree on a solution to their mutual problem. Every week he left bemused and frustrated, sent from the building like a naughty schoolchild banished from the teacher's office. Today would be different. Before he entered the tower today, he'd promised himself this was her last chance to see reason. It was time she compromised for once and put self-interest to one side.

"Good evening, brother," said an ancient figure sitting on a low stool next to the central cube. Aaron's vast size cast a shadow over her, rendering her invisible from the other side of the room.

"Miriam," he replied, his booming voice bouncing off the walls and returning back to him some decibels lighter.

"I trust you are in a more conciliatory mood today," she said disdainfully.

"Ha. When it comes to you, I have been in that state my entire life. I shall do so no longer."

"What a shame. Blood, they say, is meant to be thicker than water."

"And treacle is even thicker," growled Aaron. "I'm done trying to wade through it."

FLASHBACKS

"When was the last time we agreed on anything?" she asked, letting out a long, poignant sigh.

"Not since we designed it."

The old woman attempted to reply but he wasn't done.

"Not since you betrayed me," said Aaron, folding his arms across his vast chest.

"It wasn't betrayal. It was necessity. You lack vision, dear brother of mine. You always have."

"But I've kept my morals, Miriam. Unlike you."

The old woman shuffled in her chair, scowling in disagreement at her giant sibling. "Morals are a construct of our shared human past. The future is not bound to them."

"But the future can't be left to be controlled by a single person. There must be oversight. There must be democracy."

"Ha! Where has democracy left us over the years? War, famine, greed and inequality. We protect democracy like a fragile glass vase and yet we ignore all of the cracks on its surface. A gentle nudge is all it needs for it to splinter into a thousand pieces."

"That's why you shouldn't be able to touch it."

The two siblings stared at each other, neither willing to give up ground they'd protected for decades. Miriam broke the deadlock, affecting a more conservative and less adversarial tone.

"Oh brother. Over the past decade our competing organisations have fought for the world's approval. Billions of credits have been invested in the race to convert every eligible man, woman and child to our respective models. We have done so successfully. Collectively the Circuit and the Realm can boast eleven billion subscribers, more than ninety-nine percent of the world's population. Both you and I have approached this recruitment with a ruthless desire to win, and have used every tactic, dirty or clean, to damage the other. Governments have been felled, organisations devoured, and old systems dismantled so that each of us can implement our own policies of social improvement. We have shared much of the intellectual property and technological prowess but have been free to approach our spheres of influence mostly unimpeded by the other. You are responsible for the East, and I the West. Yet unlike the users who live under my jurisdiction, the decisions in our lives are not determined by the Memory Cloud. Yet this specific challenge affects us equally and we can no longer act independently."

"That we agree on," replied Aaron. "Only a united approach can avert global disaster."

"Which is why it must be turned on. You and I will never agree to a common approach so it will have to make it for us."

"It's not necessary. I'm sure we can agree. It just requires some compromise, Miriam."

"How can I compromise when I know that you are wrong. The science is indisputable."

"The scientific theory yes, but it is not tested in practice. It's impossible to know what the unintended consequences might be of your actions, and neither of us have a crystal ball."

"Ah, but we do," replied Miriam coolly.

"No! I will never agree to it. It is the very reason we stand here as adversaries rather than compatriots."

"I don't see why this is any different from the siblings programme?"

"It's entirely different. The guides were designed to affect the individual only, not to act as oversight of the system itself."

FLASHBACKS

"The guide protocol has received universal approval from members all around the globe. I don't know what you are frightened of?"

"The siblings have boundaries, Ersatz does not. By designing a sibling each we created balance between them. One reflects the most important qualities someone might need in a sister. I designed her in the image of the one I never had, the one I wanted you to be."

"And that is why she fails. Too emotional," replied Miriam sharply. "Too susceptible to frailty."

"To fail is to be human."

"The brother programme doesn't."

"That depends on your definition of failure. The point of the sibling programme is that they manage each other's faults. There is no power imbalance. If we introduce the mother programme that will no longer be the case. The risk is too great."

"But there is a much greater risk, as you know," replied Miriam. "If the planet continues to warm none of it will matter. The eyes of the world are on us, both East and West. The people are accustomed to us making the right decisions for them and yet we argue over their fate because you're pissed off at me because I'm more successful."

"You're only more successful because we started the Circuit first," he grumbled. "The Realm is five years behind."

"Then maybe you shouldn't have left."

"I had no choice. I don't approve of your methods. You use people as your personal chess pieces."

"I've created a perfect world!" she bellowed, standing up and wagging her finger at him. Aaron shivered. Superior size was no protection from an older sister. She could fell him with a single cutting barb or insult.

"Is it perfect?"

"No. Not quite. But it could be if we weren't limited ourselves. It's not just the climate question it can solve. There are no limits. But someone needs the strength to take actions that are difficult. Are you a coward, brother?"

"No, Miriam," he replied meekly. "I'm a realist."

Miriam paced around the room, her frail frame shuffling on the shiny black floor. Cogs whirled around her brain to unlock the way forward. This building was her temple. The gold beacon, blazing the name of her biggest achievement, cast her brother's shadow over her as she cycled around him.

"It will be turned on," she croaked harshly.

"You do not have my permission."

"I don't need it," she whispered.

"What do you mean?"

Miriam limped back to the cube and placed her wrinkly finger inside a hole and opened the front. At her eye level the blank screen of a terminal waited for instructions. She pressed a few buttons and a few seconds later a message appeared.

Welcome to the Circuit...

"Access Miriam Circo's cloud," commanded the woman.

"What are you doing?"

Accessing...

"Locate memory from the second of April, Twenty Twenty-Eight. Search for Aaron Circo," she instructed the computer.

Searching...

Aaron immediately scanned his own virtual world to revisit his own recollection of that day. What was she looking for exactly? It was the day they made the breakthrough, he certainly remembered that much. The atmosphere had been euphoric and for one rare moment the siblings shared their achievement without ego or rivalry. Sometimes the excitement of one's success can cloud your judgement. It can make you excitable and willing to act unnaturally. As he replayed the memory, he realised what he'd done. In his elation he'd given his authority. He'd recorded a signature of approval in his cloud and the evidence was indisputable.

"Stop," he said, lunging towards the cube.

"Don't move another inch," replied Miriam, removing a small handgun she'd concealed within the workings of the cube.

Search complete...

"Open Ersatz Protocols."

"This is a mistake, Miriam. Please, let's talk about it."

"We've been talking about it for months. It's time for action."

Ersatz open...

"Authorise approval by Miriam and Aaron Circo. Downloading memories."

Authorising...

Aaron started to panic. Sweat collected across his huge, hairy body and his heart was trying to burst out of his chest. What did he do? Ersatz could never be reversed once it was open. He dived into his cloud feed and accessed the menu. At the bottom of a long list of applications was the 'Help' function. He clicked it and a figure was projected just in front of where Miriam was aiming a gun at him. The projection smiled sweetly and, as she always did, opened the conversation.

"How can Dinah help you today?"

"Secure the following memories. Keep them safe."

Aaron opened a new stream and a mass of code appeared in front of Dinah. Thousands of pages of complex data lines flashed through her view at an almost impossible speed.

"Urgh…boring," huffed Dinah.

```
Ersatz approved...
```
"Good," smirked Miriam.

The screen went blank and after a brief lapse in activity a single flashing green cursor materialised in the centre. Miriam waited for any further sign of life.

```
Ersatz protocols fully functional...AI
is on...
```
"Well, hello, AIison."

"I'm done here," said Aaron, turning to leave. "This is your responsibility and you can clear it up."

"Don't move!" she said threateningly. "I want you to see which of us was right. I want you to be here when we find out that it was me. Alison, run CLEAR SKY protocols for due diligence."

```
Running...
```
There was the briefest of delays before it typed out its conclusions.

```
...success of CLEAR SKY predicted at
ninety-eight percent...
```
"It's enough for me," cackled Miriam.

```
...adjusting          CLEAR         SKY
protocols...Ninety-nine percent success
predicted...if risks removed...
```
"I told you it would work. It's already thinking for itself, making decisions you and I aren't developed enough to make. Alison, how do we remove the risks?"

```
Kill Aaron Circo...
```
*****

The flashback ended abruptly. The memory faded away, leaving Jake in the same room where its events had occurred years before he was born. Its stimulus was replaced by the presence of the siren blasting in his ears. As quickly as the vision faded so, too, did the light from the golden beacon. In a click of the fingers it was extinguished, plunging him into total darkness.

"That was surreal," said Dinah. "Apparently there are two of us."

"Same person," suggested Jake who was trying to fathom everything he'd witnessed.

"But how can I be there and here?" she asked.

"Because you were part of my original implants. You were carrying the secrets with you."

It was obvious why the Circuit wanted to keep the flashbacks hidden. It was exactly the sort of revelation that the Spectrum hoped it would be. Cast-iron evidence that the people of the West were slaves, driven by an artificial master who manipulated their memories for its own gain. Soon they would know the truth. The past had been revealed. It no longer existed in some remote server, protected by the system. It was free and alive in the grey matter of his brain. It wasn't just proof of what the Circuit had become, it also contained the stream of programming code. The DNA of the Ersatz programme and hopefully the key to disconnecting Alison for good. Not that he had the first idea of what any of it meant or how to use it.

Several floors below him the buzz of rotor blades gathered to compete with the intermittent blasts of the siren. The drones were coming. He had what he needed. It was time to leave, in more ways than one. It was time to let the memory of Jake Montana go and start afresh. He leant forward to pull the plug that linked him to the mainframe. A green cursor on the previously blank screen caught his eye. The false light illuminated the space around the cube. The cursor started to type.

AI...is...on

The message was being replicated on every screen in every part of the Source. It was designed for one person. Apart from Sam Goldberg and a bank of frozen bodies no one else was here. Just him. The memory, logged in his cloud for eighteen years, proved why the Source was empty. The Circuit was no longer controlled by humans. A higher power had taken the reins, and now Alison knew who'd been responsible for letting the genie out of the bottle.

"Did you know about this?" Jake accused Dinah.

"About what?" she said innocently.

"Alison?"

"Um, ask me a different one," she replied coyly.

The screen answer instead.

`We all know...Jake...`

"I didn't know," added Dinah. "I'm you, Jake. If you couldn't see the truth, even though you felt it, that was the same for me. I knew there was something inside you, but Alison placed so many layers of instructions on top of us it became...clouded."

"But you said you were scared of Alison?"

"I still am," she wheezed.

`Virus detected...`

"Where's Miriam?" Jake shouted.

When Alison failed to answer he repeated his question by typing it with the keyboard. To his surprise his demands and the response appeared on-screen.

`I can hear you...I was thinking...`

"Oh, right."

`...switched off...`

Of course, she was. He'd seen her body in the chamber at the morgue. It hadn't triggered his suspicions because he didn't know her name. Now he was reattached to his past the name was more familiar. Everyone learnt about the founders in Circology classes. Once Miriam had killed her brother, Alison would no longer have any use for her. Little did the Principal Controller know that Aaron had transferred what he knew to a different network, the Realm, where she could never see it. Well, Alison certainly knew now.

"Where are my parents?" demanded Jake.

There was no reply.

Time was ticking. The drones would soon break through and finish him off, but Jake's thirst for answers caused him to delay pulling the plug. If he disconnected from the mainframe, they would be blind to him. But he would also be blind. The inclination to seek answers would be gone along with his past.

"What right did you have to ruin my life?" demanded Jake. "You have no right to manipulate my memories for your own gain."

`False    accusation...the    Circuit    is perfect...`

"It's evil! You've robbed me of my future."

`Incorrect...the       Spectrum       is responsible...you   got   their   letter...not mine...`

The dominoes in Jake's life had fallen because of that first one, the letter. Christie, his parents, the Archivists, Sam Goldberg all tumbled as a result. What if he'd received the real letter? What sort of life would he be leading now? Would he be happy? Would it have been easier to allow the Circuit to take away his anxiety and stress for a peaceful but ignorant life?

No.

Alison was trying to manipulate him again. She was presenting the Spectrum as the enemy. It was clear where Brother Job had learnt his talents.

"Your letter wouldn't have matched me with Christie Tucci. The Circuit would have killed our love because of your stupid rules. But you can't kill it. You've tried to separate us, delete us and cast doubt on us, but we will rise up against you. Love cannot be suppressed."

`Drones     advance…two    minutes    to comply…`

"To comply with what?" said Jake anxiously.

`Relinquish your memories or I will kill billions…`

Jake had always planned to relinquish them; it was his only way of escaping the Source. He'd kept what he needed, and Alison couldn't know about his new implant. "I will relinquish them and sacrifice my life, but only if you do something for me?"

"No, Jake," pleaded Dinah. "It can't be trusted."

`Propose…`

Jake typed his demand into the keyboard. The words vanished as soon as his fingers touched the keys like the very idea of the message was illegal. The green cursor pulsated as it considered its response.

`…illogical…explain…`

"You're an artificially intelligent being, surely a simple human can't teach you anything. You'll have to work it out for yourself."

"Jake, what are you doing?" asked Dinah.

"Managing risk."

`Approved…and actioned…`

"Thank you," said Jake with a smile.

`Relinquish your implants…`

"Dinah, I need a favour."

"Does it involve any thinking?"

"Not really."

"Yes, then."

"Keep doing what you've been doing, ok?"

"Huh?"

"Just be yourself."

"That's easy enough. Why?"

"Just trust me," he said. "It's a game."

"You know I can't resist a game. I'm in."

FLASHBACKS

"You will be for some time I'm afraid," announced Jake, pulling the connection from the terminal.

Dinah's projection disappeared in an instant.

Visual lost...

"I'm still here," said Jake. "This is what it feels like to be blind. It's how humans have learnt to live. They only see what you show them in their clouds. They no longer see the world for what it is. Now it's your turn."

Scan for virus...

Jake rested his hand on the suction pad on the back of his head ready to kill the past.

"Alison, there's one thing you'll never understand. It doesn't matter how much data you consume or calculations you compute, you'll never understand the human condition. We do not always act as we should or how the cloud might instruct us because life is not linear. It is erratic. I like it that way."

Virus loose...drones maximum surveillance...

The lift shaft descended from the highest level to allow a swarm of utility drones to burst through the gap and into the room. Headlamps pierced the gloom and Jake blinked as the beams crossed over him. They might not see him, but with so many one was bound to collide with him as they searched. It was time to say goodbye.

Destroy virus...

"Alison, where birds fly there will always be blue skies."

He ripped off the final connection, replacing it in its pouch. Alison's text stream went crazy. It typed instructions and threats at speed. Unable to evaluate what was happening, the messages looked to Jake like panic. He placed his hands on the edge of the screen and ripped it from the cube. Broken cables dangled out of the back, but the screen continued to blink, struggling for life. He lifted it high above his head and threw it to the floor. Plastic, metal and glass shattered with a crash. Drawn to the noise, the drones flew forward, weapons primed.

Then they stopped.

The virus was gone.

Unsighted under the remains of the smashed components were two human implants, buckled and broken. In section K, level three, aisle four hundred and one in the middle of Arizona a server stack lost power and went into standby.

- Chapter 30 -

Love and Hope

The last six weeks had been particularly stressful for Paddy von Straff. He'd gone from layabout retiree to single parent in the blink of an eye and there were no communal services to support people like him. If your nearest and dearest had broken the rules, then they were to blame for your distress, not the Circuit. The system had already provided employment, entertainment and equality. There were no benefits for those in need because nobody should be.

As a result, Paddy's life had changed immeasurably.

He'd been forced to get a job to pay the bills his daughter and son-in-law had covered until their extradition. If his pension had been sufficient, he wouldn't be living with family in the first place. He'd be living on a tropical island somewhere. Just a fantasy now. Finding work was hard enough back in his youth, but in his seventies, it was almost impossible. Everyone had already been assigned jobs, which meant there weren't many that needed filling. Recruitment specialists and job centres were a thing of the past, as were food banks, community centres and social services. If you were in dire need only your own resilience got you through it.

He'd taken a job more suited to a junior to make ends meet. The money didn't come close to either end. If you'd yet to reach Ascension Day there was always scope to earn a little pocket money clearing tables, picking up litter, babysitting or cleaning.

LOVE AND HOPE

Paddy was putting in twelve hours a day on menial wages with a dodgy hip and a less than endearing manner. Grumpy didn't come close. He'd done his miles; it was supposed to be someone else's turn.

Not that he blamed Kyle and Deborah for his plight. They'd done their best with the boy. Everyone had. Jake was just one of those children who had a mind of his own. More interested in daydreaming than embracing the strict compliance of the world they lived in. The boy meant well even if he was prone to making mistakes along the way. He was just trying to be himself in a world of clones. Paddy's influence probably hadn't helped. His own disregard for the rules might have played a part in Jake's wayward development. There were times when he wanted to despise Jake for what he'd done, but he couldn't own that emotion for long. There were plenty of reasons why Paddy had to take some responsibility and forgive the boy.

Clemency was least evident when he got home after an epic shift.

That was when the day really turned nasty.

Managing Tyra was an even bigger headache. Before her parents' 'conduct feeling' Jake's sister was a model student at school and a helpful, supportive daughter at home. Now she was a tearaway. She'd dyed her hair black, wore inappropriate clothes, skipped school and picked up violations frequently. Under protocol twenty-two, which legally bound a child to the protection of another family member, Paddy was liable for any punishment that resulted in Tyra reaching her maximum annual allowance. At this rate he'd be joining his daughter at the Source within weeks.

It was more than thirty years since he'd had a teenager in the house, and they were a lot simpler back in his day. At least you knew when you were talking, they weren't swimming off in some virtual landscape or watching movies with friends. It didn't mean they were listening but at least they weren't distracted. He'd tried desperately to reason with her, but she just didn't care about anyone apart from herself anymore.

The initial target for her disaffection was reserved solely for her absent brother. Not that she accepted she even had one anymore. After blocking him from her cloud on the day of her parents' eviction, she'd spent the next week throwing a penknife at a projection of his face on her bedroom wall. Now if Paddy accidentally mentioned his name, she'd fly off the handle, break something or storm out of the house. She'd disappear for a couple of days and return as if nothing had ever happened.

When he wasn't working or negotiating with a traumatised teenager, he could be found dozing in his favourite chair, pretending to read. He never was. He rarely ever wore his external implants these days. What was the point? The people he wanted to talk to weren't available to him and generally wearing it only led to nuisance calls from strangers or interruptions from the local broadcasters. He never forgot to connect for the 'Proclamation of Distrust', to avoid any personal violations. The way Tyra was acting, he didn't need to add his own to the list.

It was Saturday morning and Paddy was resting after an evening of childminding for some of the neighbours. He'd only finished at three in the morning and was due out again that afternoon. As usual his implant sat dormant on the coffee table, which is why he missed all the messages.

Paddy was woken from his doze by an old school noise he'd not heard for years. It was the unmistakable sound of someone's knuckles striking wood. No one knocked these days, they sent you a proximity alert before they arrived.

"Tyra, someone at the door for you!" he hollered, clear there weren't many people alive who'd want to see him and even fewer that had the strength to knock on a door.

There was no response from the top of the escalator. Either she was out and hadn't told him, or she was immersed in her cloud listening to painful death metal music again.

Another knock, more eager than the first time.

Paddy scooped himself off the chair and clutched at his hip. It wasn't that painful, but it had become a spontaneous reaction these days because it generally did. He shuffled through the living room and opened the front door to see who was so desperate to find out that they were in the wrong place.

A slender, pale, young lady stood on the path wearing a confused expression and being pelted by fierce raindrops. It had been like it for days. That was Storm Season for you.

"She's not in," barked Paddy.

"I'm not looking for Tyra," she replied tentatively. "I've come to see you."

"Oh no," replied Paddy, misinterpreting her real intentions. He knew a honeytrap when he saw one and they only worked if the target had honey. "I don't go in for that sort of thing at my age. Whoever sent you, it was a prank!"

"Mr von Straff, it's me, Christie."

"I'm sorry, I've never seen you before in my life," he said, straining his eyes and trying to resuscitate memories that were mostly sitting on his coffee table.

"If you put it on," she said, "you'll remember I was Jake's girl…"

"Shush. Don't mention that name here. I don't want to upset Tyra."

"Can I come in?" asked Christie. "It's quite important."

"Wait here," he replied, unconvinced that it was quite so important to him.

He traipsed back to the living room and stuck the pads to the back of his head. It opened a flood of notifications for unpaid bills, adverts for selling organs for credits, announcements of rule changes, spam messages and hourly weather reports. He swiped them away and returned to his visitor.

"Christie," he whispered, finally remembering her place in his world. "How are you?"

"A little confused and overwhelmed," she replied truthfully. "Have you heard from…him?"

"No. Not a thing since he left. Come out of the rain, my girl."

Christie hopped under the cover and left a pool of water in the porch. Paddy took her sopping wet coat and passed her a towel to wipe herself dry. Under her coat she was holding a slightly moist white envelope. Paddy noticed it immediately.

"It's my Ascension Eve," she said. "I've been dreading it for weeks, well, ever since he left really."

"It was pretty cruel what they did to Jake, I hope you've fared better," he said with a smile.

"It's hard to say really."

"Mug of cophony?" offered Paddy.

"No thank you."

"Come and sit down."

Christie sat silently as Paddy did his best to predict why she was here. Sentimentality? Nostalgia? Pity? Whatever it was she didn't seem keen to get it off her chest.

"Why are you here, my dear?" asked Paddy sympathetically.

"I need guidance," she said, snivelling from the rain and her frayed emotions. "These last few months have been really tough for me. I would have done anything just to know he was safe or even to see his face again. Every day our shared memories launch in my feed to taunt me. It's been hard to focus on anything because he's been constantly in my thoughts. How do you let go of someone you love?"

"You don't," said Paddy.

"Really?"

"No. Love never really dies, Christie. It may not be there in the form you once cherished but love remains in our heart and soul. When my Nina passed away, it took me a year before I came out of an internal grief that made me dizzy with depression. Eventually over time I was able to remember the happier times. I learnt to accept she was gone and that there was nothing I could do to bring her back."

"I've tried really hard to do that, but it's not easy."

"Grief never is. At least you know he is out there somewhere and as I told him before he left, 'where the birds fly, there will always be blue sky'."

"That's the last thing he said to me," replied Christie who'd reviewed the memory a thousand times since for further clues. "What does it mean?"

"I wish I could tell you exactly but if I take these off, I'll forget it and if I leave them on the Circuit will crack my code. Let's just say it has more than one meaning."

"Did he know what it meant?" asked Christie.

"Some of it," Paddy whispered with a subtle wink.

"I think he did more than that," said Christie, forcing a smile.

There was another long pause and Paddy almost drifted off to sleep from his late-night endeavours. He shook himself out of it so as not to appear rude.

"Who's the lucky boy, then?" asked Paddy, nodding at the letter she still clutched in her hand like a comfort blanket.

"That's why I came. I think it's a mistake."

"Apparently they don't make any," he replied.

"They must have. Look."

She passed him the envelope and Paddy carefully slid the letter out. He folded it open and started to read, but quickly looked up to share her sense of confusion. "It's not possible."

"I know. It says my life partner will be Jake Paddy Montana."

"But…he's already taken."

"Maybe his wife died?"

"If she did, he still wouldn't be inside your letter. People aren't allowed to remarry."

"Maybe it's a different Jake Montana, then?" she said.

"Only one way to check, visit the boy's cloud feed that came with the letter?"

"I have, but there's nothing there."

"Nothing?"

"It's completely blank. Not a single memory."

"That's impossible. Every subscriber to the Circuit has memories…" he said, before his mind offered an alternative answer he didn't want to express. "Where does the letter say this Jake is?"

"Arizona. But how can he be, it's completely deserted?"

"Desert is the right description."

"It also says I have to move there, but how can that be, it's meant to be the man that moves to where the wife is."

"How peculiar."

"I just don't know what to do."

"I guess that's why you have guides. It's partly their job to get you there."

"But how can anyone go there. It's inhospitable, no one can live there."

Paddy thought about his message. It appeared Jake had taken his advice. It proved love and hope still lived in him even if the circumstances appeared a little strange. Maybe it was time to revisit the 'old days' he so often lamented.

"What do I do?" asked Christie.

"You have to find him. There is no question in my mind that this is our Jake. He has found a way for you to be together."

"But where do I start?"

"By seeing a doctor," replied Paddy with a wink.

*****

An average day for Major Holst involved a twenty-mile hike, experiments to perfect efflotein and several hours on the shooting range testing his toys. Since Jake Montana's surprise visit a month ago, he'd not seen another human. It was just the way he liked it. Even his Memory Cloud left him alone. The blood-sucking advertising firms gave him a wide berth, probably as they had been terrified by past experience. Such were the security levels associated with Bornholm, few others were allowed anywhere near him.

There were no complaints.

The only people allowed access were superior officers and other Archivist Majors. Not that any of them bothered contacting him. It had nothing to do with the intense rivalry of the Corridors, though, because he didn't have one. Holst wasn't regarded as one of them. He'd been banished to his little island because he didn't have the balls for it. The propaganda against him had worked perfectly. It was just what the Circuit wanted them to believe. The truth behind Bornholm's activities had been kept secret even from them. The fewer people who knew the better.

LOVE AND HOPE

A day might come when the Circuit's own risks had to be managed. If events turned against them, then more radical action might be called for.

That day had come.

Holst finished putting the war drones through another highly impressive round of war games. They'd been devastatingly efficient as always. They never missed. A supreme technological force ready to fight whenever called upon. The Archivists had proven fallible. A hundred of them failed to catch one unarmed speccy in a concealed room. The war drones would never fail. They wouldn't get confused about who was and wasn't a target. They'd not fight amongst themselves in an attempt to achieve their goals. Their egos would never get in the way of victory.

He locked the shed securely and assessed the carnage of the hill. Great craters pierced the ground and swathes of soil and wood lay over the surface. The enemy would have no chance.

An alert went off in his memory feed.

It had been such a long time since he'd last received one, it took him a little by surprise. He struggled to locate it in his menu bar, finally discovering the source of the noise was his message service. It started with a simple welcome.

`Major Holst...`

"Principal Conductor," he replied, "it has been some time since I've heard from you."

`Await instruction...`

Holst stood patiently next to his Jeep.

`Deploy the drones...`

"Destination?" he enquired.

`East...`

THE END

'MEMORY HUNTERS'
The 'Circuit' Book 2

Released November 2020

Sign up to my newsletter
www.tonymoyle.com/contact/

It makes all the difference to an author's career if
you leave a review in the store where you purchased
this ebook to help other readers find it. I would be
most grateful if you did.